You'r

Book 1
Adventure Into Truth

Book 2
Souled Out

By Michael J. Arend

◆ FriesenPress

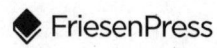

Suite 300 - 990 Fort St
Victoria, BC, V8V 3K2
Canada

www.friesenpress.com

Copyright © 2019 by Michael J. Arend
First Edition — 2019

Edited by Stacey D. Atkinson
Front Cover Art by SelfPubBookCovers.com/andrewgraphics

All rights reserved.

No part of this publication may be reproduced in any form, or by any means, electronic or mechanical, including photocopying, recording, or any information browsing, storage, or retrieval system, without permission in writing from FriesenPress.

Disclaimer - This is a work of fiction. Names, characters, businesses, places, events, locales, and incidents are either the products of the author's imagination or used in a fictitious manner. Any resemblance to actual persons, living or dead, or actual events is purely coincidental.
Attention - Quantity discounts are available to your company, educational institution or writing organization for reselling, educational purposes, subscription incentives, gifts or fund-raising campaigns.

ISBN
978-1-5255-5553-4 (Hardcover)
978-1-5255-5554-1 (Paperback)
978-1-5255-5555-8 (eBook)

1. FICTION, ACTION & ADVENTURE

Distributed to the trade by The Ingram Book Company

Dedication

As I thought about all the possible people, I would have loved to dedicate this book to, I decided to dedicate it to me. Yes, that's correct, I have decided to dedicate my first book to myself.

"Do you remember as a young boy lying awake at night and wondering what you would do when you grew up? You weren't sure, but you knew that whatever it was, you were going to do something big. Later, in high school, you developed a fondness and a knack for creative writing. Some of your English teachers prodded you to write more, while others chastised you for writing essays that were far too descriptive. Finally, as a grown man you decided to follow your heart and take the plunge by ordering a writing course, only to have that course thrown in the garbage by a misunderstanding partner. Stay the course my friend, and never give up. It will seem like a very long time, but all your dreams, and so much more, will finally come true."

Author's Note

Can you feel it? I certainly can. Human spiritual awareness has grown to epic proportions in just the last number of years. I remember when I hit my lowest point in 2011. A point at which I no longer had the desire to continue on. Somehow, through meditation, spiritual readings, and a plethora of self-help books, I made it back to the world of the functional and decided I needed to give back. I was on a journey to become my greatest version and wanted to help others on their journey's as well. As I discovered new avenues from which to help others, I started to notice that so many people had gone through similar circumstances, and wanted to do the same thing.

Now, eight years later, I have witnessed the number of people that have adopted this new consciousness grow exponentially. Even science now agrees that our lives are about a spiritual unfolding. They now know, as the ancient spiritual traditions have known for thousands of years, that we can create our own reality with our thoughts, words and actions.

I wanted to write a non-fiction spiritual manual for helping people find their way through this new consciousness, that contained a short and reoccurring adventure story at the start of each chapter. As I began to write, however, it became clear this short story had become much too large. And so, I started to write an adventure parable that contained thoughts and principles I fully believe in.

The story and characters contained within these two books are fictional, but the message behind the story, in my opinion, is true. I would ask that you keep an open mind when reading these books and if a thought or idea resonates with you, hold on to it. If it doesn't, let it go. We are all at different stages in our spiritual journeys and there is no right or wrong. What we understand to be true for each of us is merely based on our perceptions and beliefs at that particular moment.

All you have to do is suspend your beliefs, perceptions, and self-doubts just long enough to take in the story and discover that, you, and indeed all of us, are The One.

MAY 30/20

To FITZ,

MAY THE WINDS
OF THE UNIVERSE
ALWAYS FILL YOUR SAILS!

love,

MPH 3/20

To Billy

May the winds
of the winters of
Finn You last short.

[signature]

Book I

You're the One: Adventure Into Truth

By Michael J. Arend

Chapter 1

The Seclusion Room was dark. Coughing and sputtering, she slowly regained consciousness. She saw only the faint outline of a toilet bowl protruding from the far wall. Her only light source was from a night light left on in the main corridor that shone through the inverted Plexiglas inspection bubble bulging into the room.

What was that? thought Raven. Something was crawling across her cheek.

"Damn centipedes!" she said aloud as she brushed it off her cheek.

She knew they were harmless, but with their long legs and antennae, they brought back memories of prehistoric monsters that had scared her so much as a child. The bugs were something she didn't want to deal with right now.

Just need to rest for a second, thought Raven. But as she closed her eyes, all she saw were visions of that big black bird again.

"Enough!" she shouted as she sat up straight.

Why do I keep seeing that damn bird? She didn't want to think about birds or bugs; she had other things to think about.

How did I even get here? she wondered as a sudden wave of déjà vu spread over her like a warm blanket.

This has all happened before...oh man, my head, it's killing me! Can't think straight. Ahh, that's the reason, she thought as she rubbed her hand over her scalp to see where the pain was originating from. Nice goose egg. Someone let me have it all right. But why are my clothes and my hair damp? Why am I in this despicable place?

Her memory was starting to come back now. All I was trying to do was prevent that Neanderthal from beating that poor man to death.

Then she felt her mind go to a deeper place as if commanded to do so. Don't they realize that we're all connected with each other and our environment? No, even better, that we're all one? We all came from the same source, and we're all going back there when our time here on earth is done. It can be no other way. The story we were told about Adam and Eve when we were young is really just a story about us. When we finally decided to make the trip from our spiritual realm to Earth, amid much fanfare and celebration I might add, we lost all recollection of who we truly were and still are.

"Where is this stuff coming from? Why do I know this stuff?" questioned Raven aloud.

Long, long ago, those that were in the midst of their journey could not comprehend this either but felt as if they were here for a reason and that they were somehow connected to everything else in this world. As the ancients before them used stories of Gods to fill the void of knowledge, so did they. They crafted a very clever story about a man and a woman who came from a spiritual source, or God. They were finely crafted by God, in his likeness, and put here on the earth to enjoy all there was, have fun, and be happy.

"Damn it! Why won't it stop? My head feels like it's about to explode!"

Then, as inevitably happens to us all as we live our lives here on this spinning orb in the middle of nowhere, they forgot that they were really just spiritual beings. They started to believe they were separate from everything else. They believed they were all there was. They found comfort in their new friend, the false self. This false self began Edging God Out and was nicknamed the EGO. Soon they believed that it was all about me, me, me! And thus the challenges began.

"For Christ's sake! I never even went to Sunday school!" yelled Raven.

The ones that lived long ago could not explain this, of course, so they fabricated a story of a serpent that tempted Eve to bite the apple to reveal the knowledge that was being kept from her (really just the amnesia we all suffer when we make the trip). She inevitably manipulated Adam (some things never change!) to do the same, and then all hell broke loose, literally. God was pissed and sent Adam and Eve (us) out of the garden (spiritual realm) to live a life of constant struggle (challenges), here on earth (hell), never to be happy again (not!).

Once we know this, how can we even lift a hand in anger or hatred against another? We are all related. We are all sisters and brothers. We must be like what we came from. We are all one.

Raven shook her head. Stop thinking like that! That's what got you thrown into this room to begin with. If you hadn't told them the truth about being God, you wouldn't be in this mess!

"What the hell are you talking about, Raven?" said Raven speaking aloud now. "You're here to get your daughter because she's the One. That's it! I remember now. Simone, she's the one that will lead us."

Raven thought back to when Simone was just a child. She always had a way of knowing things before you told her; even their family doctor, Doc Adams, thought she was special. After all, Simone's the one that taught both of them how to read a person's aura.

Their minds are far too small to comprehend any of that. If only they could see what I've seen. That's where the truth is ultimately revealed. Energy, that's all. It's all just energy.

"Got to figure out a way..."

Raven fell silent as she heard a key slide into the lock. The door creaked open.

"Get up, girlie. You're coming with me!" In the doorway stood the silhouette of a large, very muscular man.

"Chief wants to see ya," grumbled the man as he began to move toward her.

A long, thick arm reached out to grab her, and she instinctively pulled away. She ran to the far side of the room looking for anything to defend herself with, but there was nothing in the room except a thin mattress and the stainless steel toilet bowl bolted to the wall. His outstretched arm found its mark, and his hand closed around her throat.

"Don't fight it, girlie; you'll only make it worse!" barked the man.

She pulled back while grabbing his wrists and found enough leverage to bite his hand. He grimaced with pain, and then she felt a piercing pain in her neck.

A needle! He just injected me with something. Got to act fast before...I...slip... As he dragged her through the Seclusion Room door, the last thing she saw was a billy club hanging by his side and what looked like a green frog giving her the finger tattooed on his inner forearm.

Raven felt herself slowly coming back to the realm of the living and wondered how long she had been out for. As she regained consciousness, all she could feel was an excruciating pain in her neck. That's where that bastard injected me, she thought. He'll get his, that son of a bitch!

"So, Raven, we finally meet."

A female voice, thought Raven. I wasn't expecting that.

"So this is the great Raven. You don't look so great lying on my floor!" said the woman.

Raven. Why did my parents have to give me such a stupid nickname? I prefer Jane.

"Get her up, and put her in the chair!" commanded the female voice.

Two very large men picked Raven up as if she were weightless and deposited her on a hard oak chair. One of the men was sporting a bandaged hand with a faint bloodstain showing through. Raven tried not to smile.

"Where's your daughter?" demanded the woman.

Raven, struggling to clear her vision, looked up and saw a pale-skinned, red-lipped, black-haired woman wearing a tight black leather jacket. She was strangely beautiful, but her aura showed only negativity and darkness.

"I don't have a daughter," Raven managed to say.

"Bullshit! You have a daughter, her name is Simone, and it's well known that she's the One, your so-called savior—the Avatar that will lead the human race to the next level of the multiverse."

"I don't know what you're talking about." Raven felt a slap across the back of her head. Her world went black for a second, and her ears were ringing. "I'll die before I tell you!" exclaimed Raven with conviction.

"That can be arranged," said the chief. "Take her to the room, and give her sodium pentothal."

"Yes, ma'am," answered one of the men dutifully.

Why did they call her ma'am? wondered Raven as the two men dragged her through the door. Was she military?

"You will tell us what we want to know, my dear," asserted the chief, "or you'll die like the rest of them."

Raven sat bound and gagged in what looked like a dentist's chair.

Fitting, she thought, I've always hated the dentist.

One of the huge men was still in the room by the door, and a tall, slim man busied himself with getting things ready on a stainless steel dental tray. Seemingly satisfied with his creation, the tall man turned and walked toward Raven.

"So, you don't want to tell the truth, eh?" said the tall man. "That's OK; we can help you talk. First I'm going to inject you with some sodium pentothal, and then we'll have a little chat. If you don't talk, then we'll start pulling your teeth out one at a time. If you still don't talk, we'll move on from there. Sound good to you? I knew it would."

Raven thought she saw a small wink from the tall man. Was it a wink or maybe a twitch? She wasn't sure.

"Oh, I forgot to tell you my name," said the tall man. "You can call me Dennis. Dennis the Dentist. Has a nice ring to it, eh?"

His English is near perfect, no perceivable accent, and that "eh." He must be from—

"I'm from Canada," said Dennis with a huge grin. "We Canadians are very friendly, you know." Another wink.

"But I really enjoy my job. Don't I, Tex?" said Dennis turning to look at the man by the door.

"Yes sir, you do," answered Tex in a southern drawl.

"He's a good boy," said Dennis after turning his attention back to Raven.

Why did he call Dennis sir? And what's with the winks? thought Raven.

"OK, let's get started, shall we," said Dennis as he picked up a long, slender syringe from the tray.

As Dennis began to speak, he winked one more time. As he drew closer, Raven could sense the man's goodness. His aura confirmed to her that Dennis was not all bad. As Dennis pressed the needle against Raven's skin, he leaned closer to her so the man by the door couldn't see him unbuckle her arm restraints. Dennis winked one more time.

"OK, Missy, let's take that gag off and see what you have to say."

For some reason the man called Dennis was helping her. Got to take a chance and go for it! thought Raven.

Raven started to slowly move her head back and forth and cry out as if she were in pain. Suddenly her body was contorting in every direction, with inhuman noises coming from her mouth.

"She's convulsing. She must have had a reaction!" yelled Dennis looking at Tex.

"Get over here, you fool, and give me a hand."

Tex was at the dentist's chair in an instant and grabbed for Raven's hands. Just as he did, Raven threw a punch with all her might that caught Tex squarely in the Adam's apple. As Tex grabbed his throat, Dennis hit Tex on the back of the head with the Texan's own billy club. Tex crumpled to the floor in a heap.

Dennis quickly released Raven's foot restraints and helped her to her feet. Dennis motioned her to the door, and as Raven stood beside him, she looked back at Tex lying motionless on the floor.

"Told you you'd get yours!" whispered Raven under her breath.

As much as Raven was glad Tex got what was coming to him, she couldn't help but feel sorry for him. He was just a man following orders. A man trained to do despicable things. He needed help too, as we all do, to realize who we truly are. She felt remorse for having hurt him but knew it was necessary to save Simone—the One that would save us all.

Chapter 2

Raven followed Dennis as they twisted and turned down hallway after hallway. They were going to the lower floors in the building, the basement. When they got to a long grey hallway lined with barred doors on either side, Raven started to feel Simone's presence.

"Wait!" shouted Raven breathing heavily now.

"Who the hell are you, and why should I trust you?"

"I'm Dennis the Dentist, now let's go."

"No, not until you answer me," said Raven.

"We've been following you and your daughter for a very long time. We are a splinter group of mercenaries that are trying to change the world for the better, OK. Now can we go?"

"That's not good enough; I need more."

"OK, OK. My real name is Wayne, and I was a Canadian commando for the JTF2 squad. Our group is made up of former military members from around the world that have joined together to help mankind make the quantum jump."

"The quantum jump? What the hell is that?" asked Raven.

"I'll tell you later; it's really important that we keep moving, so can we go now?"

"Yah sure, of course. Let's go," said Raven, still not fully understanding why Dennis or Wayne or whatever his name is, was helping her.

Raven could really feel Simone's presence now.

She must be close, she thought. Even as a baby and a little girl, she and I have always had a special connection.

"Mom?" shouted Simone.

Raven stopped abruptly and looked to her right where the sound had come from.

"Simone, baby! Are you all right?"

"Other than being held against my will, with no access to my phone, yes, I'm fine," said Simone sarcastically.

Wayne pushed Raven out of the way.

"Sorry to break up the little family reunion, but we have to get you out of here. They'll follow us down here and soon find out that we hid you under their noses the whole time. Stand back, Simone, while I blow the door."

"Blow the door?" said Raven. "Isn't that kind of spy movie stuff?"

"Yes, it is, and there's a reason for that," answered Wayne as he busily readied a small, strategically placed charge near the door lock.

"You just carry around little cubes of C-4 explosives with you?" asked Raven.

"Doesn't every dentist? Now stand aside. Ready, Simone?"

"Yup."

Wayne blew the lock, and the door opened a few inches amid smoke and dust.

"Boy, that stuff stinks!" coughed Simone.

"Shhh," whispered Wayne holding his finger over his lips.

They could hear people coming down the stairwell at the end of the hall.

"They found Tex, and now they've heard the charge go off. Hurry this way," whispered Wayne.

Wayne led them to the other end of the hall hoping to find stairs there.

"Damn it! This is just a pump room. There's only one set of stairs. We're trapped here!"

They could hear voices coming from outside of Simone's blown-open cell and now heading their way.

"OK, we only have one chance. Raven, remember I spoke of the quantum jump?"

"Yeah."

"Well, you're going to find out what it is right now. Simone, they keep telling me you're special. I hope to Christ you are. This is what we have to do..." Wayne could hear people running down the hall toward the pump room. "OK, each of you grab one of my hands. Now I want you both to think happy thoughts."

"Happy thoughts? At a time like this?" blurted Raven.

"Yes, relax and start to feel gratitude about something. Feel how thankful you are to have each other. How thankful you are to be alive. To be able to breathe. Start to feel the energy around us. There's energy in everything," explained Wayne

"Even these concrete walls?" spewed Raven again.

"Mother!" interjected Simone.

Wayne continued as if he hadn't heard the exchange.

"Everything is matter, and matter is just energy. We manipulate this energy to look like concrete, steel, and even the electric pump motors. Focus on the motors. Imagine the infinite supply of electricity within us. It's one and the same."

Wayne started to feel the familiar feeling of light-headedness that always seemed to accompany the beginning of the quantum jump. Although he had never actually made the jump, he had experienced many times the "ghost" phase that accompanies the change to beings into light.

"Hold my hand...the transition has begun," said Wayne.

Suddenly the door to the pump room burst open. Raven felt oddly light as if she were floating, yet still standing there, and she felt good. She had never felt this much love before. She looked over at Simone and Wayne. They looked beautiful. They were surrounded by a gorgeous blue-white aura, and they looked as if they were meditating—eyes closed and a smile on their faces.

Movement caught Raven's eye, and she saw Tex, another man, and the pale dark-haired boss-lady bursting into the room.

Oh no, she thought. We're doomed!

The henchmen and their boss scurried about the room, looking right in their direction but didn't even look twice.

Don't they see us? thought Raven. She could see that the boss was shouting at the men, waving her arms all over the place.

"You fools! There's no one here. They must have doubled back. Back to the staircase!"

Raven watched as the men left the room followed by the black-haired beauty, but then she stopped. She stood in the doorway and turned her head as if she had heard something. She was looking right at them. Raven noticed her feelings of love were being overtaken by hatred toward this black-haired bitch.

Raven felt a funny feeling in her right foot. She looked down to see it was now in colour instead of being engulfed in the blue-white aura. Raven looked up once again, but the woman had vanished. Suddenly Raven felt as if she had fallen to the ground and was now out of the aura altogether and back to her colourful self.

"Whew! That was close," said Wayne.

"What just happened?" demanded Raven.

"Whoa, relax. We just made the first step toward a quantum jump, that's all."

"That's all? They burst into the room and looked right at us, but they didn't see us. And you say, 'That's all?'"

"Simone, doesn't this seem strange to you?" asked Raven.

"No, Mom, actually I've been able to do this my whole life. I use it as a form of meditation," answered Simone matter-of-factly.

"Holy crap, I always knew you were special, but this just blows my mind! Why didn't you tell me?"

"Look, it's simple," interjected Wayne.

"I told you to focus on the energy in everything around us and then take my hand. I knew you'd have trouble focusing, so I kept feeding you energy from Simone, through me."

"Like Reiki?" asked Raven.

"Kind of," replied Wayne.

"We all have the ability to do what we just did, but if you are still asleep and haven't awakened yet, you won't be able to."

"That's why they didn't see us," said Raven rhetorically.

"That's right," answered Wayne.

"But near the end, I was starting to revert back to my old self."

"Yes, and I'm glad we stood behind these barrels of antifreeze so Sarah didn't see your foot starting to drift from the aura."

"You saw that?" asked Raven, embarrassed now. "Wait a minute—Sarah? That's the woman's name? Who is she? You know her?"

"Yes, that's her name, she used to work with us, I know her, and yes, I saw that," answered Wayne.

"Your feeling of hatred toward Sarah brought you out of the aura. You see, to make the quantum jump to the next level, you must only focus on the energy that surrounds us. And that energy is the energy of the universe. The energy of our creator. The energy of infinite, unconditional love," concluded Wayne as he took a deep breath, closed his eyes as if he was about to meditate, and smiled.

"As much as I concur with everything you said, Wayne, I can sense they have left the stairwell, and I think it's time for us to get out of here," interrupted Simone.

"You're absolutely right, my princess," said Wayne as he started toward the door.

Raven looked at her daughter and mouthed the word "princess?"

Simone just shrugged her shoulders and turned her palms toward the sky.

The trio made their way up the staircase and out of the north door at the rear of the building and into the night. Once they felt clear of danger, they paused to look back at the building they had come from.

"It's a hospital," said Simone. "Just a regular old hospital."

"Well, no, not exactly," said Raven. "It's a mental hospital. Your friend, Jessica, told me you were looking for a place to hide and thought you had gone there. Little did I know that Wayne had found you and was keeping you safe. Anyway, once I started asking questions about you, they put me on the forensics ward with all the criminally insane. Then they threw me into the Seclusion Room for trying to help that poor bugger."

"Help who?" asked Wayne.

"Well, this guy was walking around saying he was Jesus Christ, and the staff largely ignored him, but then some orderlies, or at least that's what I thought they were, started beating on him. They all had the same tattoos. You know, the one with the green frog giving you the finger."

"Ex-Navy Seals," added Wayne.

"Well, whatever they are," continued Raven, "I couldn't stand to see a person mistreated like that, so I started yelling at them."

"What did you say, Mom?"

"I told them I was Jesus too, that's if Jesus even existed at all. That got their attention, and they turned to listen.

"I told them that Christ is the supreme dramatic symbol of the divinity in all of us. But did he ever live at all? Horus, from the ancient Egyptian tales, had an almost identical journey, thousands of years earlier. From the three kings present at his birth to his betrayal and crucifixion, the story is the same. So who is, or was, Horus or Jesus? Christ is the divine essence of our nature. His story is a dramatic representation of a deep element of human consciousness. The scriptures are just symbolic. They were never meant to be taken literally as the churches elected to do around the third and fourth centuries, just to silence the vulgar masses."

"Holy shit, Mom! Where did you learn all that stuff?" asked Simone in disbelief.

"I don't know, darling. Ever since I woke up in the Seclusion Room, I've been able to spout off all kinds of spiritual stuff."

"Is there more?" asked Simone.

"Well, then I quoted a portion of a William Wordsworth poem."

> Our birth is but a sleep and a forgetting:
> The Soul that rises with us, our life's star,
> Hath had elsewhere its setting,
> And cometh from afar:
> Not in entire forgetfulness,

And not in utter nakedness,
But trailing clouds of glory do we comeFrom God,
who is our home.

"So, yes, 'I am Jesus Christ,' I told them, 'and so are you and you,' and that's when they came after me, and then everything went black."

"I hate to interrupt the latest edition of *Theology Now*," said Wayne, "but we really should be going. I'm supposed to bring you back to base, but I want to make a stop along the way."

"Where are we headed?" asked Simone.

"To see someone that hopefully will give us an answer to the question we all have."

"What's that?"

"Are you really the One?" said Wayne. "We better get going."

Chapter 3

Wayne led them to a car in the parking lot of a nearby apartment building. The trio drove through the night and the following morning, stopping around one o'clock in the afternoon at a small roadside motel.

"OK," said Wayne, "we're only about a half-hour away now. We'll stop here, get cleaned up, grab a bite to eat, and then go see the Oracle."

"What did you say her name was?" asked Raven.

"Pythia. She's a direct descendant of the Oracle of Delphi in ancient Greece. She has given us many correct readings in the past," answered Wayne.

"OK," said Raven grudgingly, "but I still think it's a waste of time. We already know she's the One. Why else are these people after us, and look what she was able to do back at the hospital?"

"I know, I know, but we need to be certain," said Wayne.

"Don't I have a say in this?" shouted Simone. "What if I'm not the One? What if I am? Then what?" Simone ran into the bathroom crying and slammed the door behind her.

A few minutes later, Simone emerged from the bathroom, having regained her composure, and apologized for her emotional outburst. Raven hugged her, and then they all left to go see the Oracle.

Simone looked nervous in the backseat of the car.

"Not to worry, honey," said Raven. "We're almost there."

Wayne parked the car in a visitor's spot in front of a very nondescript seven-story apartment building. They got out of the car and entered the lobby.

"Which one is hers?" asked Raven, staring at the occupant list for the building.

"Not sure," answered Wayne. "They said I would know it when I saw it."

"Here it is: Rhoda Delfy." Wayne pushed the button and waited. The inner door clicked, and all three of them looked at each other. Wayne quickly grabbed the door handle before it locked again and pulled it open.

"Let's go," he said as they filed through the building's inner door.

"How did you know that was her name?" asked Raven.

"Rhoda is a Greek derivative of the name Pythia, and the last name is Delfy. Too easy."

They entered the elevator, and Wayne pushed the button for the seventh floor.

"I can feel her now," said Simone stoically. "And she can feel me."

They stood staring at door 707. Wayne knocked, but as he did, the door pushed open.

"I'm in here!" said a grandmotherly voice.

Wayne led the way toward where her voice had come from. It was a typically designed apartment with a hall leading to the living room at one end and bedrooms at the other. Wayne turned toward the living room. Beads hung from the entrance, and he could smell incense burning and hear the faint sound of music. After entering through the beads, Wayne stopped, put both hands together in prayer fashion at his chest, and took a half bow forward.

"Namaste," said Wayne.

"Namaste, my friend," replied Pythia softly.

"This is—"

"I know their names," said Pythia as she stood from the lotus position. "Let's take a look, shall we." She walked up to Raven first. "So you are Raven."

"I prefer Ja—"

"You prefer Jane, I know, dear. Raven, however, is more suitable."

Pythia held Raven's hand for what seemed to Raven like an eternity.

"You are a strong one. Easy to see why Simone chose you."

Wayne suddenly realized he knew the music playing in the background.

"Is that John Lennon's—"

"'Imagine,'" said Pythia. "It most certainly is. It's one of my favorites."

"Sorry, I didn't think you would be listening to semimodern music," said Wayne.

"That's OK, dear. Some tunes transcend time, and this one is timeless. And besides, that dude got it all right in that song." Pythia now turned toward Simone.

"Well, look who we have here!" Pythia reached her hand out to Simone, and Simone's hand met hers halfway. Instantly the room grew brighter, and Wayne could clearly see the blue-white aura around them. He could see their lips moving but couldn't make out what they were saying. Wayne felt confident that Simone was, indeed, the One, and their search would finally be over.

The room dimmed again, and Pythia turned and walked away from Simone. Wayne looked at Simone, and she seemed visibly drained.

"Well?" asked Wayne impatiently. "Is she the One?"

Pythia stopped and turned toward Wayne.

"Sorry, big guy."

"What do you mean?" said Wayne. "I was certain—"

"She was the One?" said Pythia.

Wayne was starting to get annoyed at her habit of always finishing people's sentences.

"Wayne, let me tell you a secret. I feel I owe it to you since you've brought me so many candidates."

"There were others?" questioned Raven.

"You will never find the One because there isn't one," continued Pythia, ignoring Raven's question.

"I don't understand," said Wayne.

"I know you don't, dear. You are a good man, and that's why I'm going to tell you what you've come to find out." Pythia once again assumed the lotus position.

"The One does not exist in singular form. Your search has been futile. What you refer to as 'the One' is a 'collective.' A collective of human souls that have awakened enough to vibrate at a high frequency. If enough souls do this together, in harmony, the future of mankind can be altered, and many can make the jump to the next *lokas*. The people who remain will still be in their version of hell and will need to continue their journey over and over until they attain the enlightenment they require to make the jump themselves."

"So it's not one person, a savior, if you will, but a collective of human spirits that is the One?" asked Wayne.

"I think you're on to something there, champ," said Pythia smiling coyly.

"But how many people do we require to become the One?" inquired Wayne.

"No one knows for sure," said Pythia. "But nearest we can tell is the square root of one percent of the population."

"So if there are seven billion people on earth, that's—"

"Eight thousand three hundred and sixty-seven. If you round it up," interjected Simone.

"Simone knows what to do, my friend," said Pythia. "Now leave me alone so I can enjoy my favorite song and meditate." She looked at each one of her guests. "Nice to meet you, Raven. And Simone, you have a gift, so use it. And Wayne..." Wayne turned to look back at the Oracle as she paused. "This will be our last visit my friend. Namaste"

"Namaste," replied Wayne as he half-bowed, hands in prayer fashion at his chest.

The three of them left the Oracle's apartment and walked solemnly toward the elevator. Wayne wondered what she meant by "last visit," as he pushed the button to summon the elevator. They got in, not saying a word to each other, and just stared at the descending lights.

Outside the building, a black SUV had just pulled up, and two very large men, one with a bandage around his hand, emerged from its doors.

"I'll take the front. You take the back," said one of the men in a Texas drawl.

Tex was very light on his feet for a man of his size, and he quickly made a beeline for the front door.

The trio left the elevator without saying a word and stepped through the front doors of the building. Wayne came to an abrupt halt as soon as he heard the mechanical noise of an automatic pistol being cocked.

SIG P226, he thought, used by the Seals and his own JTF2.

Raven and Simone stopped as Wayne did, only to hear the large Texan speak.

"Thought y'all got away, didn't ya?"

All three turned to see the Texan's gun at the end of his outstretched arm.

"Turn around!" ordered Tex. As he spoke, a black van pulled up behind the SUV.

"Walk slowly toward that black van over there," continued Tex. "And no funny business. Especially from you, dentist boy!"

As they walked toward the van, the back door of the SUV opened, and a pair of red high heels and two very long legs appeared.

Sarah! thought Wayne, even before the black-haired beauty emerged.

"Eyes front, Canuck!" barked Tex.

The trio continued to the open back doors of the van and came to a stop at the vehicle.

"Well, well, well!" remarked Sarah as she walked to the rear doors of the van. "Thought you'd seen the last of us, eh?"

There's that "eh" again, thought Raven. She must be Canadian too. Instantly she could feel there was a connection between Wayne and Sarah. More than a casual connection.

"We've been following your every move, hoping you would lead us to the Oracle," continued Sarah.

"You'll never find her!" shouted Simone.

"Oh, and look what we have here. The great Simone. Savior of humankind," replied Sarah majestically.

"No matter, honey, we have you now. That's what we really came for."

"You black-haired bitch!" yelled Raven.

"Oooo, feisty are we? No worries, you'll die like the rest of them." She looked over at Wayne. "And as for you, lover boy, you're almost worth keeping around. Almost!" She then commanded the men. "Shoot Raven and Wayne while the One watches, and put them all in the van."

"Yes, ma'am," answered Tex. "My pleasure!"

"Wait!" shouted Wayne. "Sarah, you know how I hate guns."

As Wayne spoke, he took hold of Raven's hand, who in turn took Simone's hand.

"Yes, I remember," answered Sarah. "So fitting an end for you then, eh? But pray tell—why is it you hate guns so much anyway?"

"It's not that I hate the actual guns so much; it's what they make me do that I hate," answered Wayne.

"Oh really..." started Sarah, but as the words were leaving her mouth, Wayne could feel the surge of energy flowing from Simone, through Raven, and into him.

He moved swiftly, energized with source energy, and grabbed the gun in the Texan's hand, twisted it toward his head, and pulled the trigger. As Tex fell, Wayne pointed the gun at Sarah's feet and shot her in the right foot.

Wayne heard the sound of heavy steps coming toward him and turned to see the other henchman running at them. Wayne aimed at this left leg and squeezed off another round. As the large man fell to the ground, the door of the van opened, and another clone appeared, fumbling with his gun.

Wayne fired two more shots. The first hit the man's gun and knocked it out of his hands, the second catching him in the upper right arm. As the man writhed in pain on the ground, Wayne picked up the man's weapon, another SIG, expelled the magazine, and removed the slide all in one easy motion. Wayne did the same to the SIG he got from Tex and threw the weapons in the ditch.

"Get in!" yelled Wayne as he jumped into the driver's seat. Raven and Simone jumped into the back of the van and closed the doors.

"I didn't think you were going to shoot all those people!" exclaimed Simone, speaking loudly over the sound of the revving engine.

Wayne glanced in the rearview mirror to see Tex running after the van, clutching the ear Wayne had shot off.

"They'll be fine," offered Wayne, feeling remorse for having had to resort to violence, especially guns. God, how he hated guns.

"We have to ditch the van," said Wayne. "It's too dangerous to go back for our car. There's a car rental place a few klicks from here. We'll need to rent a vanilla car."

"A vanilla car?" inquired Raven.

"One that's plain, nondescript," explained Wayne.

As the trio left town in the rented car, Wayne was happy to see the sign "Thanks for visiting Spring Valley" in his rearview mirror.

"It's about a two-and-a-half-hour drive from here, so if you want to get some rest, now's the time," said Wayne.

"Where are we headed?" asked Raven.

"To the middle of nowhere," mumbled Wayne.

"Often referred to as Nellis Air Force Base," said Simone.

Wayne looked at Simone in the rearview mirror and gave her a knowing smile.

"OK," said Raven. "In that case, wake me when it's over."

Chapter 4

There were no signs, just a dirt road that led off the highway. Raven was fast asleep in the front seat, Simone wide awake in the rear.

"Raven, it's over," said Wayne.

"Huh, what?"

"It's over. You told me to wake you when it's over."

"It's over? We're done? The world is saved?" said Raven sleepily.

"No, dear, we're just here, sorry," chuckled Wayne.

"For God's sake, man. Make up your mind!"

Wayne glanced back at Simone.

"She's always that grouchy when she wakes up. Don't take it personally," said Simone.

"Okeydokey!"

They got out of the car and stood in front of a large lift gate and a couple of signs.

"Not even a fence?" asked Raven.

"No fence, just magnetic sensors, electro-optical trip sensors, road sensors, and remote TV cameras," said Simone calmly. "Oh, and armed guards in SUVs, just like the one on that hill to the left."

As Raven looked to her left, Wayne and Simone were focused on the dust cloud in the distance that appeared to be getting closer to them. The black SUV pulled up on the other side of the gate, and for a brief moment, Wayne had that tingly feeling in his spine that told him something was wrong.

The passenger door opened up and out jumped P-A. His real name was Pierre-Alexandre, but everyone called him P-A.

"How are you, my old friend?" offered P-A over the gate.

"Good. All of us are good," answered Wayne.

The driver of the SUV opened the gate, and they all climbed into the SUV.

"What about the car?" asked Raven.

"We won't be needing it anymore," answered Simone.

P-A turned around in his seat, looking at Wayne, and said, "Is she?"

"She is," answered Wayne.

P-A turned to face the front again. "Very good!"

Again, a small tingle in Wayne's spine.

"You know, Wayne and I go back a long time," said P-A, speaking a little louder so all could hear. "We met in basic training and later joined the JTF2 together. *Facta, non verba*, right buddy?"

"Deeds, not words, my friend."

Raven looked out the window as they drove. Nothing but dry, arid land as far as she could see. She wondered what was about to happen next. Wayne knew this P-A guy but didn't seem to trust him. She allowed her mind to drift back to all that had happened over the last few days.

"Unbelievable!" said Raven out loud.

"What's unbelievable?" asked Wayne.

"Oh, the landscape. Yeah, it's so dry and seems to go on forever."

"Sure does," agreed Wayne, knowing full well that Raven was thinking of something else.

The SUV began to slow and soon came to a stop in front of a large rounded building that looked like an aircraft hangar.

"Welcome to Nellis, otherwise referred to as Area 51!" bellowed P-A.

The driver opened the door for Simone and let the others pile out themselves. P-A led them to a small door to the right of the main hangar doors.

"Right through here, ladies."

P-A was always a ladies' man, thought Wayne. He was, after all, French Canadian.

"So this is Area 51?" queried Raven.

"This? No, this is just a faux building, my dear. The rest is—"

"Below ground. Yes, I know," interjected Simone. "I have had many dreams and visions of this place."

Just like the Oracle, thought Wayne. Always cutting people off.

"We'll take the stairs one floor down and pass through security before we go any farther," said P-A.

"Stairs?" asked Raven. "What, no fancy elevators?"

"You haven't seen nothing yet, *ma chère*..."

Wayne felt that tingle again as P-A let that last sentence trail off as he headed for the stairs.

After passing some very hi-tech and elaborate security measures, P-A finally led the group down a long hallway. The hall eventually opened up to a very large room. In the centre of the floor was painted a large red circle with a red *X* in the middle of it.

"OK, everybody stand inside of the red circle," announced P-A in a booming voice.

As soon as everyone was situated within the red circle, a bright red curtain of light sprang up from the floor and stretched to the ceiling.

"Relax, everyone; the light curtain is there for your safety." As P-A spoke, he was pressing some buttons on a control panel that appeared as the curtain was activated.

Soon they could feel the floor begin to move beneath them. Slowly at first and then so fast that everything outside of the curtain was a blur. Simone reached out her hand and let her fingers pierce the light curtain. She felt a mild tingling sensation that increased in intensity the further she stuck her hand into the red curtain of light. Not unlike our combined energy fields, she thought.

"Almost there," said P-A. Suddenly the elaborate elevator began to slow and came to a Swiss-like precision stop.

"We're here," said P-A in Raven's direction. "Five thousand five hundred and eighty-five feet—over one mile below the surface. Cool, eh?"

"If you like that sort of thing," quipped Raven.

The light curtain dropped, and P-A started walking.

"Follow me!" commanded P-A.

P-A led them down another long hall and up to a large set of black doors with curious stainless steel symbols on them. They looked alien somehow.

"OK. Beyond these doors lies things and information that are highly classified. You all have clearance to be here, but there are armed guards present, and they will shoot you if you stray from the group and go where you are not allowed. Understood? *Oui?* Let's go."

P-A placed his hand into a slot in the door while simultaneously looking into a retina scanner. It triggered a *clunk*, and the doors began to open.

Everyone stood in awe in what they saw. People were moving about busily in front of them, some in doctors' scrubs, others in coveralls like mechanics, but it wasn't the workers that were holding their attention. Past all the people, through a huge twelve-inch-thick glass window, hovered a flying disc.

The Frisbee-shaped craft pitched and yawed and seemed to be rotating and moving about its centre.

"Wow!" offered Raven.

"Unbelievable!" mouthed Wayne slowly.

"Old technology," added Simone.

"Are you serious?" questioned Raven.

"She's right," interjected P-A. "We've had this for a while now. They're just testing—"

"The new guidance system to allow the craft to be used for war," said Simone in a monotone.

"She can be very annoying, can't she?" said P-A rhetorically.

"Tell me about it," offered Wayne sympathetically.

∞

Not that far away, at the Las Vegas airport, a blond bombshell wearing red sneakers was making her way through security at the Janet Terminal, toward the classified aircraft servicing Area 51. Sarah passed with no problem and made her way to the waiting area to have a seat.

Her right foot was killing her even though the doctor had frozen the pain nerves for her before she left. It felt like walking on a stump, except it still hurt.

That son of a bitch! He'll get his. Had to shoot me in the foot, didn't you, asshole? she fumed. "You know how much I like my high heels!"

A couple of other passengers turned to look at her.

Oops. I guess I said that last part out loud, thought Sarah. "Sorry. I...I forgot my heels," she offered with one of her patented smiles. Whew! Don't draw attention to yourself, honey. Hang in there; you'll soon see Mr. Wayne Offenshaw!

Chapter 5

"Offenshaw!" shouted P-A.

"Eh? Yeah, OK, I'm coming." Wayne was still staring at the disc as the group left and headed down another corridor.

"You're going to have to keep up, *mon ami*. Don't want anything to happen to ya!" said P-A smiling.

Wayne felt another tingle, and he still wasn't sure why. He was in a very secure facility that was run by the people he worked for and trusted. Keep your eyes and ears open, Wayne thought to himself. Anything is possible.

The group had stopped and waited for Wayne and P-A to catch up.

"Right this way," said P-A as he took the lead once again.

P-A led the group into a large boardroom complete with nice, comfy high-back leather chairs, a huge oak table, and a video screen.

"There's someone you folks need to meet, and he will be here shortly, but until then, we eat!" As P-A finished his words, two women and a man brought in food and drinks for the weary travelers.

Raven and Simone looked relieved and began to eat. Wayne hesitated but then realized how hungry he actually was and began to eat too.

"Now that you've all had a chance to rest and enjoy some sustenance," started P-A, "I want to introduce you to our head scientist on the project, Dr. Jian Shi."

A thin man entered the room. "Good afternoon, ladies and gentlemen," said Dr. Jian with a slight Chinese accent. "I know you have had a long and arduous journey to get here, but we have no time to waste, so I will dive right in. You were brought here to fulfill a role in a very important project. A project so important, the survival of our species hangs in the balance.

"Simone, not to put undue pressure on you, but you were identified as the missing element we need to complete the transfer of humankind to the next lokas, or level within the multiverse, if you will. You see, all is not as it seems. Many of the people on the earth today just go to work, get paid, spend money, sleep, eat, and repeat—totally unaware of the power each one of us has within us. The power to create our own reality. The power to be our own God. I see you are a bit perplexed, so I will start at the beginning."

"Excuse me, Doc, but I'll leave you folks alone for a bit. I've got a few things to tend to," interrupted P-A.

"Sure thing, Pierre-Alexandre," obliged Dr. Jian.

I hate when he uses my full name, thought P-A.

"OK, thank you. Excuse me, folks." P-A muttered to his assistant to follow him and left the room. Once in the hallway, P-A gave his orders to his subordinate. "No one in, no one out of that room until I return, got it?"

"Yes, sir," answered the man dutifully.

"Good. I'll be back shortly," said P-A as he was walking away. He was happy he didn't have to listen to all that airy-fairy, mumbo-jumbo stuff again. Now to get some work done.

Wayne didn't much care to let P-A out of his sight like that but settled in to listen to what Dr. Jian Shi had to say.

"So, as I was saying, in the beginning, there was nothing but energy, source energy, the energy of the cosmos. It matters not what you call it, it just is, and there was nothing else. Yet the energy could not know itself because it was all there was; there was no reference point. So in the absence of nothing else, 'all that is' was not. This is the great 'is or is not' that mystics and all the great teachers have referred to since the beginning of time. Now, this energy source knew it was all there was, but that was not enough because it only knew this conceptually, not experientially. It wanted to know what it felt like to be so magnificent, but it could not know what it felt like to be so magnificent unless that which is not, showed up. Everyone with me so far?" asked Dr. Jian.

"Yes!" said Simone.

"Yes," answered Raven, and a wavering "I think so" came from Wayne.

"Good, let's keep going then," said Dr. Jian.

"Since this pure, unseen, unheard, and unknown energy decided to experience itself as the utter magnificence it was, it realized it had to use some sort of reference point. It then decided that any portion of itself would have to be less than the whole, and if it simply divided itself into portions, each portion, being less than the whole, could look back on itself and see magnificence. So, 'all that is' divided itself, becoming, in one glorious second, that which 'is this,' and that which 'is that.'

"For the first time, 'this' and 'that' existed separate from each other, but so did something else. That which was 'neither.' Therefore, three elements suddenly existed: that which is 'here,' that which is 'there,' and that which is 'neither here nor there' but which must exist for 'here' and 'there' to exist. It is the nothing that holds the everything. It is the nonspace that holds the space. It is the all that holds the parts.

"Everyone still with me? Good." Dr. Jian didn't wait for a response this time; he just kept right on going, gathering velocity like a snowball rolling downhill.

"OK, let's take this a little further now," said Dr. Jian.

"Now this 'nothing,' which is also 'everything,' is what some would call God. There are differing opinions on this, depending on whether you subscribe to the great Eastern traditions or the more practical Western description of God. However, the one that is correct is the one for those who believe that God is 'all that is' and 'all that is not.'"

Wayne slid down in his chair and released a sigh. When will this torture end? he thought.

∞

"Now boarding Flight Six to Nellis, leaving from Gate Two," said the announcement.

Good, just in time, thought Sarah as she returned from the ladies' room. If I have to adjust this stupid blond wig one more time, I'm going to burn the damn thing!

Sarah walked to the gate with her small bag, wondering if P-A had lived up to his end of the bargain.

∞

"Now, in creating that which is 'here,' and that which is 'there,'" continued Dr. Jian, "God made it possible for God to know itself. In that moment of great expansion from within, God created relativity. The greatest gift God ever gave itself. So, from the 'nothing' sprang the 'everything.' An event we scientists like to call the big bang theory. Isn't this exciting?" asked Dr. Jian, again not waiting for a response.

"And as the elements of all raced forward, time was created because something was first 'here,' then it was 'there,' and the period of time it took to get there was measurable!"

Wayne felt compelled to jump in. "OK, Doc. Thanks for the history lesson, but what has this got to do with us, with Simone?"

"Ah, Mr. Wayne, you ask a good question. Patience for a little more, and then we will get to that, OK?"

Oh goody! thought Wayne as he nodded and smiled at Dr. Jian.

∞

P-A had moved swiftly and gained access to the main security control console. One man dead, another just injured to get access. Acceptable, thought P-A. Just need to plant this bomb under the console, put everything in autosurvey, and wait for Sarah to arrive.

He already had half of the agreed sum in his personal account and was looking forward to the rest. He wouldn't even mind a crack at Sarah, if possible. Wayne had his turn and screwed it up.

"My turn now!" said P-A aloud as he left the control centre.

∞

"God now knew for love to exist, and to know itself as 'pure love,'" continued Dr. Jian, "its exact opposite had to exist as well. So God created the great polarity, the first of many dichotomies and parables we humans would have to navigate—he created fear. In the moment love's opposite, fear, existed, love could exist as a thing that could be experienced. Do you see how this is all tying together now?"

P-A returned to the boardroom door. "Anyone enter or leave?"

"No, sir, not a soul," said his assistant.

"Interesting choice of words." The lock on the door clicked as P-A ran his card through the scanner.

Wayne heard the click and was thankful for P-A's return. There goes that tingle again, he thought.

"Hello, Pierre-Alexandre. We are just finishing up here," said Dr. Jian.

P-A nodded and sat down quietly.

"OK, people, getting close to the end now." Without a breath, Dr. Jian launched into the last session.

"In rendering the universe as a divided version of itself, God produced, from pure energy, all that now exists, both seen and unseen. God's divine purpose in dividing was to create sufficient parts of itself so that it could know itself experientially as the creator, and there is only one way for the creator to know itself as a creator, and that is to create. And so, God gave to each of the countless parts of itself—its offspring, spirit children, or in other words us—the same power to create as the whole. Yes, people, we are of the same essence as God. We are the same stuff. We must be like what we came from, yes? And with all the same properties and abilities, including the ability to create physical reality out of thin air!"

"Why would he do that?" blurted out P-A.

"Ah, Pierre-Alexandre, good question. God's purpose for creating you, its spiritual offspring, was for it to know itself. It had no way of doing so except through us. God's purpose for us is that we should know ourselves as being part of God. But conceptual awareness was not enough, so God devised a plan, or rather a 'collaboration' because we were all in on this with God, to allow us to enter the universe just created, in physical form. This is because physicality is the only way to know experientially what you already know conceptually. Once in the realm of the physical, you could experience that which you know, but first you had to know the opposite.

"Simply put, you could not know yourself as tall unless you became aware of short. And you could not know yourself as fat unless you became aware of thin. Therefore, you cannot experience yourself as what you are until you become aware of what you are not. This, we scientists like to say, is the purpose of the theory of relativity and all physical life. And as such, you cannot experience yourself as a creator unless, and until, you create. And you cannot create yourself until you uncreate yourself. Put simply, you must first 'not be' in order to 'be.' This can be very subtle, but you all are clear on these distinctions, yes?"

"As if," mumbled Wayne. "Yes!" said Simone. "I'm pretty sure," said Raven.

"Don't worry," said Dr. Jian. "It will become much clearer when we get down to the lab."

"Can't wait!" mumbled Wayne again, followed by a laser-beam-like stare from Simone. "What?" mouthed Wayne.

P-A arose from the table and said, "OK, people, from here we go down another floor to the lab. Let's meet out in the hall, and we'll go from there."

Everyone got up from their cushy chairs and gave a big stretch.

"Thank you, Dr. Jian," said Raven as she moved past him.

"Thanks, Doc," said Wayne.

Simone walked up to Dr. Jian and extended her hand. Dr. Jian shook her hand and said, "Nice to finally meet you, Simone—oh! I...I wasn't expecting that!"

As Simone's hand met Dr. Jian's, a transfer of energy took place that Dr. Jian had never felt before. It caught him totally unaware.

Expecting what? asked Simone. Dr. Jian had heard her speak but didn't see her lips move.

The energy coming from you—the connectedness, thought Dr. Jian, realizing he too was communicating with her through his thoughts, and his lips weren't moving either.

You're not like the others, communicated Dr. Jian.

Others? thought Simone.

Yes, sorry, there were others before you. We've been searching a long time. Some have been male; some have been female; all either Simon or Simone. They all had abilities but not like you.

Wayne stopped at the door to look for Simone, and he could see Dr. Jian and Simone locked in a handshake and staring at each other. Then he noticed the slight blue-white aura surrounding them.

They failed where I will succeed, commented Simone. *Your name, your full name is Jianghu Shi, which means "architect" in Chinese.*

Yes, I was given that name by my lab parents. I was given up for adoption by my real parents. They were too poor to keep me, and they were only allowed one child in those days. I was raised by scientists. Good people, they were, but not full of love, like you.

Simone thought, *Thank you for your honesty*, and slowly pulled her hand away.

"Thank you so much for your lecture, Dr. Jian. I learned a great deal," said Simone.

Dr. Jian heard Simone speak and saw her lips moving once again. *The connection is gone*, he thought. *What a glorious experience!*

"You are very welcome, my dear. I look forward to our future interactions," said Dr. Jian.

"I as well."

Dr. Jian turned toward the door to see Wayne in the doorway looking back at them. *What seemed like minutes to Mr. Wayne must have been only a few seconds for us*, he thought. *Perfect!*

Dr. Jian could barely contain his excitement as he made his way to the hallway to meet the others.

Chapter 6

"Good afternoon, ladies and gentlemen. This is your first officer speaking. Today we're flying at twenty-five thousand feet instead of our customary twenty thousand to avoid a little bit of turbulence in the area. Better to be stirred than shaken, right? Sorry folks, couldn't resist. We should be landing on time, in about thirty minutes from now. Relax and enjoy the flight."

"Oh, things will get shaken, all right. If you only knew, Mr. First Officer; if you only knew!" mumbled Sarah to herself.

∞

After another ride in the supersecure elevator, the group entered the main laboratory wing. Dr. Jian was leading the group now and took them down a long corridor to another set of big doors.

Dr. Jian placed his hand in the slot and his eyes in front of the retina scanner. After a series of *clunks*, the right-hand door opened slowly.

"Motorized?" asked Wayne.

"Hydraulic," answered Dr. Jian. "These doors are very strong and heavy. Good for keeping people out, but also for keeping them in."

"Everybody follow Dr. Jian, please," said P-A. Sarah should be landing soon, he thought as he made his way through the heavy twelve-inch-thick steel doors.

When they arrived at the main lab area, there were many other scientists dressed in lab coats busily working on things.

"What's all the fuss about?" asked Raven.

"It's all for you, Miss Raven, or more correctly, all for Miss Simone," replied Dr. Jian as he smiled at Simone.

Dr. Jian walked over to say something to P-A and then walked back to Simone. "Please, let's go to my office so we can communicate some more."

"Where are you taking her?" objected Wayne.

Dr. Jian needs to talk to Simone in private, my friend," said P-A. "The rest of us will wait in here."

P-A opened a door to what looked like a staff lunchroom. "Come on, *mon ami*; they'll be fine."

"I'll be fine," said Simone. "Go with P-A; I won't be but a few moments."

"Are you sure?"

"Yes. Now go!" Simone said using a more direct tone this time.

"OK. Just yell if you need anything, literally," said Wayne. Simone smiled then turned and walked with Dr. Jian to his office.

Three doors down on the left, counted Wayne as he watched them enter Dr. Jian's office.

Dr. Jian motioned to Simone to sit at a small round table to the right of what she assumed to be his desk.

"I have many more things to tell you, Miss Simone, and time is of the essence. Can we once again engage in the energy transfer?"

"Of course!" said Simone. "It will be much quicker that way."

"Good," offered Dr. Jian as Simone reached across the table and held his hands.

Dr. Jian felt a warm, tingly feeling, then felt Simone say, *Where shall we start?* Again, her lips were not moving, but Dr. Jian heard her as if she were right in his head. *Was she?* thought Dr. Jian. *Yes, I am!* communicated Simone.

I can hear everything you are thinking, but I can't read your memories. OK, that is good, thought Dr. Jian.

When we were communicating before, you mentioned that there were others, both male and female. Can you expand on that?

Yes, yes. But I must tell you about why you are here too.

Certainly, but first about the other mes.

Dr. Jian began. *We are not just living in this universe. We are, instead, existing in an infinite number of universes that we call the multiverse. Within this multiverse is an alternate version of you and me. Some male, some female. Since we are a piece of God, we can do all she can do. So our primary function, if you will, is to create. But in order to do this, we must access both our male and female side. Each of us has male and female energies within us.*

The female part is our intuitive self. This is the receptive part. Those inner gut feelings, promptings, or images that come from deep within us. She is the source of our higher wisdom within us, and if we learn to listen to her, she will guide us perfectly.

The male part is action. To think, speak, move, and do things. Whether you are a man or woman, your male energy is your ability to act. The female part of you receives the universal creative energy, and the male part of you puts it into action. The union of feminine and masculine energies within the individual is the basis of all creation. Female intuition and thought plus male action equals creativity.

Therefore, since we are here to create, we must have well-developed sides of both male and female, without each one fighting each other for dominance.

Different versions of you, Simone, have come to us from different multiverses, through an energy field not unlike this one, to try to help us gain the energy we need to make the quantum jump to the next level or lokas. Each one of them, however, has failed because they did not have the correct balance of male-female in order to create what we need.

And what would that be? thought Simone.

The ability to channel the energy of our universe to many people simultaneously.

Like a conduit?

Exactly!

∞

The nondescript white with red stripe Boeing 737 taxied to a halt near the passenger section of the hangar at Nellis Air Force Base. The stairs were brought over to the front exit, and everyone just stood up en masse to retrieve their overhead luggage.

"Can I get your bag for you, ma'am?" asked a middle-aged slightly overweight man.

"Why, thank you, dear," fired back Sarah with a huge smile. "How very kind of you!"

Sarah gave the man an inviting look, and he smiled back, but he'd seen this look many times before from women, and he knew it was hollow.

"There you are, ma'am. Have a wonderful day!"

"Oh, I plan to!"

∞

Tell me about the multiverse, communicated Simone.

Well, I haven't travelled it myself, yet, but from what I have been told by those that have, you travel through an energy tube of some sort, but in order to do so, you lose your physical form and become a sphere of energy, like an orb, bright and brilliant. Then you travel down the tube, made of the same energy as you and me, by the way, but it twists and turns, goes up then down, until you reach the plane of the multiverse you are seeking. Once out of the tube, you can see the planes of the multiverse in action. It looks like a tall building that has endless height and width. A matrix, if you will. There are no walls on the building, so you can see what is taking place in people's lives as they act them out.

Who are all these people? thought Simone.

They are you. Some are male, which in your case are the Simons, and some are female, which are the Simones. We are living more than just this life, and we are living them all simultaneously. You see, every time you make a major decision in your life, you—that is, the earth you—goes one way and another version of you goes the other way. So your life is playing out differently in each level of the multiverse. Cool, huh?

Way cool!

Now you see why we need you. Not only to communicate with people on earth but to summon all of the Simons' and Simones' energy from the multiverse as well."

∞

Sarah made her way through security without issue.

Well, at least Emily Cartwright served her country when she gave up her life. Her ID worked perfectly, thought Sarah. "Now to find a spot to hide so no one recognizes me, and contact the others," she mumbled as she made her way to the elevator. "Someone has to stop these nuts. Quantum jump—not on my watch, you don't!"

∞

I feel like we're communicating very quickly. I mean, I don't think much time is passing. Does that make sense? thought Simone.

Yes, you are correct. Thought is very fast; it knows no distance. Your thoughts traverse the universe faster than you can say the word. And that is good because we have more to cover before we go live.

Go live?

Yes, within the hour we will know if we can save our species from extinction and move on to the next higher plane in the multiverse. Just like the Mayan, the Harappan, the Khmer, the people of Atlantis and Easter Island, and many more did. If not, we will live our lives out here on earth, doomed to self-destruct, thought Dr. Jian.

What happens to those that are left here on earth? Obviously not all will make the journey.

Again, you are correct, thought Dr. Jian. *Those left behind will live out their lives like many have before, then die, and then their souls will return to the realm of the absolute. The place of perfect love. And when they are ready, they will choose their parents and begin another adventure.*

Tell me more about our souls, thought Simone excitedly.

Of course, but first I must explain some history to you and go over the three laws of the universe.

You mean, like, the law of attraction? communicated Simone.

No, not really, no. That does exist, but it is very elementary. I'm talking about the three laws of creation.

You see, the first people to come to our earth needed to allow their souls to know themselves experientially, not just conceptually. You know them as Adam and Eve. They were the father and mother of the human experience, once they discovered good and evil as it is told, or as I like to say, love and fear. You see, one cannot exist without the other. We can experience love because we know it's the opposite of fear. But what has been described as the fall of Adam or even humankind was really the greatest single event in the history of humankind. Adam was perceived to have made the wrong choice, and so Adam and Eve provided our ability of making any choice at all.

In our mythology, we have made Eve the "bad" one, the temptress, who coyly invited Adam to eat the fruit after she herself had done. This mythology was deliberately set up to allow us to make women man's downfall, resulting in warped opinions and distorted sexual views. How can we feel so good about something so bad? So now we have love and fear. This leads us to the three laws of the universe.

∞

Raven and Wayne watched closely as seemingly hundreds of computer programmers worked feverishly at their terminals. All working on something different yet connected in some way.

P-A grabbed his cell phone from his pocket. It was the text he was waiting for.

"Dinner at five, my dear? Emily."

"I should be done my work by then, so sounds good. I will be very hungry! P-A."

"Texts in the facility?" asked Wayne.

"Yes, just inner office stuff. Nothing in or out because of the signal jammers," offered P-A.

"Of course, I knew that," said Wayne. Wayne now knew something was definitely up with P-A. Cell phones use GSM frequencies 860 and 1900, and all those signals were jammed here. It had to be a "ghost" frequency of some kind.

P-A politely excused himself and said he would be back shortly.

Got to keep my eye on that one, thought Wayne. "Frickin' turn-coat!" he mumbled under his breath. Maybe I can turn him into a useful idiot, but how?

∞

The three laws are really very simple, began Dr. Jian. *First, thought is creative. Second, fear attracts like energy. Third, love is all there is.*

OK, I get most of that, but how can love be all there is when fear attracts like energy?

Good question, Simone. Well, love is the ultimate reality. It is all there is, and all there will ever be. It is the All. The realm of the relative, the earth, was created in order for God to experience herself, as I mentioned previously, but this doesn't make it real. It is a created reality that you and I have cocreated with God, in order to know ourselves experientially.

This creation can seem so real that we accept it as truly existing. God endured an environment in which you may choose to be God yourself, because you are her. But rather than just being told you are her, she allows us to experience that which we know is intrinsically, but only conceptually, true. This allows for the primal polarity of fear, the opposite of love. It is, in essence, the ultimate dichotomy.

Dr. Jian continued. *In the realm of the relative, the physical plane, there are only two places of being: fear and love. Thoughts about fear will produce one kind of manifestation in the physical plane, and thoughts about love will, similarly, produce another. You must remember this. It is the law, and it will always be true no matter what.*

Throughout time, this truth has been whispered by all the masters that walked the earth: Love is the answer. Yet, we continually do not listen. To make the leap to the next lokas, fear must be abolished from our minds. If there is fear or anger or any of the thoughts fear brings with it in our minds and hearts, we will not make the quantum jump. I can't impress this upon you enough.

Yes, I understand, communicated Simone. *Can we talk about the soul now?*

Yes, now we can talk about the soul.

∞

P-A didn't like returning to the scene of the crime but had to make sure all was good with the charges he had set earlier. He accessed the security room and stood silently as he assessed all the cameras and other security devices.

Good, all is still in auto and functioning normally. Not for long though! thought P-A. Then he glanced at his watch—4:35 p.m. Twenty-five minutes to go, and then all hell will break loose. Can't wait!

∞

The soul, your soul, began Dr. Jian, *knows all there is to know all the time, but knowing is not enough. The soul seeks to experience, as I mentioned before. It is your soul's desire to turn the grand concept of itself into its greatest experience. Until this concept becomes experience, everything is just speculation.*

That is the goal of your soul. To fully realize itself while in the body. And as the soul realizes itself, so does God since we are all one and the same. In this way, the concept of itself is turned into experience.

So our soul and God are experiencing themselves through the body? asked Simone.

Exactly, but you must remember that you, your soul, and God are one and the same. You are the One, no matter if we are successful today or not. You're the One; I'm the One; we're all the One."

So I'm not that special after all then?

Oh yes, you are. You have the ability to be an energy conduit like nothing we've ever seen. And we've been looking a long time. It is you who will make our quantum jump possible. So you are the One, but we are too. Understood?

Yup, and now that you've put it so plainly, I understand it.

Good. Very good! thought Dr. Jian. *Let's disconnect and rejoin the others. It's time to make our way back to the lab.*

"Thank you for all you've done and for everything we are about to do," said Simone.

Dr. Jian could see Simone's lips moving once again. "It is my life's work. You are welcome."

Chapter 7

Simone and Dr. Jian arrived back at the lab to find Wayne and P-A arguing.

"So, where were you, then?" shouted Wayne.

"I told you; I was checking the main security station. It's part of my job!" fired back P-A.

"How are you able to receive text messages, P-A?" retorted Wayne.

"You're receiving texts?" asked Dr. Jian. "That's impossible. All the signals are jammed."

"Exactly!" added Wayne.

Dr. Jian instinctively moved in front of Simone.

"So it's you!" blurted Dr. Jian. "You are the Judas. They said there would be one who would betray us."

"Come on, Doc, lighten up with the mumbo jumbo now, OK? I'm far from perfect, but I ain't no Judas."

"Let me see your phone then!" said Wayne.

"Gentlemen, gentlemen, all your yelling has got to stop!" growled a deep voice coming toward them.

"General Wales!" said P-A. "We're so sorry for any disturbance we may have caused."

"I should hope so," said General Wales in his trademark southern drawl. "We need quiet so our boys can concentrate because this here experiment is about to start."

"You must be Simone?" asked General Wales, looking past Dr. Jian.

"Yes, I am," said Simone, clearing her throat.

"Well, pretty lady, come with me," said General Wales, offering his elbow to Simone.

"And you must be her mother, Raven," said General Wales as he offered his other elbow to Raven.

Wayne, P-A, and Dr. Jian stood in disbelief as the general strolled away with mother and daughter hooked to his arms.

General Wales stopped and looked back. "Dr. Jian!"

"Yes, sir?"

"Let's get this show on the road, shall we."

"Yes, sir. Of course, sir."

"I'm watching you!" said Wayne to P-A.

"And you!" Wayne switched his glare to Dr. Jian. "This experiment— Is this some sort of military operation?"

"It's the only way I could get the funding," offered Dr. Jian.

"Does Simone know?"

"I told her all she needs to know," said Dr. Jian.

P-A took the opportunity to turn and walk toward the door.

Wayne started after him. "Where do you think you're going?"

Dr. Jian grabbed Wayne's arm. "Let him go. You are needed here, and we need to do this *now*!"

Dr. Jian and Wayne hurried to catch up with the general and his newly acquired entourage.

"OK, Doc," said General Wales. "Simone is all yours, and I will keep Miss Raven company while the show begins."

"Yes, yes, of course, General Wales," said Dr. Jian. "But may I have a word with Miss Raven before we begin?"

"Certainly," answered the general. "When you're done, Raven honey, you can join me right over here."

Dr. Jian reached out for Raven's hand and led her about ten feet from the general.

"Holy shit, big ego or what?" blurted out Raven as soon as they stopped.

"Yes, yes, I know. I apologize," offered Dr. Jian. "I need to talk to you about what is about to take place."

"I'm listening," said Raven. "I don't want you to be afraid," continued Dr. Jian. "And no harm will come to Simone."

"I should hope not!" asserted Raven.

"Simone will be acting as a conduit for universal energy," started Dr. Jian. "Her body will be channeling large amounts of energy from the universe to twelve others that are all hooked up to transmit this energy over the Internet."

"Over the Internet? Is this some kind of online game?"

"No. I mean, yes. Well, sort of," said Dr. Jian. "The universal energy will travel worldwide reaching millions of people. These people will instantly awaken from the slumber they have been in and realize they, too, are the One. They, too, are God. When that many minds think alike, we can make the quantum jump to the next level in the multiverse, the next lokas."

"Yes, Dr. Jian, I get that, but the Internet? I always thought it was just for spreading lies and crap," said Raven.

"Yes, well, it's actually going to save humankind. Who knew!" said Dr. Jian.

"So when I signal to you," continued Dr. Jian, "come over to me so you can make the jump too. Understood?"

"Yes, I understand," said Raven nodding. "But what about the others in the room?"

"Most are just military clowns!" said Dr. Jian. "They don't believe or are just too deep asleep to remember who they truly are. They will be left behind."

"What will happen to them?" asked Raven.

"They will continue their lives here on earth," said Dr. Jian, "but it will not be pretty. The world is poised to be taken over by a new world order. Disguised as an entity of truth and justice, they will decimate anyone or anything in their way of global domination. Ultimately, they will destroy most of the life left here on the planet."

"How many will make the jump with us?" asked Raven.

"We are hoping one-third of the population will make it."

"Won't they wonder where we went?" asked Raven.

"They will for a while," said Dr. Jian. "But most people will be too busy trying to stay alive to care."

∞

P-A had left the lab area and was making his way to the upper level. He would need to get the SUV and drive to the main hangar and wait for Sarah.

Sarah glanced at her watch 4:50 p.m. Won't be long now, she thought. Time to ditch this stupid wig and clothing.

Sarah quickly changed into the clothes she had brought in her bag. The only thing she kept was Emily's radio-frequency ID card.

"Where are you?" said Sarah aloud as she fumbled in the bag. "Ahh, here we go." Sarah pulled out the special bag that rendered anything inside it undetectable.

"Nice to see you, old friend," said Sarah as she unzipped the small bag to reveal her SIG P226 pistol.

∞

"Dr. Jian!" bellowed General Wales. "Can we *please* get this thing started."

"Yes, sir, of course, sir."

"Come sit over here with me, Raven honey. You can sit back and enjoy the show," said General Wales.

Dr. Jian shot her a knowing glance, and Raven reluctantly walked over to sit beside the general.

"Your daughter is our missing link to make all this work," said General Wales.

"Oh?" said Raven, trying to sound surprised.

"And what will you do with her after the experiment?" asked Raven.

"Oh, she'll continue to work for us. We'll pay her, of course," said General Wales, seeing the concern in Raven's eyes. "And you, too, little Missy; we'll take care of the pair of ya."

"That's what I'm afraid of," mumbled Raven under her breath.

Wayne was watching Dr. Jian give orders to his fellow scientists and assorted military personnel. They all seemed to know what to do, as if they had done this many times before.

"OK, Mr. Wayne, we are ready to start," said Dr. Jian when he walked over. "I just need to bring Simone in and place her in her chair."

Wayne grabbed Dr. Jian's arm. "You've done this before, haven't you?"

"What do you mean, Mr. Wayne?"

"This whole setup. It looks well rehearsed."

"Well, yes, we have tried it but were never successful," said Dr. Jian.

"And what happened to the stooge you put in that chair?" asked Wayne. "Answer me, damn it!"

"Please settle down, Mr. Wayne."

"They didn't make it, did they? These people died for your experiment!" exclaimed Wayne with clenched teeth.

Dr. Jian saw the anger in Wayne's eyes. "They gave their lives willingly to save us. To save humankind. You should be thankful. Besides, I am quite confident this Simone is the one we have been waiting for," said Dr. Jian coldly.

"If she dies, you die. I promise you that."

"We are all in this together, Mr. Wayne. If she dies, we all die." Dr. Jian's words rang true in Wayne's soul, and he released his grip on Dr. Jian.

"I will need your help with Raven," said Dr. Jian. "She must keep the thought of love in her mind. If she, or anyone, thinks thoughts of fear while making their jump, they will drop out."

"I understand."

Dr. Jian picked up the intercom headset and spoke into the tiny microphone that covered his mouth.

"Bring in Simone," boomed the lab speakers.

Wayne looked up to see Simone entering the room. She was being guided by a person on either side of her so she wouldn't trip on the plethora of wires dangling at her sides. The wires were connected to points on what looked like some kind of gold-coloured bathing cap that Simone was wearing. It seemed like hundreds of tiny tentacles stretching out from the body of a jellyfish.

Wayne watched intently as the helpers guided Simone to her chair. As soon as she sat down, other workers appeared and began strapping her in and connecting all the wires to different points on a control board in front of her. Simone slowly turned her head, glanced around, and found her mom. Simone gave her a reassuring look as if all would be just fine.

"I love you," mouthed Simone.

"I love you too!" mouthed Raven back as the tears began to well up in her eyes.

"Is she going to be OK?" sniffled Raven.

"Now don't you worry, honey. Your little filly will be just fine," said General Wales.

Raven detected a slight tone of condescension in the general's voice.

"I hope you're right!" she said.

Me too! thought General Wales as visions of past experiments flashed through his mind.

Wayne walked over to Dr. Jian. "How will she transfer all the energy to people outside of here?"

"Through the Internet," answered Dr. Jian, speaking louder now as the first series of electrical transformers began to hum away.

"Yes, but how?" asked Wayne again.

"I haven't got time to go over everything now, but basically we start with solid-state Tesla coils to provide initial excitation and wirelessly send high voltage to a zero-point energy device. Then we feed it though a crystal oscillator to create an electrical signal with the precise frequency we want. After that we fine tune the electrical signal to the exact frequency of blue light, about 380 to 500 nanometers. We use blue light because it is one of the shortest and highest energy wavelengths. It also is naturally emitted from televisions, computers, laptops, smartphones, tablets, and florescent and LED lightbulbs."

"So the blue light will attract people to their screens?" asked Wayne.

"Yes," said Dr. Jian. "But in order to access the true potential of the zero-point energy in the universe, we must use a conduit. We can boost the voltage, but not the amperage, with the Tesla coils to make the blue light much stronger, and since light is made up of electromagnetic particles and travels in waves, even if you are not at your screen, you will be attracted to it. We estimate anyone within twenty-five metres of a screen or lightbulb will be affected."

"Sounds like you're not sure if it'll work," said Wayne. "And what about this zero-point energy? Is that not just theoretical?"

"Oh, it will work. The theory is sound, and the mechanics and calculations prove it," said Dr. Jian.

"And yes, zero-point energy has yet to be tapped, but it does exist. Nikola Tesla stated that 'if you want to understand the secrets of the universe, think in terms of energy, frequency, and vibration.' Zero-point energy is the point from which vibration is created. It is resistance-free and has instantaneous flow. It is consciousness itself. At its full expression, it is unconditional love. It is the source. The God Point, if you will."

"Hmm, never thought of it that way," said Wayne.

"I know," replied Dr. Jian with a slight smile.

"So what are you using as a conduit to access the zero-point energy?" asked Wayne, speaking even louder now as Dr. Jian had energized the second set of transformers.

"That's where Simone comes in, Mr. Wayne," answered Dr. Jian.

Chapter 8

P-A stopped the black SUV in front of the back entrance into the main hangar and looked at his watch 4:55 p.m.—just about show time, he thought. P-A entered the back door and made his way to the main level and looked around. No sign of Sarah.

"Almost dinnertime. Where are you now?" texted P-A on his smartphone.

"Women's head" showed on his screen.

"OK. I'm parked out back waiting to take you to dinner," replied P-A.

"Sounds good. See you soon" flashed on his screen.

P-A went back down the flight of stairs he had just climbed and slipped back into the SUV and started it.

"Air conditioning on max and fan on full. Why do they give us black SUVs anyway?" said P-A to himself. "Man, it's a hot one today, and it's about to get a lot hotter!"

∞

Simone looked around her. There were twelve young men and women, six of each, arranged around her in a circle. *They're all Simons or Simones from another universe,* she thought.

Yes, we are, replied one of the males.

Cool, so we can use telepathy to communicate. Why are you all sitting around me in a circle?

We were selected from our levels of the multiverse because we share our soul with you. Because of this, we will be able to collect the excess energy you will not be able to process and send it on to its destination, thought Simon #5.

And you came here of your own free will?

Yes, communicated Simon #5. *Earth is in a transitional phase right now, and if enough people can make the jump to the next lokas, then the earth will have a chance to be rehabilitated and survive. Otherwise, we will lose the earth as a destination for our souls to discover themselves. That would be a great tragedy because the earth is one of the only places that our souls can experience so many feelings all at once. It is the best place for our souls to know themselves experientially. And that is the soul's sole purpose.*

What was that? communicated Simone.

Did you feel a slight shock?

Yup, sure did!

Not to worry. That is normal, communicated Simon #5. *They just energized the third Tesla coil—the resonator coil—a very cool system, to use your language. They finally figured out that the third coil was the key to generating enough energy to open the portal to the multiverse, to zero-point energy, if you will.*

You've been through this before, Simon?

Many have sat in your chair, dear Simone, but none have succeeded, communicated Simon #5. *But I can tell you are different. I believe you are the One.*

Let's hope so, communicated Simone as the tingling in her extremities started to increase.

∞

"How much farther, mate?" shouted the gruff voice from the back of the long white bus. Sergeant O'Malley got up from his seat and turned to look toward the back of the bus.

"OK, you ornery bunch of bastards, we should be there in about five minutes. We have to wait for confirmation that the security systems are down before we enter the zone. And remember, we want the girl alive; everyone else is expendable."

"Ya mean dead, don't ya?" shouted the gruff voice from the back again.

"Affirmative," said O'Malley over the chuckling of the other men as he sat back down.

"Nut bars. And with itchy trigger fingers too!" remarked O'Malley under his breath as the white bus continued on its way to Nellis.

∞

The entire room started to fill with a low-frequency hum as Dr. Jian busily checked some settings, then conferred with his colleagues. "OK, we're ready to start ramping up the energy," he said.

"God help us all!" said Wayne.

"Mr. Wayne, you are god, as we all are, so you just need to help yourself," said Dr. Jian smiling.

Wayne managed a slight smile. "All righty then."

Dr. Jian turned up the power, and the clamshell-like roof back on the surface automatically started to open. Wayne started to squint as the light from the late afternoon sun began to cascade in after being magnified by the many mirrors along the way down to their level.

"The show's about to start!" said General Wales to Raven.

"So far, so good," said the general, speaking a little louder now as the frequency began to climb.

"Holy shit!" yelled Wayne as the floor began to vibrate beneath him.

"Not to worry, Mr. Wayne. This is normal," shouted Dr. Jian.

Simone felt numb. She had lost all feeling in her extremities a few minutes ago, and now she couldn't feel her body anymore. All she had left were her thoughts. She tilted her head back.

Just relax, she told herself. *This is why you were born. Let's get it done!*

An admirable attitude, thought Simon #5.

You're still there, are you? communicated Simone.

I AM you, how can I not be?
Good point!

Suddenly, Simone's head was thrust violently back and became enveloped in light. Within seconds a bluish-white beam of light entered through the open clamshell-style roof, and almost instantaneously, twelve smaller beams of light were diverted from Simone and found their mark in the forehead of each of her circling brothers and sisters.

"Jesus Christ!" shouted Wayne.

"Not to worry, Mr. Wayne!" yelled Dr. Jian. "This is all normal, and you are—"

"Jesus Christ," interrupted Wayne. "I know, I know. Apparently I'm him too!"

∞

"We're going to be late for our reservation. I'm outside the north door. Black SUV," read Sarah as she checked her screen. "No kidding, schmuck, what else would you be driving? No need to answer that imbecile now—almost there."

P-A looked up from his phone and saw Sarah coming out of the north door of the hangar. Sarah, still limping, moved as fast as she could and climbed into the waiting SUV.

"*Bonjour, ma belle fille,*" offered P-A.

"I'm not your beautiful girl," said Sarah as she closed the heavy black door behind her, "and if you ever call me that again, I'll shoot you on the spot. Now put this thing in gear!"

"Yes, ma'am," said P-A mockingly.

"What's that smell?" asked P-A, sniffing the air.

"It's Emily," said Sarah.

"Emily?"

"Yes, Emily. The girl who gave her life so I could use her ID to get in here. Her perfume was in her purse, so I used it. She seemed like a nice girl too," said Sarah with a twinge of regret in her voice.

"You gettin' soft, boss?" P-A said with a smirk. It took less than a second to bring her SIG P226 to P-A's temple.

"No, I'm not *gettin'* soft. You want to *get* dead?"

"No, ma'am."

"Then drive, asshole!" asserted Sarah.

"Guess dinner's off then, eh?"

"You are an imbecile, aren't you?"

P-A put his foot to the floor while letting out a hearty laugh and headed toward the incoming white bus.

∞

"Excuse me, General Wales, sorry to interrupt, but security shows a white bus heading to the main gate, and it seems one of our vehicles is already heading out to meet it," said Lieutenant Davis, General Wales's chief aid.

General Wales motioned to Davis to bring his ear down to his level. "Check with the main security station and have them do a sweep of the entire area. Keep a close eye on that bus, Davis. We can't afford to screw this up now. Keep me informed."

"Yes, sir, absolutely," replied Davis before turning to leave.

"Problem, General?" asked Raven.

"Now don't you go worrying your beautiful black locks, honey. It's nothing we can't handle."

"Of course, what was I thinking?" said Raven. Asshole, is what I was really thinking, thought Raven. Look at what you're doing to my daughter!

Dr. Jian moved the slide control to 80-percent power. It was getting hard to see Simone and the twelve others.

"I can't make them out anymore!" shouted Wayne. "You'll have to throttle back."

"No, Mr. Wayne. This will be our last chance," yelled Dr. Jian as he moved the slide control to 90 percent.

∞

Lieutenant Davis slid his pass card through the lock of the security station door and then checked his watch. "1659. Let's see what we can see," said Davis as he opened the door. Davis stopped in his tracks and stared in disbelief—one man down and another tied up in the corner on the floor.

Corporal Birk was wide awake and struggling against his binds and gag. As Davis moved to ungag Birk, he noticed that Birk was pointing at something with his eyes. Lieutenant Davis turned his head and saw the blinking LEDs under the main control panel.

"Oh shi—" were the last words Lieutenant Davis would utter.

∞

"What was that?" shouted Wayne.

"Probably just a bump in the energy field," offered Dr. Jian. "We've never had the power this high before." He moved the slide control the remaining 10 percent to full power.

Raven felt the ground shake as well. "Is she going to be OK?" shouted Raven to General Wales.

"Of course, honey."

"Where the hell is Davis!" muttered the general under his breath.

∞

Sergeant O'Malley had stopped the white bus at the front entrance area, just before the main ground sensors. The black SUV skidded to a halt with a plume of sand enveloping it. P-A jumped out and yelled to O'Malley.

"Let's go. All systems are down."

"Right!" retorted O'Malley as he jumped back on the bus.

"OK, you sons of bitches. Lock and load!"

∞

Simone felt nothing anymore.

How are you doing? asked Simon #5.

I'm feeling like I've never felt before. I feel wonderful! I mean, my body is numb, but I have never felt so much love and energy before. They must have just ramped up the power. Sorry. Need to concentrate now.

∞

Sarah looked at the screen on her phone. That's odd, she thought. "Such a strange glow coming from my phone."

"What are you going on about now?" barked P-A.

"The screen on my phone. It's giving off a strange blue-white light, and as I look at it, I feel really good!"

"Don't look at it!" shouted P-A as he snatched the phone from Sarah's hand.

"It's part of this energy transfer stuff, from the universe to everyone on earth."

"The what?" asked Sarah calmly.

"It's actually working," said P-A excitedly, ignoring Sarah. "We have to hurry!"

∞

"I can't see any of them anymore!" yelled Raven.

"Me neither, honey," shouted General Wales. "I think we're actually going to get this to work this time!"

"This time?" yelled Raven. "You've tried this before? What happened to the others?"

"They didn't make it," yelled General Wales. "I salute you, honey. You should be very proud your daughter is giving her life for her country!" he shouted with a smile.

Raven got up and ran toward the control panel where she last saw Wayne and Dr. Jian standing. Everything was so bright now she could hardly see anything at all.

"It's working; it's working!" shouted Dr. Jian. "Look at the computer screen, Mr. Wayne. Do you feel it?"

"Actually, I do feel it. It feels like endless waves of unconditional love."

Dr. Jian smiled in agreement.

"Raven!" yelled Wayne unexpectedly. "What are you doing?"

"General Wales is planning to kill my daughter, and I won't let him! You have to shut this thing down right now!" shouted Raven.

Dr. Jian and Wayne just stared at her.

Why are they so dreamy-eyed? thought Raven. "Get out of the way then. I'll shut it down myself!" she yelled as she tried to shove Wayne out of the way.

Wayne gave his head a quick shake and grabbed Raven before she was able to touch anything.

"Take it easy, girl!" yelled Wayne as he restrained Raven.

"Miss Raven, it's OK; look here at this screen," shouted Dr. Jian. "Here are Simone's vital signs. They're all within the normal range. She's fine!"

Wayne could feel Raven's muscles relax as she looked at her daughter's vital signs.

Strange, she thought. I feel so good. Love like I've never been loved before.

∞

The black SUV stopped outside the north entrance to the hangar with the white bus pulling up just as P-A jumped out. O'Malley met him on the tarmac.

"OK, so all the security systems are down and all the doors should be open. There will be some resistance, but you know what to do," instructed P-A.

"Copy that, boss!" retorted O'Malley as he turned back toward the bus. O'Malley was back on the bus in three quick strides.

"OK, listen up!" yelled O'Malley. "It's show time! Shoot to kill, including the girl. And anyone else that gets in the way of us taking over this air base. This is our time, boys; let's do this!"

As P-A and Sarah reached the north entrance, they heard a loud "OO-RAH!" coming from the bus.

"Wonder what that's all about?" asked Sarah.

P-A led the way to the elevator and down to the lab. O'Malley and his men followed closely behind, shooting security guards and scientists as they went.

Jesus! thought P-A, feeling sorry for having to take innocent lives. I've known some of these guys a long time. It's got to be done though, in order to stop these spiritual radical types from taking over the world!

∞

Simone never felt better. *I can't feel myself anymore, but who needs that fragile body anyway. Certainly won't need it where we're going.*

Simone could feel that many souls were being affected by the light force, and they would soon make the jump to the next lokas.

You're doing it, thought Simon #5. *We're almost there!*

Yes, thought Simone. *Just a few more seconds!*

∞

P-A and Sarah arrived at the huge lab doors with O'Malley and his men in tow. Sarah turned and stared intensely into O'Malley's eyes. "I want that girl alive. Do you hear me?"

"Yes, ma'am," answered O'Malley dutifully.

"Everyone else can die," continued Sarah, "including that good-for-nothing jellyfish of a general in there. Pass it down to your men."

O'Malley turned and faced his men. "You heard the pretty lady, lads. Everyone but the girl," O'Malley said with a wink.

"Good to go, boss," said O'Malley, turning back to face Sarah and P-A.

P-A didn't bother answering. He quickly swiped his radio-frequency card through the sensor to deactivate the secondary security system that would have kept the lab secure when the main system failed. A system he had designed.

∞

The entire lab was enveloped in a bright blue-white light now, and Wayne could feel himself becoming lighter.

"Feels like I'm starting to float," yelled Wayne.

"Me too!" added Raven.

"This is sensational!" shouted Dr. Jian. "I mean, yes, it's absolutely normal. Remember to keep your eyes on the screen to ensure you keep that feeling of unconditional love. We will soon make the jump. Any thoughts of fear, anger, or hate, and you will drop out."

Concentrate now, thought Simone. *Almost there.* "Ahhhhhhhh" was the only sound she could make without moving her lips. *The sound of God*, she thought. *We're ready!*

Dr. Jian glanced at the statistics screen, paying attention to only one number. The estimated number of souls saved.

Forty-three percent! Even with a correction factor of plus or minus three percent, it has far surpassed our wildest dreams! thought Dr. Jian.

Dr. Jian let his mind, his third eye, open now, allowing the feeling of perfect love to fill his every cell. He could see how it was affecting the world. People stopped what they were doing and were mesmerized by the light. Many people had been open to it. The worldwide spiritual movement over the last few decades played an important part in raising people's vibrational frequency.

Then he saw the chaos taking place by the people that were still vibrating at a lower frequency. Pushing, shoving. People fighting each other. Dr. Jian started to feel a little heavier. He quickly stopped his train of thought.

"Are you ready, Miss Raven, Mr. Wayne?" yelled Dr. Jian.

"I am," said Raven, followed by a "Yup" from Wayne.

"Good, because here we go!"

Within seconds, the trio found themselves floating above their bodies and looking down on the room. Wayne turned and looked at Raven. He could still see her facial features, but they were no longer flesh and bone. They seemed to be made up of light, like a hologram. Wayne felt something behind him and new it was Dr. Jian.

We're vibrating at a much higher frequency now than we were in our physical bodies, thought Dr. Jian.

Wayne had understood Dr. Jian but never saw his lips, or what was left of them, move.

It's OK, Mr. Wayne; we communicate with telepathy in this form. Words are much too slow.

Oh yeah, I knew that, thought Wayne.

Dr. Jian looked around the room and could see many of his scientist friends hovering as well. Sadly, some were still at their stations, filled with fear and unable to make the jump.

How can we be here and yet still down there? communicated Wayne.

Those are only our physical bodies, thought Dr. Jian. *They have only been our vehicle, a shell of sorts, while we were here on earth. We are becoming our true essence again.*

They don't seem to be moving, communicated Raven.

Oh, they are, Miss Raven; it's just that they are vibrating at such a low frequency when compared to us, so they appear to be standing still.

Are they dead or dying then? thought Wayne.

No, Mr. Wayne, in essence we are still half in the world of the physical and half in the world of the absolute. When we make the final jump, they will cease to be alive.

It just seems like our lives are really just all an illusion, thought Raven.

Indeed, thought Dr. Jian. *That they are.*

Dr. Jian looked down at General Wales. He seemed to have moved from his last position. It looked like he was now facing the main door.

∞

"GO, GO, GO, GO, GO!" shouted O'Malley as his men surged through the lab door and opened fire.

Dr. Jian, Wayne, and Raven could see the muzzle flashes, but everything seemed to be happening in superslow motion. They felt helpless as they watched the mass slaughter below. All the staff, scientists, and even General Wales all became victims to O'Malley's men.

Wayne started to feel a little heavier now, like he was sinking. He looked at Dr. Jian and Raven, and they were starting to adopt a bit more of a flesh tone. Wayne looked down at his hands.

"Shit! What's happening?" said Wayne.

"Don't think any thoughts of fear or anger!" shouted Dr. Jian, surprised by his use of language again. "Fear makes us vibrate at a very low frequency."

Wayne closed his eyes, concentrated, and soon found himself feeling lighter again.

"Help me!" yelled Raven.

Wayne turned, then looked down to find Raven a couple of feet below him.

Think thoughts of love! communicated Wayne. *Think of Simone!*

She can't hear you! thought Dr. Jian. *We are back to telepathy, and she is using language.*

Raven looked around the room as she was sinking. "There's that black-haired bitch, and she's going to try to kill Simone!"

Wayne looked toward the door and saw Sarah enter the room, a SIG P226 at the end of her outstretched arm.

Dr. Jian began to think of his old life in China and quickly found himself sinking.

A delicate balance, he thought. "Not too much or you'll drop out. Just enough to—"

"Miss Raven!" shouted Dr. Jian. "You must let it go! It might seem like holding on will make you stronger, but the opposite is true. Letting go makes you stronger. Then you can move on!"

Simone could feel the need now for one final push. She concentrated on seeing herself as a newborn, looking up at her mom through cloudy eyes, yet feeling nothing but love from this person that had carried her for nine months and allowed her access to the physical realm. She had chosen her parents, as we all do, and now a smile crossed her lips and a tear formed in the corner of her eye as she pushed, birthing an entire new generation onto a higher plane.

Chapter 9

Wayne suddenly felt as if he were ripped through a small hole in a jet airliner suffering from depressurization. Then calm. Wayne looked around and saw nothing but green pastures, green trees, and green grass. Blue!

There's some lakes! thought Wayne. Everything shone with a brilliance that Wayne had not seen before. *This must be heaven!* He looked down at himself and saw that he still had a physical form, complete with arms and legs, yet he was floating high above everything.

Raven! Dr. Jian! thought Wayne suddenly as he remembered his friends.

I am still with you, Mr. Wayne. Wayne twisted and turned in his weightless form but saw nothing but paradise.

Where are you, Dr. Jian?

Where am I not? would be a better question.

Don't get cute with me, Dr. Jian. What's going on?

I am everywhere, as you soon will be too. We move as our thoughts move, so as soon as I think something, I'm there and it appears.

Yeah, but it feels different. It feels like you're inside me too.

Well, we are all one, remember?

Yes, I remember that lesson, thank you very much.

Oh, Mr. Wayne, still a touch of sarcasm? Soon you will lose that too.

How come you're so far evolved?

Because I spent my life remembering who I was. I am still waiting to transition to my true essence, my soul, as you are. Let's just say I read all the right books!

So where are we then?

Once we made the jump, we went to our own idea of a perfect dream place. It's the same place you would have gone had you died normally. It's like a holding or normalization zone before we make the final transition to our true essence, thought Dr. Jian.

You mean like purgatory?

Yes, exactly. Many earthly religions and wisdom traditions had a name for it, and purgatory is certainly one of those.

I am soon about to make my transition, Mr. Wayne, so I don't have much time, but I must leave you with one last piece of advice.

Go ahead, my friend.

When your transition time comes, it will be easier if you think and repeat the following words. "Aham Brahmasmi."

Sanskrit words for "I am the universe."

Very good, Mr. Wayne. You are gaining access to the knowledge of all things in the realm of the absolute. It won't be long now until you transcend as well.

Wait, what happened to Raven? I don't feel her presence.

She was caught between the two realms and didn't complete the jump.

Will she return to the lab?

No, she will likely start her journey again in order to try to complete it. I must go now, Mr. Wayne.

Will I see you again?

Of course, we are one, my friend. Nothing is separate here. There is nothing but "us."

I love you! thought Wayne, but there came no answer. That was fine with Wayne because he now knew he was really only saying he loved himself.

So utterly perfect!

∞

Raven was doing her best to think thoughts of love and assure herself that Simone would be all right.

Starting to feel better, she told herself assuredly, Yes, I'm feeling lighter now. Wait! That man, that tattoo, that bandage—it's Tex. And he's headed toward Simone! Raven felt herself drop like a stone to the floor. Ughhh.

In all the chaos, no one seemed to notice. All Raven could hear now was gunfire, and she knew what she had to do.

"You son of bitch!" screamed Raven as she ran across the room, determined to stop Tex from shooting into the circle of light. Raven ran with the ferocity of a mother bear protecting her cubs and leapt into the air to cover the last six feet between her and Tex.

Raven felt nothing as the bullets ripped into her left side.

"What the hell!" shouted Tex as Raven landed in a pile at his feet.

"You! Say goodbye to your daughter, girly!" Tex emptied the clip of his SIG P226 into the blue-white light.

Simone and the others were already floating high above the scene with only their flesh and bone shells left behind. Some of the bullets found their mark, but they were of no consequence. The final jump had begun. Simone looked back one last time and saw her mother lying dead, a black-haired woman at her side.

"I wanted to kill her!" shouted Sarah. As Sarah started to get up, she felt the bullets pierce her spine. As she fell forward, she turned to look back just as she hit the ground.

"Sorry, baby!" said P-A. Sarah's eyes grew larger, and for a split second, P-A wondered what she was looking at.

"Sorry, boss!" growled O'Malley as he pulled the trigger three times. "This place belongs to us now!"

As Sarah drew her last breath, she somehow felt a strange sense of completeness. She had always wanted to be part of a double, double cross.

∞

Wayne continued to see nothing but lush green hills and pastures dotted with clear blue lakes and streams. He felt so complete here, not wanting for anything. It felt as if he were wrapped up in a warm, cozy blanket of love. Up ahead he saw a small speck that appeared to be a light.

As he drifted toward it, the green hills and blue lakes started to disappear.

No! Don't go away! But all he could see now was a bright blue-white light. Strangely, he felt no need to enter it. A voice he hadn't heard in a very long time spoke to him now.

Wayne, I've waited so long to see you again!

Dad?

Yes, son, it's me.

But how? I mean, I never thought I'd see you here. I figured you had gone to hell with the rest of the drunken losers that leave their wives and children!

I understand your thoughts and feelings, my son.

Please don't call me your son. That just reminds me I came from you!

I understand, Wayne, but search yourself for a moment. You know there is no hell or devil, and you didn't come from me or your mother. You came from here—a place of divine love. We were just the vehicles you picked in order to make the journey into the physical realm.

Wayne allowed it all to sink in and knew his father was telling the truth. The divine truth.

OK, so it's all true, but I'm not calling you Dad. I'll use your name, Quincy. But that doesn't answer why you had to leave us like that. Dan and I were only seven and nine. Mom didn't even have a job.

I know, son.

No, you don't know! You just jumped into your truck and drove off. You didn't say goodbye or nothing!

Wayne could feel a few remnants of his physical emotions coming through again. And he liked it.

Who does that sort of thing! I'll tell you who, a man that doesn't give a shit about anything, that's who!

I did try to contact you, Wayne.

Don't give me that bullshit, Quincy.

Many times I watched you and your brother from afar, hoping this time I would have enough courage to come home, but every time I chose to hide behind the bottle instead.

You followed us around? Because we moved a lot.

Twelve times, to be exact.

So you did love us.

With all my heart.

Then why did you leave?

I didn't know it at the time, but it was all a part of your evolution. If I would have stayed, you would have become dependent on me and maybe even turned out like me. You had to learn self-reliance by taking care of not only yourself but your brother and mother too. Don't you see, Wayne? You were born to evolve to a point to where you could help lead almost half the human race to the next level in the divine dimensions. You chose your mom and me as parents, knowing you had chosen to be alive at a time when so many were so deeply in the dark. That's an incredible challenge you could only have accomplished if you learned how to take care of yourself and others at such an early age.

Wayne was silent for a moment to let it all sink in and knew it was all true.

If that's the case, then you chose your journey as well, knowing full well it would lead to ruin in the physical world.

Yes, that's true, Wayne, but none of us truly know how our physical lives will turn out; it's not all preordained or destiny. We have been blessed with the power of free will and can create our own reality using our thoughts; however, we did come to the realm of the physical in order to evolve, and we are part of a much larger tapestry in the cosmos. It's like we are making a movie where we are the star, yet we are also the extras, and we fit into everyone else's movies as well.

Wayne once again let it all sink in and began to feel that incredible feeling of unconditional love.

Dad?

Yes, son.

Where do we go from here?

I'm glad you asked that, son.

How so?

Your journey's not over yet, son; you have more evolving to do.

∞

Raven found herself floating above the mass carnage that was taking place in the lab. She saw her body lying at the Texan's feet as he blasted away at the light. She saw Sarah, then P-A, fall to the ground. She no longer felt any fear or anger toward anyone or anything, just pure, perfect unconditional love. She thought about Simone, Wayne, Dr. Jian, and the others and intrinsically knew they were safe and had made the jump successfully.

But why didn't I go? she thought.

Raven noticed the bright light from the lab was fading quickly now, and soon all was dark around her. She felt no fear, of course, and knew all would be fine but was wondering where she was going.

Simone! thought Raven. No answer came back. *Looks like I'm alone and transitioning to...*

As Raven thought it, it appeared. She found herself floating over beautiful golden fields of grain. The sky was still bright, but the sun was setting. In the distance, she could see something flying ahead of her. As she drew nearer, she realized it was her old friend the black raven she used to see as a child. She remembered the bird used to come to her and seemed to want her to follow. This inevitably led her to becoming lost in the woods that surrounded her country home, and her parents would have to search for her. She would always blame the mysterious black raven, and her parents would laugh and tell her no one had ever seen a raven in the area. Maybe a few crows, but a raven was a much larger and smarter bird.

That's when they started calling me Raven!

The big black bird buzzed closely by her and beckoned her to follow. And as she had done so many years ago, she did once again now.

∞

Quincy had told Wayne to follow him into the light. As he did, Wayne could feel a slight tingling sensation similar to the pins and needles he used to feel in his old body when he temporarily lost circulation to one of his limbs. Suddenly the bright light disappeared, and Wayne saw a perfectly round blue-white orb floating in front of him with nothing but a sea of black behind it. It looked like one of those scientific experiment balls you used to see in the movies with a centre nucleus that was very bright and veins of electricity arcing toward the outer surface and back again. It looked very much alive.

We have to stop here, son.

Dad? Is that you? You look like a science experiment.

Have you checked yourself out lately?

Wayne expanded his awareness and could sense he was now an orb too.

Wow! So that's what I felt back there.

This is the form we take when we return home, son. We are all part of Source energy. We are all one. I am you, and you are me.

Yes, I've been told that before, but now I believe it. I can feel it's true. In fact, I feel like I now have answers to all of the questions that have ever been asked.

It will come slowly, son, and you will soon know all there is to know, but first we must go on a journey.

Wayne followed his father through the sea of black until he saw a faint light up ahead. Wayne was gaining more knowledge by the minute and knew what lay ahead. Quincy stopped at the entrance.

Here we are at the—

Portal to the multiverse, interjected Wayne.

No, well yes, but that's not what I call it. I call it the "Space Tube." Once we finish our journey, you can tell me if you know why I call it that.

Deal!

Quincy moved toward the opening of the portal. As he did, Wayne took a good look at this wondrous device. It was just barely larger than they were in diameter and seemed to be made from the same blue-white energy. It was transparent with only thin beams of light to form its outer skeleton. It seemed to stretch out into the sea of black forever, twisting and turning as it went. Suddenly, Quincy was gone.

Whoa! It just sucked him right in. Well, here goes!

As Wayne moved forward, he felt himself being sucked into the tube like a marble into a vacuum cleaner hose.

Holy sh—I mean—crap. This is awesome!

Wayne rode the tube up, then down, left, then right. Now he knew what his dad was talking about. When they were younger and Quincy wasn't hitting the bottle quite so hard, he and Mom had taken them to Disney World in Florida. The highlight of the trip was his ride on Space Mountain. This was just like that ride inside the mountain—up, down, twisting, turning, lights whipping past against a black backdrop—all done to make you feel like you're hurtling through space. The designers of that ride should be proud of themselves. They pretty much nailed it!

Wayne could feel himself accelerating now and could see specks of light beyond the skeletal structure of the Space Tube.

Stars? Nope, those are galaxies!

As quickly and abruptly as the ride had started, it stopped. Wayne was still reeling from his wondrous adventure when Quincy thought, *We're here!*

Wayne expanded his awareness and could see that the Space Tube was gone.

Where's here?

Look again, son. Wayne expanded his awareness even more and saw it.

It's the multiverse, thought Quincy.

Oh my god!

You mean, Oh my you!

Yes. Yes, I guess I do. How does it work? thought Wayne, as he admired the most magnificent thing he had ever seen.

It looked like the side of an apartment building that stretched upward into infinity. On each level were rooms, and he could see people in each room acting out their lives. It was all constructed of the same blue-white energy beams as the Space Tube, forming the structure or skeleton only. There were no walls; it was totally transparent. Wayne focused on some of the life-forms on each level of the building and noticed something familiar about them.

They're all me!

Yes, son, they are all you.

But how?

Well, we are all just a piece of greater source energy. This energy found that the only way to experience itself was to split itself into many small fragments to populate different worlds and experience itself physically. By doing this, it would then come to know itself experientially, not just conceptually.

Yes, I get that, but why are they all me?

They only appear to you, as you. To me, they appear as me. This is an illusion of sorts because here in the realm of the absolute, there is no separation. There is no you and me—only us.

Of course. I get it now. Dr. Jian tried to explain that earlier.

He was a good man, and he is "us" too, as are all life-forms.

So what's happening here then, Dad?

This is a graphic illustration of time. You see, on earth man thought time was linear, laid out in front of him from left to right on a page. This seemed practical at the time, pardon the pun.

If I had eyes, I'd roll them, Dad!

Yes, I know. I do apologize. Let's continue then, shall we. The point is, time does not exist. Humans concocted something that worked for them, but the past and future do not exist. There is only one moment that exists and will ever exist, and that is the "now" moment. This structure you see before you illustrates that perfectly. It stands straight and tall and goes on forever. It's as if you took man's left-to-right linear time scale and stood it vertically on its end. The rooms you are able to see into are the different levels of the multiverse, and you are alive and well, living your life simultaneously in each one.

So I'm living out other lives, on other planets, all at the exact same moment.

That's my boy. I knew you'd get it!

But are my lives all the same?

Ah yes, you were always endlessly inquisitive. No, you are not living the same lives; however, each of your lives affects all the others.

Really, how?

Well, let's say that you decide to move to another part of the country in one life; that means there is another part of you in another life that decides to stay. In one life, you make a left turn, in another you make a right. Each decision you make in one life will affect your decisions in another life. This allows you to live out different lives with different results and all the while experiencing different emotions and, therefore, experiencing yourself more fully which is—

The reason we're here.

See, I knew you'd get it!

So why have you shown me all this?

Well, son, since you evolved sufficiently at the last level of the multiverse, which was a very primitive level, I'd have to say, you now have a choice to make.

A choice?

Yes. You can choose to continue to evolve at the next level, or lokas as it is known, or you can come home and stay with the rest of us and choose to return at another "now" moment.

I see. I take it since you're here, you decided not to go on to another level.

That's right, son. I had a particularly tumultuous life last time, so I shall wait for the right moment. Besides, I had to wait for you.

Wait for me?

Yes, we all need someone we knew in our former lives to lead us to this decision moment.

You're not really my father, are you?

No, Wayne. I am you. But for all intents and purposes, I am merely serving as your guide.

What about Mom?

Oh, she went to the next level right away. You know how much of a go-getter she is.

Yes, I do!

Much like you, son. But you must make your own choice. You have been given the divine gift of free will, and the choice is always only yours. We really must get on with it, son. What will you choose?

∞

Raven followed the big black bird for what seemed like eons, across endless fields of grain divided by beautiful blue rivers, all seemingly flowing to the same source.

This place sure is beautiful, thought Raven. *But it doesn't feel like any type of heaven. I wonder where this bird is taking me?*

An old saying she used to hear suddenly popped into her thoughts. "Always it's the one in motion, with something to do, whether humble or grand, that gets to see the ocean."

Wow, that was from a long time ago. That was something Grandma used to say!

The big black bird changed direction, and as Raven changed course to follow, she could see, up ahead at the horizon, a field of blue.

∞

Wayne tried to think about what he should do but then realized he no longer had conscious thought. For a moment he missed his earthly body, and then he knew what he must do.

I'm going back, Dad!

Well done, son. I knew you'd make the right choice.

The right choice. What do you mean? I thought there was no past or future, only the now. If the future doesn't exist, why do you feel it's the right choice?

Because, son, you have much to do in your new life. No one knows your future because the choices you will make will form your future. You need only decide who you want to become. To be, or not to be, that is the question.

Really, Dad, you're quoting Shakespeare now!

Shakespeare might have said those words, but where do you think they came from? The point is, choose who you want to be, do the things you need to do in order to become that person, then allow source energy to deliver all you will need to be you.

Sounds easy.

It is. It's creation 101, and you, son, are the greatest creating machine ever thought of—you are your divine self, a piece of source energy, a piece of us. Now, one piece of advice I need to give you, son, is to pick your parents wisely.

Pick my parents wisely—what do you mean?

Once you get to the next level, you will be able to detect what is presently going on in your prospective parents' lives.

You mean I get to choose my parents?

Absolutely!

That means I picked you! Holy crap, why would I have done that? You were a terrible father!

We went over this already, son, remember?

Yes, I remember. You left so I could learn self-reliance. Big frickin' deal, it still hurts! And I don't know why it hurts because I've left my physical body! Man, this is still so confusing.

I know, son; it happens to all of us. There are still remnants of your physical past, especially your emotions. That's why if souls choose to cross over and go back quickly, they retain certain memories and attributes from their former physical lives.

You mean like the young piano virtuosos or kids remembering flying planes in a former life?

Exactly!

So if I choose to go now, will I retain some of my former memories?

Yes, it's still early, so you probably will, but they will fade as you unlearn who you truly are while living your new life.

Why would I want to do that?

It's not that you really want to; it's that you need to, in order to evolve further. That's part of the deal. The soul already knows itself conceptually but longs to know itself experientially. This can only be done once you forget who you truly are and then go on a journey to remember who you truly are, all the while experiencing emotions and thoughts you could only experience in physical form. It's kind of fun, actually! I think I may have talked myself into going back sooner rather than later!

Oh, no you don't! Me first!

That's why I mentioned picking your parents again. It will feel right when you find the right couple. During your search, hold the thoughts of love and compassion deep within you, and you will be attracted to parents with the same values.

OK, I get it, but I thought we create our own lives with the thoughts we think?

Of course, that's absolutely true; however, from the ages of about zero to seven, your brain will be thinking only in theta waves, which are meant for us to absorb, like sponges, all of our surroundings. This is where much of your programming will be done. Your subconscious mind, which will run eighty-five percent of your daily life once you grow up, will now be programmed by its environment, which at those ages, is mostly your parents.

I see. It makes perfect sense now. OK, I'm ready. Let's get this party started!

Chapter 10

Sergeant O'Malley had a smile on his face as he surveyed the situation.

"Oh, how I love the smell of gunpowder in the afternoon!" he said, laughing out loud.

"SIMPSON!" shouted O'Malley.

"Yes, Sarge," answered Corporal Simpson dutifully.

"Sit-rep. I want a report on the entire complex!" ordered O'Malley.

"Copy that."

We did it! thought O'Malley. We're in charge of Nellis Air Force Base. The famous Area 51!

"DUNCAN!" shouted O'Malley.

"Right here, Sarge."

"You're the comms expert, so get your little derriere down to the communications room, and tell our Russian friends we have control and we await their arrival."

"Copy that," answered Corporal Duncan.

Derriere. Nice touch! thought O'Malley. Almost makes me want to shed a tear for my old French-Canadian buddy, P-A. "NOT!" laughed O'Malley out loud.

Corporal Simpson caught O'Malley laughing as he started into his report. "Complex is secure. We have complete control, Sarge."

O'Malley was surprised to hear Simpson behind him but kept on laughing anyway. It had taken a lot of negotiating to get this deal done with his Russian friends, and now it was all coming together. They would all be rich men once the Russians pay him for all this quantum junk, thought O'Malley.

"Excellent!" responded O'Malley. "They will be here soon. In the meantime, check all these bodies for valuables. No use leaving our tips behind!"

O'Malley started checking some of the bodies himself.

All these kids and the so-called One all gone for nothing, thought O'Malley.

Wait a minute. Only a few have any bullet wounds. Most of them, including the One, have no injuries whatsoever. How did they die then? thought O'Malley.

Must have been electrocuted by all this bullshit machinery. "Oh well, I won't tell my Russian pals this crap doesn't work. They can find out all on their own. After they've paid me!" mused O'Malley out loud.

"SARGE!" said Duncan excitedly over O'Malley's radio.

"What's up?" answered O'Malley, somewhat pissed Duncan had broken his train of thought.

"We've got incoming bogeys, and by their radar signature, I'd say they're F-35s."

"F-35s? Those are ours!" shouted O'Malley into his lapel mic.

"Yup. And they just went hot," added Duncan.

"Holy shit! Missiles away! We've got incoming! Maybe thirty seconds!" screamed Duncan into his radio.

"Goddamn it!" yelled O'Malley, stomping his feet. O'Malley keyed his mic and told Duncan to get his derriere back to the lab. Maybe we can survive the blast down here, thought O'Malley.

Sergeant O'Malley looked skyward and said aloud, "This wasn't supposed to happen. Just make one final deal, sell this crap to the Russians, and then retire."

Just as he finished his sentence, O'Malley noticed the light was still pouring in from the surface. "That damn clamshell roof is still open!"

"SIMPSON!" yelled O'Malley. "Get that roof closed. Pronto!"

"On it," answered Simpson.

O'Malley knew nothing would save them now. He plopped himself down and relaxed in one of the leather chairs, knowing the missiles would find their mark in just a few seconds. As he glanced over toward the bodies of Sarah and P-A, he began to squint as he noticed something flashing. He got up quickly and rushed over to P-A's body. In P-A's right hand was a small device with a red flashing LED.

"He signalled them! Son of a bi—" were the last earthly words Sean O'Malley would ever utter.

∞

Wayne barely got the thought expressed when another Space Tube appeared before him.
I get to go for another ride?
Yes, you do, son, but this time you go alone.
Where will it take me?
To the next level in the multiverse, the next lokas, the fourth dimension.
How will I know when I'm there?
The fourth dimension is much more magical than the material-based third dimension. It's very unique and has a somewhat hypnotic quality. Many beings feel liberated as they move from the limitations of the material world into the expansiveness of the magical world.
Sounds like fun!
Oh, it will be, but you have to remember to feel your way while on the Space Tube. When you feel it's right, just have that thought and get off the ride.
That easy, eh?
You'll know when it's time. Remember, keep thoughts of love and compassion in the forefront.
How can I not? That's all this place is!
How true, son. A twang of leftover emotional sadness came and went quickly as Quincy knew this was his goodbye to Wayne.
Now you must go while you still have some remnants of your past life within you.

Before Wayne could say goodbye, he found himself hurtling down the Space Tube once again.

Man, you just think it and it happens. It looks like thought is the only thing faster than the speed of light. I need to remember that in my next life. Thoughts become things, and fast! No reason that won't work back on earth or wherever I'm going.

Wayne's thoughts drifted for a moment, and he thought of his time with his father.

Not such a bad dude after all. Terrible father, but he was on his own journey and did what he had to do, with what he had, from where he was.

Instead of the intense hatred that dogged him since he was a boy on earth, Wayne felt nothing but love now for the soul that had been labelled Quincy.

I love you, Dad!

Wayne felt a sudden turn to the left that jarred him back to task.

OK, OK, settle down here...whoa!

Wayne felt absolutely glorious as he rode the Space Tube through the corkscrew section.

Yeeeeee-haaaaaaw! All right, what was I supposed to remember? Oh yeah, Aham Brahmasmi, Aham Brahmasmi, feel love and compassion; Aham Brahmasmi, feel love and compassion; Aham Brahmasmi...

Wayne felt the corkscrew come to an end, and he sensed he was now on a level plane.

Here it is, STOP!

As soon as Wayne had the thought, the ride stopped, and the Space Tube disappeared. Wayne had felt a funny "fizzy" feeling and knew this was the place.

I'm feeling so much love and compassion right here. This must be the spot.

Wayne's thoughts grew cloudy now as if he were losing consciousness.

Water—I feel like I'm surrounded by water. The womb! That's it; I'm in the womb of my new mother!

These were the last thoughts in the realm of the absolute that Wayne would have for quite some time.

Chapter II

Karl, as he was now labelled, was the firstborn son to Anika and Peter. His new parents brought Karl up surrounded with love, joy, and compassion for all life, allowing him the free will to make his own mistakes and go down his own path. Karl grew up and found he had a knack for helping others and gravitated toward a teaching career.

During school, he was often ridiculed when he talked of the "multiverse" or the "Space Tube."

"I remember being there!" he would say, and his fellow students would just laugh and call him Cuckoo Karl.

Karl decided to repress some of those memories that still seemed so clear to him while he attended university.

I guess the magic Quincy had spoken of in the fourth dimension doesn't exist after all, thought Karl.

Karl's first teaching gig was at a north-end part of town that was known to be a little rough around the edges, but Karl had asked to go there because he thought he would enjoy the challenge.

Man, that janitor looks familiar, Karl thought to himself.

"Hello, I'm Karl Dunitz, one of the newbies around here," Karl said to the young Hispanic janitor.

"Oh yes, hi. I'm Jorge, head custodian."

"Head custodian, eh? You seem so young." Karl looked into Jorge's eyes and knew he had known this man before.

But from where? thought Karl.

"Are you Canadian?" asked Jorge.

"Ah, what? What do you mean?"

"You said 'eh' after your sentence. That's often a Canadian trait."

"Well, no, I mean, yes, but it was in a former life," Karl said jokingly, trying to ease the tension of the moment.

"I see. Very interesting, Mr. Karl."

"What was that you just said?" asked Karl forcefully.

"I said that was interesting," answered Jorge.

"No, no, after that. You called me Mr. Karl."

"I do apologize. I have that habit it seems. My parents taught me respect for others was very important and to address others by their title first before their name," answered Jorge. "I hope I didn't offend you."

"No, not at all. It's just that...it's just that I knew someone who used to do that a long time ago," offered Karl.

"But you are not that old, Mr. Karl."

Karl looked deep into Jorge's eyes now and said, "Dr. Jian?"

"What's that, Mr. Karl?"

"Oh, nothing. I just thought that perhaps I knew you from somewhere."

"That's impossible, Mr. Karl. We just met!" said Jorge smiling.

"Yes, yes I know," answered Karl.

"Well, it was nice meeting you, Mr. Karl. I'm sure I'll see you around. Please excuse me, but I must get back to my work," said Jorge.

"Of course!" conceded Karl. "I'm so sorry to have kept you from your work."

"No problem, Mr. Karl. Bye for now," said Jorge as he turned to continue his work.

Karl turned and started to walk down the hall. He took a few steps and then looked back at Jorge. Karl noticed Jorge had a paperback book in his back pocket, and he could just barely make out the title: *Life: A Spiritual Guide to Making It Amazing*.

It has to be Dr. Jian, thought Karl. "I can't explain it, but I can feel it!" said Karl under his breath.

Karl quickly walked through the teachers' lounge, ignoring the hellos of his fellow teachers, and went straight into the men's restroom to plunk himself down on the toilet in the first stall. Karl sat, elbows on his knees, fingers rubbing his temples. His head was killing him.

What's going on here? Karl asked himself. Is this part of the magic Quincy talked about?

"You all right, Karl?" came a voice from the doorway. Karl recognized the voice as that of the gym teacher, Fred Souza, whom he had met earlier that day.

"Yes, I'm fine actually. Just some first-day jitters," answered Karl quickly.

"OK, just checking, buddy." Fred always called everyone "buddy" even if they weren't.

Karl closed his eyes and concentrated. The memories came back quickly now. Everything he had repressed came flooding back with renewed intensity.

Yes, that's right! This is the fourth dimension. The magical, not material, world. I picked my parents, and I came here for a reason—to raise the vibrational frequency of this world and use the magical powers of this dimension to help others remember who they truly are and become their greatest versions!

Feeling better now, Karl left the stall and stopped to wash his hands. Karl looked at himself in the mirror.

"You were here before, my friend, and you came back to make a difference in people's lives," Karl whispered aloud to himself. "That had to have been Dr. Jian. I wonder who else I'm going to meet!"

Karl rejoined the other teachers in the lounge. He moved quickly and quietly to an open chair as the principal had already begun her annual address to the teaching staff. Karl hadn't had the pleasure of meeting the principal yet, so he was looking forward to hearing her speak. Karl sat down, smiling politely to some of the others that looked perturbed at his late arrival.

Karl looked toward where the principal's voice was coming from and his jaw dropped. "Simone!" Then he smiled reassuringly to the teachers around him. "Looks like someone I used to know," he whispered to the teacher closest to him, who just shook her head in disapproval.

My god! thought Karl. She made it, and she's the principal! I don't know how, but I'm able to recognize others from my past life!

The principal concluded her annual address to a round of light applause. The teachers then all started to get up and mill about, introducing each other to the handful of new teachers.

"Don't think you're going to change the world" seemed to be the topic of most of those discussions between the young and the established. Karl made his way through the group, shaking hands and smiling accordingly. As the room started to clear, he noticed a teacher he hadn't met yet. She was petite but muscular.

"Hi, I'm Karl," he offered, extending his hand.

"Hi Karl," said the redhead as she turned toward Karl.

"I'm Sabrina, girls' phys ed teacher."

Karl was speechless.

"Do I know you from somewhere?" asked Sabrina.

"Sarah?" was all that Karl could manage to slip out of his lips.

"I'm sorry, it's Sabrina."

"I apologize," said Karl, not believing what he was seeing. "I've met so many people today."

"I here ya," responded Sabrina. "Hey, you want to get a cup of coffee or a glass of wine somewhere after this day's finally through?"

"You don't mess around, Sabrina."

"Never have, never will!" she said smiling and in a semiserious tone.

"I know!" added Karl.

"Are you sure I don't know you from somewhere?" asked Sabrina again.

The chemistry was still there, thought Karl. "I'd love to!" answered Karl finally.

"Love to what?" asked Sabrina.

"Get a glass of wine later. This whole thing has been a little overwhelming, and I'd love to find out how we can work together this time."

"This time?" asked Sabrina.

"Yeah, you know, better friends than enemies!"

"Somehow I think I do!" laughed Sabrina.

Let the magic begin! thought Karl.

∞

Raven followed the big black bird until they were flying over the open ocean.

I love the water, thought Raven as she dutifully followed the bird. *I wonder where we're headed?*

Just as Raven entertained those thoughts, the big black bird tipped itself forward and began diving straight for the water as if it were an osprey. Raven did the same, trying her best to keep up with the bird, but it seemed to be increasing its lead.

With the ease and grace of an Olympic diver, Raven entered the water in search of the big black bird, but it was nowhere to be found. Raven reversed course and headed for the surface.

Raven awoke, coughing, sputtering, and spitting water from her lungs.

Where am I? thought Raven.

The Seclusion Room was dark...

Book 2

You're the One: Souled Out

By Michael J. Arend

Chapter One

They say you never hear the shot that kills you, and Karl had never heard a thing.

"Jesus Christ!" screamed Hilary, Karl's manager and all-purpose assistant. "Call 911!"

Hilary knelt down beside Karl and told him everything would be fine. "The ambulance is on its way, honey. You just hang in there!"

Karl was having trouble breathing and began to spit up blood.

"Don't try to talk, honey. Lie still and conserve your energy."

Hilary moved Karl's suit jacket aside and could see where the bullet had entered, evidenced by the frothing pink blood as Karl struggled to breathe. She called out for someone to get her a plastic bag or something, but it just fell on deaf ears as the thousands of people that gathered to hear Karl speak were running in every direction to escape the scene.

Hilary reached under Karl and felt the warm wetness of his blood. The bullet went straight through, she thought.

"Hilary..." managed Karl.

"Shhh...It's OK, honey; I'm here."

She always called everyone honey, thought Karl. It used to bother him, but now he was happy to hear it.

"Hilary, I know where I'm going next."

"What are you talking about?"

"When I die...I'm going back to the third dimension."

"First of all, you're not going to die!" said Hilary with conviction. "And second of all, you said that we move forward through the dimensions, not backward."

"I was wrong; we can go backward or forward," coughed Karl. "Depending on where we feel the need or are drawn to. It's part of the Process."

"OK, Karl, you can tell me all about this new theory of yours once you've recovered. Right now, you have to rest. Save your strength, honey. They'll soon be here."

Karl looked up at Hilary with nothing but love and admiration. She had been by his side for the last ten tumultuous years. She'd given him the best years of her life. She should have been starting a family, thought Karl. She was a very attractive woman.

Karl felt himself getting weaker as he struggled to breathe properly. Must have been a lung shot, he thought.

Suddenly, Hilary leaped up and was shouting and waving her arms.

Karl felt the paramedics at his side, hooking him up to an array of tubes and wires. One of the paramedics slipped an oxygen mask over Karl's mouth and nose.

"This should help you breathe a bit better," he said.

"Looks like a lung shot," said Ruth, the senior paramedic on duty. She had seen a lot in her last eleven years and knew exactly what to do.

"Hand me the plastic ten-by-ten sheets and some tape. We have to get him breathing better or we're going to lose him."

Karl felt them cutting his shirt out of the way and begin wiping up the blood to allow the tape to stick.

As the paramedics continued to work feverishly to save him, Karl felt himself slip into a dreamlike state, where he began to remember what brought him to this moment.

∞

"I don't care what you say, Sabrina; it's just something I have to do!" said Karl with conviction.

"Really, you don't care?" answered Sabrina. "You don't care about what we've been through the last three years!"

"You know that's not true. I'm sorry, I do care, but I came here for a reason, and there are some things I have to do. It's just the way it is."

"So, you'd rather spend your days traveling around the globe, trying to convince people about your theories of multidimensional living, than stay here and live with me?" Sabrina didn't wait for an answer. "Well, that's just great. And here I thought we were going to start a real life together, not live some fantasy version you created in your mind."

"Sabrina, I love you. I always will, but I have to do this. Why won't you come with me; it's going to be an awesome adventure! We can do this together, like it was meant to be."

"I can't, Karl."

"Why not?"

"Because I'm a teacher, and that's what I love to do!"

"Sabrina!" said Karl as he grabbed her arms and turned her toward him. "I have to tell you something, and I'm not making this up. I knew you in my former life. Your name was Sarah."

Sabrina just stared at him blankly.

"And as far as I can tell," said Karl, turning and walking a few steps then turning back to face her, "I've known you in the life before that, and the one before that, and…"

"Karl!" shouted Sabrina. "Get your head out of the clouds. You have to stop talking all this mumbo jumbo, airy-fairy stuff. People are going to think you're nuts!"

"Then let them! Do you really think I care about what others think about me?"

"Maybe you don't, but I do!"

"Oh, so it all comes down to what they think of you!"

"Karl, do you think I will ever be taken seriously as a teacher if we're together and you continue to come up with these silly notions about things that don't, and will never, exist?"

"Wow. The person you were in my past life would never have allowed others to sway her opinion. She was strong and acted on what she believed in."

"You want strong? OK, how's this—I need you out of my life so I can live mine the way that I want to!" Sabrina struggled to hold back the tears now.

Karl stood there stunned. He felt as if a boulder just crushed his chest.

"I just thought we were meant to be, that we'd be together, in some form, forever."

"It's time for you to go, Karl. My journey is not your journey. Do what you need to do, and if we were truly meant to be together, as you say, then perhaps it will all fall into place. Now go."

Karl continued to stand there stunned.

"I said, GO!"

Karl shook his head as if he had just woken up and took one last look at Sabrina, then turned and left.

Sabrina finally let it all out and began to sob uncontrollably. "I just let the only man I ever loved walk out of my life! What the hell am I doing?"

Sabrina felt the urge to run after Karl, jump into his arms, and tell him she'd go with him until the end of time, but somehow her feet would not move. Her heart wanted them to, but her mind wouldn't allow it.

∞

"What's the matter, Ruth?" asked the junior paramedic.

"He just started to twitch, and his heart stopped for about ten seconds, but it's going again," said Ruth calmly. "I thought he was going to convulse, but his EEG has settled out."

"Have you seen that before?"

"Not like this. We need to get his blood oxygen level up so we can transport. Take the mask off and start bagging him."

As the paramedics continued to work away on Karl's physical body—the garage where he stored his soul during this lifetime—Karl began to slip into a neutral place. The paramedics called it a "coma," but it was just a place of reevaluation, a place where the reintegration process begins.

This is the realm that ghosts, or at least what people like to think of as ghosts, inhabit, thought Karl. Really, they aren't ghosts; they're just people who were very afraid of dying and not sure where they would end up or what would happen to them. They often just stuck around for a while, in limbo, until eventually they would continue with the integration process and return home to source energy. This was the place where people who were aware, such as psychics, tarot card readers, and the like, could communicate with the dearly departed.

Wait a minute! thought Karl. What if someone tries to contact me? Just as Karl's thoughts were being thought, a voice rang through his head like a temple bell.

Mr. Karl? MR. KARL? Karl recognized the voice immediately. It was his old friend Jorge. They had met at the first school Karl taught at. Jorge was the head custodian, and many people couldn't understand why he had made Jorge his right-hand man.

I hear you, my friend! thought Karl.

Good, that is very good. I thought I had lost you, replied Jorge.

Just like old times, eh?

Not really, my friend, you are gravely injured and are in danger of leaving us.

Listen to me then, while we are able to communicate telepathically, communicated Karl. *I'll try to relay all that I have found out about who we truly are, where we came from, and what we must do to advance our society to the next level.*

Rest easy, my friend, do not bother about this. There will be plenty of time to tell me all that once you recover, thought Jorge.

Stop it, you fool! You know as well as I do that I'm not going to make it. I'm just so glad you're here so I can...

Karl felt a tremendous jolt of electricity flow through his body, then another, and another.

"Karl!" yelled Hilary.

"Whaaat?" gurgled Karl as he opened his eyes.

The paramedics had used the defibrillator to restart Karl's heart. Although it was risky with the condition he was in, they felt it was their only option to keep him alive.

"Why?" whispered Karl.

"What's that, honey?" asked Hilary as she brought her ear down to Karl's mouth.

"Why did you wake me? Let me sleep. I must...talk...with Jorge."

"Jorge's not here, honey."

Hilary turned to the paramedics. "He's becoming delusional; we have to do something!"

"Time to transport?" asked the junior paramedic.

Ruth took a quick look around at the mayhem and then turned to Hilary. "We're going to need a path to get back to the ambu—"

Three loud shots rang out in quick succession. By instinct both Ruth and Hilary bent over to shield Karl.

More screams from the fleeing crowd ensued as Ruth and Hilary, sitting up now, attempted to shield Karl, and themselves, as some of the frightened crowd tried to run right over them.

"Looks like we got him!" spewed Frank breathlessly as he ran up to Hilary. "Threat immobilized."

"Thank you, Frank. We're going to try to transport Karl now. Can you clear us a path to the ambulance?"

"On it," replied Frank. "Campbell! Schreiber! Get over here, now!"

Even as his men were running up to him, Frank continued to yell. "We need to form a wedge. Time to move!"

Hilary looked at Frank with respect and admiration. Frank had been with Karl almost as long as she had. She was finally able to convince Karl he needed some security to keep him safe. The things Karl was talking about made some folks very uncomfortable. And then the death threats started.

Hilary had always felt a little electricity when around Frank, and at one time had hoped to explore that, but Frank was just as devoted to his job as she was, and he would never let that happen.

Frank returned and touched Hilary gently on her arm. "We're ready. I'm so glad you're all right."

"Of course, I'm all right, honey. Let's get this show on the road," responded Hilary, smiling on the inside.

Ruth watched the gentle exchange, rolled her eyes, then commanded, "Let's move!"

Karl could feel himself being lifted onto the stretcher and then raised to transport height. Now he was moving. He could feel the stop and start of their progress and the eventual thump as the stretcher legs folded beneath him as he was slid into the ambulance.

He heard the double doors closing and, now, the siren blaring and horn honking to clear traffic out of the way.

Chapter Two

"Did we get him? Is he dead?" shouted Senator Parkinson with a slight southern accent. "Answer me, damn it!"

"Well, not exactly, sir," replied Will Parkinson sheepishly.

"What the hell does that mean, 'not exactly'?"

"Well, he's been shot, and he did go down, but the cops got to our man before he could either confirm the kill or finish the job."

"Jesus Christ!" yelled Parkinson at his son. "If you screw this up, there'll be hell to pay. First for you, then for me. This man of yours, the guy you hired, is he dead or can he still talk?"

"He's been confirmed dead, so he won't be singing any songs."

"Singing any songs...idiot," mumbled the senator to himself. Then he said out loud, "You've been watching way too many old gangster movies." He paused. "If this guy, this blasphemous prick named Karl, who calls himself God and Jesus Christ, lives, well then, we just proved him right, didn't we?"

"I...I guess so," answered Will.

"You guess so?" shouted Parkinson at the top of his lungs. "I know so!"

Senator Parkinson took a few deep breaths to compose himself. "You get your skinny little ass down to the hospital and find out if he's still alive. And if he is, you better finish the job yourself, or else you and I are as good as dead. And I don't really care about you, but I don't want to die just yet. I've got a country to make great again!"

Will Parkinson just stood staring at his father. Flashes of the caring man his father used to be went through his mind. Now he was nothing but a selfish, egomaniac fighting for a cause that was as selfish and egocentric as he was.

"WILL! Are you hearing me?" shouted the senator.

"Yes sir!" said Will automatically as he snapped out of his trance. "I'm on it."

Senator Parkinson watched his good-for-nothing son walk through the door and close it behind him. Too much like his mama, that boy, he thought. He better do what he's told, or it will be the end of this line of the Parkinson herd.

As Will Parkinson closed the door behind him, he began to wonder if this Karl guy really was special. Maybe he *is* the man to lead us to salvation, to save ourselves, from ourselves. The word on the street says he's real. And I'm supposed to kill him!

$$\infty$$

Hilary ran beside the stretcher as it burst through the emergency department doors at Southern General Hospital.

"He needs surgery, stat!" yelled Ruth as she guided the stretcher through another set of swinging, double-hinged doors. As they breached the doors, the surgical team was there to meet them.

"Is this him?" asked Dr. Hinchcliff, head of surgery at Southern.

"Of course, this is him," said Hilary. "What do you mean by that?"

"Who's this?" asked Dr. Hinchcliff.

"I'm his personal assistant, and confidant," answered Hilary.

"Nice to meet you, Miss Confidant. Now get her out of here!" said Dr. Hinchcliff to his staff.

"I don't think I like your tone, Doctor!" said Hilary as she was already being pushed back through the doors by the nursing staff.

"I'll take it from here!" said Ruth.

Hilary was trying to fight against Ruth but found out just how strong the short pudgy paramedic really was.

As Ruth got Hilary back through the doors, she gave Hilary a shove that sent her hard up against the wall.

"Are you nuts, lady?" asked Ruth, trying to restrain herself from yelling. "Dr. Hinchcliff is one of the best surgeons in town. You don't want to upset him before he operates!"

Hilary, still reeling from the push against the wall, nodded. "I...I guess I just didn't like the look in his eyes."

As the words spilled from her lips, she noticed the same look in Ruth's eyes. "I have to go!" said Hilary as she turned and walked purposefully out of the hospital.

I have to talk to Jorge, thought Hilary. Something just doesn't feel right. Karl taught me to trust my intuition, my soul, and it says something is wrong here.

∞

Karl felt the coldness flow through is left arm as Dr. Hinchcliff's team administered the anesthetic that would keep him pain-free and in a state of amnesia. He wasn't sure what they would try to do to save him, but he had the feeling that he wasn't going to make it out of this one alive.

"Karl, I know you can hear me," began Dr. Hinchcliff. "You've been injured, and we're going to take good care of you. My team and I won't let you down."

Karl could feel himself slip into unconsciousness as Dr. Hinchcliff's words faded away. It was a familiar feeling for Karl as he was used to transitioning from being wide awake and then transcending to a sleep-like trance as he meditated, but this was going further. Karl felt his muscles and eyes begin to twitch, his breathing and heart rate become erratic. Suddenly, his muscles relaxed and the twitching stopped. His body was now unconscious.

Strange, I still feel like I'm awake. But my body is asleep.

That's because you're special! came a voice from out of the ether.

Jorge! I knew you wouldn't leave me. And for God's sake, you know perfectly well I'm not any more special than anyone else!

Well, that's what everyone's been saying lately. You're the One, they say. Jorge couldn't resist a chuckle.

We've been through that already, my friend, and you and I are just as much the One as everyone else is.

I know, I know, but I couldn't resist the irony. Did I make you smile?

If I had a body, sure, answered Karl. *But it seems I'm floating above the operating room at the moment.*

Oh, that. That's just disturbed bodily multisensory integration.

OK, Jorge, dumb it down for me please.

You're having a near-death experience, or NDE. Quite common given your circumstances.

Am I getting ready to reintegrate? Is this my continuation day? Because if it is, I'm ready! exclaimed Karl enthusiastically.

Not so fast, Karl. There are five stages. Peace, body separation, darkness, seeing the light, and entering the light. Which one are you at?

You do remember I've been through this before, right?

Just answer the question!

Body separation, nothing else yet. Happy now?

Yes, thank you, I am. Hopefully you will stay in the realm where you are now until the operation is over and then return to your body as the anesthetic wears off.

Jorge?

Yes, my friend.

I don't want to lose you again. Finding you here in this dimension was such a wonderful feeling. What if I see the light? Do I enter?

I suspect you have much more to do here in this dimension and you will survive this...

Once again Karl felt the ferocity of a sudden jolt of electricity. He was back in his body but still felt somehow detached. Another shock, then another. Karl knew they were successful in making his heart beat again, and for now he wouldn't need to enter the light.

"So much damage," said Collette, Dr. Hinchcliff's chief surgical nurse. "It's a wonder he's still here."

"Tumbling bullets," answered Dr. Hinchcliff.

"Tumbling bullets?" queried Collette.

"Yes, they're meant for military use. The tip of the bullet is heavier than the end, so when it hits, the back end bends toward the front until it breaks apart. The military doesn't want rounds to go completely through the body. With the round breaking up inside the body cavity, it causes more trauma, killing the person quicker."

"But this bullet went all the way through," countered Collette.

"They were probably anticipating that he would be wearing some type of body armor."

"I didn't know you knew so much about bullets, Gene," said Collette matter-of-factly.

Dr. Hinchcliff stopped working on Karl and looked over his mask and lighted magnifying glasses at Collette.

"I was in Afghanistan, remember. I can't count how many of those boys I attempted to put back together that were shot with these types of bullets. Poor bastards."

"Sorry to make you remember," offered Collette.

"No worries."

I hope that will keep her satisfied, thought Dr. Hinchcliff. I shouldn't have said anything about the bullets. Damn it! How did I get myself into this mess? Focus now, Gene...one more connection to make and then you're done.

"OK, we've done what we can here," said Dr. Hinchcliff solemnly. "Great job, team."

"Tony," began Dr. Hinchcliff as he turned toward his trusted anesthetist, "let's set him up for VS. I don't want him to move for a while."

"Are you sure you want him in a vegetated state? I think he's at least in a minimally conscious state. He was able to respond to stimuli when we brought him in."

"He may have been in MCS when we brought him in, but I think it's best if we induce him to VS."

"Dr. Hinchcliff...Gene," said Tony, lowering his voice now, "I understand the need for total rest to recover, but he'll recover sooner and more completely in MCS, not VS."

"TONY!" Dr. Hinchcliff glanced around the room as he felt everyone stop what they were doing and look at him. "Just do what you're told! Please."

"OK, OK, I get it."

"What's up his ass?" asked Tony, looking over at Collette as Dr. Hinchcliff left the operating room.

"Something about Afghanistan, I think."

"I see."

"Well, my friend," said Tony, talking to Karl now, "I'm going to put you into a deep sleep for a while. Nighty, night."

Chapter Three

Karl had felt like he was in limbo somewhere, but now he could feel himself drift further into a deep abyss. He felt his bodily functions slowing down. They were no longer working automatically but were being kept going by machines.

It will be easy, remarkably easy. The words came through loud and clear as they kept repeating themselves over and over deep in Karl's mind.

There's just one decision to be made, continued the voice in Karl's head.

Suddenly, Karl felt the answer to that question come to him, and then he heard his spirit within, his soul, answer, To accept the reality of who we really are!

With that Karl found himself floating above his listless body that was now placed in a hospital room. There were lots of machines hooked up to him, all whirring, buzzing, and pumping to keep him alive.

He had heard the conversation between Dr. Hinchcliff and Tony and felt something wasn't right. Why had they put my body in such a deep sleep? No matter, I'm free from my physical bonds and feel absolutely wonderful!

Karl moved out to the hallway now and saw a beautiful blue-purple glow emanating from the floor. It led down the hall, so he decided to follow it. Soon he heard the sound of a human crying, so he followed the sound and the blue-purple glow to the room it was coming from.

As Karl floated into the room, he saw someone sitting at the side of a bed crying. As he looked at her, he saw the spirt of the person who had just passed away rise from its physical shell and hover there for a moment, looking back at the person who was crying. Karl could feel the spirit's pain, and he knew it would fade for him, and he would transition into an energy orb, just as he himself had done when he was Wayne.

The spirit turned and looked at Karl. *She was my wife, she was my life,* said the spirit telepathically to Karl. *I was shot at a rally today, your rally.*

I am sorry for your loss, dear one, but that is how it was meant to be, answered Karl.

I understand, but I still feel the pain. Why do I feel her pain even though I've passed on?

You are only in the first phase, dear one. It's important now to let go of the past and move forward. If you languish here, you will always feel the pain and will become a lost soul. Eventually you will transition, but not after much pain that, in the end, changes nothing.

I understand. Thank you for that. I'm beginning to feel much lighter now, answered the spirit.

Go where you feel you must; it will all lead you home. Perhaps I'll see you there soon.

No! said the spirit. *You have to stay here and fix this world. I know why you came here, and you must finish what you started.*

Karl felt surprised for a moment but then realized the spirit was now starting to have access to all the questions ever asked.

I will, dear one, I will.

I know you will, Karl. Aham Brahmasmi, I am the Universe!

Aham Brahmasmi, dear one.

Karl saw the spirit leave and felt so much love for him and his grieving wife. He thought for a moment and realized the spirit, while here on Earth, had been a supporter of his, and he was killed attending *his* rally.

Let's find out what Dr. Hinchcliff is up to!

Chapter Four

As soon as Hilary got into her car she called Jorge on her cell phone. "Jorge? Jorge? No, I don't want to leave a message after the beep!" she said as she threw her phone back into her purse.

"Jorge, where the hell are you when I need you?" As soon as the words left Hilary's lips, she turned and looked at her purse in astonishment as her phone began to ring.

"Jorge? Where the hell have you been?"

"You rang, Madame," said Jorge in his best excuse for a stiff English accent.

"There's no time for jocularity. Karl's in intensive care, and I have a funny feeling about his surgeon."

"What about his surgeon? Tell me more." Jorge knew that if Hilary's alarm bells were ringing then something wasn't right.

"I don't really know what," began Hilary excitedly, "but the tone he used with me and the look in his eyes told me he was hiding something, and I don't mean a little something. And then that paramedic. She threw me against the wall, and she turned out to have that same look in her eyes. I had to call you, I just had to speak to—"

"Hilary! It's OK, I'm here. Relax and take a deep breath." He listened to her breathing. "There, now tell me where you are right now."

"I'm still at the hospital. In the parking lot. In my car. Are you coming?"

"I'm on my way. Stay in the car until I get there. Which parking lot are you at?"

"The one beside the emergency entrance."

"OK, I know the one. I'll be there in twenty minutes, and Hilary..."

"Yes."

"Lock your doors."

"OK, I will. Just hurry up, would you!"

As she hung up, Hilary thought about what Jorge had said: "Lock your doors." *I hadn't thought I would be in danger, but I guess it's a good precaution.*

Hilary started to scan the parking lot for anything that looked out of the ordinary.

"There, what was that?" she whispered aloud as she looked out of the passenger-side window. Just a bush moving in the breeze she decided.

"Don't go getting all paranoid now," she reminded herself aloud. "You know you have a penchant for being a little 'mentally creative' as they say."

Bang! Hilary nearly hit her head on the roof of the car as she turned to see where the noise had come from.

"Aaah!" screeched Hilary when she turned to find a young man wearing a hoodie at her window.

"Excuse me, ma'am," said the voice behind the perfectly white teeth. "Do you know if I can get to the Intensive Care Unit through the emergency entrance?"

Hilary just sat there staring up at him.

"Sorry, I didn't mean to scare you. I stumbled and my hand came down on your roof as I tried to catch myself."

Hilary blinked a few times then opened her window a crack. "You scared the living crap out of me!" she began, breathing once again. "Just go in to emerg and ask how to get to intensive care; they'll know."

"OK, thanks, I thought so. There's just so many entrances; I wanted to narrow it down." The young man pulled one hand out of his pocket to wave and said, "Thanks, I appreciate it."

"Wait! You look familiar," called out Hilary after him. "What's your name?"

"Will," Damn it! Why did I say that, idiot? thought Will.

"Will Parkinson?" asked Hilary.

"How did you know?"

"I remember seeing you in the news before, standing beside your father, the senator. Is everything OK?"

"Yah, my mom's friend was injured at that wacko's rally this afternoon. Just wanted to visit," countered Will.

"So sorry to hear that. I was there too," said Hilary.

"You should be thankful you didn't get hurt."

"You don't know the half of it," offered Hilary.

"OK, thanks again," said Will as he turned and walked toward the emergency entrance.

"Holy crap!" said Hilary aloud. "Hurry up, Jorge, things just got weird."

∞

Karl took one last look at the crying widow. He felt her pain, but there was nothing he could do, and it was time to leave. Karl expanded his awareness as much as he could in his limbic state and could feel the presence of Dr. Hinchcliff. It was faint, but he was still in the building. When he got back to the hallway, that same blue-purple glowing light near the floor was there to greet him. He somehow knew all he had to do was follow it and it would lead him directly to Dr. Hinchcliff.

"He's not dead, I tell you!" yelled Dr. Hinchcliff into the phone. "And he has a good chance to live long enough to tell someone all he knows."

"Couldn't you have just botched the operation, Doc?" asked the voice on the other end.

"That's not the way it works. I took a Hippocratic oath, and besides, my whole team—who are very good at what they do, by the way—were right there. They'd know if I screwed something up on purpose."

"OK, then can't you just sneak into his room and inject something into his IV or put a sock in his mouth?"

"You've been watching way too many gangster movies, Senator."

Funny, I just said that to my son, thought Parkinson. My son! he remembered. "Have you seen my son yet?"

"No, why, should I have?"

"He's probably on his way to try to finish off Karl Dunitz."

"Jesus Christ! You're turning your son into a hit man?"

"Take it easy, Doc; he's not the sharpest knife in the drawer, if you know what I mean."

Like father like son, thought Gene.

"That's why you're going to help him."

"I don't think so, Senator; my job here is done."

"You'll be done, all right, if you don't do as you're told, Dr. Hinchcliff."

Gene's mind whirled as he tried to think of a rebuttal.

"The bottom of the river is a very lonely place, Doc. Look at the bright side; you'll be upholding your pledge of allegiance to serve the Society. You may even step up a level or two."

Gene couldn't think anymore. He hadn't joined the Society to kill people; he just wanted to rid the world of those who would expose the Great Secret.

"All right!" answered Dr. Hinchcliff finally. "I'll do what I can."

"And you'll look out for my son?"

"Yes, yes, I'll look out for your son."

That's it! thought Gene. I'll just pin Dunitz's death on the senator's son. Then Karl Dunitz will be dead, Will Parkinson will go to jail, and he'll never rat out his father, which means all will be right once again!

"OK, Senator, I've got to go. I have a plan to formulate."

Karl had been hovering in the room the whole time and couldn't believe his ears. He had heard great things about Dr. Hinchcliff in the past, and now the same man who had just worked so hard to keep him alive wanted to kill him.

But what is the Society, and what the hell is the Great Secret?

The Society, began Jorge, *is also known as the Devil's Workshop, but I'm not sure if that's a name they gave to themselves or perhaps what others have named them.*

Ah, there you are, my friend, communicated Karl with relief. *I was wondering when I was going to hear from you.*

I have been busy trying to track down the people behind your attempted murder and calming all your adoring fans. I've received thousands of emails and texts asking if you were still alive.

And what did you tell them?

I told them you were floating around somewhere in the hospital and doing fine.

Quite an apt description, my friend.

I thought so!

Well, I can tell you who's behind my attempted murder, thought Karl knowingly. *It's Senator Parkinson, and that's not all; his son, Will, is in on it too.*

Senator Parkinson? He's just a pawn. He must be working for someone else hoping to advance his political career. Besides, he's not the sharpest tool in the shed.

I've heard something like that before about him.

Anyway, thought Jorge, *back to the Society. Once an invitation is secured, membership grants a person certain consideration: political favors, appointments to influential positions, business and financial opportunities. They seem to have a more religious, or perhaps sacrilegious, bend and believe they can gain mystical abilities or accrue occult powers by being guardians of the Great Secret.*

OK, so far, they seem like every other secret society out there, but what's the Great Secret?

The Great Secret, my friend, is what you were about to make public to the world.

The Process?

That's the one. Apparently, others discovered the same thing thousands of years ago, and once the general population found out the secret, it ended in disaster for the leaders, so they decided to hide it instead. They felt the public was not, or perhaps never would be, ready to hear the truth. So, a secret society was founded in order to guard the secret of the Process and eliminate anyone that threatened to expose it.

But the Process belongs to everyone. It is what we are, how we're made, how everything in the Universe works. Everyone should know about this!

I agree, my friend, but there are those with much to lose if the Secret were to get out.

Then they'll just have to get over themselves because I plan to disclose the Process to everyone.

Mr. Karl, that is a very noble thing to do for a very noble cause, but I believe, given your current situation, you should focus on getting well, then you can think again about revealing the Process.

Karl thought for a moment about what Jorge had just said. *Maybe he's right. How could I ever disclose the secret to all of life without my body, my vehicle on this earth, to do it with?*

OK, Jorge, I'll give it some time and see if I can recover sufficiently in order to do what I need to do. In the meantime, we need to find Hilary so I can try to communicate with her somehow.

Hilary's still here; she's in the parking lot.

In the parking lot? Are you kidding me?

No, she called me and said she was concerned about your surgeon, Dr. Hinchcliff, so I told her to stay put and I'd be there soon.

So why are you wasting time discussing this telepathically with me?

Not to worry, Mr. Karl, Frank is on his way to her now. I will follow him shortly, and don't forget how much time is condensed while we communicate in this fashion.

You are right, Jorge; I'm sure Frank will be with her soon.

Chapter Five

Frank crisscrossed between cars so as not to fall into Hilary's rearview mirror as he approached her car. He stopped for a moment behind a large SUV to look at her. He could only see the back of her head, but he liked what he saw. He loved the look of her auburn hair, especially from behind. A feeling of warmth and a slight smile crossed Frank's face, but he knew he could never commit to a relationship, let alone one with a coworker.

Bang! Once again Hilary nearly jumped out of her seat as she heard something hit her car.

"Aaah! What the hell? Oh, it's you!" yelled Hilary. "You son of a bitch, you scared the crap out of me!"

As she looked out of her window, all she could see was Frank doubled over laughing.

"I'm not kidding; I think I may have to go to the restroom!" said Hilary as she lowered the driver's side window.

Frank laughed even harder now, and Hilary couldn't help but smile and chuckle as well.

"That's the second time someone's done that to me within the last thirty minutes," remarked Hilary, laughing now.

Suddenly Frank stopped laughing and the smile left his face. "What are you talking about?"

"That's the second time in the last thirty minutes someone has scared me like that."

"Yah, I heard you the first time, but what, and who, was the first time?"

"Oh, Will Parkinson, you know, the senator's son? He stumbled as he walked by and caught himself by slamming his hand down on my roof. Scared the crap out of me then too."

"Will Parkinson was here? Where did he go?"

"He said he was going to visit a friend of his mom's in intensive care and was wondering which was the best entrance to take," answered Hilary.

"So, what did you tell him?"

Hilary could sense Frank's tone get much more serious. The tone he used when he's hunting someone.

"I told him to just go to emerg and ask them the best way to get there. What's up, Frank?"

"Senator Parkinson was the one who ordered Karl's shooting. Will is involved as well," said Frank as he studied all the entrances within sight.

"Damn it! I knew something was weird. Him showing up here like that, with his hood pulled over his head," exclaimed Hilary.

"What was he wearing?"

"Navy blue hoodie, jeans, and white sneakers," answered Hilary proudly. Frank had taught her to always pay attention to things like that.

"OK, call Jorge and tell him to meet me at Karl's room and advise him that Will Parkinson is in the building. There's police protection at the entrance to his room, right?" asked Frank earnestly.

"I...I don't know. I think so. I'm sorry, I didn't stick around after my altercation with Dr. Hinchcliff and that paramedic."

"Well, I'm not sure about that paramedic, but Dr. Hinchcliff is in on it too. You might want to stay here where it's safer. I'm going to track down that wimpy little city boy!"

Jorge was just turning into the hospital parking lot as his phone began to ring.

"Hello?" said Jorge as he slipped his transmission into park.

"Hi, Jorge, it's me, Hilary. Just wanted to let you know that Frank is here and he's gone into the hospital to look for Will Parkinson."

"Will Parkinson is here? That's not good news, Miss Hilary. Did you make sure there was police protection in place outside of Mr. Karl's room?"

"I'm so sorry, Jorge, in all the commotion, I didn't check to see if anyone was assigned or not."

"Shoot! OK, I've got to go and get up to Mr. Karl's room."

"Wait! Frank said he'll meet you there. Where are you now, Jorge?"

"Just pulled into the hospital parking lot."

"Good, I'm going with you; let's go!"

"I think it's better if you wait in your..." Jorge stopped talking and hung up his phone as Hilary stepped into his view and was headed toward the emergency entrance.

Jorge quickly left his car and trotted up behind Hilary.

"Aaah!" exclaimed Hilary as Jorge drew up alongside her.

"Jumpy are we, Miss Hilary?"

"You don't know the half of it, Jorge."

∞

Frank had stopped to ask in the emergency department if anyone had seen a man with the description Hilary had given him and was now running up the back stairs, taking two at a time, to the fifth floor where Karl's room was.

Frank stopped at the door to the fifth floor, took two deep breaths, and then slowly cracked the door to have a look. He could see Karl's room from where he was and was disappointed to see no police outside of it.

"Shit! Hopefully I've beat that skinny little bastard here."

Frank slowly opened the door just enough to squeeze his muscular frame through the opening. *Oh my god, I might be too late!* he thought as he moved quickly toward Karl's door. When he arrived, he saw the figure of a hooded man leaning over Karl's motionless body.

"Freeze!" yelled Frank as he burst through Karl's door, a 9 mm pistol in his outstretched arm.

The hooded man did just that and didn't turn around.

"Hands behind your head, asshole. Slowly."

There was no movement.

"I said," Frank repeated forcefully, "hands behind your head. Now!"

Once again, no acknowledgement. Frank began to cautiously approach the hooded man from his left rear quarter, but as he got close enough, the hooded man whirled around and grabbed Frank's wrist, forcing him to let go of his pistol.

This prick has a hell of a grip! thought Frank as he instinctively threw a left hook at the man's face.

As Frank's fist quickly closed the gap to the assailant's face, the man's other hand came up to meet it and close around Frank's other wrist.

Frank stood there, stunned to have been so effectively disarmed by this person. As the man looked up at Frank, the shadows from the hood disappeared, and Frank was surprised to see the teary-eyed face of young Will Parkinson.

"I can't do it," said Will, sniffling. "I can't kill him. He represents where we need to go. Where we must go if we are to survive ourselves."

Will relaxed his grip on Frank and brought his hands to his face, crying uncontrollably now. Frank took a couple of quick steps back, still not trusting Will.

"It's OK, son, I believe you," began Frank. "But I need you to turn around and put your hands on your head, now!"

"I'll cooperate," said Will. "I don't want to cause any more trouble."

Frank reached into his pocket and grabbed his nylon cable tie he used for temporary handcuffs and placed it over Will's wrists, cinching it tight.

"Walk straight ahead to the wall and then slowly turn around and sit down on the floor," said Frank as he bent over to grab his side arm.

Will did as he was asked and sat there on the floor blubbering.

"That's one hell of a grip you've got there, son."

"What?" asked Will sheepishly through his tears.

"I said, that's one hell of a grip you've got there."

"Kyusho Jitsu."

"Martial art of pressure points," said Frank. "You know, many martial arts experts think that's cheating and don't practice it."

"It just takes a long time to master," added Will.

"Well, it looks like you have. My wrists are still sore."

"They will be for a couple of days. My dad made me take the training; he thought I was too wimpy looking."

"Well, looks can certainly be deceiving," said Frank with a slight hint of respect for Will's abilities.

∞

Dr. Gene Hinchcliff had left the break room, and Karl had followed, but then the comforting blue-purple glow appeared near the floor once again, so Karl veered off and followed it instead. That soft glow was so mesmerizing, he felt it was speaking to him in some way.

An angel of sorts? thought Karl.

When Karl reached his room where his body was resting, he was jolted out of his meditative state by the sight of Frank being held helpless by Will Parkinson. As he watched, he was glad to see the altercation end peacefully, but now he was picking up Will's brain energy impulses.

He was here to finish the job he had started, thought Karl, but couldn't do it. Funny, I'm sensing very kind and compassionate thought patterns from him now. Perhaps he can now be trusted.

Karl, Frank, and Will were all caught off guard as a tall blond nurse burst through the door to Karl's room.

"What the hell are all you people doing in here?" asked the nurse. "This is intensive care; you can't just waltz in here anytime you like. This man needs his rest so he can recover and—"

"Lead us?" interjected Will.

"Well, actually, yes. How did you know what I was going to say?"

"Never mind all that; where the hell were you?" asked Frank forcefully.

"This man," continued Frank pointing at Will, "did just as you said and just waltzed in here."

"I was filling out some charts I've fallen behind on."

"I thought the care here was one-on-one?"

"Well, it was, but cutbacks by that moron, Senator Parkinson, have forced us to be one-on-two, and sometimes one-on-three. None of us enjoy it, but it's our job."

So that's how Dad was able to save all that money on health care, thought Will. Asshole!

Hilary was trying to keep up with Jorge as he raced ahead to get to Karl's room. She had begun running again recently but obviously was still not up to her former level of fitness.

Once again, everyone in the room turned to look at the door in surprise as Jorge breathlessly ran into the room. Jorge stood motionless, consuming huge amounts of oxygen as he surveyed the situation, only to be bumped into from behind by the similarly breathless Hilary.

"What's going on?" managed Hilary between gasps for air.

"Everything's under control," answered Frank condescendingly, as he glanced at the tall blond nurse.

"Out of my way, Neanderthal," said the nurse as she brushed past Frank. "I hope you don't mind if I check on my patient."

Strangely, Hilary felt there was some sort of attraction between the nurse and Frank, although they seemed to not care for each other.

"Well, I'm glad we got here in time," said Jorge breathing much easier now.

"Not really, Jorge," remarked Frank while looking at Will. "But this young man is going to tell us all about it, soon enough."

"Dr. Hinchcliff?" called out Head Nurse Dixon.

"Oh, hi, Dixie."

"Why are you standing out here in the hall hiding behind the crash cart?"

"Oh, I was just observing what was going on in Mr. Dunitz's room. I was about to see how he was doing and then noticed there was a room full of people," replied Dr. Hinchcliff sheepishly.

"Yes, there is, so let's go see what's going on, shall we," replied Dixie in her usual in-charge tone.

"Yes, of course, what the heck is going on!"

Dixie led the way and pushed open the door to Karl's room.

"I'm Head Nurse Dixon and..."

Jorge held up his left hand as a stop sign and glared at Nurse Dixon as he was talking on the phone.

"Yes, Commissioner, I want around-the-clock protection outside of Mr. Karl's room," continued Jorge. "Of course, yes, there will be a substantial contribution to the annual policeman's ball. Thank you. Yes, I'll wait until the first policeman arrives. Thank you again."

Jorge dropped his hand, and Nurse Dixon continued unphased.

"I'm Head Nurse Dixon, and Dr. Hinchcliff and I demand to know what's going on here!"

Dixie looked around the room, but everyone was looking past her and shrugging their shoulders.

"What are you looking at?" asked Dixie as she turned around.

"Dr. Hinchcliff? Well, he was just here," said Dixie blushing now.

Ah, a chink in the armor, thought Frank.

"This man," started Frank, "was attempting to cause bodily harm to Mr. Dunitz. Where the hell was your one-on-one coverage?"

"It's all right, Nurse Dixon," interjected the tall blond nurse. "I already told them the reason. It's my fault; I was trying to update all my charts. I only left for a few minutes."

"It's all right, Judy," replied Dixie. "It's not your fault."

Judy, thought Frank. Nice name.

"OK, it looks like we're all done here," said Dixie using her in-charge tone once again. "Everybody out except Mr. Stop Sign, who is apparently going to wait for police security."

Jorge looked at Nurse Dixon and smiled his best smile. He'd been called a lot worse before.

"I haven't got the stomach for this shit anymore!" said Dr. Hinchcliff to himself as he continued down the back stairs. "Obviously Will failed. So now what?"

Chapter Six

Jorge sat down on one of the chairs in Karl's room to wait for the police. He hadn't realized how tired he was until he sat down, and now all that had transpired in the last twenty-four hours started to take its toll on him.

Karl had been in the room, seemingly hovering over everyone else. He wasn't really sure how this was happening, but it felt good. He was free of his aging and now severely damaged body and could feel the pull from the other side. He didn't want to go yet, but it just felt so beautiful, so loving, and so hard to resist. He knew the time would come when he would relent and follow that beautiful feeling of unconditional love, but for now he had to start downloading what he had discovered to someone.

How are you doing, my friend? thought Karl.

Jorge naturally looked over at Karl's body, but then realized the voice was in his head.

I'm doing fine, Mr. Karl, thought Jorge while rubbing his temples.

You don't look fine. You need to get some rest soon, but before you do, I need to download everything I've discovered to someone. The pull from the other side is increasing, and I fear I haven't got much earthly time left.

OK, communicated Jorge, *I'm ready. Download away!*

Sorry, Jorge, you're not the one.

What do you mean, I'm not the one? I know more about you—who you are and who you were before—than anyone else. I've been by your side every step of the way and now you tell me I'm not worthy?

It's not that you're not worthy, Jorge; you're just not leadership material. Your strength lies in serving others with your honesty and integrity, and using your incredible abilities to find out and assimilate information so it can be understood—all attributes left over from Dr. Jian.

Jorge let it all sink in for a moment and knew Karl was right. *OK, if not me, then who?*

Will Parkinson.

Will Parkinson! Are you nuts?

I know it seems ludicrous, but I've been privy to his thoughts, and he thinks as we do. He's not like his father; he's just been trapped trying to please him for so long he no longer knew who he was. Tonight, he discovered who he truly is.

But Frank has him now, thought Jorge earnestly. *Who knows what he'll do to him to make him talk.*

He'll talk, and Frank will get all the information he's looking for. Then he'll bring Will back here so I can start the download telepathically.

OK, I'll call Frank and tell him to take it easy on the kid, obliged Jorge.

Don't bother, he needs to find his own strength. He'll be fine.

∞

"Sit your ass down and don't speak until you're spoken to!" yelled Frank at his prisoner.

Frank had brought him down to the police station where he could borrow one of their interrogation rooms for questioning. They always said yes to Frank. Frank was ex-Special Forces and ex-FBI; they didn't screw with him.

"Who do you think you are?" countered Will. "My dad!"

"Oh, that's a good one, little boy. No, I'm not your dad; I'm your worst fricking nightmare!"

"What movie did you get that line from?" asked Will half laughing.

Frank rushed over to Will and grabbed him by the scruff of the neck, putting his face inches from Will's.

"I could break you like a twig if I wanted to, little boy. Don't make me angry!"

Will could see Frank meant business, but wasn't about to let him know it.

"Yes, I saw you in action at the hospital. How's your wrists?"

Frank swung his right fist and stopped it an inch from Will's chest. He kept his fist centered over Will's chest, gathering strength from the universal energy that surrounds all of us. His fist began to quiver and then he let it go. Will knew what was coming but could do little to prepare.

Will tried to absorb as much of the impact as he could, but the chest area has very little give. Will, and the chair he was bound to, flew back about three feet before tipping and then toppling backward.

Will had hit his head on the floor as the chair tipped back, but his chest hurt a whole lot more.

"What are you, some kind of freak?" shouted Will hoarsely. "Get me up off the floor." Will was trying to show his defiance, but that punch had really messed up his breathing.

"Are you going to say you're sorry?" asked Frank calmly.

"Are you kidding me? I should kick your ass!"

"From the floor?"

"Oh, you're really tough when you're picking on someone who's tied to a chair and laying on the floor. Why don't you get me up and untie me and then see what happens!"

Frank rushed over and started to lift the chair and Will off the floor when the door crashed opened.

"What the hell is going on in here!" demanded Detective Sergeant Smith. "What are you doing to this man? This is not the way we treat detainees in our department, and I don't care where you're from!"

Smith had caught Frank in the middle of lifting the chair, with Will in it, back to its normal position.

There was a moment of awkward silence.

"I was just trying to lean back against the wall," said Will. "And the chair fell over."

"I don't believe you," said Smith

"Honestly, I'm fine. I just tipped over, no harm done."

Frank smiled at Smith and nodded in agreeance.

Smith brought his hand near his face and curled his index finger toward himself, motioning for Frank to come to him.

"Do you know who that boy is?" whispered Smith.

"Yup."

"If you harm him, we all lose our jobs. Get your answers without killing the boy, OK?"

"Yes sir!" said Frank condescendingly.

Smith left the room shaking his head and closed the door behind him.

"I guess I'm not allowed to kill you," said Frank

"Nice try, freak. Although that was a great one-inch punch."

"You liked that, did you?"

"Not really. It hurts like hell."

"Well, so do my wrists."

"Not many people can deliver the one-inch punch properly," said Will.

"Karl taught me."

"Karl? But he's a pacifist."

"He didn't teach me the physical punch; he taught me how to harness the energy."

"He's a special person, isn't he?" asked Will.

"Very special. So why don't you help me help him?"

"You know, many of the people my age love to listen to Karl speak—his talks about love and how we all came from the same source and all that. But I'm not sure what I like more, his message or the fact that he pisses off my dad and all his cronies with their ancient ways of thinking."

"I hear you," began Frank. "I felt the same way when I first heard him. I was still in the FBI and couldn't stand the bureaucracy any longer, so I guess I was 'ripe for the picking,' so to speak, but there was just something that rang so true to me. I couldn't deny it."

"So how do you think he would propose to lead us out of this mess we're in?" asked Will.

"I'm not sure, but I do know this. The change that needs to be made can only come from our hearts. We must stop seeing ourselves as separate from our source and separate from each other."

"OK, I get that, in fact, I've heard him say that. But what else?"

"The only solution," continued Frank, "the only *real* solution is in the ultimate truth."

"And that is?"

"Nothing exists in the universe that is separate from anything else. Everything is intrinsically connected, interdependent, interactive, and interwoven into the great tapestry called 'life.' If you could just picture a huge tapestry with all its many colors of fibers all interwoven and comingling with each other, that's how connected we all are with each other."

"I can't really picture a tapestry in my mind because I don't really know what one is. Got another example?"

"OK, try this analogy. You are the star of a motion picture, a movie."

"Cool, I like where you're going with this so far!"

"You are the star," continued Frank. "But you're also the extras too."

Frank could see the bewilderment on Will's face.

"You are the star, but at the same time that you're acting out your role as the star in your film, you are also an extra in everyone else's movie where *they* are the star."

"Oh, I get it! Everyone is a star in their own independent film, but at the same time, for everyone else they have met in their lives, they are also working as extras in *their* independent films."

"Exactly! If all of the world's governments, and all politics, were based on this one simple ultimate truth, then we no longer would feel the need to compete with one another or to harm one another."

"What about love? How does that all fit into this process?" queried Will excitedly.

"Well, Karl says that Love gives all and asks for nothing."

"What do you mean? How can we require nothing?"

"I know, I didn't get it at first either, but here's how I understand it. If we all gave everything, if all we did was give, then what would we need? The only reason we require anything is because someone else is holding something back from us. But if no one was holding things back because everyone gave everything, then we'd have it all."

"I see, but that would only work if everyone was able to give everything to everybody all at once."

"Absolutely! And that's why there has to be a shift in global consciousness. And the next question you're going to ask is, 'How will that happen,' right?"

"How did you know that was my next question?" asked Will.

"Because it was mine too! This can only come about if someone starts it. Karl has already started it, but I fear he may not be physically able to continue."

"Hmmm," wondered Will aloud.

"There's an opportunity for you here, Will."

"An opportunity?"

"Yes, don't you see? There's a reason you're all mixed up in Karl's attempted murder. It's like the tapestry or movies we talked about earlier. You could be the source of this new consciousness. You could be the inspiration. In fact, you must be!"

"I must be?"

"Yes, who else? You have great connections with the people of your generation, and they're the ones who are going to make all the changes, not us old folks. Plus, you have ties to the political world through your father."

"Yeah, but I'm just touching the tip of the iceberg on all this stuff."

"Don't worry about that; Karl will see to it that you get all the information you need. Look, you don't have to make any decisions now. Why don't we go back to the hospital, visit Karl, and go from there? Sound good?"

"I'm willing to go that far, I guess," answered Will with uncertainty.

"Good, then let's get out of here."

∞

Frank turned his sports car into the hospital parking lot and selected the nearest parking spot. He got out of the car and took a quick glance around the parking lot. As he did, he noticed Hilary's car was still there.

"Stay here, Will, I'll be right back."

"Wait! Untie me first, you ignoramus!" Damn it! thought Will. Hey, he used my first name, cool. "But it would have been nice if he had untied me!" said Will talking to himself now.

Frank cautiously walked up to Hilary's car door and tapped on the window.

"Wha...what? Oh, hi, Frank. I must have dozed off," said Hilary sleepily as she fumbled for the switch to lower the window.

"What's going on? Is there a change in Karl's condition?"

Frank took a look at Hilary and couldn't help but comment. "I know you like me, Hilary, but you don't have to drool over me!" Then he smiled one of his patented smiles.

"Oh shit! Sorry, honey," said Hilary as she wiped the drool from the corner of her mouth. "I must have been leaned up against the steering wheel."

"That you were. Not to worry, I'm sure you were having a very nice dream."

Hilary pulled the latch on the car door and shoved the door hard into Frank's knees. "Asshole!"

"She's back, folks, back to the world of the living!" exclaimed Frank to an imaginary crowd in the parking lot.

"Stop clowning around and let's go check on Karl."

"OK, but I have to collect something from my car first."

As they walked up to Frank's car, Hilary could see there was another person in the passenger side, but they were sitting oddly.

"OK, let's go, Will," said Frank as he opened the passenger-side car door.

"You said you were going to untie me once we got out of the cop shop."

"I lied," exclaimed Frank rather matter-of-factly. "Now turn around so I can untie you."

"What's *he* doing back here?" asked Hilary.

"*He* has a name, Madame, and it's William," said Will in his best theater school accent while rubbing his wrists.

"I know your name, honey; I just don't know what you're doing here. They should have locked you up by now."

"Out of the mouth of babes..." asserted Frank.

Hilary punched Frank hard in the left arm. "He didn't say anything wise, Franky," started Hilary. "That verse is supposed to refer to when someone younger says something wise beyond their years."

"Franky? Oh wow, you'll never live this down," said Will laughing out loud.

"Shut up, boy! How's your wrists?"

"How's yours?"

"How's your chest?"

"Touché. Let's not go there."

"OK, enough jocularity, let's go; we have a lot of work to do," said Frank as he grabbed Will by one arm to turn him in the direction of the hospital entrance.

As they walked toward the entrance, Hilary once again punched Frank in his left arm.

"Stop it!" said Frank, surprised at how hard Hilary's punches were.

"Will Parkinson?" mouthed Hilary to Frank. "Are you crazy!"

Her eyes were as big as saucers, but Frank lifted his hand and nodded to reassure her.

"Trust me on this one, OK?"

Chapter Seven

Frank, Hilary, and Will walked up to Karl's room and were met by a young police officer at the door.

"Hello, folks. Sorry, no access to Mr. Dunitz's room."

"I'm Frank Tillitson, head of security for Mr. Dunitz," replied Frank, showing the young officer his ID.

"And I'm Hilary Lambton, Mr. Dunitz's chief assistant and aide."

"Oh, I think I've seen you on TV, ma'am!" said the young officer.

"I believe you have," added Hilary flatteringly.

"And who do we have here?" asked the officer, staring at Will.

"I'm..."

"He's Will Parkinson, Senator Parkinson's son," interrupted Frank.

"OK, wait right here while I check with Mr. Alonso."

The young officer stepped into Karl's room and flipped the lock closed from inside. "Mr. Alonso. Mr. Alonso!"

"Ah, what?" replied a sleepy Jorge as he sat up on the cot that the nursing staff had brought in for him.

"There are a few people here to see you, and they say they work for Mr. Dunitz."

"What? Who?"

"A Frank Tillitson, Hilary—"

"That's fine, that's fine, let them in," said Jorge.

Jorge stood up, stretched, and then tried to smooth the wrinkles out of his shirt the best he could.

"Ah, Mr. Frank, Miss Hilary, and Master Will."

"Master Will?" questioned Will.

"Don't worry about it. Just go with the flow," whispered Frank to Will.

"Mr. Karl has been expecting you."

"Thank you, officer. You may leave us now," added Jorge.

"Expecting us?" asked Will.

"Yes, he knew Frank would be bringing you around eventually. I just hoped it was in one piece."

"The kid can hold his own, Jorge. He's all right in my books."

Hilary shot Frank a look of disbelief.

"Yes, well let's get on with it then, shall we?" said Jorge.

After closing the door behind him, the young police officer pressed the button on his lapel radio and began to speak. "Tillitson, Lambton, and young Parkinson just arrived, sir."

"Very good. Keep an eye on them and let me know what they're up to. I'll let Senator Parkinson know," replied Detective Sergeant Smith.

Will waited until the officer had left and then asked, "What exactly are we going to get on with? I mean, how can we even communicate with Mr. Dunitz when he's in a coma?"

"First of all," began Jorge, "he would like it if you called him Karl; and second of all, you will communicate with him telepathically."

"Telepathically! I'm not into all that psychic stuff; I don't know if I'm the right guy for this," said Will anxiously.

"Mr. Karl asked to speak to you. No one else."

"But I've never even meditated, let alone talked to someone telepathically."

"Have you ever sat by a campfire, just staring at the flames, alone in your thoughts?" asked Jorge.

"Of course, who hasn't?"

"Then you've meditated."

"Really, that's meditation?"

"One form of meditation, yes. And so is daydreaming, which I'm sure you've done as well."

"Actually, I'm really good at that one!"

"Good, then you're eminently qualified," said Jorge reassuringly.

"I'm still surprised he wants to talk to me. I'm the one who arranged his assassination attempt."

"It surprises me too, Master Will," said Jorge as he remembered the discussion he had had with Karl. "But it is Mr. Karl's wishes."

"It'll be fine. Just go with the process," said Frank.

"All right, I'll give it a try, but it's just so spooky with him lying there like that and me knowing I was responsible for putting him there."

"You are not solely responsible; there are many others involved. Things will become much clearer once you begin to converse with Mr. Karl."

"OK, let's do this. How do we start?" queried Will.

"First we need to sit comfortably," began Jorge.

As Jorge began talking, Frank instinctively walked over and leaned up against the inside of the door.

"It's best if you turn your palms up, resting lightly on your thighs while making a circle with your forefinger and your thumb. This is the flow of energy from your heart, flowing outward then returning to you—the circle of life."

"Now," continued Jorge, "we need to clear our minds. Take a deep breath and relax. If a thought comes into your mind, just let it pass as if it were a cloud in the sky, being gently pushed by the breeze. It may also be helpful to think of your thoughts as a ticker tape that scrolls across so many news channels. Just let all your thoughts keep on scrolling, never allowing any of them to stick."

Will did his best to do as Jorge instructed but still felt like a fish out of water.

"At this time," continued Jorge, "we will introduce a mantra, which is just a saying repeated over and over so that we no longer focus on our thoughts. Our mantra will be 'Aham Brahmasmi,' the Sanskrit words for 'I am the Universe.'" He paused for a moment. "Aham Brahmasmi, Aham Brahmasmi, just repeat it to yourself mentally now. *Aham Brahmasmi. Aham Brahmasmi.*"

After a few moments Will heard Jorge speak.

How are you feeling, Master Will?

I feel great! I feel calm. I'm not nervous at all.

Very good. Have you noticed your lips aren't moving, but we are conversing?

Holy crap, you're right! I didn't think I was capable of this.

We're all capable of this, and much more, Master Will. We're just kept so busy earning a living and surviving that we've forgotten who we truly are.

This is freaking awesome! Can the others hear us?

Mr. Frank chooses not to as he is busy protecting us, but Miss Hilary is well versed at telethapy.

Hello, Will, communicated Hilary.

Wow! I mean, hello Hilary. This is just so awesome! I'm so excited!

Easy now, Master Will, interrupted Jorge. *If you allow too much emotion in, then your body releases chemicals that will bring you out of the meditative state.*

OK, OK, I'm calming down. Aham Brahmasmi, Aham Brahmasmi.

Excellent, Will. It's so nice to meet you.

What? Who said that?

It's me, Will. It's Karl.

I'm so sorry, Karl. I didn't want to kill you, I was just doing what my dad ordered. I'm so sorry, so sorry!

You are forgiven, Will. I know what went down, and I'm glad you were involved.

You are?

Yes, I am, and I know that your dad has held back his love for you for so very long that you would do anything to please him in order to gain his affections.

I never thought about it that way.

Frank looked over at the trio on the couch and could see tears running out of the corners of Will's eyes.

Karl's got him, thought Frank.

All any of us really want, continued Karl, *is to be accepted and recognized for who we are. We want it so bad that many times we act foolishly in order to achieve some sort of affection or acknowledgement.*

Tell me about it; I've done that my whole life!

I suppose you're wondering why I wanted to speak with you.

Yes, I am. I figured you wanted information on who asked me to arrange your death. Man, that sounds weird, communicating with you now.

No, I already know most of that and don't really need to go any deeper. The reason I brought you here is to ask for your help.

How could I possibly be of help to you? You've already done much more than any other human I know.

Thank you for the kind words, but I haven't done enough yet, and I fear that my physical body will not allow me to finish what I started. That's where you come in.

But I thought the operation was a success? communicated Will.

It went as well as could be expected. Dr. Hinchcliff, although a poor judge of character, is a very skilled surgeon.

I'm sorry, began Will, *but I'm still trying to comprehend how I'm even speaking with you right now.*

Well, they induced me into a comatose state, which has allowed me to enter the realm between the living and the dead.

You're a ghost?

Not really. Have you ever heard of people having near-death experiences?

Of course.

Well, to put it simply, that's where I am. I haven't crossed over to the next realm—what some might call purgatory—so I'm still here, able to see what's transpiring and talk telepathically with anyone that believes they can do so as well.

Cool! So, you're not dead yet?

Not at all, Will, but there are some time constraints on my condition. If it worsens, I may pass on, or if I get better, they will take me out of this comatose state, and then it will not be as easy to communicate.

Frank had this crazy notion that you wanted me to continue on for you if you pass away, thought Will.

That's true, I do.

How could I ever even begin to fill your shoes? I don't know one percent of what you know about all this airy-fairy stuff.

That's why I want your permission to start downloading telepathically what I know and have recently discovered to you.

That's all well and good, Mr. Dunitz, began Will.

Karl.

Yes, OK, Karl. But even if I had your knowledge, I wouldn't know what to do with it. I'm no leader!

Everyone is a leader, Will, and the greatest among them just plant seeds in the minds of the people they serve and allow them to believe they have done it all themselves.

You make it sound so easy.

It is.

But I'm not even religious, added Will.

Forget religion, Will, focus on spirituality.

Wow. I don't know much, but I do know that you'll make a lot of people angry with that statement.

What, you don't think I already have?

OK, so you don't care if some people won't like you, but why should I just forget religion?

Because it's no good for you, communicated Karl.

No good for me? Maybe I haven't really subscribed to the notion of a higher power that judges me, but I thought that religion has helped many people, even if just by giving them hope for a better life if they believe.

I hear you, Will, but understand this: in order to make organized religion work, it has to make people have faith in it and believe they need it. And in order to do that, they must then lose faith in themselves. So, the very first thing that organized religion does is make you lose faith in yourself. The second thing that it does is make you think that it has all the answers and you don't. And finally, the last thing religion does is make you accept all its answers without question. You see, if you start to think, you will start to question. If you think and question, you will search for answers from within, and religion can't allow that because you might come up with an answer that's different from the one it wants you to believe.

Wow, I never thought about it like that.

So, do you see that it's better just to focus on our spirituality instead of man-made religions?

I'm starting to, but do you mean to tell me that it's really all just a power play?

It's the only way they could think of at the time to try to control the uneducated and uncouth masses. Religion, or the churches, if you will, knew of the power we all possess within and certainly couldn't allow the masses or general public to have access to that secret, or chaos would ensue, and then they would lose all control and, therefore, power. It's not too dissimilar from what goes on in today's political power struggles.

You see, if they can get you to doubt yourself, then there's no way you could claim your true power. They're holding your power, and they know it. And the only way to keep it under wraps is to stave off the latest movement toward seeing and then solving our two biggest problems.

Which are? asked Will inquisitively.

Most, if not all, of the world's problems would be solved if we would, as a society, abandon our infatuation with separation and adopt a new attitude of clarity.

I'm not quite sure what you mean.

Well, firstly, you must never see yourself as separate from anything or anyone. Everything you see before you, including all humankind, all came from the same source. An energy source filled with the desire to know itself, its own existence, and to evolve. Secondly, we must adopt an attitude of clarity, as in never telling anything but the whole truth to anyone. When you adopt the first one, it will naturally bring about the second, but fear always seems to creep in and distort and destroy, so fear is one of our greatest enemies.

That seems like a utopian dream, but is it really possible?

We will never be able to produce the society that we've always dreamed of unless, and until, we can solve these two problems because they lead us to the ultimate truth.

Oh boy, here we go again. Which is?

What you do to others, you are also doing to yourself; what you fail to do for others, you are also failing to do for yourself; the pain of others is also your pain; the joy of others is also your joy; and if you dismiss any part of it, you dismiss a part of yourself. Although we live in this illusion that everything is separate from us, we can use it as a tool and see it for what it is—a way to playfully and joyfully experience any aspect of who we truly are, yet never accepting it as reality. We can then use separation to simply manifest whatever we desire because we already understand that it is an illusion and separate from us. Once you realize this, you will become totally "enlightened"—that is, a being that is filled with light. You may even decide, once you leave this physical body, to return again quickly, not to create new experiences, but to bring this message of the light of truth to the land of illusion so that others may see it. Then you will be part of the awakening, as you are now.

Is that what you did, come back right away, I mean?

Yes, it is, began Karl. *I was given the name Wayne in my former life and lived on this planet, but in a different dimension. Unfortunately, many of the same issues that faced us in the third dimension also exist here in the fourth.*

So, this is the fourth dimension?

Yes, it is, and I was told it was more magical than the third, but there are a few people in power around the world that are trying to suppress everyone's inherent ability to see the magic.

People like my father.

Your father is only someone who has given himself up to a powerful bedfellow named "greed," just like many have before him. He has enough money to buy anything he wants, so the next progression is to start lusting after power and control; however, he's really just a pawn in all of this and is taking orders from elsewhere.

I remember when he used to take the time to play with me as a kid. We even used to take long drives in his convertible sports car, just to get ice cream. I miss who he was then, communicated Will with a tone of sadness.

And that's how you should remember him because that's still who he is underneath his cloak of selfishness. But for now, he believes he's doing the right thing for the world and himself. It's not that he doesn't love you, it's just that you've never met his expectations, to follow him into the realm of total separation. Something deep inside you told you that wasn't the way to enlightenment. Just like something deep inside you now is telling you that everything I have told you thus far, and will tell you, is part of the ultimate truth.

Will tilted his head back and opened his eyes to allow the tears to flow out then quickly closed his eyes again. He saw a clouded figure standing by the door and knew it was Frank keeping them safe. He felt so safe here.

I so feel it now. This is the path I am supposed to take. This is the reason I was born.

There are many reasons you were born, Will, and many lives you are living simultaneously in other dimensions, but we'll save that conversation for a little later.

What, you mean I'm also living elsewhere besides the fourth dimension?

Will's tone changed quickly from one of sadness to one of excitement.

That's exactly what I mean, but that lesson will have to wait. Right now, we have to figure out your father's next move to buy us enough time for me to download to you what I have just recently discovered.

∞

"Yes sir. I do get it, but kill my own son?" questioned Senator Parkinson emphatically. "Surely there must be another alternative? He's a good boy and will come around if...yes sir...I heard you the first time...I'll get it done."

Parkinson hung up the phone. "What the hell have I done?" he yelled as he raised his hands into the air. "I can't kill my own son!"

Then he thought, I haven't slipped that far into the abyss. Wait a minute, maybe I can kill him. "All I have to do is fake his death," remarked Parkinson out loud now. "Fake his death, move him to some sleepy little town on the West Coast, and give him a new identity. It'll be just like the Witness Protection Program, which I happen to be in charge of!"

Aaah, Parky, you still have it!

∞

Will Parkinson felt his phone start vibrating in his pocket. He had it on mute, but it still vibrated when a call or text was coming in.

I think you should answer that, communicated Karl.

How did you know...forget it, I know how you know.

Will opened his eyes and saw Frank staring at him. He reached into his front right pocket and pulled out his phone.

"Holy shit. It's my dad!"

Answer it, thought Karl.

"Speak of the devil," added Frank.

"Wait a minute, you have been listening to what we've been talking about."

"Mr. Frank always listens," started Jorge, dropping out of his meditative state, "but chooses not to participate."

"Just answer the phone, honey!" insisted Hilary impatiently.

Answer the phone, Will, and tell your father to meet you here in my room, communicated Karl.

"What, are you crazy?"

Trust me.

Will looked up at Frank, who was motioning him to answer the phone, and then swiped the green answer arrow on the screen.

"Hello?"

"Will? It's your dad."

"Yah, I saw that on the screen."

"Then why did you answer like that, and why did it take you so long?"

"I'm not going to get into that with you right now, Dad. I'm kinda busy. What do you want?"

"I'm sorry. It's just that I'm, I mean, we're under a lot of pressure right now. We have to—"

"I'm not under any pressure," interjected Will. "I know exactly what I'm doing now and what I want to do with the rest of my life. So as far as I'm concerned..."

Frank had rushed over in front of Will, tapped him on the side of the head, and mouthed the words "play nice."

"You know what, Dad?" began Will. "Let's just stop being so mad at each other, and why don't you meet me in Karl Dunitz's room at the hospital so we can talk?"

Senator Parkinson was stunned that Will had suggested Dunitz's room, but now his mind was working overtime.

"Sure! That sounds great, son," said Parkinson trying not to sound anxious. "In half an hour?"

"I'll be there," said Will before ending the call. "Something's not right."

"Why do you say that?" asked Jorge.

"He announced himself as 'dad' and he called me 'son.' He never does that."

It's all good. We not only know where he is, he's coming to us. It will all work out, thought Karl.

"If Will's in Dunitz's room," began Senator Parkinson, speaking out loud to himself, "I can finish the job and then deal with Will after. I love it when a plan comes together!"

Chapter Eight

Sabrina had already checked her bags with the airline when she began to feel like something was wrong. She knew she needed time away from Karl and all the negative publicity he seemed to be attracting lately, so she had booked a flight to visit her mom. She always felt the need to run home for support when things went wrong in her life since her dad had passed. He had been a police officer and died from a gunshot wound while trying to protect some shoppers in one of the worst mall shootings the country had ever seen.

"Why are all those folks gathering around the TV?" wondered Sabrina aloud.

Sabrina wandered over to see since it was in the direction of her departure gate anyway.

"Four people killed, thousands injured in an assassination attempt on spiritual leader Karl Dunitz's life today," said the ticker tape running at the bottom of the screen. "The suspect has been shot and killed while Mr. Dunitz is critically wounded and is apparently in an induced coma."

Sabrina's jaw dropped as she read the news. She couldn't believe what she was seeing. The video of the shots, Karl falling, and then the crowd fleeing just kept playing in a loop behind the ticker tape.

"This can't be happening," was all that Sabrina could say in her trancelike state. She couldn't take her eyes off of Karl's body flailing backward as if pulled by some unseen wire cable in a movie stunt. Over and over again she watched the man she had just told to get out of her life fall like a rag doll to the ground. First her dad, and now the man she so dearly loved.

"I didn't mean it, Karl!" yelled Sabrina out loud. "I love you!"

Some of the people gathered around the TV turned to see who was yelling.

"Hey, aren't you Karl's girlfriend?" yelled one of the watchers.

"She is, she is!" yelled another.

Sabrina shook her head as the yelling had woken her from her trance. Some of the people started moving toward her, surrounding her.

"Why weren't you there? What are you doing, running away? Shouldn't you be at the hospital?" yelled various members of the crowd.

Sabrina put her hands over her ears as she searched for an opening in the circle of people around her.

"Leave me alone!" screamed Sabrina at the top of her lungs.

The crowd stopped making remarks and stood still for a brief second. Sabrina saw an opening and went for it. She could hardly see where she was running through the tears in her eyes, but she still remembered where the doors leading to the taxis were. She pushed her way through the crowded exit and ran up to the first cab she saw and jumped into the rear seat.

"Get me to the hospital, hurry!"

"Which hospital, Madame?" asked the driver in slow broken English.

"I don't know, the one where Karl Dunitz is at."

"Oh, OK, that would be Southern General."

"Good, whatever. Just get this thing in gear and step on it!"

Although his English wasn't very good, the cab driver relished the opportunity to drive the cab as if he had stolen it.

"You look familiar," said the cabby as he swerved around some quickly stopping cars ahead of him.

"Shouldn't you be watching the road, not looking in the rearview mirror at me?" asked Sabrina, stating the obvious.

"You his girlfriend, no?"

Why did I ever think I could just be a regular teacher. Too many people know me now, thought Sabrina

"Yes, yes. I'm his girlfriend. Just get me to the hospital, and in one piece please!"

"Yes, of course, Madame."

Sabrina didn't know who this cabby was, but he sure could drive a car.

∞

Senator Parkinson walked through the main entrance of Southern General Hospital and strolled up to the information desk to ask directions to Karl's room.

"Wow, you're Senator Parkinson," said the surprised information attendant.

"That's right," answered the senator with a smile, "and I'm here to visit Karl Dunitz." Then he added, "He's a very good friend of mine."

"Well, we're not supposed to give out his location, but since you're the senator and all, I'm sure it's OK."

"Aww, that's mighty sweet of you, my dear. I don't believe I caught your name?"

"Michelle. My name's Michelle," said the attendant, blushing now. "I've been working here for over twenty years too," she added.

"Well, I'm so very glad to meet your acquaintance, Michelle. You don't look near old enough to have worked here that long."

"Thank you for the kind words, Senator, and may I add that you are much more handsome in person than on the TV."

"Well, look what we have here, not only is she beautiful, but she's smart too!"

Even though Michelle was dark skinned, she blushed three shades of red with the senator's latest compliment.

"Now, the directions to Mr. Dunitz's room? Please."

"Oh yes, I'm so sorry. You just go over to the main elevators over there," said Michelle pointing. "Then press the button that says 'ICU,' turn left after the doors open, and he's at the end of the hall in a double room."

"Well, thank you so much, pretty lady. Perhaps I'll make your acquaintance again someday."

Senator Parkinson turned and walked toward the elevators, but stopped and turn around when he heard Michelle call out.

"Oh, and Senator, you'll know which room he's in because there should be a policeman outside his door."

Great, thought Parkinson, just great. I guess I'll have to charm him too.

"Thank you once again, my dear," said the senator with a smile as he turned and walked toward the elevators.

"What a nice man!" said Michelle as she watched the senator press the call button for the elevator.

∞

Frank was starting to pace back and forth in front of the door to Karl's room.

"You're pacing like a caged animal, honey," said Hilary with a tone of minor annoyance. "What's up?"

"I'm trying to figure out the senator's next move. That, and I have to go pee!"

Frank's remark eased the tension in the room.

"Well, go pee then, you animal!" offered a chuckling Hilary.

"Mr. Frank, please go pee before we have a puddle in the room. You remember what happened last time, don't you?" added Jorge.

The room burst into laughter with Will joining in, if only to release some of his built-up tension from the anticipation of seeing his father.

"You mean, Franky pissed himself in front of you guys?" added Will, wanting to join in the fun of humiliating Frank.

The room exploded into laughter once more.

"I'm going for a piss!" shouted Frank as he ripped open the door to Karl's room.

"OK, honey!" said Hilary, wiping the tears of laughter from her eyes. "You go for it!"

"Everything all right, Mr. Tillitson?" asked the policeman at the door. "Sounds like a party going on in there."

"Just a bunch of a-holes, that's all."

"Gotcha," offered the policeman, knowing full well the others must have made a joke at Frank's expense.

"I'll be back in ten," added Frank.

"Yes sir, I'll be here."

∞

The doors to the elevator opened with a loud *ding*, and Senator Parkinson immediately turned left and headed down the hall.

There he is, thought the senator as he noticed the policeman at the door to Karl's room. Senator Parkinson smiled one of his patented smiles as he walked up to the policeman.

"Hello, officer. I'm—"

"Senator Parkinson. I know who you are," said the policeman in a flat monotone. "How can I help you?"

"I'd like to visit Mr. Dunitz. He and I go way back."

"I see. Well, you're not on the list, so I won't be able to allow you to visit today. Sorry about that, Senator."

Senator Parkinson looked down at the young policeman's name tag. "Are you expecting to make a career of this, Henderson?" asked the senator.

"What are you getting at, Senator."

"Well, you seem like a bright young man; I just wondered if you wanted to continue being a police officer for any length of time."

"You're not on the list, so you're not getting in, simple as that," began Henderson, staring straight into the senator's eyes. "And my future plans for employment are none of your concern."

"Excellent. I love a man with resolve!" said the senator excitedly. "Have it your way."

Henderson watched the senator reach into his pocket, pull out his cell phone, and tap a couple of times on the screen.

"Detective Sergeant Smith? Yes, it's Senator Parkinson calling. I'm trying to get in to visit Mr. Dunitz, but your man here at the hospital says I'm not on the list."

Henderson just kept staring at Parkinson with disdain.

"Yes, I'll tell him. Thank you, Detective." He ended the call on his cell phone. "Well, it looks like you have to let me in after all," said Parkinson with a smile.

"How do I even know you talked to Detective Sergeant Smith?"

"Henderson?" cracked the young policeman's lapel mic.

"Go ahead for Henderson," answered the young policeman.

"This is Detective Sergeant Smith, and I want you to allow Senator Parkinson in to visit Mr. Dunitz."

"Are you sure, sir? He's not on the list."

"I made the list, dumb ass!" screeched the mic. "Let me make this perfectly clear, Henderson," continued Detective Smith. "You're going to allow Senator Parkinson in to visit Mr. Dunitz, and the only other person that can be in that room is his son, Will. This is going to be a private moment for them. Got it!"

"Just to be clear, sir, you want everyone out of the room except Will Parkinson and Senator Parkinson."

"That's what I said. Now, if you want to continue your career with us, you'll do as you're told."

"Yes sir. Absolutely!" said Henderson looking up at the senator's gloating smile.

"That wasn't so hard now, was it?" asked Parkinson.

I don't like you, Parkinson, thought Henderson.

"Just doing what I'm told, Senator, not what I want."

"Still defiant, huh. I can see why Detective Smith likes you."

∞

Sabrina had put her seat belt on long ago but was still being thrown around the back seat as the cabby continued to pick his way through traffic. Her right shoulder and chest took the brunt of the g-forces as the cab finally came to a screeching halt at the front entrance to the hospital.

"IEEEEEE!" yelled the cabby as the car came to a rocking halt. "That, was fun!"

Sabrina wanted to share in the cabby's exuberance, but she was on a mission. "What do I owe you?" she asked.

"Today, I give you ride for half price. I feel so much joy. I had forgotten what it was like to drive with passion!"

Sabrina couldn't help but smile, even under the circumstances.

"Here, my friend. Keep the change," said Sabrina as she pushed the money through one of the vent holes in the plastic protective seat divider.

"You are so generous, Madame," he said as she slammed the door and began to walk away. Then he called out to her, "Madame!"

"Yes?" asked Sabrina as she turned back to look at the driver.

"Please be careful in the hospital. It can sometimes be a very dangerous place."

"Thank you. Yes, I will," answered Sabrina anxiously. "Sorry, I have to run."

The cabby couldn't help but feel he would never see her again. "Good-bye, Madame."

Sabrina turned and half ran toward the front doors of the hospital.

"Hi, I'm looking for Karl Dunitz's room," huffed Sabrina half out of breath to the information attendant.

"I'm sorry, ma'am, but I can't give out that information."

Sabrina looked down at the attendant's name tag and said, "Michelle, hi, I'm Karl's long-standing girlfriend, and I just found out he was shot, so I need to see him."

"Oh yah, you do look familiar. I think I saw you on TV standing behind Karl. He seems like such a nice man. Is he as nice in person as he seems on TV?"

Sabrina could feel her blood start to boil but held it together for another try. "Yes, as a matter of fact, he's even nicer in person. Listen, why don't I ask Karl to stop by and say hello to you before he leaves the hospital?"

"That would be incredible! I'd love that."

"But I'll need his room number to let him know."

"I'm not supposed to give it out," began Michelle. "But I guess since you're his girlfriend and all, it'll be OK."

"Well, thank you, Michelle, that's very kind of you."

"I'm not allowed to give you the room number," said Michelle leaning forward now and speaking in a half whisper. "But I'll tell you what I told the other gentleman. Just go over to the main elevators over there, and press the button that says 'ICU.' Turn left and then look for the policeman."

"I'm sorry, the other gentleman?" queried Sabrina.

"Oh yes," started Michelle, back to her normal voice. It's been quite a day. First Senator Parkinson came in to see Mr. Dunitz, and now you!"

Senator Parkinson, thought Sabrina. This can't be good.

"OK thanks, Michelle," her voice trailing off as she started toward the elevators.

"He's such a nice man," said Michelle to no one in particular. "And good looking too!"

∞

"OK, people, everyone needs to leave Mr. Dunitz's room. Detective Sergeant Smith's orders," bellowed Officer Henderson as he walked into Karl's room.

"First of all," began Jorge, "I'll ask you to keep your voice down, and second, this is highly irregular. Why do we have to leave?"

"Senator Parkinson is here and would like to visit with Mr. Dunitz alone."

"Alone! Are you nuts?" suggested Will. "You do know my father is responsible for ordering Karl's death, don't you?"

"Oh wait, you wouldn't know that," continued Will, "because you're just a beat cop!"

"Master Will, condescension isn't necessary here, and I would ask you to keep your voice down as well," interjected Jorge.

"Detective Sergeant Smith's orders," repeated Henderson in a monotone as he shot Will a glance. "Not my wishes, folks, just carrying out orders, that's all."

"What if we choose not to comply to your ridiculous request?" asked Hilary

"Then I'll have to remove you."

"Bring it on, beat cop," barked Will defiantly.

"Violence is never the answer, Master Will. We will comply with your request, on one condition."

"I'm not in a position to grant you conditions, Mr. Alonso," said Henderson.

"We will be allowed," continued Jorge as if Henderson had not even spoken, "to remain on the outside of the door and able to see into the room at all times."

"I can arrange that," capitulated Henderson.

"Good. All right, everyone, let's step outside," said Jorge.

"You're not really going to leave my father alone with Karl, are you, Jorge?" begged Will.

"Oh, you're staying too, Mr. Parkinson," interjected Henderson.

"What?"

"The Senator asked to have you with him while he visits with Mr. Dunitz," explained Henderson.

"I'll ask you again, are you nuts?" began Will. "Do you want another attempted murder on your hands, because I may just decide to 'off' the old man!"

"Master Will!" shouted Jorge. "You will do as you are asked, and you will not use violence of any kind. Is that clear?"

Will could feel the blood rushing to his head and chest. A sure sign his body was getting ready to fight. Then he thought back to his conversation with Karl and remembered what Karl had told him about decisions and other versions of him in other dimensions making the opposite decisions.

"You're right, Jorge. Upon reflection, I feel it's better if I stay with Karl during my dad's visit."

"Excellent choice, Master Will."

∞

"Sabrina!"

Sabrina turned to look in the direction her name had come from just as she was exiting the elevator.

"Sabrina!" said the man again as he walked up to her. "Sabrina, hi, Karl told me you were leaving town for a while. Are you OK?"

"Frank!" Sabrina leaned forward and gave Frank a big hug. "I'm...I'm not that good actually. I was on the way to visit my mom for a while after Karl and I...ah...split, and I saw that he had been shot on the airport TV screen."

"Well, I'm glad you decided to come back. He took your breakup quite hard, you know."

"How's he doing, Frank?"

"Not so good," said Frank. "How did you know what floor we were on?"

"The info booth lady told me. Just before she told me Senator Parkinson is here too."

"Parkinson is here? When?" asked Frank, switching from caring to serious in an instant.

"I don't know. She just said he had asked for his room number as well."

"Shit!"

"He must be there by now," offered Sabrina. "Where were you? Shouldn't you have been with Karl?"

"I'm sorry, Sabrina," started Frank, ignoring her previous comment. "But Senator Parkinson is the one who ordered Karl's assassination attempt."

"Are you serious? Oh my god, the senator's son is up there too. What the hell is going on, Frank?"

"No time to explain," yelled Frank over his shoulder, as he had already started to run towards the opposite end of the hall.

∞

"Dad!" said Will with a fake smile. "It's so nice to see you."

"Stop with the fake niceties," said Senator Parkinson as he turned, flipping the lock on the door and pulling the drapes so no one could see in. "We wouldn't be in this position if you would have hired the right guy for the job. I gave you one task, just one task. And you managed to screw that up too!"

"Dad, I don't really care what you think of me anymore, but I know you're making a big mistake getting rid of Karl. He could be much more useful to the cause if he was working with you, I mean us."

Senator Parkinson pulled a syringe out of his coat pocket, took the protective cover off the needle, and looked hard into Will's eyes.

"These religious, spiritual, save-the-world types are all the same, son. They're all trying to take the world from us. They have to be stopped. And as far as I can tell, this man is their leader, so let's start at the top, shall we. Now, are you going to act like a man and finish him, or do I have to do it?"

Will had never seen this level of madness in his father's eyes before. He had said and done some pretty awful things, but not like this.

"Dad, I can't let you kill him."

"Yes, you can, because if I don't, they are going to kill both of us."

"They?" asked Will.

"The secret society, the Devil's Workshop. The entity behind everything that goes on in this world. This is big-time stuff, Will, but I have a plan. If we kill Karl now, that will make them happy, and then I won't have to kill you."

"What did you just say?" asked Will.

"They've ordered me to kill you because of your screw-up, but if we kill Karl now and then I just tell them I killed you, we could get you a nice, comfortable existence elsewhere. Maybe out on the West Coast where you always wanted to go."

"Through the Witness Protection Program you just happen to be in charge of, no doubt."

"Yes, of course."

"Not going to happen, Dad. I've seen how well the program *doesn't* work. And besides, if this organization is as powerful as you say, then they'll find out and come after me anyway."

"Will, listen to me now. The entity that runs the secret society isn't human. They are a race of highly evolved beings trying to control us for their own benefit. They can't be stopped!" exclaimed the senator.

"Really, Dad. Now you believe in extraterrestrials? You, the man that wants to stop all the religious and spiritual movements the world over. Not a chance, Dad. It's just not going to happen."

"Just what I thought, you pussy! You'll never amount to anything. You're just like your mom, always looking after other people's interests instead of her own."

Senator Parkinson turned and walked toward Karl's lifeless body. "Time to meet your maker, asshole!" he exclaimed as he positioned the needle to enter Karl's IV catheter. He felt a pull from behind. "Aaargh! What are you doing, Will? He has to die!"

"Drop the syringe, Dad, or I'll break your wrists."

Will had moved swiftly and used the Kyusho Jitsu lessons his father had paid for to his full advantage.

"I said drop it!" yelled Will as he applied more pressure to the vulnerable points in his dad's wrists.

Senator Parkinson's hands sprung open as if on springs, and the syringe fell to the floor.

∞

"He pulled the drapes!" complained Hilary. "We can't see a thing in there!"

"Officer Henderson, I demand you unlock the door this instant and ensure the drapes stay open while the senator and his son are in the room."

"Sorry, Mr. Alonso, nothing I can do about it now," responded Officer Henderson. "They'll let us know when the visit is over."

"That is totally unacceptable, I—"

"Frank! Thank god you're here," shouted Hilary.

"What the hell is going on here? Is that Parkinson and Will alone with Karl?" yelled Frank. "Officer, give me your keys!"

"I'm sorry, Mr. Tillitson, I can't do that."

Frank didn't wait another second. He struck the base of his right palm into the bottom of Officer Henderson's nose, letting off slightly as he knew this move could kill a man if done properly.

"You broke my nose!" yelled Henderson into his hands as they cupped his face.

"I guess you didn't hear me the first time. Give me your keys."

Officer Henderson grudgingly gave his keys to Frank, his hands bloody and shaking.

"What's going on? Is Karl all right?" asked Sabrina.

"Sabrina! How did you—"

"It's a long story, Hilary," said Sabrina breathlessly.

Frank put the key into the lock and turned it to the left as fast as he could then shoved the door open.

"Freeze!" yelled Frank as he lunged into the room.

"OK, Frank, we're frozen, but my dad was just about to give me a hug," said Will smiling at his father. "Right, Dad?"

"Yes, it's been a while since I've seen you, son."

Frank noticed the grip Will had on his dad's wrists and knew that feeling all too well.

"Sabrina, what are you doing?" asked Hilary as Sabrina barged her way past Hilary and Jorge.

Sabrina had no idea what she was doing; she was just acting on some inner instinct that had awoken within her. She reached into

Frank's jacket, pulled his 9 mm pistol from his shoulder holster, cocked the slide, and pointed the gun at Senator Parkinson's head all in one easy motion.

"Are you the son of a bitch that tried to kill my Karl?" yelled Sabrina as if possessed. "Answer me, or I swear to god I'll end you right now!"

"Just calm down, Sabrina," said Frank, speaking calmly now. "Nobody is going to die today. Just give me back my gun and no one will ever know this happened."

"Did you, or did you not, arrange the assassination attempt on Karl Dunitz's life?" reiterated Sabrina, moving to her right to stay just out of Frank's reach.

"I did. And I'm proud of it," said Senator Parkinson defiantly. "These spiritual fanatics, the so-called raise the frequency of the world types, must be stopped at all costs." He paused. "But of course, you'll need proof, which you'll never find, so I'm going to hug my son and walk out that door."

"Not so fast, Senator," came a nasal voice from the corridor. Officer Henderson held up his phone over Jorge's shoulder for the senator to see. "As you can see by the moving sound waves on the screen, I've recorded everything," said Henderson reassuringly.

"Ma'am, please put the gun down, and Senator, could you please walk toward the door."

Senator Parkinson turned back toward his son and gave him a pseudohug. "This isn't over yet, cream puff!" he whispered into his son's ear.

As his dad turned to face the door, Will gently kicked the syringe under Karl's bed. A move that didn't go unnoticed by Frank.

"If Karl doesn't make it, I'm coming for you, asshole!" said Sabrina as she lowered Frank's gun.

"Let the man through please!" ordered Henderson.

As Senator Parkinson walked through the door, he noticed Henderson's bloody nose. "What happened to you?" he asked.

"I fell. Now this is what's going to happen..."

Frank moved toward Sabrina, took the gun from her shaking hand, and gave her a big hug. "What the hell got into you?" he asked.

"I...I don't know," said Sabrina sounding a bit confused. "I just did it. I've never even handled a gun before."

"Well, not in this lifetime anyway," added Frank with a smirk.

"You believe in that stuff too?"

"It's true, Sabrina. What Karl's told you is all true. You just have to allow it in."

"Frank! The Senator is getting away!" yelled Hilary from the corridor.

Frank quickly made his way through the door and ran into Officer Henderson's outstretched arm.

"Hold on, ace," said Henderson. "I had to let him go."

"What do you mean, 'let him go'?"

"I didn't get his confession on my phone. I turned it on after the fact, but he doesn't know that."

"So, you're hoping he leads you to some bigger fish?"

"Exactly. I told him I would release him on his own recognizance and discuss the matter with Detective Sergeant Smith."

"You're not as dumb as you look, Henderson."

"I'll take that as a compliment, but why did you have to break my nose?"

"Well, you're in a hospital. Get it fixed!"

Chapter Nine

Karl was glad everything was starting to calm down. He had witnessed the whole scene while quietly hovering above.

Being able to observe all this while being, for all intents and purposes, invisible, is cool, but creepy all at the same time, thought Karl. *Man, do I miss the emotions my body would have felt. Jorge?*

Hello, Mr. Karl. Sorry about all the ruckus.

It's not quite over yet, communicated Karl. *Look out, here comes Nurse Dixon.*

"Mr. Alonso!" ordered Nurse Dixon. "In case you have forgotten, this is a hospital and this floor is the Intensive Care Unit. Peace and quiet is not only recommended, it's essential to my patients' well-being!"

"I do apolo—"

"And furthermore," she continued as if Jorge hadn't spoken, "you will abide by this hospital's policies or I will have you removed from the ICU so your friend can get the rest he needs. Is that clear?"

"Yes, Nurse Di—"

"Good! Because the next time I have to leave my desk to speak with you about this you'll be leaving on the end of my shoe!"

Nurse Dixon, not waiting for a response, wheeled around 180 degrees and walked purposefully back to her office.

Told you she was coming! thought Karl. *If I was in my body I'd laugh my ass off!*

Ha-ha, very funny. She's the least of our worries. Where do we go from here?

There isn't much time, communicated Karl. *Bring Will back in and I'll begin the download.*

Jorge turned, walked back into Karl's room, and found Will and Frank in a heated discussion.

"I couldn't let him do it, I tell you!" said Will earnestly. "He wanted to finish off Karl, and then he mumbled something about witness protection."

"Are you sure you weren't in on it until the moment we burst onto the scene?"

"Look, I don't care if you believe me or not, but I told you what happened."

"Gentlemen, please let's try to get along, shall we?" began Jorge. "Now, Master Will, please tell me what happened."

"Well, as I was just telling Franky here"—Will felt it necessary to get one last jab in at Frank while Frank shot Will the death stare—"my dad tried to blame me for botching up Karl's assignation, and then I tried to persuade him to work with Karl instead of seeing Karl as an enemy."

"Nicely done, Master Will. Please continue."

"Then he rambled on about how these 'spiritual types' are trying to steal the world from them and pulled a syringe from his pocket."

"You mean this syringe?" asked Frank as he held up the syringe he had picked up from under Karl's bed.

"That's the one. And when he tried to inject it into Karl I immobilized him, and that's when Franky here burst into the room. Followed by that crazy lady."

"Sabrina," said a voice from behind Jorge.

"Pardon?" asked Will, not sure where the female voice was coming from.

"That crazy lady's name is Sabrina. Nice to make your acquaintance, Will," said Sabrina as she brushed past Jorge and extended her hand toward Will.

"Nice to meet you too," said Will cautiously. "You don't have any more hidden weapons, do you?"

"Not to worry, I'm unarmed," said Sabrina blushing now.

"Man, I've never seen a move so fast and slick. Who taught you that?"

Sabrina looked over at Frank before saying, "Self-taught, I guess."

"Wow, that was awesome!"

"Yes, well, as awesome as that was, Master Will, Karl has asked to begin his download to you now. He fears there may not be much time left."

"What do you mean, not much time, Jorge?" asked Sabrina earnestly.

"He was referring mainly to the actions of the Society, but also feels his condition is quite precarious, and he's not sure how much longer he will be in his NDE state."

"Who the hell is the Society, and what the hell is NDE?" demanded Sabrina.

"The Society," interjected Will, "is a secret group of people trying to keep the upper echelon of the world's rich elite in power. My dad's been a member for years."

"Also known as the Devil's Workshop," added Frank.

"And Karl is experiencing disturbed bodily multisensory integration, otherwise known as near-death experience, or NDE," added Jorge.

"OK, I don't really understand any of what you guys just talked about," said Sabrina, "but, I have faith you're doing the right thing. Karl trusts you implicitly, which means so do I."

"Thank you, Miss Sabrina," said Jorge. "You are more than welcome to join us in the meditation and listen in on what Karl is talking to Master Will about."

"Sorry, Jorge, I never allowed myself to go there; that was Karl's domain."

"I respect that, Miss Sabrina; however, if you can just be still and quiet your mind, you may begin to hear excerpts of our communication with Karl."

"I'll try, Jorge, thank you."

"Mr. Frank, could you get the door?"

Frank stepped outside the room then shut the door behind him so he could talk with Officer Henderson.

"How's your nose?"

"It'll be fine," said Henderson sporting a new bandage and tape job on his nose.

"Any news on Parkinson?"

"Nothing yet, but Detective Sergeant Smith has a couple of men working on it."

"Do you think your boss is doing all he can?"

"What's that supposed to mean? Are you implying Detective Sergeant Smith is part of this?"

"Easy now, Henderson, I'm just keeping an open mind."

"Well, he's not. He's a good man," said Henderson, suddenly realizing he sounded like he was trying to convince himself.

"I'm sure he is," added Frank. "Have you seen Hilary?"

"Miss Lambton? Oh, she said she was going to the cafeteria to get some coffees."

"Excellent, I could use some right about now."

∞

Dr. Gene Hinchcliff was lying on the couch in the doctor's break room fast asleep.

"Dr. Hinchcliff. Dr. Hinchcliff."

"I didn't do it, I didn't do it..." mumbled Gene.

"Dr. Hinchcliff. For God's sake, Gene, WAKE UP!"

"What? What's going on?" asked Gene as he sat bolt upright, looking around the room.

"Dr. Hinchcliff, I think you need to have a look at Mr. Dunitz."

"Dixie? Holy crap, you scared the shit out of me!" said Gene as he wiped the drool from the corner of his mouth with his sleeve. "I must have dozed off."

"If you call cracking the plaster with your snoring and forming a river with your drool, dozing, I guess you did," said Nurse Dixon sarcastically.

"What didn't you do, by the way?" added Dixie.

"What do you mean?" answered Gene cautiously, rubbing his temples.

"When I tried to wake you, you were obviously dreaming, but you kept saying, 'I didn't do it. I didn't do it.'"

"Oh, that must have been a leftover memory from Afghanistan or something. No biggie. So why did you wake me again?" asked Gene, trying to change the subject.

"I thought you might like to have a look at Mr. Dunitz. There's been quite a commotion in his room recently, and now his friends are in there meditating or something."

"That's it? They're just meditating?"

"Well, yes, but Mr. Dunitz is doing some twitching as well, and I wondered if he was coming out of his VS," queried Dixie.

"Twitching? He's in a vegetative state, there shouldn't be any twitching. Unless..."

"Unless he's waking up," said Dixie.

"Thanks for waking me. I'll be down in a bit. I think I need to clean up a little first."

"Yes, you do. It stinks in here. I hope that's not all coming from you!" said Dixie jokingly.

"I think it is!" added Gene with a smirk.

∞

"Master Will, please sit comfortably on the couch and begin your deep breathing. Miss Sabrina, you may sit in that chair over there, and I will sit beside Master Will."

Jorge?

That was quick, Master Will. Very Impressive.

I just thought of Karl and how much I appreciate the opportunity he's giving me, his ability to forgive, and how much love you all have shown me.

Ah yes, gratitude. One of the best ways to clear one's mind of all the daily rubble.

Mr. Karl, are you with us?

Jorge, so nice to communicate with someone again. I see Will is with us, and you have invited someone else too!

Yes, I thought she might want to try to communicate with you as well.

Did you see her in action, Jorge? That was some of the old Sarah getting through; it was awesome!

Yes, from what I remember, she was quite a pistola caliente!

What's that? communicated Will.

A hot pistol, thought Karl. *And she certainly was, in more ways than one!*

Karl looked down on his beloved Sabrina and wished he could hold her tight. How he missed the ability to touch, to experience a physical embrace.

We better get a move on, Jorge. I can feel things are progressing, communicated Karl.

I agree, wherever you want to start.

How about we start with how everything works? Would that be all right with you, Will?

Of course, I want to learn it all! thought Will excitedly.

What if I said you already know it all, you've just forgotten it?

You mean, like amnesia?

Exactly! So, let's start with our past.

But what does the past have to do with our future? Shouldn't the past just be used as a learning tool so we don't repeat our mistakes?

Very good question, Will, and indeed you are right as well.

He's a quick study, interjected Jorge.

That he is, my friend. OK, let's ramp it up then, shall we, thought Karl.

When we know about our pasts, we can make better decisions on how to create our future. In that regard, let's talk about what man has created in the past, things like power, strength, and this guy called the Devil.

You see, our societies have been doing it all wrong. We've been repressing our five natural emotions, which has imprisoned us and turned these very natural emotions into very unnatural ones. This has brought us nothing but unhappiness, death, and destruction. The model of behavior we've chosen to follow is the exclusion of our emotions. If you're feeling grief, get over it; if you're feeling angry, stifle it; if you're feeling envious, be ashamed; if you're feeling fear, conquer it; if you're feeling love, control it, hide it, limit it, run from it—do whatever it is you have to do to stop showing it, right here and now. Truth be told, all we have done is imprisoned ourselves, imprisoned our souls.

This all sounds kind of sad, thought Will.

It is, continued Karl, *but it stems from our not remembering who we truly are. Let's go back to the time when our society decided to reorganize itself, back when men decided to become the dominant species, and decided that showing emotion was inappropriate, because in earlier times we used to live in a matriarchal society.*

Wait a minute, you mean a society where women were the boss?

That's correct, Will. There was a massive shift in society, whereby men exerted their natural superior strength and started to dominate the world. This is when we moved away from showing our emotion, and it was during this time that males invented the Devil and the masculine God.

Men invented the Devil?

Yes, essentially the Devil, or Satan, was a male invention. It was all a part of a male rebellion against the matriarchy, a period during which women ruled over everything with their emotions. They also held all governmental positions, all religious posts, and all places of prominence in commerce, science, academia, and healing.

Then what did the men do?

Men were forced to justify their existence. They really had no use except to be used for fertility, do the heavy labor, and offer protection. They were very much like worker ants or bees, doing all the physical labor and making sure children were produced and protected. It took centuries before males were even allowed to participate in their clan's affairs or to have a voice or a vote in community decisions. They weren't considered intelligent enough to understand those types of things.

Pretty much the reverse of what's taken place in our world. Wow, it's hard to imagine a society that would not allow a whole class of people to vote based only on their gender.

Says Will, tongue firmly planted in cheek! communicated Karl.

Well no, I mean yes, but, well you know what I mean!

Yes, I do, and point well taken.

But hold on a minute, communicated Will. *You said that men were very much like the worker bees and ants, doing all the heavy physical work and producing and protecting the children. If that's so, then nothing has really changed.*

Except that men have all the power now, thought Karl.

OK, I get that, but there's a price to pay for all that they do. I'm sure it goes both ways though: men resent today's women that are trying to take back some of the power, and women resent men because they want to keep all the power. It's an endless struggle.

Again, you are correct, Will, but there is a way to end this struggle.

There is?

Yes, and it's all about strength.

I thought we just established power corrupts?

We did, but I said strength, not power. Let me explain, communicated Karl. *Life is about unity, not separation, and it's also about strength, not power. Unity brings inner strength, and separation leaves us feeling weak and powerless, therefore struggling for power. If we are able to heal the rift between the sexes and end this illusion of separation, we will all find our inner strength. This is where we will find true power—the power to do anything we put our minds to, the power to have anything we desire, the power to be anything we want to—for the power of creation comes from inner strength that is produced from unity.*

Wow, I've never heard it described like that before, thought Will.

I know, but remember, right now we've got it all wrong. Society feels inner strength comes from individuality and from separateness, but that's totally wrong. Separation from each other and from our higher source is the cause of all our suffering. It has pretended to be strength, and our politics, economics, and even our religions have perpetuated the problem. But we seem to want to cling to this model no matter where it leads us, even to our own destruction as a species. So, remember Will, true power comes from inner strength. Inner strength does not come from power. It's about power "with," not power "over."

Awesome! You're a great teacher, but let's get back to how the men were able to get all the power or turn the tables, so to speak, communicated Will excitedly.

Of course. Well, the women were caught off guard because they felt that the men weren't intelligent enough to figure out a way to gain any of their power, and indeed they were right. But what the men lacked in intelligence, they made up for in cleverness. They decided it wasn't the women they had to convince to give them some power, it was the rest of the men. After all, life was pretty good back then: do some work and then have sex. Not a bad life, some would say, so it wasn't easy for powerless men to convince other powerless men to seek power. Until they discovered fear. Fear was the one thing that women hadn't counted on. The fear began to take shape in the form of men that were disgruntled. These were usually the least desirable of the men and, therefore, the ones that women paid less attention to. So, they began by planting seeds of doubt among the other men: What if the women were wrong? What if their way of running the world wasn't the best? What if it was leading us all into certain oblivion?

Many of the men disregarded this however; after all, didn't the women have a direct line to the higher source, the source of all life, which they were an exact copy of? So, men had no choice but to invent the antithesis of the Great Mother, who was worshiped by the people of the matriarchy, and invented the "evil one."

How did they ever manage to convince anyone, let alone people of the matriarchy, that an evil one even existed? communicated Will.

Simple, continued Karl. *Everyone in their society understood that occasionally there was one bad apple among them, especially a boy child that would not want to do the right things and be kind to all. This person was usually labeled as "bad" because he could not be controlled, so a myth was created. One day, the myth went, the Great Mother bore a child, which turned out to be "not good." No matter what the Great Mother tried, this child would resist. Finally, one day he fought with his mother for her very throne, and that was way too much even for a loving, forgiving mother. And so, he was banished forever but kept showing up in clever disguises, sometimes posing as the Great Mother herself. This myth then laid the foundation to ask, "How do we know the Great Mother we worship is actually the Great Mother and not the evil one in disguise?" This prompted the men to worry, then to be angry because the women were not taking their worry seriously, which ultimately led to a rebellion. Therefore, the being we call the Devil, or Satan, was created.*

But did everyone just buy into that idea? I mean, weren't the women supposed to be more intelligent than that? thought Will.

It wasn't hard to create a myth about a bad child, especially a male, because males were the inferior gender. This also had another profound effect: if the bad child, or evil one, was male, who would there be to challenge him? The women were clearly superior in matters of thought, clarity, compassion, and planning, but in matters of brute strength, a male was needed, and now males were needed for protection of the females from this evil one. So gradually, over time, the male protector also started to be seen as an equal partner, standing alongside the women. From this, a male god was created to coexist along with the Great Mother, and for a while these gods ruled mythology together, but after some time the need for protection and strength overshadowed the need for wisdom and love, and soon a new type of love was born, a love that protects with brute force. Unfortunately, it was also a love that covets what it protects, which allowed jealousy and fear to really gain a foothold in that society.

Wow, that's fascinating! I never would have thought that the Devil was just created out of thin air, communicated Will.

Hold on, there's more. It wasn't long before this jealousy and fear really took over. Soon, more and more people began to think that the male god was the superior god, since males were the most powerful species, and stories of those that did argue, and lost, with this new idea appeared, and the God of Wrath was born. Now the whole idea of a god that was the source of love became a god that was the source of fear. The god of love, an inherently feminine model of the endlessly tolerant love of a mother for a child, was replaced with the jealous, wrathful love of a demanding, intolerant god that wouldn't put up with any interference, allow a do-not-care attitude, or ignore no offence. The gentle smile of the Great Mother, experiencing endless love and gently submitting to the laws of nature, was replaced by the stern countenance of the not-so-amused male god that proclaimed power over the laws of nature, which, forever after, limited love to an afterthought. This is the God that exists and is worshiped now.

Amazing and totally fascinating, but—and I don't mean to be ungrateful—what's the point of telling me all this?

Because, Will, before we dive into the future, it's good to know where you came from and where you are now. And most of all, it's important to realize that you made it all up. The idea that might is right or that power is strength was born in our male-created theological myths. The God of Wrath, jealousy, fear, and anger was born in the imagination of men. Yet, because it was imagined *for so long, it became people's reality. Some people still consider it their reality today, but it has nothing to do with ultimate reality or what's really going on here.*

Which is?

Your soul has a purpose. It came here to experience the highest experience of itself it can, to realize itself, to make itself feel real. You see, your soul is part of the energy source that makes up everything that now exists, has existed, and will ever exist. I'll refrain from calling it "God" here because of what I told you previously, and I don't want you to think that this source was merely imagined by well-meaning human beings. This energy source had no way of knowing itself because it just was. But it decided that if it split itself up, it could then look back at itself and know what it was. This experiment worked to some degree, but source energy, which is always evolving, decided it should split itself up into many small entities and allow these entities to experience themselves as they saw fit, and then when they returned home again, or became reunited with source energy, the entire experience of the smaller entities, known to us as souls, would be assimilated by the whole, allowing source energy to know itself more and more while the evolutionary cycle just kept rolling along.

I see, thought Will. *So, the history lesson is over, and now we're getting into some of the juicier stuff. I can't wait!*

History is never really over because we are constantly making more by what we do in the present moment. But what I was attempting to do was tie it all together for you. It's really quite simple, Will. The purpose of your soul, it's reason for coming to the body, is to be and express who you really are. The soul absolutely yearns to do this, since it's a piece of source energy, and it yearns to know itself and its own experience. This yearning to know is life itself seeking to be. The real point of the history lesson was to explain that the God of our histories is not the God who really is. Your soul is the tool that source energy, known to some as God, uses to express and experience itself, and since you are a piece of this source energy, or God, if you will, then you are also, by extrapolation, God.

Holy crap! I never thought of it like that. It really is quite simple, isn't it?

Yes, it is, Will. Source energy's purpose in creating you was so that it might have an experience of itself as the creator of its own experience.

I get it now, but some people won't understand. Is there another way you can put it to help me help others understand?

Well, source energy is not the God of our mythologies, or the goddess, the Great Mother, or any other of the plethora of names we have labeled it; it is simply the creator—that which creates—but it chose to know itself by creating its own experiences. As a creator, it knows its magnificence through the design of a snowflake or the beauty of a rose, but most of all it knows its magnificence through the creation of you. You have been given the same creative ability as source energy. In fact, that's why you're here—to know who you truly are by creating your own experience. You also possess one thing that the other creatures do not: consciousness. With consciousness you now have the ability to be aware of yourself, which makes us self-conscious. Source energy is aware of itself, being itself, because of you and me and all the other souls out there. So, what we create and experience, the creator is also experiencing and, therefore, continually evolving.

Does that mean the creator is constantly changing, that we are constantly changing?

Yes, Will, we are always changing and evolving. We know it on an individual basis, but we do it collectively too. You are the creator of your experience but are also the cocreator of the collective's experience.

Oh yes, I remember now, communicated Will. *Frank had explained this to me at the police station. He likened it to being a movie star in our own film, but at the same time we are also the extras in everyone else's film.*

Exactly! Good man, that Frank.

Yes, he is, added Will.

Chapter Ten

"I brought you a double-double," said Hilary as she walked up to Frank and Officer Henderson. "And for you, a black coffee with the fixings on the side since I didn't know what you took."

"That's perfect!" said Henderson appreciatively. "That was totally unnecessary, but very kind of you."

"Thanks for the coffee, Hilary," added Frank, feeling a little obliged to thank Hilary after Henderson's groveling.

"What's going on in there?" asked Hilary as she looked around Frank and into Karl's room.

"Karl is busy downloading information to Will."

"Is Sabrina able to communicate with them as well? I thought she shied away from a lot of that 'mumbo jumbo,' as she called it?" asked Hilary.

"I'm not quite sure," started Frank, "but it seems she's trying. Probably shaken up by the shooting and has decided to try to communicate with Karl."

"What's all this about downloading information?" queried Henderson. "I don't see any computers in there."

"They're using their minds to communicate through telepathy," answered Hilary.

"You mean that stuff is really possible?"

"It sure is, and much more too," responded Hilary.

"Uh-oh," said Frank. "Here comes trouble."

Hilary and Officer Henderson looked quickly at Frank and then in the direction he was looking. Coming toward them was a defiant-looking Nurse Dixon, followed closely by Dr. Hinchcliff.

"Officer Henderson, I'd like you to allow us in to assess our patient," commanded Nurse Dixon.

"Of course, no problem," answered Henderson.

"Wait a minute!" said Hilary. "Is this a scheduled visit for a given reason, because the nurses have been checking on him and they say he's fine."

"Miss Lambton, may I remind you—"

"One of the nurses," interjected Dr. Hinchcliff, "alerted Nurse Dixon that Mr. Dunitz was starting to twitch, so I wanted to check him myself to make sure he wasn't waking up from his induced coma."

Hilary scanned Dr. Hinchcliff's eyes and looked at Frank with a "no" look.

"Dr. Hinchcliff, can I ask you a few questions before you go in?" queried Frank.

"Sure, fire away."

"What is your relationship with Senator Parkinson?"

"I guess it's a friendly one, why?"

Frank stared directly into Dr. Hinchcliff's eyes without acknowledging the doctor's previous answer and asked, "And what do you know of the secret society known as the Devil's Workshop?"

Dr. Hinchcliff couldn't help but take a step back and stare wide-eyed at Frank.

"Well, what do you know about them?" demanded Frank.

"Mr. Tillitson!" scolded Nurse Dixon. "I will not allow you to speak to a senior member of our staff in that manner. This is not the time or the place for an interrogation as we are trying our best to keep your friend alive."

Frank shifted his steely-eyed gaze over to Nurse Dixon. "Are you?" he said. "Or would you be just as pleased if he was to never wake up!"

"That's enough!" yelled Dr. Hinchcliff, surprised by the volume of his own voice. "I know nothing about any secret societies," he said quieter now. "And if you'd like to interrogate me, then we can go down to the police station. But until we do, my entire focus is on keeping Mr. Dunitz alive. So, if you'll excuse me, I'm going in to check on my patient now."

Dr. Hinchcliff pushed by Frank and stood quietly by the door for a brief second before Henderson opened it for him.

"Hmpff!" growled Nurse Dixon as she followed the doctor into Karl's room.

"Dr. Hinchcliff, Nurse Dixon, what a lovely surprise," said Jorge as he stood to greet them.

∞

"That was an unexpected line of questioning, honey," said Hilary looking at Frank.

"Well, I had to do something, and I was hoping to put him off his stride. His reaction to the Devil's Workshop question was very telling. He knows about it, all right, but how much I don't know."

"What the hell is the Devil's Workshop?" asked Henderson.

"Exactly," said Frank. "What the *hell* is it?"

∞

"Hello, Mr. Alonso," began Dr. Hinchcliff. "We have been informed that Mr. Dunitz has been twitching, and I wanted to make sure he wasn't coming out of his induced coma."

"I see," started Jorge. "You don't want him to wake up?"

"It's not that I don't want him to wake up," answered Dr. Hinchcliff. "It's the timing. His body needs complete rest to recover from a very invasive surgery, so I'd like to keep him under for a while yet."

"Well, I haven't noticed any twitching lately, and he's not twitching now," said Jorge.

Dr. Hinchcliff strolled over to the neurological monitoring machine and pressed a few buttons. "True, he's not twitching now, but it looks like he was quite lively even just a few moments ago."

"I see," said Jorge. "I'm sorry if we didn't notice. As you can see, we are all quite tired and have been resting on the couch. When do you think you will be able to bring him out of his coma?"

"I'm not sure, Mr. Alonso," said Dr. Hinchcliff as he turned toward Jorge. "Maybe in a few days, but I would think he'll be under much longer than that."

"Is that really healthy for him?"

"I...I mean, we," responded Dr. Hinchcliff, "need some time to sort out his condition before we bring him back, but I promise you will be the first to know."

"I think we're done here, Nurse Dixon," said Dr. Hinchcliff as he started out of the room.

Jorge followed the two of them out into the hallway. "Thank you for the telepathic warning, my dear," said a smiling Jorge to Hilary.

"Anytime, honey. You folks about done in there?"

"There is much more to go, Miss Hilary, but it will seem very fast since the information is passed so much faster when using thought energy."

"Well, you better get a move on then. By the way, are you hungry? I can get us all some breakfast."

"Not right now, Miss Hilary, but thank you. Why don't you and Frank get some breakfast together. We'll be fine; Officer Henderson is here."

"Actually," interrupted Henderson, "my shift is over in a little less than an hour, so I won't be here much longer, but not to worry, someone will be here to replace me."

"Very good," said Jorge as he turned, walked back into Karl's room, and closed the door.

"Everything all right?" asked Will.

"Yes, I believe we are OK to continue our downloading. Thank you for pretending to be asleep when the doctor was here."

"I wasn't pretending. As soon as Karl stopped communicating I drifted off."

"Looks like Miss Sabrina has joined you," said Jorge, nodding toward a slouching, heavy breathing Sabrina.

Mr. Karl, we are back, are you there? thought Jorge.

Yes, hello Jorge. That was an unexpected interruption. It sounds as if Hinchcliff is in no rush to wake me up.

I believe he needs to figure out his, or should I say the Society's, next move before he makes any decisions. For now, you're out of the way, and they can tell the public that you are as good as dead.

Makes sense, but for now we must focus on educating our number one student.

Your only student! communicated Will.

You're the one! thought Karl.

I've heard that somewhere before, thought Will.

Of course, you have. There's nothing you don't already know; it's just a matter of remembering. Ready to get started?

No time like the present!

I'm so glad you said that, Will, because that's what we're going to cover next: time. Time, as you know it, doesn't exist. It's not some sort of continuum or time line like people have made it out to be—running horizontally from left to right across a page with arbitrary numbers along it—because there exists only one moment, the "now" moment.

What about yesterday and tomorrow? communicated Will.

If you took that horizontal left-to-right time line and stood it vertically on its pointy little end, then at the bottom of this vertical line you would have the now moment. Now, pardon the pun, picture leaves of paper on this vertical spindle stacked one on top of the next. This represents the different dimensions. Each one separate and distinct, yet existing simultaneously with the others. Still, at the bottom only one moment exists, that one moment—this moment—the eternal moment of now. Right now, this very second, everything is happening at once; there is no beginning and no end because time does not exist. It—source energy, infinite consciousness, God, or whatever you want to call it—just is. And within this "is-ness" is where your experience lies. You can move to any conceptualized time or place you choose, whenever you want.

Are you trying to tell me I can time travel?

Of course, you already have many times.

I have?

Sure, where do you think you go in your dreams? Most people cannot remember their travels from dimension to dimension because they can't retain the awareness. But there are always trace elements of this energy left that sticks to us like glue, and sometimes there's enough residue so that others, who are sensitive to this energy, can pick up on it and sense our past or future.

You mean like psychics?

Exactly. Sometimes there's even enough residue left that even you, in your limited consciousness, are aware that you've been here before. Your entire being is suddenly shaken up to the notion that this has all happened before.

Déjà vu!

You said it! Or that spectacular feeling when you meet someone and you just know that you've known them before. And that's a true feeling because there is only one of us, and forever is actually a right-now thing. Many times, you have looked up or down from your piece of paper on that spindle and seen yourself on the other pieces as well because a part of you is on every piece.

Whoa, this is starting to get a little bit unbelievable!

I know some of this is going to challenge your comprehension of everything you've been taught, but you have to remember that you have always been, are now, and always will be. There has never been a time when you were not, and there never will be such a time. Take a second to search your heart, your soul. You will know this is all true.

I do feel it's true, but does this have any application in real life?

If you have a true understanding of time, then it makes it easier to live within your reality of relativity, where time is expressed as a movement. In actual fact, it's you who is doing the moving, not time. Time has no movement, there's only one moment.

I'm sorry, but I'm finding this a little hard to believe, thought Will.

Have you ever had something significant happen to you, and then things just seemed to slow down, and it seemed as if everything was standing still?

Yes, I have, just recently actually. I believe one of those times was when I watched you get shot and fall over on TV, knowing I was responsible.

OK, good example. It felt like time was standing still because it was such a significant moment in your life that you lost track of the arbitrary boundaries you have set for yourself as a physical entity on this planet. It felt as if time was standing still because it does. And when you stand still too, you often have one of those life-defining moments.

I don't know, it still seems awfully coincidental.

If you are needing some sort of proof, you just have to look at science; it's already proven mathematically. If you were to get into a spaceship and fly far enough and fast enough, you could turn around and come back to watch yourself take off! This clearly demonstrates that time is not doing the moving, you are. Time is merely a field through which you move. In our case, we're on a spaceship called Earth. For example, take all the arbitrary numbers we've given to things, like one rotation of our planet or one rotation around our sun. We chose numbers like 24 and 365, which make no sense. Then we divided those 24 hours into minutes and chose the number 60. We could have based everything on 10, but that would have been too simple. Wait, it gets worse. Then we picked 12 for the number of months in a year, which led us to having some months with more days in them than another because 12 didn't divide equally into 365. Oh, but wait, let's try to make it simpler again, and then we'll start referring to decades and centuries using the 10's scale we should have used earlier. Time, as we know it on Earth, is simply a human construct to count moments. Everything that's ever happened, or is going to happen, is happening right now. The ability to observe all this simply depends on your point of view, your place in space. Is this starting to make any sense now?

I think so. What you're really saying is that time doesn't move, we are doing the moving, and that physical objects are limited because of their speed. But that means nonphysical things, like my thoughts or my soul, could theoretically move through time and space at insane speeds, communicated Will.

Precisely! And that's what happens in dreams, when you feel that déjà vu feeling, and even what we're doing now, communicating telepathically.

But if all this is true, and everything has already happened, that means I'm completely powerless to create or change my future?

This is the now moment, so nothing in the future has happened yet. If you see an event in the future you don't like, don't go there, choose another one. You have to change or alter your behavior to avoid that future outcome you don't desire, thought Karl.

But how can I avoid it if it's already happened?

I'm sorry, Will, let me come at this from another perspective. Remember I told you that you already know everything there is to know, you just don't remember it?

Yes, but what has that got to do with the future or passing of time?

Right now, here on Earth in the fourth dimension, you are at a place in the space-time continuum where you are not consciously aware of the whole of the Universe. Your existence has been dumbed down, if you will, so that you can consciously experience yourself creating your own world. This dumbing down, or forgetfulness, is one of the greatest secrets of all time. It's the reason you're able to play this great game we call life! What you don't know can't be so, and since you don't remember your future, it hasn't happened to you yet. Something can only happen when it is experienced, and a thing is only experienced when it is known. Now sometimes, and this happens to all of us, we get a brief glimpse, or knowing, of the future. When this happens, that means our spirit, or the nonphysical part of us, has sped ahead of us and gone to some other place in the space-time continuum and has brought back some residual energy of that particular moment. This causes us to sense something about what is about to happen that feels odd. If you don't like what you sense, then just step back and reevaluate if you should do it or not. In that instance, you have just changed your experience, and all the others that are you breathe a sigh of relief.

Hold on a minute! You mean I exist in more than one place? communicated Will.

Yes, and you're ready to hear this, Will. You exist at every level of the space-time continuum, simultaneously! And just so you don't think you're special, this goes for all of us, not just you.

No, of course not. It's just that this is so hard to comprehend. It just seems so, so...

Huge? communicated Karl

I was going to say enormous, but yeah, huge is good too.

At the level of your soul, Will, you, and indeed all of us, have always been, always are, and will always be. A world without end.

Oh, so now you're slipping religious references in, thought Will.

It's hard not to when we sit back and ponder the enormity of it all.

That brings me back to something I thought of when you mentioned that things have been dumbed down so I can experience myself creating my own world. Is this not a direct comparison to God? communicated Will.

Most certainly. And I believe the biblical quote said something like "He who believes can do everything that I can do, and even greater things." You are a divine being, Will, capable of doing whatever you desire while experiencing all of it at the same time.

Wow, there's so much to know.

You already know—

Everything there is to know. I heard you the first time, thought Will. *But what about our spirit or soul speeding ahead of us and coming back. Is there a way we can speed up this whole learning process?*

Did you ever watch any of the early episodes of Star Trek, *Will?*

Not really, they were before my time. I loved the later ones though, and all the movies.

OK, well, there was this one episode where they encountered alien beings that came aboard their spaceship, but these aliens moved in what they called "hyperaccelerated time." To the members of the crew, these aliens could not be seen, but they could be heard as a buzzing, like an insect, when they were nearby. To the alien beings, the entire human crew of the spaceship seemed as if they were standing still, like statues. This, in effect, is what's taking place when your soul leaves your body. You are moving so slowly through the space-time continuum, which is part of the dumbing down process by the way, that your soul can leave and return in what we would term milliseconds.

You mean my soul just takes up and leaves my body whenever it wants? communicated Will.

Not whenever it wants, although it could do that. You see, since your soul is used to moving very quickly through the space-time continuum, or "ether," as it's sometimes called, it's hard for the soul to be locked into your physical body for long periods at a time. Although your soul has chosen to be you and loves to learn, evolve, and experience itself creating its own experience, it also longs to be free again and return home. When you sleep, or sometimes for brief periods when you are not consciously creating, your soul leaves your body to travel to other dimensions where there are others that are you and to just kind of check things out. This is why you sometimes get glimpses of the future or déjà vu.

Incredible!

It is, isn't it. I just love telling people about it. Gives me goose bumps! thought Karl.

So, what happens when I die? Does that mean my soul has left for good to return home?

Yes. When the soul decides it has evolved to the next level, or "lokas," as it's sometimes called, it will know it is time to return home. But it will often stay as long as it feels there is more you need to experience in order for the soul to evolve further.

I see. Does that mean then that many of the elderly are still here to experience things?

Absolutely! If you are still alive in your physical body, then you are here to experience new and exciting things. Your soul feels you still have more to do, more people to help, or more to create. After all, we are the Universe's best creating machines!

OK, just to recap, there is a past me and a future me, and if the me that exists now decides to change something he doesn't like in the future, the me in the future no longer has the benefit of that experience, yes? communicated Will.

Well, not really because the past and the future do not exist. But just for the purposes of illustration it works.

But you said there's more than one of me!

There is only one of you, but you are much bigger and more dynamic than you think you are. And to answer your other question, yes, in fact, the whole tapestry has changed, but the "future" you, as you call it, never loses the event he has experienced; he's just happy you don't have to go through the same thing.

But then the me in the "past," as I call it, hasn't experienced that thing yet, so he walks right into it?

I love your spunk and determination to get to the bottom of things, thought Karl. *In a way, yes, but you can help him.*

I can, how? thought Will.

Of course, you can. By changing what the "future you" experienced, the "past you" may never have to experience it at all! This is the way that all souls evolve through experience. It's why we're here!

I love it! It's starting to make more sense now, but what about past lives? There are people that try to get in touch with their past selves, and they say they were a totally different person. If I've always been me, how could I have been someone else in a past life too?

You're talking about past-life regression, and yes, people are able to look back, if guided correctly, at who they were because they are the same soul. You are a divine being who is capable of more than one experience at a time, and you are also able to divide yourself into as many different selves as you want. You can live the same life over and over again, as we just talked about, or you can live different lives at different times in the space-time continuum, or any combination of the two!

Holy crap! I thought I was starting to understand this, but it just keeps going and going.

Yup, and that's just the tip of the iceberg! communicated Karl. *Just remember, you are a divine being that knows no limitation. A part of you has chosen to know itself as you in your present identity, but this is by no means the limit of your being, although the you in the here and now thinks it is.*

Why, why do I have to think it is?

If you didn't think it is, communicated Karl, *you wouldn't be able to do what you came here to do.*

And that is?

You are using this life, and indeed all of the lives you've chosen to live, to be and decide who you really are, and you do this through creation and experience.

Is that it? Just to be and decide? Sounds kind of lame.

Nothing lame about this journey, Will. You have attracted all the people, events, and circumstances to you to use as tools so as to design the grandest version, through the grandest vision of yourself. This process of continual creation is always ongoing, never ending, and it's all happening right now on many levels. In our earthly definition of time, we see it as something linear with a past, present, and future. You imagine yourself having one life and then you die. Or, at best, you imagine yourself having more than one life, but only one at a time. But what if time didn't exist? You'd be living all those lives, all at once, which is what's actually taking place!

Now that sounds more like an adventure! thought Will.

Indeed, it is! You see, it would be very difficult to play this game of life if you had full awareness of what's actually happening. If you did, the game would be over, no more creation. The Process, as we have coined it, absolutely depends on the process being completed exactly as it is and always has been, including our lack of total awareness of it taking place.

But now that I'm aware of this, doesn't it screw the whole process up?

Not at all, Will. Being aware of how the game works by no means makes you a master. Just because you know the rules of baseball doesn't mean you can jump on the field and play at a high level. You have been given all this knowledge at an accelerated level, through me, because you were ready to hear it. You have lived enough lives already and have started to know there is more to all of this. This is referred to as starting to become "awake." I will impart enough knowledge onto you so you may become wide awake, but that in no way means you know all there is to know. I, myself, am still learning a great deal with every passing lifetime. So, you should feel blessed and accept knowledge of this process as a great gift from divine universal creation. Embrace the Process, and move through it with grace, peace, joy, and wisdom. Use this incredible process and transform it from something we just endure to something we use as a tool to create the most magnificent experience of all time—the fulfillment of your divine self.

It sounds like such a grand journey. What's the best way to ensure I don't mess this up and do the best that I can do?

There's no way to mess anything up, Will. The decisions you make in one life will affect your other lives, and the Process will continue. It can never stop. And don't forget that all this is happening simultaneously, even as we communicate now, your other lives are being affected. The best thing you can do is to use your "now" moment wisely and for the highest purpose.

Which is?

The creation and the expression of who you really are. Come to a decision about who you are, who you want to be—and then do everything in your power to be that. If a way presents itself to create and express your divine self right here, right now, then follow that way. That's what got you here now, although you didn't know it.

It did, how?

Because you asked. Just by questioning your father's actions, the actions of the world around you, and thinking there must be a better way, you have put dormant forces into motion, which caused me to recognize something in you no one else saw. Everyone is constantly creating, whether they choose to acknowledge it or not. What you have done yesterday created your today, and what you do today is creating your tomorrow.

Although it's happening all at the same time!

Absolutely! See, this stuff's not so hard. Are you starting to see the perfection, the symmetry in all this, Will? I hope you are, because the grand truth of it all is that there's only "one" of us!

Chapter Eleven

"I'm glad you decided to come with me for some breakfast, honey," said Hilary.

"Me too, I'm starving!" answered Frank.

"Is that all you men think about, your stomachs?"

"We have to keep ourselves fed and strong in order to protect you lovely ladies," said Frank with a wry smile.

"Bullshit! You're just thinking of yourselves!" shot back Hilary.

"Well, I can't help anyone else if I don't help myself first."

"That was something Karl would say. You men are all—"

"Shhhh!"

"Don't you try to shush me; I'm not done yet!"

"Hilary! Please!" said Frank with tight lips and clenched teeth as he leaned forward toward Hilary.

"What is it?" asked Hilary, sensing Frank had seen something.

"That man over there. The second in line at the cashier," indicated Frank with his eyes.

"The man in the overcoat?

"That's him."

"Who is he?" asked Hilary.

"He's the top assassin for the Society, that's who!"

"I thought that was the guy that shot Karl."

"No, luckily Will hired someone else. If this guy would have done the job, Karl would be dead for sure," asserted Frank in a half whisper.

"What's he doing here in the cafeteria?"

"These guys are lone wolves and have their habits. Some, like him, like to eat before a kill."

"Holy shit! You mean he's here to..."

"Finish the job? There's no other reason a guy of his caliber would be here."

"Let's go, we have to warn Jorge!" said Hilary half standing up.

"Sit down, Hilary," said Frank calmly, as he moved his hand in a downward motion. "We don't want to spook him."

"Spook him! He's spooking me!" strained Hilary through clenched teeth.

"Let's finish our breakfast, and then I want you to go tell Henderson and Jorge what's happening," decided Frank.

"What are you going to do?"

"I'm going to let him make the first move," said Frank.

"Why would you do that? You said yourself he's their top man!"

"Exactly. Which means he'll have more than one plan. I need to see what develops first. Now enjoy the rest of your breakfast."

"Yah, right."

∞

So, what's actually going on here? thought Will.

We're communicating telepathically so that you will gain enough knowledge and understanding to lead the human race to the next level. Is that not plainly understood?

No, I'm talking about what is really going on as we live our lives here on Earth. Wait a minute, what did you just say? You want me to lead the human race somewhere? You must be kidding me?

No, I'm not. There's no time for kidding. My time has come and is slipping away as we speak. You are "the one" to continue the education of the people of Earth. You should be glad you're on the fourth dimension, where people are much more open to these types of teachings. You should have seen it on the third dimension, that was a tough one! People knew there was something else, a higher power that they belonged to, but all they would do was deny, deny, deny, even when the answers were hiding in plain sight. In the end, we were only able to save about forty percent of the population, and we had to resort to methods that used the latest technology we possessed.

Where did the forty percent end up?

Many of them decided to return to physical form right away and are here in the fourth dimension. Others decided not to return to physical form just yet and are enjoying the overwhelming love, peace, and joy in the spiritual realm, communicated Karl.

And what about the others that stayed behind?

They will live out their physical lives in the third dimension, being who they need to be in order to experience what they need to experience.

Poor buggers.

There is nothing poor about them, Will. They are the same as us, doing what they can, with what they have, from where they are. There is no right or wrong way to experience physical life and learn what we need to learn. We're all on the same journey and we're all headed in the same direction.

That goes back to what I was trying to ask you, what is really going on here? None of this is really real, is it?

No, it's not. You are living one big illusion. Think of this as one big magic show. A show that's taking place right before your eyes, and you know how all the magic tricks are done, but yet you refuse to believe it, even though you are the actual magician!

I always wanted to be a magician!

Well, you always have been. We're all magicians. But it's important to remember this because otherwise you will believe very deeply that this "show" is very real.

So, you're trying to tell me the things I can see, hear, smell, touch, and feel aren't real? thought Will.

You need to keep in mind that what you are looking at, you are not actually "seeing." You see, people often think that our brains are our source of intelligence, but they're not. Our brains are nothing but a data processor. It takes in data through receptors in our bodies called "senses." It then compares this data to what it has received before and assigns a label to what it perceives it to be, not *what it really is. Based on these rudimentary perceptions, you now think you know the truth about something, when actually, all you are doing is creating the truth that you think you know.*

Whoa, I think that last bit just flew over my head! thought Will.

Well, you can't comprehend something new if all you are doing is thinking within your current values, concepts, and understandings. If you want to learn something new, you have to accept that you have limited data on the subject, instead of thinking you already know all there is to know.

I didn't know I didn't know that.

I know! communicated Karl. *And here's the kicker: you are making everything up! Life is the process by which everything is being created. This source energy, divine consciousness or God, if you will, is pure and raw energy, which we call "life." So, by knowing this, we now become aware of a new truth. This energy is the Process.*

But didn't you say we are also this energy?

Yes, I did, and thank you for remembering that. You 'are' this energy, which means you are not a result of the Process; you 'are' the Process. You are the actual process itself. You are the creator, and you are the Process by which you are creating.

So, I'm the creator, and the created, all at the same time.

You got it, Pontiac! thought Karl.

Pontiac? What the heck are you talking about now?

Sorry, strike that last remark. That was a common saying in the third dimension, the 1970s I believe.

The 1970s?

OK, strike that too. That's just how we counted our years back then.

That just sounds so ancient! Anyway, getting back to being a creator, how does one go about creating things? asked Will.

It all starts with a desire. Desire is the key to all creation. Desire leads to something called "intention." Intention is desire transforming itself into a force. This force brings about something called "thought." Thoughts then lead to feelings, which lead to actions, which ultimately lead to results or outcomes. Put into terms you may better understand:

desire = intention

intention = thought

thought = action

action = outcome

I shouldn't waste time waiting around for my ship of dreams to show up then, right?

You are absolutely correct. In fact, your ship of dreams will never arrive, no matter how long you wait for it, because it doesn't just show up out of the mist; it's built beneath you as you move along until one day you realize you're sailing your own ship with full sails.

I really like that nautical reference, thought Will.

I was in the Navy in a former life.

Really? That must have been exciting.

All our lives are exciting, Will. It's what you make of them. Now, I want to get back to the Process. I just recently started to put this all together and need to get this information out to the public, so this is important stuff. Are you ready?

Yup, ready as I'll ever be!

Good. "The Process" is really just another term for the cycle of life. It is the sacred rhythm by which we continually connect to our paths, both to and from, the all of everything. It is the path that our souls joyfully play along throughout eternity. Most of us have always thought that there are lower and higher places within the levels of the Universe, but it's not a ladder; it's a never-ending wheel!

So, it's not levels we strive to achieve and then feel superior to others, but a constant moving wheel where we travel along and meld with others to form our individual experiences, communicated Will.

You are starting to get this stuff, excellent! But we must remember there is no separation of any kind. You are never separate from source energy. You cannot be, because you are pure energy: infinite, inexhaustible, and irresistible. Even at the end of our lives—what we call "death"—we won't see ourselves letting go of life, but simply enjoying it once again on a different path along the wheel. Once we finally understand this—that there is nothing we are not because we are the energy of the Universe—then we can finally let go of the man-made invention we spoke of earlier: Satan. You and I and everyone else are One, and our purpose is to evolve, to grow, to love, and to Be. There is no need to worry what will happen after you die anymore.

Wow! That's powerful. People are so hung up on not wanting to die, but really, it's not an end, just a continuation. We should just call it our "Continuation Day"!

Well said, Will. I'm so glad you are allowing this to sink in.

Yes, I do feel I'm starting to grasp it, but I still think back to what you said about everything being an illusion and wonder how that fits in?

OK, then let's see if I can break it down a bit more for you. When we look at the sun, moon, or stars, they aren't actually there, began Karl. *What we're really seeing is what has already taken place, the past. Because of the distance, there is a time delay for the light to reach us, plus another short delay for our eyes to take it in, our brains to process what we're seeing and label it, and then for us to actually acknowledge what we're looking at. For example, it takes about 1.3 seconds for the light to reach us from the moon, 8.3 seconds from the sun, and about 3 years from the closest star. It can take tens of thousands of years for light from stars in our galaxy alone to reach us. What this means is that what we're actually seeing isn't there. We're seeing what was there, the past. A past we have all participated in. As we discussed earlier, time, as we know it, does not exist. If you look at a traditional time line that runs from left to right and has arbitrary start and end numbers along it, we logically come to the conclusion that "time" has a beginning and an end. However, if we tip this time line up 90 degrees and cause it to become vertical, all that exists is that one single moment, or zero point, in time that is at the bottom of the now vertical time line. This is actually how the Universe operates—everything is taking place right now. The only movement is vertically up or down along what is now called the "dimension line." You see, many other dimensions exist other than our own, and many people have labeled them with numbers. For example, the third dimension—where I was—and the fourth dimension—where I am with you now. The labels don't really matter because we're living our lives simultaneously in every single one of them! Now remember I told you that we're living in the now or present moment, right? Well, now I'm going to appear to contradict myself by telling you that it's impossible to see the present. Why? For the same reason that when you look at the sun, the image, or information, is already 8.3 seconds old.*

OK, I thought I was getting it, but you're losing me again, thought Will.

Hang in there, it's just starting to get good! communicated Karl. *When the present moment happens, energy is dispersed, and there is a sudden burst of light formed by the energy dispersing. This light, just as the light from the sun did, takes time to reach the receptor cells in your eyes. Your receptors then have to send the image they have received to your brain, which then has to interpret the data and search its files to see if it knows what that image is or if it's a brand-new image, which in that case, also has to send warning signals to other parts of the body. Now, what do you think was happening while you were seeing and interpreting all this data? Did the earth stop rotating? Did the sun stop shining? No, the Universe just keeps on doing what it does best, which is evolve and create. So, what you're now seeing in front of you is not in front of you at all. It's what you think you are seeing. You've been busy thinking about what you have seen, telling yourself what it is, and deciding what you're going to call it. And while all this is happening, the now moment has moved on. Therefore, we are always fractionally behind universal creation or what is actually taking place. Even when you are looking at what's right in front of you, you are looking at what we define as the "past." Following that same principle then, what we define as the "future" is simply our vision of what we would like our lives to be like. A definition of the "now" then is simply the difference between the past we remember and the future we see.*

Yes, and I love your explanation of this, but that doesn't delineate time at all, communicated Will.

I'm getting there; we're going to discuss that next, thought Karl. *Now, I said that time, as we know it, doesn't exist, and I'm going to prove it to you now. Because we know something already exists, that means it is in our past. The greater the distance we place between ourselves and that thing, event, or physical location, the farther into the past that thing, event, or location recedes. But this effect is due to the distance, so it's only the physical distance that has created the illusion of time and allowed you to experience yourself in the "here and now" while also being in the "there and then." The simple high-school mathematical formula of distance equals speed multiplied by time bears this out. If we manipulate the formula, we find that time equals distance divided by speed. Therefore, the time is merely a function of the distance to a thing or event and the speed at which these things and events are traveling. For example,* the sun is about 152 million kilometers away. Divide this by the speed of light, which is about 18 million kilometers per minute, and we get approximately 8.3 minutes for the light of the sun to reach Earth.

So, if you've been paying attention, you will now be able to deduce that nothing we are seeing is real because it has already taken place, and we are simply seeing the image of what was once a thing or event. We can also deduce that time, as we know it, doesn't exist because it is simply a function of space, distance, and speed. And space, distance, and speed can be manipulated to allow our consciousness to make the present appear to exist at different times in different places throughout the Universe. Accordingly, there is a relationship between space, distance, and speed, but only in the physical reality, and the physical laws of the Universe only apply to physical things. Consciousness is not something that is physical, so therefore the laws of physics do not apply to it, and it is not restricted by them. This means that it is possible for consciousness to exist anywhere and everywhere in the Universe simultaneously, which is the now moment. Therefore, we are able to travel to anywhere in the Universe instantaneously, showing us once again that time does not exist.

Getting back to the images that we see aren't real, your personal interpretation of those images is called your "imagination," and you can use this imagination to create anything you desire because your imagination works both ways. Not only can you interpret energy, you can manipulate it as well. You see, your imagination is a function of your mind. If you hold the image of something in your mind long enough, a force is created that acts on universal energy, and the image begins to take physical form. The longer you imagine it, the more physical that form becomes until the increasing energy you have given it causes it to literally burst into light, flashing an image of itself onto what you call "reality." You then see the image, decide what it is, and what to label it. This then is called "the Process." This is what we are. We are the most incredible creating machines in the Universe! I am the Process, you are the Process, we're all the Process because everything in the Universe functions this way. It is a never-ending process; it's the mechanics of the Universe. I like to call it "Soul Mechanics." Therefore, you are both the created and the creator. You are a creator, and thoughts become things. Armed with this knowledge, indeed the greatest secret of all, you have no more excuses. You have created, you are creating, and you will always be creating your life. The Process never ceases; it is infinite and so are you.

Holy shit, I get it now! Is that why these so-called secret societies don't want us to know this stuff? thought Will.

Yes, it is, and the more of us that hold the same image allows this image to be created quicker because we're giving it more power. That's how things are manifested on a grand scale, and that's why the power of the people is so important, and that's also why so many leaders and secret societies have wanted to keep this a secret. They'd rather have us keep our heads down, go to our jobs, and make some money to buy things that advertising tells us we need. This way, we won't have the notion to ponder the secrets of the Universe because we're too busy eking out some sort of living for ourselves. This also keeps us in debt so that we need to keep going to work and repeating the consumer cycle. The whole while, governments, secret societies, or perhaps even intervening alien life-forms can fulfill their agendas without any real influence or resistance from the people.

So that's what they're up to. But why?

Once you have more than enough money that you could ever spend, there's nothing left to gain except power over others. It's really just an ego-building power play.

I hope you don't mind, began Will, *but you said that time doesn't exist and that everything is happening at the same time, right?*

Yes, go on.

Well, if everything is happening at once, then the future has already happened, which begs the questions, what is this thing that's already happened? How did it happen? What the heck happened?

All of it has already happened. Every possibility already exists as completed events, communicated Karl.

But how can that be? I just don't understand how that could work.

OK, let's go over it a little differently because it's important you understand this. You've seen people playing video games, or perhaps you've played them yourself, right?

Of course, who hasn't?

Good. Have you ever wondered how the computer or program knows how to respond to every move you make with your game controller?

Yes, I have wondered that, but I never gave it a great deal of thought, communicated Will.

The game knows how to respond because it's already all in the program, on the hard drive, memory chip, CD/DVD, or whatever the latest format is. It knows how to respond because every possible move has already been placed in the program, along with its appropriate response.

That's nuts! And kind of spooky, actually.

It's not spooky; it's just technology. Every ending and every twist and turn that produces that ending is already contained within the program. The Universe is just waiting to see which ending you choose this time. And when the game is over, it doesn't matter if you win, lose, or tie; the Universe will simply ask you, "Do you want to play again?" The program doesn't care whether you win or not—it doesn't have your human emotions—it just wants to know if you want to play again. All the endings already exist, and which ending you experience depends on which ending you choose.

So, the Universe, source energy, or God is nothing but a program?

I apologize, I didn't mean to make it sound like that; I simply wanted to use an example that would make more sense to you. But in many ways, life is like a program. All possibilities exist and have already happened. Now you get to choose what you want to experience.

And that's what the soul is here to do, thought Will.

Exactly. Just because what is currently happening in our world at the moment seems so bleak doesn't mean we can't think some new thoughts, perceive our world to be different than it is, and alter our experience.

You mean I can change how the world I am currently living in unfolds?

That's exactly what I mean, communicated Karl. *All the endings already exist, and remember, time—*

Doesn't exist. I know, I know.

Well then, if you know, what does that mean?

Everything is happening at once.

Bingo. Give the boy a prize! All that has ever happened, is happening, and ever will happen exists right this very moment. Just like all the moves and endings in the game program exist on the hard drive, memory chip, or CD/DVD right now, no matter how you choose to play. You are merely sliding up and down the dimensional pole as you choose, no time references required.

Awesome, I can actually choose my own destiny!

Absolutely. So, if you would like to experience what it would be like to live with corrupt governments and secret societies in power, focus all your attention on that, then you will attract that experience to you. And if you feel you'd like to experience a different reality where that doesn't take place, then focus on that, and that will be the outcome you attract.

But I guess you can't tell me which one will happen for me, can you, oh wise one! thought Will.

Very funny, I love your sense of humor! Actually, I could tell you, if you were to tell me all your thoughts, words, and actions you're going to take, but they haven't happened yet. This is why I've been stressing the fact that we have to let everyone know about this process. Once people know they can control their own future and are free from the oppression of power-hungry magnates and societies, then, and only then, will we experience true freedom.

That's all well and good, but how am I supposed to do that? This was supposed to be your job, remember?

Ah, but our lives have changed direction, haven't they? I am about to move on to a new adventure somewhere else in the Universe, and you are about to become the leader of the free world, communicated Karl.

Holy crap. That just sounds so daunting. How do I even start?

Search inside yourself, that place of inner wisdom. Listen to what that calls you to do. Then do it.

Chapter Twelve

Hilary ate the rest of her breakfast quickly, while Frank just picked at his.

"Frank? Frank!"

"I heard you the first time. What do you want?" responded Frank annoyingly.

"You should eat the rest of your breakfast; you might need your strength."

"What, you're my mother now?"

"No, I'm not your mother, thank god," asserted Hilary. "You must have killed her with that loving attitude of yours."

"I did kill her."

"What? What did you just say?"

"I killed my mom," deadpanned Frank.

"I unplugged her from the BPAP ventilator. I was the one who made the decision to take her off the machine."

"Frank, I'm so sorry. I didn't know," said Hilary apologetically. "But the doctors must have recommended it, right?"

"They did. But it was my decision."

"Frank, honey, you didn't kill her, you just let her continue on to a better place."

"I know all that, and sometimes I tell myself that just to justify my actions, but the fact remains that it was my decision to end her physical life here on Earth."

"What condition was your mom suffering from?" asked Hilary.

"Lung cancer. She smoked for forty-eight years then quit after my dad died from the same disease."

"I'm so sorry, honey. I had no idea. But there was no hope of survival for your mom, was there?"

"No, there was nothing left to do."

"Then you simply allowed her to transition over to the realm of the absolute. I'm sure she was very grateful for that."

"Not sure about that, but all I know is my mom's not around anymore and I pulled the plug."

"Frank, let yourself off the hook. She's forgiven you a thousand times over."

"I tell myself that too, but the feeling never seems to go away," said Frank sadly as he looked down at his unfinished meal. Then he looked up and checked on the assassin as Hilary began to speak.

"I just want to come over there and give you a big—"

"Hilary!" said Frank curtly. "It's time to move."

"Just let me finish what I was saying, you insensitive ignoramus!"

"Our man is on the move. You need to get upstairs and warn the others. Now go!"

Hilary stared at Frank for a second and saw that he was deadly serious. She felt so much compassion for him, he had never opened up like that before. As she stood up to leave, she started to turn to look toward the assassin.

"Don't look! Just go. Now!"

"Whatever you do, please be careful," asserted Hilary with a loving tone. She turned to her left and casually walked out of the cafeteria before sprinting to the elevator after she was clear of the cafeteria doors.

∞

But there is just so much uncertainty, thought Will.

What are you uncertain about? communicated Karl.

Well, for starters, how I'm supposed to lead people when I have trouble leading myself? And for another, this whole thing about you not being here anymore. How can I be expected to fill your shoes? A young privileged son of a senator. Yah, like that's going to go over well.

So, you're lacking clarity? You'd like to see how it's all going to turn out before you even start. Is that it?

I know that's impossible, but yes, I would like to know that all the effort I'm going to put into this will actually pay off.

Pay off for whom?

Well, for others, the people, society. The whole world, I guess. And yes, for me too.

You'd like to know what's in it for you, is what I'm hearing.

It just seems that if I'm going to sacrifice my life to this cause, then I should also receive something in return, right?

You've come a long way, Will, but you've just shaken my confidence in you. You've just taken a step back into your old programming that was installed as you grew up. You've slipped back into your old self, the self that feels entitlement. The self that wants before it gives. The self that becomes a successful person, but ultimately grapples with being eternally unhappy because it never reaches that feeling of real fulfillment. Is that what you would prefer over the chance to help millions of people give themselves back to themselves?

Give themselves back to themselves? What do you mean?

You have the chance to become the difference maker in people's lives, Will. The one who inspires others to live a brand-new life, free from the clutches of big business and corrupt governments. You will do the inspiring and empowering, but they will do the transforming. That is the hallmark of a great leader. Once all has been accomplished, the people feel they have done it themselves. You won't have to lord over them, you just need to point them in the right direction because right now they are wandering around aimlessly, looking for the very thing you will provide for them. Clarity. Have you ever noticed that having a lack of clarity is actually clarity itself?

Ah no, sorry to say that has escaped me, communicated Will slightly sarcastically.

If you're not sure about something, continued Karl, *that alone has allowed you to have clarity about one thing. You now know, without the shadow of a doubt, you don't have clarity.*

So, in other words, I'm clear about not being clear.

There you go, you've got it! Take the time to honor uncertainty. It's the seed from which all-knowingness comes.

That makes some sense, but that doesn't help me do anything.

Will, you don't have to do anything. You have to be something.

What do you mean?

Doing is a physical act, so if you are busy doing something, that would be in the present. If you "have" something, that would be the past, because as soon as we have something, that moment has moved on, and the thing we have is in the past. Most people try to live their lives from the past. They wait until they have something before they do anything. But the creation of your life begins in the "be," which is your future. You need to decide who you want to be, and once you decide that, you can then do what a person like that would do and then allow the Universe to deliver your "have."

You're starting to lose me. Can you give me an example?

Sure, let's say you decide to be a giving person. Now, you say to yourself, "If I am a giving person, what would a giving person do?" You decide that a giving person would help others, so in this case, you decide to give a little money to charity.

That's the "do" part, right?

Exactly! Then you allow the Universe to deliver to you based on your choices and actions, and that will be your "have." You see, if you want to live an exciting future where anything is truly possible for you, then you must begin in the future, not in the past. It's impossible to run into the future when you're dragging a ball and chain from the past. Therefore, you must decide who you're going to be, and then if you're going to become that person, do what a person like that would do. The have part will take care of itself because it will come naturally to you based on the choices you made and the actions you took. That's why I said you just have to inspire and empower people; their transformation will happen on its own!

That sounds so simple, but I know it's not.

Simple yes, easy no. Nothing worth doing is easy, Will. It's the challenges in life that make life worth living, not how easy we make it. That's the rub: the easier life is, the unhappier we become.

I don't know if this is the right time or not, but I want to talk a bit about what happens when we die.

The time for a discussion about death is always right because it's also a discussion about life.

The two are interwoven, aren't they? thought Will.

Indeed, they are. Every moment actually ends the instant it begins. Every interaction starts to end as soon as it starts. Once you understand this, the true depth of each moment in our lives can start to be understood. If you don't understand death, life will never truly appear for you. But you must do more than understand death; you have to love it just as much as you love life.

Love death? That's a little farfetched, isn't it?

The time you're able to spend with anyone would be truly enhanced if you thought it was the last time you would see them, right?

Of course.

Then by extrapolation, your refusal to think about your own death leads to your refusal to think about your own life. We talked earlier about life being an illusion; well, death is an illusion as well. When you look at something deeply enough, you start to see it for what it is, in this case, an illusion. When all you do is look past it, not through it, you can't see it for what it is, which is what pretty much everybody is doing. It's like a movie, shown on the screen of your mind. You are creating the story, and you are writing the lines the actors are speaking, but you are not the story. You are the creator of this and many other stories while playing a bit part in everyone else's story. Once you understand this and realize that nothing is real, then nothing can be painful anymore.

So, death is an illusion too.

Absolutely! You are not the illusion but merely the creator of it. Death is never an end, it's a beginning. Life is eternal and death is an illusion, but we have been taught that when the body dies, we die too. But you are not your body, so the inevitable destruction of your body should be of no concern to you. In this way, we should be using this illusion of death to allow us to better experience life. If, for example, you see some flowers on a tree that are wilting and dying, you could feel sad. But once you realize that this flower dying will soon allow the tree to bear fruit, you then can appreciate the flower's true beauty. However, you are not the flower or the fruit; you are the tree with roots firmly planted within the Universe, which in turn acts like the soil in which we are all planted. This life-and-death cycle just adds to the richness of the soil, which means you can never die, you merely change state.

That's a good analogy, communicated Will. And I'm glad you included that because I was starting to get a bit confused. But what do you mean by changing state?

Well, as I mentioned before, we are nothing but pure energy, what some would call "spirit." When this energy chooses to do so, it slows itself down by lowering its oscillation or vibrational frequency to a point where it starts to become matter. In this way, your energy, or spirit, is embodied in physicality. This splintering of the energy field, some would call God, is what leads to souls. But in truth, there is really only one soul that is always reshaping and reforming itself because it never stops evolving. We never stop evolving. So many of us just want to stay the same—just live a comfortable life and not change a thing—but that goes against the natural flow of life. The only constant is change, but yet we abhor the very thought of it.

So, once we've splintered off, as you put it, then what are we here to do?

Nothing. Just be, thought Karl.

Nothing? That makes no sense; we must be here to accomplish something?

Ah, there's your old programming again! Let me try to make this easier for you to comprehend.

Yes, please do!

All righty then. Agreeing to slow your oscillation down and take physical form means that you also agree to share everything that you experience while in that physical form. Source energy is just that, energy. It knows it exists, yet it can't experience itself. So, it splits itself up so it can look back at itself and experience what it is. This is the root of all desire. The desire for you to do or accomplish things in your life comes from this innate feeling within you. But you don't have to do anything because just you being you is already enough. You are contributing to the evolution of the whole because, as you move through physical life, all your experiences are being transferred back to the source. People *get so hung up on having to accomplish certain objectives in life, but really just moving through life, communing with others, sharing, serving, and experiencing is all that ever needs to be done.*

In essence then, what you're saying is that what society calls "hippies" or "good-for-nothing lazy people" have had it right all along, thought Will.

In many ways, yes, but remember, there must be no agenda; there should just be: feed people, love people, serve the greater communal good.

And that's what you want me to do.

By George, I think he's got it!

What?

Never mind, just another old third-dimensional saying. Yes, my friend, that's what I want you to do.

Chapter Thirteen

Frank watched the assassin take his overcoat off and put it around the back of the chair he had been sitting in, return his tray to the used tray cart, and then slowly start to walk toward the cafeteria doors.

What the hell is he up to? The only reason he'd leave his coat there is if he was coming back for it, thought Frank.

Frank pulled out his phone and dialed. "Schreiber? Tillitson. Where are you now?"

"I'm at the city morgue trying to get some info so we can identify the shooter," replied Schreiber. "What's up, boss?"

"Forget about that for now; I need you at the hospital."

"I'm on my way," replied Schreiber dutifully as he turned and started walking out of the morgue.

"When you get here," began Frank, "go straight to the main cafeteria and look over to the southwest corner of the room, right beside the window. There will be an overcoat over the back of a chair, and I want you to keep an eye on it and let me know if its owner returns."

"Must be an important owner."

"Horst VanDerbleek," said Frank as he breathed out.

"Holy shit! The Dutchman?"

"The one and only. I think he's here to try to finish off Karl."

"Then the coat is part of an escape plan. This guy's one of the best," asserted Schreiber.

"Get here as quick as you can. I've got to go; he just left the cafeteria. I'll be wired up, so let me know when you get here."

"Roger that. Be careful with this one, boss."

"Aren't I always?" responded Frank as he got up from his chair.

"That's why I had to remind you," said Schreiber as he hung up and pressed the button on his remote to unlock his car.

∞

If I hear you correctly then, began Will, *there really is no end to life; we just change state.*

That's correct, communicated Karl.

So, reincarnation is real.

It is.

Do we decide when we want to come back?

Yes.

Are you just going to talk in one- or two-word sentences from now on?

Yes...I'm just kidding! Sorry, I was just answering your questions truthfully.

Care to explain on any of your answers then?

OK, yes, reincarnation is indeed a fact, and you can decide when and if you want to come back.

Cool. I knew there had to be something to it, thought Will. *But does that mean we also choose when we want to leave or die?*

The soul never desires that the body dies. In fact, it would prefer if you would live forever. But the soul will leave the body—that is, change its bodily form—in an instant when it sees no purpose in remaining in its current form.

If the soul wants to stay, then why do we die?

You don't, you merely change form.

Yes, but if the soul's desire is to never leave, then why does it?

It's not your soul's desire to leave, but when there is no further usefulness in staying in that particular form, the soul simply changes form and moves on. And it does so willingly and joyfully.

Joyfully? There's no remorse felt for leaving behind an empty rotting shell?

No, why should there be? thought Karl.

Because the physical form they are leaving behind is about to die! communicated Will.

I see where you're going with this. First of all, the body never dies; it too just changes form. Whether buried or cremated, it merely returns to whence it came. Ashes to ashes, dust to dust. The body is completely an organic, carbon-based entity, which when it dissolves, returns its energy to the earth, just as so many trees and plants do, feeding all sorts of organisms as they decay and become one with the earth. Secondly, no soul can ever die. It is pure energy, and energy can never be destroyed; it can only be transformed. Therefore, neither body nor soul ever dies; it just changes form. Do you remember some of the comic book characters you used to read about?

Used to? I still read them.

Really? Well, whatever. Anyway, some of them were classified as "shapeshifters." They could change their form whenever they wanted and assume another form as it suited them. That's basically all your soul is doing.

I never thought someone would compare my soul to a comic book character!

Me neither, and it may be a little farfetched, but it does aptly describe what's going on. Is it any clearer now? thought Karl.

Actually, your comic book reference has helped, believe it or not. I tried to tell my mom that comic books would come in handy one day!

∞

Frank walked along the wall as he came to the cafeteria doors and paused to peek out one of the windows in the dual sliding doors.

He's taking the stairs, thought Frank. *I hope Hilary has already warned them.*

Frank moved through the cafeteria doors and quietly opened the door to the stairwell.

"I had such a good time at the party last night, but I have to get some food in my stomach!" said one of the hospital cleaning staff as she and her coworker hurriedly pushed past Frank to go on their break.

Jesus! thought Frank as his heart pounded in his chest. *I wasn't expecting that.*

Frank stood just past the entrance to the stairwell and listened. He's a few flights ahead of me, he thought. Got to move!

∞

I'm assuming then that my soul and my physical body all put together make up what we call a "human being," communicated Will.

Yes, you are correct, started Karl, *but something you must always remember is that a "being" is not a thing, it is a process.*

I am the result of a process then?

Well, yes and no. You, we, are not just the result of a process, we are the process itself. You are a creator and you are the process by which you are creating.

Oh boy. This is where I get lost again, thought Will.

Everything you see in both the heavens and earth is being created as we speak. The process of creation is never ending and is never complete. Nothing ever stands still because everything is energy and everything is always in motion. Some have called this "e-motion." When you look at something, you're not looking at a static object that is just standing there, you are looking at an event that is taking place. Everything is constantly moving, changing, and evolving. Everything! We have called this event "life." Life is a process, and that process is observable, knowable, and predictable. The more you observe, the more you know, and then the more you can predict.

So, to summarize, life is change, communicated Will.

Yes. Life is a process that never ends, is always changing, and is you, since you are the process and are creating it all.

I am the creator and the created, thought Will.

Once again, it leads us back to this one truth.

∞

"Who are you and where's Henderson?" asked Hilary slightly out of breath.

"I'm Henderson's relief; his shift is over," responded the tall young police officer.

"OK, whatever. I need to see Mr. Alonso right away."

"Your name, ma'am?" asked the officer.

"Look, I'm Mr. Dunitz's personal assistant, and I need to see Mr. Alonso right now. It's very important and I haven't got time to play the name game with you," said Hilary as she started to walk around the young officer.

"Sorry, ma'am," said the officer as he stuck his arm out to stop Hilary. "I'm only allowed to let you in if your name is on the list."

Hilary hated when people called her ma'am, and she wasn't sure why. Then it hit her. It was ever since that bank employee came to the house to give her mom their final notice of repossession. Mom was yelling at him, pointing at me and saying we had nowhere to go. All that bastard said was, "Yes, ma'am, I understand, but we're still taking your house, ma'am. To be honest, ma'am, I don't care where you go, but you must go." Hilary suddenly remembered it like it was yesterday.

"Fine. Hilary, Hilary Lambton," she said, shaking her head to try to erase her memory.

The officer searched his list, checking all the papers carefully on his clipboard. "Sorry, ma'am, I can't let you in. You're not on the list."

"That's impossible! I'm the one who made the list and gave it to Detective Sergeant Smith!" yelled Hilary.

"Is there a problem here, Officer?" asked a voice from behind Hilary.

"Dr. Hinchcliff, I'm glad you're here!" said Hilary with conviction.

"Yes, well first of all, I must remind you both that this is the ICU ward, not some kind of recruit training facility, so I must insist that you keep your voices down. Is that clear?"

"Yes, of course, I apologize," began Hilary, speaking quieter now. "But this imbecile can't seem to find my name on the list and won't let me in to see Mr. Alonso, whom I need to see right away because it's an emergency."

"Emergency? What type of emergency?" queried Hinchcliff.

"Life and death!" exclaimed Hilary.

"Officer, check your list again. Miss Lambton's name should be there." asserted Dr. Hinchcliff.

"I made the stupid list. It better be there!" added Hilary over Dr. Hinchcliff's shoulder.

The young officer began flipping pages and searching for names. As he did, Hilary noticed that the officer wasn't wearing a name tag. Something wasn't right.

"Give me that list!" shrieked Hilary as she reached around Dr. Hinchcliff and grabbed the clipboard right out of the officer's hand.

Hilary turned and started to walk a few steps away from Hinchcliff and the officer and then stood dead in her tracks.

"Miss Lambton! I can't have you acting like this in my hospital," said Dr. Hinchcliff, yelling himself now.

Hilary turned to face Hinchcliff, mouth agape.

"What's the matter?" asked Hinchcliff.

"There's only one name on this sheet," began an astonished Hilary looking at Hinchcliff, "and it's yours!"

Chapter Fourteen

You are the creator and also the created. If you haven't figured it out yet, I'm trying to hammer this point home because we have precious little time left together.

What do you mean, "little time"? thought Will.

There is a plan afoot to end my physical existence here, and it is soon coming to a conclusion, communicated Karl.

We have lots of time. You're on life support, and we're communicating at hyperspeed, so let's keep it going. Don't bother about the future, let's focus on the now.

Very good reasoning, my friend, and I like your reference to the now. However, this is all part of the Process as well, and we can't stop it.

But I'm not ready. I haven't done enough learning or got enough information to lead anyone else. I can barely lead myself, thought Will.

You learn best by teaching, and that is what you are about to do. To teach others of the Process and allow them to remember who they really are.

I...I don't think I can do it alone. I need you here to guide me.

The Process is eternal, as you and I are as well, and it will always continue, with or without our help. It happens automatically. You just need to let go of trying to control everything in your life, to get out of your own "way." Because the way is the Process, which is life itself. Trust the Process, Will. Trust the Process, or in other words, trust yourself.

But how can I trust the Process, or myself for that matter, when the Process just keeps bringing me crap!

You have to start liking the things that the Process, or life, is bringing you, began Karl. *You must know and understand that you are bringing these things to yourself. Do you see the perfection in all of this?*

I'm sorry, but by definition if I could see the perfection, then that would mean everything is perfect, and this situation is far from perfect! communicated Will.

Ah, but it is perfect! I was only meant to be here long enough to awaken the people just enough to accept a new leader. One that will guide them to new heights in conscious awareness, which will allow them to finally banish greedy and power-hungry businesses and corporations that are destroying the earth and all life-forms that live there. Something we were never able to accomplish in the third dimension.

I thought you said you saved close to half the population by using a human conduit to spread energy via the internet?

We did, but getting back to perfection, there is no one that can create your experience of anything but yourself. Oh sure, other people can create your external circumstances and events of your life, but no one else can ever cause you to experience anything you don't choose to experience. You, and you alone, are the creator of your experiences. You are a divine being, you are the Process, and you are the One. The world will constantly present you with circumstances, but only you determine what those circumstances mean.

Well, right now I don't like my external circumstances! thought Will.

Learn to like what—

The Process brings me. I know, I know.

See, you've got this stuff! Oh, and thanks for the reminder about the internet.

The internet? Why? thought Will.

Let's just say, the internet will be your friend!

∞

"I want you both to relax, don't make any sudden movements," said the tall young officer in a low half whisper.

Hilary moved her head to the left and could see the young policeman had his right hand on his gun. She looked into Hinchcliff's eyes and nodded slightly.

"Ah, ah, ah! Easy now, Doc. Turn around slowly and walk toward Dunitz's room."

Dr. Hinchcliff had no choice but to obey, but he had no intention of letting this good-for-nothing fake cop get away with this.

"Miss Lambton, follow your friend."

"So now you get my name right!"

"I knew who you were. Just keep moving, and Doc, the door's unlocked, just give it a push."

"Walk straight to the far wall and sit down on the floor," said the policeman as Dr. Hinchcliff started to push open the door.

"What are you going to do to us?" asked Hinchcliff with a shaky voice.

"Oh, it's not what I'm going to do *to* you, it's what you're going to do *for* me."

Dr. Hinchcliff didn't know what the policeman had in mind but knew it didn't sound good. He also had a feeling that none of them were going to make it out of this one alive.

∞

Mr. Karl, Master Will, I'm so sorry to interrupt the download of information, began Jorge, *but we are running out of time. I feel a disturbance that is coming closer and will soon interrupt us. This may be the last moments you have.*

Thank you, Jorge, and yes, I have felt it too, communicated Karl.

What do you mean, Jorge? thought Will. *Are we done communicating already?*

I am sorry, Master Will, but there isn't much time. Please finish up now. I will try to keep the others at bay for as long as I can.

Thank you, Jorge. OK, Will, ready for our last session?

No. No, I'm not, but I guess there's nothing I can do about it, so let's get it done.

Very well, let us begin. Do you remember we talked about opposites? About that which you are and that which you are not? That you cannot experience hot if you don't know what cold is like, or up and down, or good and evil?

I do remember some of that, but what has that got to do with anything now? At the moment it just seems like such a meaningless concept.

Au contraire, mon ami!

Is that your attempt at speaking French at a time like this?

Yes, it is. Now *pay attention*, mon jeune homme plein de promesses.

Not sure what you're saying, but it sure sounds nice!

You can look it up on the internet later. You'll have lots of time for that, believe me. So, as I was saying, these seemingly opposite concepts, or dichotomies, exist only in your mind. In fact, you have made them all up! You are the one who is deciding what is hot and what is cold, what is good and what is evil. And your ideas about these things are changing all the time. The Universe simply provides you with a field of experience, but you decide what to label them.

OK, I get that, thought Will. *But what significance does that have at the moment?*

Patience, my good man. This is leading toward a great secret.

Which is?

It's not necessary for an opposite condition to exist right next to you in order to experience it. The actual distance between the contrasts is irrelevant. The Universe, in its entirety, provides all those experiences for you because they all already exist. This is the purpose of the Universe, communicated Karl.

But how could I experience hot if I don't physically experience it myself? I can't get the experience of hot just by looking at a picture.

Ah, there's the rub. You have experienced it. You have experienced all of it! If you haven't experienced it in this lifetime, then you have in a past life. Or the one before that. Or in the ones you're living simultaneously right now, and so on. You have already experienced every opposite element that there is, and these are all burned into your memory.

You mean I don't have to experience them again if I don't want to? communicated Will.

That's right. You just need to know they exist and then remember them. All of us, every being in the Universe, has already experienced everything because we are everything. We are "all" of it. You are that which you are experiencing and you are causing the experience.

I'm not sure I got all of that, thought Will.

That's OK, began Karl. *What I want you to understand is that what you are doing now, this very instant, is remembering everything you are and choosing the portion of that which you prefer to experience in this moment, this lifetime, on this planet, and in this current physical form.*

Holy crap! I think it just clicked. I have separated myself from the body of the collective souls, or God, or whatever, and am experiencing what I choose to experience in this form, while all the time making my way back to the collective once again. Wow, it's like a process within the Process!

I wish I could hug you right now. You are making me so proud! And yes, you are absolutely correct. It is a cycle that you will repeat over and over again. Some would call it "evolution," but actually, it's more like a revolution. Just as the moon revolves around the earth, and the earth revolves around the sun.

∞

The Dutchman gently pulled the staircase door leading to the ICU ward open just enough for him to use his ninety-degree spotting scope. As he peered through his scope, he saw the policeman ushering Dr. Hinchcliff and Hilary into Karl's room.

"Damn it!" said the Dutchman under his breath. "What the hell is that cop doing there; it's supposed to be shift change! He had his hand on his gun. Something's not right."

As the Dutchman planned his next move, he heard someone approaching quietly up the stairs.

Got to move! thought the Dutchman. He suddenly pulled the door open, turned to his left, and walked quickly toward Karl's room. Once within six feet of the policeman, he pulled out his automatic pistol and pushed its barrel hard into the right temple of the policeman.

"Don't say a god damn thing and get into the room!"

Dr. Hinchcliff felt Hilary bump into him from behind, who similarly felt the policeman shove her into the room.

"Take it easy, buddy!" said Dr. Hinchcliff as he turned around.

"Holy crap!" added Hilary as she swung around to face the policeman. "Who the hell are you?"

"All of you over to the far wall!" said the Dutchman with a deep gravelly voice.

"Except for you, cop. Stay right where you are and put your left hand on your head. With your right thumb and forefinger, I want you to gently lift that revolver out of the holster and hold it away from your body."

As the policeman did what he was told, the Dutchman grabbed the revolver and stuck it down the front of his pants.

"Now, with the same two fingers, gently grab your handcuffs and hold them away from your body."

Once again, the policeman complied, and the Dutchman quickly grabbed the cuffs.

"Miss Lambton, do you know how to operate these cuffs?"

"You...you know my name?"

"Of course, I do. I always know everything there is to know to complete my assignment."

"Which is?" asked Hilary.

"No more questions! Do you, or do you not, know how to operate these cuffs?"

"I do," offered Hinchcliff.

"I didn't ask you, Doc, so keep your mouth shut!" commanded the Dutchman while pointing his gun at Hinchcliff.

"I can operate them," interjected Hilary in a calm voice, hoping to ease the tension.

"Good. OK, cop, take two steps forward and put both hands behind your back."

The Dutchman bent over slightly to drop the cuffs on the floor then gave them a kick.

"Miss Lambton, take those cuffs, put them around his wrists, and cinch them tight. Then show me what you've done."

As Hilary moved forward to pick up the handcuffs, she saw the Dutchman pull an object out of his pants pocket and screw it onto the barrel of his pistol.

"Is this tight enough?" asked Hilary, turning around to look at their assailant.

"I didn't see him flinch. Squeeze them tighter."

As Hilary squeezed the cuffs closed another couple of notches, she felt the policeman squirm.

"That's good," said the Dutchman. "Now go back over to the far wall. And you, cop, can go over there too, but I want you to sit on the floor cross-legged facing the wall."

"You know, we're here for the same thing," said the policeman as he started to move toward the far wall. "Why don't we just do the job and then we can both go our separate ways?"

"I don't think you understand, cop, or whoever you are. I only work alone, and I'm not working for the same people you are, so as far as I'm concerned, you're just one more meaningless piece-of-shit obstacle in my way. Would you like to become a dead obstacle? Because I'm happy to oblige!"

"Once my people find out about this, they won't be too happy," offered the policeman.

"The end result will be the same, and that's all they care about. You don't actually think they care about you, do you? You make me laugh, cop. Now get on the floor!"

The policeman, with hands cuffed behind his back, tried to sit down, but fell back awkwardly, hitting his head on the hard terrazzo floors.

"Maybe that will knock some sense into you!" laughed the Dutchman. "You should be a comedian because you certainly suck at being an assassin!"

The policeman recovered, sat upright, legs crossed, staring at the wall.

"Miss Lambton!" said the Dutchman.

"Yes."

"What's with these folks? Are they meditating or something?" asked the Dutchman moving his gun barrel in a wide arc encompassing Jorge, Will, and Sabrina.

"Something like that," answered Hilary.

"Something like that? That's way too nebulous for me, my dear. Tell me exactly what they are doing!" commanded the Dutchman, changing from a sweet, understanding voice to a dark and serious one in an instant.

"They're communicating telepathically."

"And why would they be doing that?" asked the Dutchman.

"To exchange information quickly and..."

"And what?" demanded the Dutchman.

"Read your mind," answered Hilary confidently. "They know everything that's going to happen before it happens, so why don't you leave now to save yourself."

"Ha-ha-ha! You're funnier than the cop! I like you, Hilary. Maybe I'll kill you last!"

Hilary shuddered as he spoke her first name out loud.

"Whatever your soul wishes will be our pleasure to provide for you," said Hilary.

∞

Mr. Karl, please excuse my interruption, but there is much unpleasantness in the room. I fear someone is here to harm you, thought Jorge.

Yes, I feel it too, communicated Karl. *See if you can defuse the situation so Will and I can finish up here.*

Of course, communicated Jorge.

I fear the end is near, Will, so we must press on; there is a few more things you will need to know.

I don't like this. I don't like it at all! Why do you have to leave? Surely there must be some way you can stop it.

Your planet is in the middle of its greatest spiritual revolution, and they need you to lead them. I got the ball rolling, so to speak, and you will ensure it continues to roll. The people will figure it out. You must have faith in that.

Well, we need this new spirituality now, not later. Isn't there a way to make these people stop wanting to kill you?

My death will help ignite the next uprising of the people. It must be like this, Will, so let's press on.

Chapter Fifteen

Jorge opened his eyes and couldn't believe the number of people in the room. He counted eight.

"Excuse me," began Jorge as he stood up. "What is going on here? This is a hospital ICU ward, and Mr. Dunitz requires his rest."

"Oh, look who just woke up! And who do we have here?" asked the Dutchman.

"My name is Jorge Alonso, and I am Mr. Dunitz's right-hand man. I'm not sure who you are, but it appears you are in control here."

"Very astute of you, my little Hispanic friend, especially after being asleep for so long and not being privy to what's going on here. Or were you?"

"What do you mean, Mr...."

"VanDerbleek. Horst VanDerbleek, but you can call me the Dutchman."

"And what is the purpose of your visit today, Mr. Horst?" asked Jorge.

"First of all, what I meant was that the fine Miss Hilary over here told me you could read minds while in your transcendental state."

"Ah, I see. Do you practice transcendental meditation, Mr. Horst?"

"Secondly, I ask the questions around here, Jorge, so back off with the interrogation. And I told you to call me the Dutchman!"

"Yes, of course, Mr. Horst, I do apologize. I have this habit of always using people's titles and first names. Once again, I do…"

Jorge's world turned dark as the Dutchman pistol-whipped him across the right temple.

"Jorge!" screamed Hilary as she fell to the floor to be by Jorge's side. "Look what you've done, you son of a bitch!" she said as she held up her hand covered with Jorge's blood.

"Didn't see that coming, did you? Read my mind, my ass! Don't worry, Hilary, he'll live. It was just a backhand. Now, anyone else feel like asking questions?" shouted the Dutchman.

∞

What's the matter, Karl? thought Will.

Something's happened to Jorge.

Should we help him?

No, we must finish this. To expand on what I was talking about earlier, we are already living in a contextual field that is called "the Universe," yet almost all of us try to create our own smaller contextual field around us.

What do you mean? thought Will.

It's possible for you to become aware of who you "are" without creating any negative experiences to prove it. You can merely notice who you "are not" by observing it elsewhere in the contextual field or Universe. What this means is that you can change people's lives right now and eliminate all which you are not, without worrying about your abilities to know and experience that which you are.

If I follow that, began Will, *then what you are saying is that I don't have to keep calling forth or manifesting the opposite of what I want, in order to experience the next version of who I am. I don't have to manifest evil in order to experience good. I can just manifest good and remember that I experienced the same type of evil before, in another life.*

Exactly! communicated Karl. *You don't have to create the opposite of who you are and what you choose in order to experience it. You simply observe* that it's already been created elsewhere. You just have to remember it exists; you don't have to go through the pain of experiencing it if you don't want to. This is what you need to communicate to the people.

They're not going to believe this stuff right away. It's going to take time. Time, I fear, we don't have, thought Will.

The mighty oak springs from the acorn. Plant the seeds, Will, and they will respond.

Yes, but how do I start to plant the seeds?

Tell them to look up, communicated Karl.

I think you mean look within, don't you?

No, look up at the planets, the stars, the galaxies.

How is stargazing going to help us? thought Will.

You will be observing your own past.

What???

As we spoke about before, when you look up and see the light from the stars, it could be hundreds or even millions of light-years old. What you are seeing isn't actually there. You are seeing what was there. You are seeing the past, and it's a past you participated in.

I did? Are you saying that it's possible to exist in two places at once?

Yes, of course, did we not talk about time not existing before? You are not seeing the past at all; it's all happening NOW! I know I just told you that when you look at the stars you are seeing the past, and now I'm telling you the past doesn't exist, which seems hypocritical, but remember time, as humans have constructed it, does not exist, so therefore, how could the past or the future exist. All we're left with is the timeless now. You, in essence then, are living right this very second, lives that you refer to as your "future" and your "past." The illusion of time is created by the distance between your many selves. The now is simply the difference between the past we remember and the future we see.

Wow. That's incredible!

It sure is, and one more thing. There is only one of us. So, when you look up at the stars, you're not seeing your past, you're seeing our past.

∞

"I'm in the cafeteria and in position," came Schreiber's voice into Frank's right ear.

"Copy that," responded Frank. "I may need you up here on the ICU ward. I'll let you know."

"Roger that, boss."

Frank slowly opened the stairway door and peeked around the corner just in time to see the Dutchman escort Dr. Hinchcliff, Hilary, and a policeman into Karl's room.

"Shit!" said Frank out loud, closing the door. "He had a gun to his head!"

I don't think that was Henderson. He looked too young. Must have been a shift change, thought Frank.

"Schreiber?"

"Go for Schreiber."

"The Dutchman has started his act. I need you to call Detective Sergeant Smith and tell him we need police backup here right now. After that, use the east entrance to the ICU ward and tell the nursing staff to keep everyone out of the hallway until this is over. Gunfire is imminent."

"Roger that, boss. On my way."

Schreiber dialed the police station while walking out of the cafeteria.

"Detective Sergeant Smith please," said Schreiber to the person that answered his call.

"One moment, sir, I'll connect you," said the female operator in a monotone.

"Smith here," said Detective Sergeant Smith as he placed the telephone receiver between his shoulder and neck.

"Smith? Schreiber. Tillitson is requesting immediate backup at the ICU ward. Assassin is in play; gunfire is imminent."

"Assassin?" answered Smith, sounding surprised.

"Yes sir."

"What about the police protection?"

"It's been compromised," answered Schreiber matter-of-factly.

"Jesus H. Christ! OK, I'm sending backup now."

"Roger that, sir," responded Schreiber.

Detective Sergeant Smith slammed the receiver down and stared at the phone.

"What's going on?" asked Senator Parkinson.

"Looks like our boy isn't the only one at the hospital today. Someone sent a professional to finish Dunitz off."

"A professional? What do you mean?" asked Parkinson.

"A hit man."

"A hit man, are you sure?"

"Schreiber said an 'assassin,' so to those Special Forces types, that means a professional hit man."

"What about the police officer we sent to do the job?"

"Schreiber said he was compromised, which means he's either dead already or he's going to be," said Smith glumly.

"What do we do now? What if the cop we sent spills his guts before he dies?" asked Parkinson shakily.

"Don't get your knickers in a knot, Senator; I've got this under control," replied Smith.

"We can't let this become a newsworthy affair, Smith. Do you hear me?"

"I hear you loud and clear, Senator; that's why I'm not sending any backup to the hospital."

"So, what do we do now?" asked Parkinson.

"Nothing," began Smith. "We do nothing. The assassin will finish off Dunitz for us, and if the cop lives, we'll deny everything and take care of him ourselves. Question is…who sent the assassin?"

∞

So, I have told you the truth as I understand it, and I am hoping it has had an effect on how you see yourself, and the world you live in, thought Karl.

It has! These communications have totally changed how I think and feel about society. I'm thinking that all I need to do is tell people the truth.

You are absolutely correct, Will. Just tell them the truth, and they will follow. The way to "get" there is to "be" there. There's nothing you have to do, just be where you choose to get to.

I have one more question for you, if you don't mind? thought Will.

Shoot!

After all is said and done, do you believe the human race is inherently good or evil? And before you say it, I already know that good and evil don't really exist—they are just opposite ends of a contextual field we ourselves created—but humor me here, would you, communicated Will.

Yes, well, this is the crossroads our race has come to, and really the future of the human race depends on which way you go. If you and your society believe that you are inherently good, then you will make decisions based on constructive behavior. Conversely, if you and your society believe they are inherently evil, you will make decisions that will reflect your evil, destructive ways. Now, a question for you: What is your present opinion of the human race? What is your present opinion of yourself?

Since I've had these communications with you, I have drastically changed both my idea of myself and society. Before, I was quite negative about pretty much everything, but you have helped me see and understand how we all fit into the vast energy field of the cosmos. And I also understand that I can create my own future by the way I think, feel, and act. Thoughts become things, remember!

Yes, they most certainly do! communicated Karl. *What you see for your future and for the future of society, you will create, and remember this: You are always "a part" of the whole because you are never wholly "apart" from it.*

Thank you so much for all you have done for me and humanity, Karl. I love you, and will never forget you!

Nor I you, dear one. For we are truly one and the same.

Chapter Sixteen

Sabrina had been awake for quite some time and was looking through the slits of her eyes to try to find a weakness in the Dutchman.

So hard not to follow his movements with my head, thought Sabrina. When the hell are the good guys going to show up? Maybe I've watched too many movies. Going to have to handle this myself.

Will Parkinson slowly started to come out of his meditative state and opened his eyes. He couldn't believe what he saw and quickly closed his eyes again.

Is what I just saw real or is it just something I conjured up during my meditation with Karl, thought Will. My mind is still in that blissful state. OK, open your eyes slowly and assess the situation.

Will looked through the slits of his eyes and saw Jorge on the floor with Hilary over him, a cop with his hands behind his back and legs crossed as if doing yoga, Sabrina sitting on the couch either sleeping or meditating, Dr. Hinchcliff leaning up against the far wall, and a pacing, half balding, skinny man with a silencer on his pistol.

Holy shit! thought Will as he quickly shut his eyes again. This must be some sort of dream. All this was taking place while Karl and I communicated? Impossible!

Will slowly allowed his eyes to open slightly once more, and the whole scene just repeated itself.

This is like some sort of perverse scene from a B-movie horror film. Going to have to do something. But what?

Frank quickly made his way along the wall to Karl's room, bent over so he wouldn't be seen through Karl's window, even though the drapes had been drawn.

Going to have to chance taking a look, thought Frank just before he popped his head up. No good, can't see a thing. Need to find a slit in the drapes.

Frank moved along the wall and was very nearly at the door when he saw a small opening in the drapes.

Will had just opened his eyes again and was still hoping that somehow this odd collection of characters in Karl's room would disappear.

Wait! What was that? thought Will. There it is again! It's Frank. I know it is!

Will had noticed a movement in a small opening of the drapes near the door. He's popping his head up to get a glimpse of what's happening, and he's formulating a plan. Got to give him some time!

"Ahem." Will cleared his throat, and the Dutchman spun around with his pistol pointed at Will's head.

"So nice of you to finally join us!" said the Dutchman.

"Who are you and why are you holding us at gunpoint?" demanded Will.

"Another pseudo-mind reader, I see."

"Mind reader? What are you talking about?"

"Never mind! I'm the guy that has to finish the job that you screwed up, that's who!" said the Dutchman sarcastically.

"Then what are you waiting for?" asked Will.

"I've been waiting for you!"

"Me?"

"Yes, that's right, you're going to witness me finishing off the job that you didn't have the guts to do yourself," said the Dutchman as he tucked his pistol down the back of his pants and pulled something from his right pants pocket.

"What's that?" asked Will.

"A little cocktail I got from a veterinarian friend for your much-loved leader," said the Dutchman as he screwed the needle onto the end of the syringe.

The Dutchman walked purposefully over to the IV catheter in Karl's arm, stuck the needle in, and began pressing the plunger.

"Nooooo!" screamed Sabrina as she jumped off the couch and started toward the Dutchman.

The Dutchman calmly stopped injecting Karl and pulled the pistol from behind his back and fired.

Sabrina had flung herself toward the Dutchman to cover the distance as fast as possible, but suddenly felt a searing pain in her head as all went black.

Sabrina's lifeless body fell onto the foot of Karl's bed then slid down to the floor. Blood oozing from the Dutchman's head shot.

"Ahhhhh!" screamed Hilary, now surrounded by bleeding people on the floor.

Dr. Hinchcliff was biding his time against the far wall but now felt compelled to move. He rushed toward the Dutchman as fast as he could, but the Dutchman was faster. Gene Hinchcliff felt the bullets rip into his chest and knock him backward. As he lay on the cold terrazzo floors bleeding, Hinchcliff couldn't help but wonder, *So, this is what it feels like to get shot. All those bullets I pulled out of those young soldiers. This is what they went through.*

Dr. Hinchcliff's world went black as the Dutchman sent one more bullet into his brain.

Frank heard the silencer-muffled shots, then Hilary's scream, and jumped into action.

The Dutchman laid his smoking pistol down on Karl's bed and continued to push the syringe plunger that would empty the drug cocktail into Karl's veins.

Will knew it was now or never.

Frank kicked the door down to Karl's room and burst in with gun extended only to find Will holding both of the Dutchman's wrists in a submissive Kyusho Jitsu posture.

The Dutchman looked at Frank, then back at Will.

"What are you going to do now, tough guy?" asked Will.

The Dutchman smiled knowingly then pulled back his head and drove it into Will's nose.

Will's nose immediately started to bleed, and his eyes welled up with tears. He felt the Dutchman move for his gun and then remembered he saw a revolver in the front of the Dutchman's pants. Will, fumbling while looking through the tears in his eyes, found what he was looking for and squeezed the trigger.

The Dutchman writhed in pain, but the bullet had gone through the meat of his inner thigh and was far from fatal. He threw a right elbow into Will's already broken nose and turned to run out of the door.

"Freeze!" yelled Frank, but the Dutchman kept coming, knocking Frank's extended arm out of the way as he went by.

Frank turned to follow him out of the door, but by the time he got out into the hall, the Dutchman had already made it to the stairwell. He's a slimy little prick! thought Frank.

As Frank turned to go back to Karl's room, he spoke into his mic. "Schreiber!"

"Go for Schreiber."

"He's on the run and no doubt heading toward the cafeteria."

"On it."

"Has the police backup arrived yet?"

"Nothing yet, boss," said Schreiber, his voice already partly muffled as he ran.

"What in the Sam Hill is going on here!" shouted Nurse Dixon. "Oh my god! Dr. Hinchcliff?"

"He's dead!" asserted Frank. "Now go back to your office and call the cops. Tell them there is an assassin at large and to roll the SWAT."

Dixie stood in the open doorway to Karl's room, staring at Hinchcliff's lifeless body. I was just talking to him a little while ago, thought Dixie.

"Nurse Dixon!" yelled Frank. "Did you hear me?"

"Um, yes, I'm sorry. I'll call them right away."

Frank rushed into Karl's room to find Will, Hilary, and Jorge looking down at Karl's body. Will and Jorge were both holding cloths up to their bloodied heads. There was complete silence now, which made the constant flat-line tone of Karl's heart monitor even more ominous.

"Turn that machine off," ordered Frank.

Frank walked over to the handcuffed and still sitting cop and kicked him hard in the lower back.

"Argh!" yelled the cop as he fell over backward onto the floor.

Frank pushed the barrel of his gun into the cop's left eye at the same time as he turned his head into Dr. Hinchcliff's blood on the floor.

"Is today the day you want to die, asshole?" yelled Frank. "Well, is it?"

"No," responded the cop feebly.

"Then tell me who you're working for."

"He's not with the Dutchman," offered Hilary. "He's working for someone else."

"I swear to god I'll pull this trigger in three seconds if you don't tell me who you're working for!" shouted Frank.

"I...I can't," answered the cop. "They'll kill me."

"Die now, or take your chances later. Three...two..."

"Parkinson!" yelled the cop. "It was Senator Parkinson pulling the strings."

"And who's his man on the force?"

"Smith. Detective Sergeant Smith."

That's why no backup arrived, thought Frank. "Schreiber?"

"Go for Schreiber."

"Smith is in the game, that's why no backup. SWAT should be here soon."

"Roger that," answered Schreiber.

∞

Karl watched helplessly as the scene in his room played out. He had no physical connection to his body anymore, but still felt a chill as the Dutchman pushed the cocktail of death into his arm.

Sabrina? Sabrina? thought Karl, hoping to get an answer.

Yes, my love. I can hear you now, answered Sabrina. *I can't see you, but I can hear you.*

That is good, my dearest. I'm so sorry to have put you in harm's way. It was not my intention that you get harmed in any way. I love you!

I love you too. It was my idea to come back to you. I had to. You know that we will always be together.

I know. Somehow we have been stitched together in this great tapestry of life, communicated Karl.

My heart still aches for you, yet I'm not in my body. I can't help it. I yearn to hold you in my arms one last time!

I know, my love. It has always been this way between us, and it always will be. What do you see where you are? asked Karl.

I see nothing but miles of beautiful beaches, and the sound of the waves are so inviting.

Good, you are in your place of transition.

I won't stay here then? asked Sabrina.

Each of us goes to the place that we have envisioned for ourselves during our lifetime. Soon you will lose all sense of your physical body and transition into your true self. Your soul, communicated Karl.

What will happen then?

You will have the choice to return to physical form right away or stay "home" for a while and enjoy that blissful loving feeling.

I want to go back as soon as possible. Don't you?

I thought you might! communicated Karl. *Yes, I'm going back right away. Perhaps to the third dimension.*

Then that's where I will go, thought Sabrina.

You must go where you feel you can experience all you can in order to keep evolving. The Process will never stop.

You're the One: Souled Out

I will see you soon, my love. Remember me!
I will never forget you. I love you!

Chapter Seventeen

Frank stood quietly beside his friends and looked down on Karl's lifeless body.

"He was a great man," offered Frank.

"I can't believe he's gone," sniffled Hilary.

"He has just transitioned. He is not dead," said a stoic Jorge. "Today is merely his continuation day. Continuing on to the next stage of his, and our, soul's evolution."

"Funny," started Hilary, "he mumbled something to me about going backward and not always having to move forward to another dimension when we die. Is that possible, Jorge?"

"The universe is cyclical. It is constantly expanding, it never stops. That is part of the Process."

"That's exactly what Karl said right after he was shot," added Hilary.

"It was his new discovery, and he wanted to let everyone know in his speech," said Jorge.

"Then who will tell them now?" asked Hilary.

"Karl has chosen to confide in Master Will. He will be our new leader."

"No offence, Will, but you've barely lived yet. How can you take us to the next level of consciousness?" asked Hilary as she turned toward Will.

"Karl has put his faith in me," began Will, "and has told me all I need to know to become my greatest version, but I will need your help."

"We are at your disposal, Master Will," added Jorge.

"When do we start?" asked Hilary.

"Right after I get my nose fixed!" said Will emphatically.

"Tillitson?" rang in Frank's earpiece.

"Go for Tillitson," said Frank as he turned and took a few steps away from the others.

"The Dutchman has retrieved what seems to be an Uzi from his coat in the cafeteria and is now headed to the parking lot. SWAT has just arrived, cutting him off."

"Hold station there, Schreiber. Do not participate in the gunfire. I'll be right down."

"Copy that," answered Schreiber.

"Got to go, folks," said Frank as he headed toward the door to Karl's room.

"Frank!" yelled Hilary after him. "Be careful. We don't need any more dead people today."

"One more would suit me just fine," said Frank as he stopped in the doorway.

∞

Jorge, can you hear me? Jorge?

I am here, Mr. Karl. So nice to communicate with you once again.

Yes, it is, but I haven't much time. I will soon transition, and we will lose contact.

I have to tell you, began Jorge, *that it has been an absolute honor to serve you in this past lifetime. I can only hope that we will be able to work together again in our next lives.*

There is no doubt that we will, my friend. I have already communicated with Sabrina, and she has transitioned. I wish things could have been a bit different, Jorge. I feel like I have left things incomplete.

You are supposed to feel that way, thought Jorge. *There must always be things that we want to still accomplish when we reach continuation day; otherwise we have not lived a full and proper life while in physical form.*

So true, my friend, communicated Karl. *I will miss your profound wisdom.*

Where will you be going next? asked Jorge.

I will be going back to the world that you and I left behind.

The third dimension? Are you sure you want to go back there? I can't imagine there is much left there for anyone, thought Jorge.

I just feel like I'm being drawn back there. I guess I'll find out.

Karl started to feel the pull of the Universe and resisted it, but it felt oh-so welcome.

I must say good-bye now, my friend. It is time for me to start the transition process.

I will miss you, Mr. Karl, thought Jorge with a frog in his throat.

And I you, communicated Karl. *Please give my love to Hilary, Frank, and the rest of the team. There were many things we could not have done without them.*

I will, my friend. Until next time!

Until next time!

Karl gave in fully now to the pull of the Universe, and he could feel himself transitioning to the place he had envisioned.

∞

People in the cafeteria started to panic and run out of the main doors of the cafeteria.

They've got him surrounded, thought Schreiber. He'll never get away.

"Tillitson?" spoke Schreiber into his wrist mic.

"Go for Tillitson," answered Frank.

"Looks like SWAT has him surrounded. I'm going to check out his coat."

Frank was busy dodging people running toward him. He assumed they were running from the main cafeteria.

"Schreiber!"

"Go for Schreiber."

"Do not touch that coat! It could be a—"

Frank felt the floor shake beneath him when the blast went off. He flung himself against the wall in an attempt to avoid any shrapnel from the bomb.

"Jesus Christ!" yelled Frank, although he couldn't hear himself or the fire alarm that was triggered by the blast.

His ears were ringing so loudly that he could no longer hear the screams of the people that had fallen on the floor in front of him. Many of them with shards of glass in their backs.

"Got to get to the cafeteria," growled Frank through his clenched teeth.

Frank ran toward the formerly beautiful glass main doors to the cafeteria that no longer existed and stopped in his tracks just inside.

"Vaporized," said Frank glumly. "He was just vaporized."

Frank stood and stared at the ceiling above where the Dutchman's coat had been.

"Nothing but pink," whispered Frank to himself.

Frank let out a blast of air from his nose as he thought back to what he had said to Hilary. This was not the one more death he was hoping for today.

"What the hell?" said Frank. "That slimy prick Dutchman is getting away!"

Using the blast as a diversion, the Dutchman was able to slip through the SWAT team perimeter and find his car in the parking lot.

"You son of a bitch!" growled Frank as he ran through the carnage and the water from the sprinkler system to get outside.

Frank pulled his SIG 226 pistol from its holster, stopped to aim, and then started pulling the trigger. The first few rounds pierced the driver's door but seemed to have no effect. Frank aimed a little higher and caught the Dutchman in the side of the neck.

"Not today, scumbag, not to-fricking-day!" said Frank as the Dutchman slammed into a parked car.

Frank held his ID badge out from his body and put down his weapon as a member of the SWAT team ran up to him.

"Nice shooting, Mr. Tillitson," said the young constable.

"I've had lots of practice," said Frank matter-of-factly as he bent at the knees to pick up his weapon, keeping his eye on the young cop.

"Are you new here?" asked Frank, noticing the absence of a name tag. "What's your name, son?"

"VanDerbleek!"

Frank grabbed the muzzle of the Colt M4 carbine the young cop was pointing his way and pushed it away with his left arm as he stepped forward with an elbow to the young cop's nose with his right.

"Not as tough as your old man, I see," said Frank now towering over the young man as he lay on the ground. "Just getting started in the family business, are we?"

Frank flipped the crying and bleeding young man over onto his belly, placed his arms behind his back, and handcuffed him with the zip tie he always had in his pocket.

"This one's not one of you guys," said Frank as a couple of SWAT team members ran up. "He's the assassin's son, Max VanDerbleek."

"You know my name!" barked young Max into the dirt.

"It's my job, boy," asserted Frank. "Now, do yourself a favor and take some courses while you're in prison so you can get a real job when you get out."

"Take him away, Danny."

Frank knew most the members of the SWAT team by first name as he had trained many of them.

"I'll remember you. You killed my father!" screamed Max as the SWAT team members dragged him away.

"Yeah, yeah, blah, blah, blah. Whatever, kid," mumbled Frank. "Don't forget to go to school!" he yelled after them.

∞

Karl could see nothing. All was completely black.

I think I remember this from last time, thought Karl. *Just relax and allow.*

Soon the blackness gave way to a beautiful sunrise on a white sand beach.

Ah, that's more like it, thought Karl. *Now this is my version of heaven! I just love the way the waves gently lap the gorgeous white sands. And listen to the calming sounds the waves make!*

Karl felt himself slowly gliding effortlessly along miles and miles of endless white sand and turquoise waters. He knew, of course, that this was purgatory, his calming place, and it would soon come to an end. But until then, he was going to savor every last moment.

Karl? spoke a familiar voice. *Karl, can you hear me?*

Mom? Is that you? Oh my gosh, I had forgotten that someone always comes to meet us when we transition. I'm so happy to hear your voice. I love you so much!

I love you too, son! We have been watching your latest journey in the fourth dimension and are very proud of the progress you were able to make there.

Thank you, but I owe it all to you and Dad. I couldn't have had more supportive and loving parents. Is it OK if I call you Mom, or do you prefer Anika now?

Both of those are merely labels, son. You can call me anything you wish.

I want to call you Mom.

Then so be it.

Chapter Eighteen

Frank arrived back to the ICU to find it in total chaos.

"What's going on, Dixie," asked Frank as Nurse Dixon rushed past him.

"Fire department is evacuating everyone because of the terrorist bombing," replied Nurse Dixon.

"It wasn't terrorists; everything's under control now."

"No time to talk, sorry," said Dixie as she continued on her way.

Frank returned to Karl's room to find it totally empty, clean, and fresh smelling.

They've already been here, thought Frank. The cover-up has begun.

Frank's mind was reeling, his head already hurt from the blast, and now it hurt even more as he tried to focus. Where would they evacuate to? The front of the building!

Frank joined countless others as they ran out of the main entrance of the hospital.

"Hilary!" yelled Frank as he caught a glimpse of her about fifty yards away. "Is everyone all right?" he asked as he ran up to the group gathered around Karl's gurney. "Holy shit, you brought Karl with you!"

"Oh, Frank! I'm so glad you're OK," exclaimed a surprised Hilary as she threw her arms around him. "I thought you got caught in the blast."

As Hilary pulled away from Frank to look at him, he pulled her back into his chest and held her tight.

"Mr. Frank, you are bleeding," said Jorge.

"I am?" answered Frank.

"Yes, you are, honey," added Hilary. "On your face and down your arm."

"Must have been some of the glass fragments from the main doors of the cafeteria."

"You better get that looked at, Frankie," said Will, feeling the need to chime in and lighten the mood.

"I will, Will," answered Frank, grasping for a comeback. "But first I need to tell you that the Dutchman has been neutralized, so we can all take a deep breath and relax, for now."

"What do you mean, 'for now'?" asked Will.

"Well, we know that your dad and Detective Sergeant Smith sent the fake cop, but who sent the Dutchman?"

"Does it really matter, Mr. Frank?" asked Jorge. "Karl is dead now."

"You are correct, Jorge, but they will soon figure out that someone is taking up the torch, so I really don't like being out in the open like this."

"Speaking of that fake cop, where is he?" queried Frank.

"We left him in Karl's room," answered Jorge.

"Well, he's not there now!" said Frank. "In fact, it's as if none of us were ever there!"

"Frank," started Will, "I will not hide in order to get the message out there that needs to be heard."

"I understand that, and kudos to you for your bravery, but you're now my responsibility to keep safe, and I think we should move under the emergency entrance roof for safety from above."

"OK, whatever you think," said Will as he grabbed one end of Karl's gurney to turn it in that direction.

"I can't believe you guys brought Karl out here with you!"

"What else were we supposed to do?" answered Hilary. "We couldn't just leave him!"

"I know, I know," replied Frank. "Karl would have liked that you brought him with you."

The group wheeled their leader and friend toward the emergency entrance while tears welled up in their eyes.

∞

"I've got them in sight," said a voice in a helicopter disguised as a news chopper hovering overhead.

"They're wheeling a body with a sheet pulled up over its head, which I assume is Dunitz."

"Dunitz is dead," came a voice over the headphones of the man in the chopper. "It's the boy we want. Kill him now!"

"Copy that, sir." replied the man in the chopper as he gave the signal for the pilot to land.

∞

Mom? thought Karl.

Yes dear.

Are we going to go for a ride in the Space Tube?

Space Tube? What in the Universe are you thinking of?

The multiverse portal. My father from my past life called it the "Space Tube," and I must say, it's an apt description.

I see. Of course we are. It's how we get around out here. Distances are so vast that we must use a method to find the creases in the space-time continuum. It just makes sense, don't you think? communicated Anika.

Yes, of course. You were always so smart, Mom. I would sometimes lay awake at night and dream of knowing all that you knew.

Thank you, son, that's very kind of you, and I'd say that was flattering, but currently I do not possess an ego, and as of now, you do know all that I do.

Yes, I can feel the tingling in my extremities. A wondrous feeling! And I can feel my awareness expanding as we communicate. I can't decide which feeling I love more. This feeling of knowing all and in a total state of bliss or having the ability to feel human emotions, thought Karl.

I think you are not done with your evolution, my son. You are choosing to go back again soon?

Yes, I am. I just feel drawn to going back to the third dimension on Earth.

A very dangerous place at the moment, son, but you must follow your desires. Now follow me, my little orb! communicated Anika with a chuckle.

I'm an orb again. Yee-haw, I'm coming, Mommy!

Karl was totally consumed by a feeling of love and compassion for his mother, himself, and indeed everything. As he playfully chased his mother across the heavens, he once again realized that we are all one. He was his mother, and she was him.

How utterly perfect once again! thought Karl.

∞

As the group reached the emergency entrance, Frank felt relieved that they were out of the sun and out of view from overhead.

"Nice to be out of the sun," said Will.

"I agree, honey," added Hilary.

"Frank?" came a voice from over Frank's right shoulder.

Frank turned around to see Derek from the city morgue walking his way.

"I thought that was you," began Derek. "Who have we got here, Mr. Dunitz?"

"Yes, unfortunately. He was murdered, lethal injection," said Frank glumly.

"I see. I'm so sorry to hear that. I followed his teachings closely and was so looking forward to his speech."

"You're from the morgue, right, honey?" asked Hilary.

"Yes, ma'am." Derek noticed Hilary wince after he called her ma'am. "Unfortunately, it's a busy day for us," continued Derek looking back at Frank now. "Three deaths so far from that explosion. What was that anyway?"

"The assassin that got Karl left a C-4 booby trap in his coat in the cafeteria. Lost my best man."

"So sorry for your multiple losses today, Frank," said Derek with no emotion. "We should get Mr. Dunitz on ice though. It's going to be a hot one today, and he shouldn't be out here any longer than he needs to be."

"I agree," said Frank.

"On ice. Not exactly a friendly term, is it?" stated Will.

"I do apologize," began Derek. "It's just a figure of speech we use. We don't actually put people on ice, we just—"

"I get the picture," said Will.

"OK, sorry, again," offered Derek.

"Do you have room in your truck now, Mr. Derek?" asked Jorge.

"As a matter of fact, I do. Would you like to ride along?"

"Yes, as long as I don't have to ride in the back."

"No, no. You will ride up front with me," answered Derek with a smile.

"OK then," began Jorge turning to the others. "I will go with Mr. Derek to the morgue and ensure Mr. Karl is handled with care and dignity."

"Thanks, Jorge. Keep your phone on so we can stay in touch," said Frank.

"I will do that, Mr. Frank; however, I believe it needs to be charged as well."

"You can charge it at the morgue, Jorge," interjected Derek.

"Ah, very good, Mr. Derek. Then let us go."

As they watched Derek and Jorge wheel the gurney carrying Karl's physical body to the morgue truck, Will was struck with an uneasy feeling.

"How well do you know Derek?" asked Will.

"I've known him for ten years or so. Always respectful and treats the dearly departed with care and dignity."

"But can we trust him?"

"I was thinking the same thing, honey," added Hilary.

"My, my, starting to get a little suspicious of people, are we?"

"Well, so much has happened in the last twenty-four hours, and many things have turned out to be not what they seem," responded Will.

"You're absolutely right, Will. But that's my job," began Frank. "Your job is to gain the people's trust, and you're never going to do that by second-guessing everyone you meet."

"You're right. I apologize."

"No need to apologize; I like that you're aware of things. Speaking of which, standing around here is giving me the creeps. Hilary, is your car still in the parking lot?"

"It should be, unless it was towed for expired parking."

"Good, let's make our way over there and go for a ride."

"Where are we going?" asked Will.

"To introduce you to your new team."

"New team? You mean Karl had a team? I mean, other than you guys?" asked Will.

"You'll find out," said Frank knowingly.

∞

The helicopter was back to circling overhead after dropping off the two commandos on the hospital roof.

"It looks like they're headed toward the parking lot. Where are you now?" asked the man in the chopper.

"Almost down. Two more flights of stairs," responded one of the commandos.

"We cannot let them leave the property. Primary target is the boy."

"Copy that."

∞

"Crap!" yelled Hilary

"Is that your car?" asked Frank.

"What's left of it, yeah. I just bought it six months ago!"

"Well, it did a good job of bringing the Dutchman's car to a halt," added Frank with a smirk.

"It's not funny!" exclaimed Hilary.

Frank and Will looked at each other and broke out laughing.

"Where's your piece-of-crap car, Frank. You drove here didn't you?" asked Hilary.

"Sorry, Hilary, we didn't mean to laugh."

Frank looked back at Will, and they both broke out laughing once again.

"You two are acting like little boys. Now where's your pile-of-crap car so I can have a good laugh?"

"It's over here," said Frank, wiping the tears of laughter from his eyes.

"Sorry, Hilary, just letting out some pent-up emotion," said Frank, still trying to hold back another outburst of laughter.

"You expect all three of us to fit in that?" asked Hilary as they walked up to Frank's car.

"Yes, I know, it only has two seats. That's why I wanted to take your car," responded Frank.

"OK, I'll drive and you two can snuggle in the passenger seat," said Hilary.

"I don't think so!" said Will.

"Not a chance, my dear," began Frank. "Let me put the top down before you get in, Will, and then Hilary will have an easier time climbing on top of you."

"I don't like the sound of that," said Hilary.

"You don't like the sound of that? What about me!" exclaimed Will.

"What, there's something wrong with me?" asked Hilary.

"No, I didn't mean that. It's just that..."

"You may as well stop there, my friend," said Frank as he got into the older but timeless roadster and hit the button to lower the roof. "You're never going to win that argument!"

Frank waited until everyone was aboard then started the car and pressed the button to put the top up again.

"Why don't you leave the top down, Frank? It gives us more room," asked Will.

"I'd like to be a bit more discreet as we leave the area."

"Discreet? In this piece of junk?" added Hilary.

"I'll have you know that this is a classic roadster that has been impeccably maintained," answered Frank as he shoved the gear lever into reverse and let out the clutch.

The two commandos burst through the ground-level door just as the man in the chopper began to speak.

"They are all in a red sports car. Just backing out now. Do not let them leave!"

"Copy that. We have them in sight."

As Frank moved the gear lever into first gear, he heard the bullets hitting the car.

"Shit! Everybody down!"

Frank revved up the engine and violently let the clutch out as Hilary and Will slid down in their seat as far as they could. The little roadster responded with both rear tires struggling for traction and sending off plumes of blue tire smoke.

"Stay low, stay low!" yelled Frank over the sound of bullets hitting steel and whistling through the convertible top.

The two commandos switched their Colt M4 carbines to fully automatic mode now as the little roadster left the parking ramp and turned hard left onto the street.

"Jesus Christ!" screamed Frank as his driver's side window exploded and the bullets whistled just over his head.

Frank changed hard into second gear, which threw the little roadster sideways, exposing even more of the car to the shooters.

"Damn it!" yelled Frank as he heard the bullets rip into the front fender, hoping none of them had hit anything vital under the hood.

The two commandos ran to try to get a better angle while changing magazines in their weapons as the little roadster started to speed away.

"Everyone OK? Anyone hit?" yelled Frank as two more bullets hit the trunk lid.

"I'm good!" yelled Hilary.

"I think I'm fine," said Will cautiously.

"What do you mean, you 'think'?" asked Frank.

"I feel a warmth at my back."

Frank took one hand off the wheel and stuck it behind Will's back to feel for blood and then looked at the dashboard.

"You're going to be fine," said Frank as he leaned forward and pressed a button on the lower dash. "Seat heater was on."

Chapter Nineteen

Karl playfully chased his mom for what seemed like a lifetime. Eventually, she came to a stop, and as Karl arrived, so did the Space Tube.

Ah, there it is! I was wondering when we were going to find it. It's so beautiful! thought Karl.

Karl stared at the wonder of this tube-like structure. Blue-white energy beams made up its circular frame, interspersed with a cross brace every now and again, made of the same blue-white energy, and the whole thing seemed to stretch out into the Universe forever.

There is no finding it, son, communicated Anika. *You merely need to think that it is here and it will be.*

Then you weren't thinking of it then obviously.

No, I just wanted to play with my boy!

Thank you for that, Mom. I still feel some remnants of my physical emotions and would probably cry if I had tear ducts. I certainly do miss our daily playful interactions.

I do too son.

Mom? communicated Karl. *Have you already had more children in another life?*

Oh yes, of course. We all live our lives simultaneously as you'll soon see.

With that, Anika boarded the Space Tube and was whooshed into seemingly oblivion.

Well, I guess it's my turn!

Karl expanded his awareness to include all that surrounded him.

Yee-haw! I forgot how incredible this multiverse portal is, thought Karl.

Karl enjoyed his ride immensely as he looked out at other stars and galaxies as he passed through them. Then, as quick as it started, it was over.

How was that? thought Anika.

That was absolutely out of this world! communicated Karl.

Nice choice of words, son. It truly is out of this world. Now expand your awareness and tell me what you see.

Karl relaxed and opened himself to everything around him. *Yes. I see it. It's the multiverse.*

Absolutely correct, son, but what you are envisioning is just a graphical representation of the multiverse. In actuality, the multiverse exists everywhere. In fact, there is nowhere it is not. You are always part of it. This representation is just something your energy field has concocted in order for it to make sense to you.

So, the same goes for the Space Tube? thought Karl.

Yes, the Space Tube is also everywhere all the time. As I stated before, you merely have to think about it and it appears.

And you don't see them then?

No, this part of my soul, what some might call my nucleus, is always here in the realm of the absolute. Other parts of my soul, however, would experience exactly what you experience.

I take it then that this part of my energy field, which I am experiencing at this moment, is split off from my nucleus and is constantly making journeys to other realms, communicated Karl.

Yes, son, you would be correct. If the split-off part of your soul that you are now decides to stay in the realm of the absolute, then you will begin to know all there is to know and will understand all of this, just as your nucleus does.

Incredible! So, because I'm constantly returning to physical form to know myself experientially through feelings and emotions, I have lost the ability to truly know myself conceptually, thought Karl.

Well, no, you haven't lost the ability, you're just a little rusty, shall we say. If you decide to stay and not go back this time around, it will all come back to you. You see, one of the first caveats that exist when you decide to make the switch to physical form is that you agree to not remember who you truly are. This ensures that you have a new experience every time. Your mission, so to speak, during each lifetime is to discover this truth before you reach the end of your physical body.

I did that this last time around! communicated Karl.

Yes, you did, son, and we're all very proud of you.

We?

All the angels, all the orbs, all the souls, all the energy fields, all that is. Put it all together and it's just US. We're all one and the same. Individuality does not exist; it's merely an illusion in the game we play called "life."

That's so cool! In some way, I already knew that though.

Of course, you did! Now look upon your multiverse and tell me what you see, thought Anika.

I see a tall vertical structure, like an apartment building, but with blue-white energy beams used for the frame, with divided rooms in which I am experiencing all my other physical lives in other realms.

What else do you see?

I see that some of the rooms in the building are dark. There's no energy at all in those rooms.

Exactly. One of those rooms is from the fourth dimension that you just left.

It is? thought Karl.

Once your physical life is over in one realm it is now devoid of your energy because you are now here in front of me.

I see. So, when I go back to another physical realm, one of those rooms will once again be full of energy.

You bet! communicated Anika.

Then because there are many dark rooms that means there are a lot of pieces of my soul doing this all at the same time.

Once again you are correct. You are constantly renewing and reshaping you. It can be no other way because energy is constantly evolving. It's what we call "the Process."

What did you just think?

It's called "the Process."

That's exactly what I discovered in my last lifetime!

I know, thought Anika. *Who do you think nudged you in that direction? The discovery of the Process will serve you well in your next lifetime.*

Chapter Twenty

Jorge was just sitting down with Derek to enjoy a cup of coffee when his phone he had put on Derek's desk to charge began to ring.

"Hello, Jorge here."

"Jorge, I'm so glad to hear your voice!" shouted Hilary over the sound of the roadster's roaring engine and squealing tires.

"Miss Hilary, is everything OK? What's that dreadful sound?"

"We just barely made it out of the hospital alive. Someone sent more assassins to finish us off."

"Where are you now?" asked Jorge.

"We're in Frank's car trying to evade a helicopter that's following us."

"Frank's car? Is Master Will with you?"

"Yes, he's beneath me, trying too...sorry, another corner...hang on to me so I don't slide over to Frank's side."

"Yes, it's only a two-seater. Fun car though, yes?" smiled Jorge.

"Well, right now it's full of bullet holes, and Frank is really pushing it hard, but so far it's holding together. Everything go OK with Karl?" asked Hilary.

"Yes, yes, all is well. He is on ice, so to speak."

"We're headed to the tunnel; can you meet us there?"

"I will have to procure some transportation, but yes, I will meet you there in about an hour," answered Jorge.

"OK, great. See you then," said Hilary as she hung up.

"Everything all right?" asked Derek.

"Yes, I believe so. Is there a car I could borrow for a couple of hours, Mr. Derek?"

"Why don't I give you a lift to wherever you need to go?" countered Derek.

"That would be nice of you, Mr. Derek, thank you, but I wish to go on my own."

"Well, I could lend you my personal vehicle, I suppose. But I need it back here by five o'clock because that's the end of my shift."

"Of course, by five o'clock then. Thank you, Mr. Derek. But first we need to finish our delicious coffee, no?"

"Yes!" answered Derek.

$$\infty$$

"Shit!" yelled Frank.

"What's the matter, honey?" asked Hilary.

"Smoke—starting to come from under the hood. I'm afraid this old girl isn't going to last much longer," answered Frank as he revved the W54 in-line six-cylinder engine to redline once again before shifting.

"How much farther to the tunnel?" asked Hilary.

"About two miles according to the GPS," answered Will, trying to hold his cell phone steady enough to read the small text.

"Starting to lose power now," yelled Frank over the roar of the engine.

Just as Frank spoke, .50 caliber bullets ripped holes in the pavement ahead.

"Jesus Christ! Those looked like fifty cal rounds. They'll tear this car to shreds," said Frank as he jerked the wheel from side to side to try to take evasive action.

"Take your next left!" yelled Will.

Frank heel-and-toe downshifted, working the brake and throttle at the same time, and hit the apex of the corner perfectly.

"That was smooth, Frankie. Now put her down, the tunnel is just ahead."

"I see it!"

Frank felt the car shudder violently as more .50 caliber bullets hit near the front of the car and one tore through the front fender and into the left front tire.

"Aaah!" screamed Hilary.

"We're going to be OK!" yelled Frank. "Run-flat tires!"

Smoke was now pouring out from under the hood as the little roadster made it into the tunnel.

"OK, Hilary, send the signal," said Frank as he started to slow the car down.

Hilary pushed a sequence of buttons on the screen of her smartphone, and a light began to appear on the right side of the tunnel. Frank slowed to a crawl then turned sharply to get into the entranceway of the opening.

"What the...?" exclaimed Will. "Where the hell are we?"

Frank stopped the car just inside the opening and quickly got out as the huge concrete door was closing behind them and headed for a switch on the far wall.

"Had to start the fans," said Frank, talking louder now because of the noise. "My little girl is smoking pretty bad!"

Frank popped the hood of the little roadster to assess the damage.

"Damn it!" he yelled, waving his hand to clear the smoke. "She's done. Game over."

"Bad damage?" asked Will after Hilary was able to peel herself off him and he was able to squeeze out.

"That one round went through the fender and hit the oil filter housing. There's oil everywhere." Frank pulled the dipstick and shook his head. "No oil left in her. I don't know how we even made it here."

"I guess these guys build great engines, huh."

"This was one of their best—W54 in-line six cylinder. Voted best automobile engine in the world two years running when it first came out."

"OK, boys, that's enough of the motor head stuff; let's get a move on, shall we," interjected Hilary.

"Holy crap!" said Will as he walked around the car. "Look at all the bullet holes in the top."

"That's why I told you to stay low!" began Frank. "I knew they'd be going for head shots."

"I'm glad you put the top back up. If they could see us they probably would have hit us."

"There's no probably about it, Will. They were professionals."

"OK, guys, I've entered the code," said Hilary. "Get your buns over here."

As Frank and Will made their way over to Hilary, a small concrete section of the wall opened, and a retina-scanning device moved into place.

"Ok, I'm done. You're up, honey," said Hilary.

Frank moved up to the scanner and placed his eyes into the viewer while simultaneously putting his right index finger into the fingerprint reader.

"Your turn, Will," said Frank, gesturing with his right arm toward the scanner.

"How will they know it's me? I mean, how would they already have my data?"

"They don't," said Hilary. "But they will now."

Will stepped up to the scanner, placed his eyes into the viewer, and allowed the laser scanner to make multiple passes in order to get a root scan. While busy doing that, Hilary lifted his right hand and placed his index finger into the fingerprint scanner.

"All done. Scan complete," said Hilary.

Will heard a huge clunk and felt the ground vibrate beneath him as a huge concrete slab moved back and then to the right to reveal the red-lit corridor.

"What is this place?" asked Will.

"Welcome to my lair! Mwah-ha-ha!" said Frank jokingly as he came back from shutting off the fans.

"Seriously. How did this even get here. I've been through this tunnel a hundred times and never even saw this being built."

"Remember about five or six years ago when the tunnel was declared unsafe and went through a six-month rebuild?" asked Frank. "Well, the tunnel was fine, and this is what they built!"

"This is our command center, or HQ if you will," added Hilary.

"And Karl knew about this?" asked Will.

"Knew about it—it was his idea!" answered Frank.

"Unbelievable!" said Will as he took his first step beyond the huge concrete slab of a door.

"You ain't seen nothing yet, as the old saying goes," offered Frank. "Come on, let's introduce you to everyone."

As the trio made their way into the command center, the chopper was hovering overhead trying to keep an eye on both exits of the tunnel.

"I don't get it. They went in but didn't come out!" said the pilot of the chopper.

"Over there!" said the man in charge.

"Where?" answered the pilot.

"I guess it was nothing. I thought I saw some smoke coming from the top of the tunnel. Go back down so we can have one more look into the tunnel."

"Rodger," replied the pilot.

If there's no car or sign of wreckage, then there must be some sort of secret entrance, thought the man.

"On second thought, put the chopper down over there," said the man, pointing to a clearing near the exit of the tunnel. "I want to get out and see for myself."

"Rodger that, no problem."

Chapter Twenty-One

Anika expanded her awareness and started to move away from the graphical representation of the multiverse.

Are you coming? thought Anika.

Karl couldn't stop looking at the endless structure that contained all the other pieces of him living out different lives in different dimensions.

And it's all made of the same energy that I am right now. Incredible! thought Karl.

Karl, it's time to move on, son.

What? Yes, of course, I'm sorry. I just got taken in by the majesty of it all.

I know, I still do as well, but it's time to move to our decision point.

Anika and Karl drifted toward a small light in the distance that soon became much bigger and brighter.

OK, son, here we are. It's decision time.

So, I guess this is the part where you tell me my options, thought Karl.

Yes, it is. At this point, you must make a decision to return to physical form right away or stay home and enjoy a total feeling of unconditional love and bliss.

Karl could feel the pull of his true and natural form. The longer he stared at the light, the stronger it became. Soon he found himself drifting toward the light.

Have you made your decision? communicated Anika.

Karl suddenly stopped his drift toward the light and focused on the orb that was Anika.

If I go home I can leave anytime, right? thought Karl.

Of course, you have free will to do anything you desire. Desire is the fuel of the Universe. Without the desire to evolve, our energy would implode, collapsing upon itself.

You mean like a black hole?

Something like that, yes. You left the fourth dimension with a desire to return to the third. This is highly irregular since most souls desire to evolve forward onto higher planes of existence. You, my son, are an anomaly, which the Universe very much enjoys. You see, the Universe is very pattern oriented, everything fits and works with everything else. But every once and a while an anomaly, or "disrupter" as we call it, comes along and forces a new pattern to emerge. Thus, the Universe evolves a little more, like a new branch growing on an old tree.

I see, began Karl. *So, you don't want me to return home but to continue with my original plan?*

Not at all, the choice is yours, my son. You, as we all, have been given the divine right of free will. Whatever choice you make will be assimilated by the Universe, and it, as you, will continue to evolve no matter what.

So, you wouldn't be disappointed if I just came home and rested for a while? thought Karl.

How could I be disappointed in you exercising your free will? There are no expectations of you, my son; that is still a leftover feeling from your past physical life. And besides, I am you, and you are me. We are all one, remember? The only thing I can tell you is that once you make the decision to go home, you will stay longer than you think. You will be reunited with all the souls you have ever loved, including your pets. The feeling of unconditional love is all powering. Indeed, it is the jet engine that drives the Universe, with desire as its fuel. Your desire to stay could become overwhelming, and you would miss your chance to affect the third dimension in a way that will change many lives.

I see, thought Karl. *I believe I need to stick to my original plan and return to physical form in the third dimension. I can sense that I will be able to help other souls there and cause myself to evolve much further.*

As Karl thought those thoughts the Space Tube appeared.

Looks like you've made a decision! communicated Anika.

∞

Jorge was on his way to the tunnel but found himself getting very frustrated as he drove.

"Darn traffic lights!" said Jorge out loud as he came to a stop at another red light.

I didn't really want to leave Mr. Karl with Derek. Something tells me he can't be trusted, but I need to help Hilary, Frank, and Master Will, thought Jorge.

"OK, OK!" yelled Jorge as the horn from the car behind him honked at the green light. "I'm going, already!"

∞

Frank led the way down the red-lit corridor to a metal spiral staircase with Will, then Hilary trailing behind.

"It's like we're in some old abandoned bomb shelter or something," stated Will.

"Something like that," said Frank over the sounds of their footsteps on the metal stair treads.

The trio continued to descend the staircase for two more stories then went through the opening in the far wall and turned sharply left.

"Just about there," said Frank.

As Frank, Will, and Hilary walked up to what seemed to be a wall, a bank of bright white LED lights turned on, blinding them all. The wall gave out a huge clunk and began to open.

"Frank, Hilary! So good to see you, my friends!"

"Collin, the lights!" yelled Frank.

"Oh yes, sorry about that," said Collin as he reached for the switch inside the door. "Just had them installed last week. What do you think?"

"I think I'm blind!" said Hilary.

"Good, good! They work then."

"Yes, Collin, they work well."

"And who do we have here?" asked Collin.

"Collin, meet Will Parkinson. The heir apparent."

"Nice to meet you, Will," said Collin, sticking his hand out.

Will tried to shake Collin's hand but had trouble finding it.

"All I can see is white spots in front of my eyes, sorry."

Collin grabbed Will's hand, gave it one pump, then wrapped his thumb around Will's and pulled him close for a partial hug.

"You're black."

"Even though they are blind, they shall still see," said Collin using a preacher-like tone. "Is that going to be problem, mother sucker?"

"No, not at all. It's just that everything's still white."

"Hey, I just turned myself into a white man with them lights. Cool! Maybe I'll soon get equal pay too!" said Collin with a hearty laugh.

"Don't push it, Collin," said Frank.

"What's with the 'mother sucker'?" asked Will. "Can't you just say motherfu—"

"SHHHH!" shushed Collin. "There's a lady in the building. Mind your manners, kid."

"But it means the same thing," said Will, stating the obvious.

"I know that, but I respect the female gender, seeing they brought us into this world and all!"

"You may as well quit while you're ahead here, Will. Collin has an answer for everything," advised Frank.

"And that's just the way you like it, Frankie," said Collin with an ear-to-ear grin as he put his arm around Frank's shoulder. "Come on in to our humble abode!"

As soon as they were inside the room, the door shut behind them with a huge clunk and a young lady walked up to them.

"Will, this is Clara, our surveillance specialist, computer nerd, and all-around IT guru," said Collin. "Any questions on how things operate around here, she's the one to ask."

"Hi, Will, nice to meet you. Hi, Frank, Hilary," said Clara hurriedly. "Collin, we have a problem."

"What's up, Clara?" asked Collin, knowing full well Clara wouldn't have said that unless there was something truly wrong.

"The chopper that was chasing you guys has landed in the clearing near the south end of the tunnel, and a man has gotten out and is checking out the tunnel. We have them on the screen over here."

Clara walked them over to a large rectangular monitor showing a split-screen image of the chopper and the man inspecting the tunnel.

"Chopper's still running and...why is that guy dressed in a black suit and tie with dark shades?" asked Frank. "Wait a minute, he looks familiar. I think I know that guy!"

"Who are these creeps?" asked Will.

"Creeps?" whispered Clara to Collin.

"He's new, what can I say," whispered Collin back.

"If you guys are done whispering sweet nothings to each other," began Frank, "perhaps you could run the name Christian Bennet through the system."

Clara moved swiftly to her keyboard and began typing. "Yup, that's him. He hasn't been heard from for quite some time. Odd name for a *bad guy*, isn't it?" added Clara.

"He wasn't always bad, although I had heard they had gotten to him and he was dead," said Frank with a slight tone of remorse.

"Wow, he's really giving the door area a good look," said Hilary.

"He's a smart cookie, very thorough," added Frank.

"You know him, then?" asked Hilary.

"Went through basic together. We were basically inseparable all through our years in the JTF2. Graduated number one and two in our class."

"You were number one?" asked Hilary.

"No, I wasn't. This guy's good. He won't miss a trick."

"What if he finds the door opening?" asked Will.

"He won't," said Collin. "Nobody ever has."

"He's out on the road now checking something and sniffing it," said Clara.

"He found the engine oil, and the trail leads right to the door!" said Frank. "We're going to need some help with this."

"Hilary, call Jorge on his cell, now!" ordered Frank.

"Jorge? Hilary. I'm giving you to Frank."

"Jorge, we have someone inspecting the main door in the tunnel, and I need some sort of diversion. Are you getting close?"

"Yes, Mr. Frank, I'm almost there. I will attempt to lead our visitor astray," said Jorge then hung up.

Jorge rounded the final turn and entered the south entrance to the tunnel.

Christian Bennet immediately leaped from the road and onto the narrow curb as soon as he heard the car coming.

"Hello, my friend," said Jorge as he pulled to a stop in front of Bennet. "Are you in need of some assistance?"

"Why would you think that? And it's Agent Bennet to you."

"Well, Mr. Agent Bennet, you are standing in the middle of a narrow tunnel all alone, so I thought you might need some help."

"No, I'm fine. Now buzz off!"

"I see you're checking the oil on the road," began Jorge. "Very bad accident here two days ago. Oil, antifreeze, and all sorts of fluids all over the road. This is a very narrow and old tunnel. If you are off a foot or two either way, you will hit the wall or another car. There's not even room for a car to turn around in here. So, you don't require my assistance then, Mr. Agent Bennet?"

Bennet took everything in that Jorge had said and decided it was bullshit.

"Listen, I don't think for a moment that there was a crash here two days, or two months, ago, so I'm not buying what you're selling. If I were you, I'd bugger off before I lose my patience."

"I'm sorry you feel like that, my friend. I wish you a very nice day. *Adios amigo.*"

"I'm not your friend," said Bennet under his breath as he watched Jorge drive away. "I'm not anyone's friend, anymore."

Bennet turned around and took a long hard look at the concrete wall of the tunnel. Can't seem to find any sign of an opening, he thought. "Wait a minute!" he said out loud now. "I think there's a seam over here."

"Agent Bennet," came the voice over his earpiece.

"Go for Bennet."

"We've been ordered back to base. Cops are on their way here as we speak. I think all my fancy flying and your not-so-good shooting has attracted some attention."

"Really, well maybe if you could have held that bird a bit steadier, I might have hit something!" responded Bennet.

"Doesn't matter now. We have to go."

"Rodger that. On my way."

Bennet took one last look at the concrete wall and then turned and started toward the chopper.

"Not-so-good shooting," said Bennet under his breath. "Asshole!"

"Looks like he's leaving," said Clara to the others.

"Told you he wouldn't find anything," said Collin.

"Don't kid yourself. He'll be back," answered Frank. "Hilary, call Jorge and tell him to circle back and come in through the service entrance."

"Calling now, honey," answered Hilary.

Chapter Twenty-Two

Mom?

Yes, Karl, what is it?

Before I go I have something I want to ask you that I have thought about for quite some time, but could never come up with an answer.

Of course, dear. What is it?

Well, I've been wondering why time, as we know it while in physical form, exists but no longer seems to exist when the soul is released?

That's an easy one, son.

It is? I've been struggling with that my whole time in the fourth dimension.

I know you have. You always seemed to be obsessed with watches and clocks as a youngster, and then later you always wanted to know what time it was.

I guess I already realized my life would be cut short, and I had limited time to work with, thought Karl.

Perhaps. Or maybe you were just some sort of time freak!

What?

Just kidding, son. Just trying to keep things on the lighter side.

Oh yes. Sorry.

No need to apologize. Here in the realm of the absolute I can't be offended. There's enough of that going on while we are in the realm of the physical.

Anyway, to answer your question, time is really just perspective. It neither exists nor ceases to exist, but as the soul alters its perspective, we experience our reality in different ways.

You mean altering our perspective as we change back from the physical to the spiritual once again? thought Karl.

That's right. What the soul realizes at the moment of what human's call "death" is simply a change of perspective. You begin to see more, so you understand more. Now there will be newer and bigger mysteries for you to ponder as you move through the cosmos. But the one thing you must remember, and it's best to remember this before you leave your body, is that your perspective creates your thoughts, and your thoughts create everything else.

And the way to control your thoughts is to change your perspective, thought Karl.

Exactly! I knew you understood this already. If you assume a different perspective, you will have a different thought about everything. This will help you control your thought, and as far as the creation of your experience goes, controlled thought is everything.

I wish I had told my protégé, Will, all this before I left, but I just didn't know how to put it into words.

I wouldn't worry about William, dear. He's going to be just fine. Besides, if you want to, you can still tell him.

I can?

Certainly. When he thinks of you, you will feel it and you can be by his side in an instant. While there, you simply whisper your message into his ear. He will hear it, but it will be up to him to acknowledge it and act on it. It's called "free will." Pardon the pun!

That's wonderful, I will do that, but I don't remember you being so comedic when I was growing up, thought Karl.

That's true. I was always the voice of reason, wasn't I?

A loving voice of reason.

Thank you, dear. Now to finish off our discussion, everything that has occurred, is occurring, and ever will occur is the outward physical manifestation of your innermost thoughts, choices, and ideas about who you choose to be. Therefore, the aspects of your life you do not agree with should not be condemned but changed by altering your perspective. Bring light into the darkness and the darkness will become light. In that way, those that stand in the darkness will be illuminated by the light of your being, and all of you will see, at last, who you really are.

Wow, that's deep!

Shine on, my son, so that the moment of your greatest darkness will become your grandest gift, and you will then share this gift with others, giving them the grandest gift of all: giving them back to themselves. A new world awaits you, my son. Heal it. There is so much that you can do.

∞

With the threat to them over for now, Clara walked over to Will.

"You're looking a little tired," said Clara

"Yes, we've been on the go for quite some time now, and so much has happened in the last forty-eight hours," answered Will.

"Looks like that bandage on your nose could use changing too."

"No time for that; we have to figure out our next move."

"Frank, I'm going to change Will's bandage and get him something to eat," announced Clara.

Frank was busy conferring with Collin and Hilary and seemed almost annoyed that Clara had interrupted them.

"What? OK, whatever. Hey, Clara, could you bring us some coffee when you come back?"

"I'm not your maid, Frank. You know where the coffee is," answered Clara as she was walking back toward Will.

"See, Frank says it's OK to take a break. Follow me, Will."

"Before we do, can we look something up on the internet?"

"Sure, what do you want to look up?" asked Clara inquisitively.

"Something Karl said to me in French during the download."

"Oh really, and what would that be?"

"He said, 'mon jeune homme plein promesses.'"

Clara typed what Will said into the computer and hit enter.

"It means, "My young man full of promise."

"Wow. I still can't believe Karl selected me to put his trust into."

"I think I see a few of the reasons he selected you. Now come on, let's get that bandage changed!"

As Will followed Clara into another room, it was the first time he noticed Clara's curvy figure.

"So," said Will and Clara simultaneously as they reached the break room.

"You go first," said Clara smiling.

"No, ladies first," said Will returning her smile, but then winced.

"Does it hurt?" asked Clara.

"Only when I smile. Which I haven't been doing much of lately, until I met you."

"I see you're sweet as well as handsome."

"You just cut to the chase, don't you," said Will.

"I've learned that if you don't communicate what you feel, you won't get what you want."

"And what do you want?" asked Will.

Clara took a moment to look deep into Will's eyes. "To bring peace to the earth."

Will looked back into Clara's eyes and could see she was serious, and he loved that about her.

"And have about six children!" added Clara.

Will was stunned by her last remark and had to shake his head before he responded. "Really! I've never heard a girl say that before."

"Like I said, communicate what you want!" began Clara with a wry smile. "Now let's have a look at your nose."

"Wow, nice job. Who did this to you?" asked Clara as she carefully peeled off Will's old bandage.

"Some guy called 'the Dutchman.'"

"The Dutchman?" said Clara. "He's like number one on the hit man parade. So, you took on the Dutchman?"

"Not really. I thought I had him in a submissive posture, but then he head butted me."

"And he let you live?"

"Well, even though I couldn't see anything anymore because my eyes immediately started tearing up, I remembered he had a revolver stuck in the front of his pants, so I felt for it and pulled the trigger."

"Oh my god! You killed the Dutchman?"

"Not exactly. I think I got him in the leg because he was trailing blood as he ran out of the room."

"And where was Frank during all this?"

"He was just outside Karl's door and rushed in just before the Dutchman head butted me."

"So, he wasn't much help to you then. I'll have to have a word with him."

"It wasn't like that. It all happened so fast. The Dutchman ran out of the room like a flash, there were dead bodies on the floor, and the Dutchman had given Karl a lethal injection."

"You have had a busy time of it, haven't you?" said Clara.

"That's just one snippet of what went down."

Will's voice started to crack, and Clara could see the tears coming in Will's eyes.

"Are you OK, Will?"

"I just miss Karl. And I never even met him in person!"

As Will spoke about Karl, he felt an odd comforting feeling and heard a very slight buzzing sound.

"He was a great man," said Clara. "We all loved him and would have followed him to the ends of the earth. But it's your time now. It's your time to shine."

"How could you say that?" began Will. "You don't even know me!"

"Karl saw something in you, and I see it too, in your eyes. You're the one, Will."

"Funny, I've heard that before but never believed it until you said it."

Will reached out, pulled Clara close, and hugged her tight. She hugged him back, and he could feel that she was the one, too.

"Hungry, are we?" asked Frank as he breezed into the break room.

Will released his hold on Clara as she did the same.

"As a matter of fact, I am!" began Will. "We were just lamenting over Karl."

"No need to explain, my friend," said Frank.

"No really, Clara was about to change my bandage," said Will blushing now.

"I heard you weren't of much use to Will when the Dutchman was in the room."

"He said that?" asked Frank nodding in Will's direction.

"No, he didn't say that. I deduced that from his story of what went down. I thought you were there to protect Karl, so how was the Dutchman able to give Karl a lethal injection?" queried Clara.

"Because he created a diversion with some C-4 in his coat that he left in the hospital cafeteria, which vaporized my best man! Any more questions, your honor?"

"I'm sorry, Frank, I didn't know."

"There's lots you don't know living here in this protective bubble while the rest of us are living the dangers on the street."

"Frank, I think we all need to take a step back here," interjected Will. "We've all been through a lot in the last little while. Clara, Frank has done an outstanding job protecting all of us. I was on the couch communicating telepathically with Karl during most of what was going on so I was completely useless. Frank was doing everything he could."

"I'm sorry, Frank," offered Clara. "You're right, living here you lose touch with what's going on in the front lines, and I didn't mean to imply you weren't doing your job."

"No offence taken," said Frank. "Like Will said, we've all been through a lot, and thank you for the kind words, Will. I'll just get my coffee and leave you two alone."

"I'll bring a pot out and a tray of some goodies," said Clara as she reached out and touched Frank's arm. "I love you."

"Thanks Clara, I love you too," said Frank as he turned and walked out of the break room.

"You two were, or are, an item?" asked Will a little embarrassed.

"No, never!"

"Why did you tell him you loved him then?" asked Will.

"Because I do. I love you too, and Collin, and Jorge, and Hilary, and everyone else on this planet."

"You really mean that, don't you?"

"Yes, I do because love is the only thing that's going to save us."

"I've never met anyone, let alone a beautiful woman, like you before."

"I know. Now let's have a look at that bandage before I make the coffee."

Clara carefully peeled back the bandage on Will's nose to reveal a very angry-looking cut complete with five stitches.

"Ow!" cried out Will as Clara ripped the bandage the rest of the way off. "What are you trying to do, rip my nose off!"

"Nope, but pain is the precursor to love."

"What did you just say?"

"Pain is the precursor to love," repeated Clara. "Why?"

"I think you just gave me an idea for our next move!"

Chapter Twenty-Three

Detective Sergeant Smith and Senator Parkinson were just leaving the police station when a big black SUV pulled up to the curb.

"This doesn't look good," said Smith, reaching out with his left arm to stop Senator Parkinson in his tracks.

"Should we run for it?" asked Parkinson.

"No, it's useless."

As Smith finished his words, a large man dressed in an expensive black suit complete with white shirt, black tie and dark sunglasses appeared from the front passenger door and opened the door to the back seat of the SUV.

"Gentlemen," began the man in a deep voice, "your presence is required elsewhere."

"I'm a United States senator, and I don't go anywhere I don't want to go," responded Parkinson.

"That's wonderful, Senator," said the large man as he took a few steps and quickly closed the gap between them. "But you still only have two choices. Die here now or come with me and possibly live to see another day."

"We better do as he says," said Smith feebly as he backhanded Parkinson in the arm. "Let's go."

The large man took a step to his left to stand directly in front of Smith.

"Jesus, you are a big bugger, aren't you?" said Smith looking up at the man in black.

"I'm going to need your service revolver in your shoulder holster, Detective."

"All right, I figured that."

"And the peashooter in your ankle holster too."

"For God's sake! Is there anything you guys don't know?" exclaimed Smith as he handed over his firearms.

"No sir, there's not. Please step into the vehicle," said the man in black, turning and pointing the way with his outstretched arm.

"Where are you taking us?" asked Parkinson as he climbed into the back seat.

The man in black closed the door behind them and then got into the passenger side of the vehicle.

"I said, where are you taking us? I demand to know!"

As the big black SUV pulled away from the curb, the rear doors automatically locked and a voice came over the rear speakers.

"We're going to a very important meeting, gentlemen. The whereabouts of which you cannot know. There are two black hoods on a hook in front of you, and yes, you will be able to breathe normally. Put the hoods on and leave them on until I tell you to take them off."

"I'm not wearing any hood, you ignoramus. I'm a United States senator. Now stop this car immediately, and I will think about not charging your ass with treason and serving up your head on a platter!"

Detective Sergeant Smith leaned over toward Parkinson and looked him in the eye.

"These guys don't work for the government, and they certainly don't give a rat's ass about the United States of America. I think we should do what we're told, for now, Senator."

"Did you hear me up there!" said Parkinson defiantly as he banged on the thick plexiglass partition between them and the two men in black.

"Senator," began the monotone voice over the rear speakers again, "we don't work for your government nor have we pledged allegiance to your flag, so your threats mean nothing to us. My orders were to bring you in dead or alive. If you like, I can stop the truck and make it the former instead of the latter. Which one will it be?"

"Put on your hood, dumb ass, and shut the hell up. You're going to get us both killed!" reinforced Smith.

Senator Parkinson reached for the door latch and pulled it hard. "Damn it!" he yelled. "I guess you got us over a barrel, son. I'll take the latter."

"Good choice, Senator, although I would have enjoyed the other option."

Parkinson could swear he heard a smile in the man's voice.

"Now settle in and relax, it's a bit of a drive."

Parkinson looked over at Smith who already had his hood on and then slipped his hood over his own head.

"Goddamn sons of bitches!" said the senator under his breath as he settled in for the drive. "They will pay for this!"

∞

"Jorge! So nice to see you again," said Collin as Jorge entered the lab through the big concrete and metal door.

"Yes, yes, Mr. Collin, nice to see you too. That is, if I could see," answered Jorge as he stuck his arms out in front of himself to prevent bumping into things.

"When did you install the eye-piercing lightbulbs?"

"They're the latest technology, Jorge. Instead of LED, they're LEDC!"

"OK, I'll bite, Mr. Collin," said Jorge, knowing Collin was dying to tell him more. "What is LEDC?"

"Well, it's still a light-emitting diode, but enhanced by a small sliver of grandidierite, a very rare gemstone found almost exclusively in Madagascar."

Jorge nodded his head in appreciation, hoping that Collin was finished with his explanation.

"Grandidierite," continued Collin without taking a breath, "like alexandrite and tanzanite, is pleochroic and can transmit blue, green, or white light. These particular crystals have been cut so fine that they only transmit white light, and once exposed to the already high six-thousand-five-hundred kelvin color of the diodes, produces over forty-five thousand lux, which is almost as bright as looking at the sun!"

"Incredible!" announced Jorge.

"I knew you would appreciate the finer aspects of our new lighting system, Jorge."

"Will it keep the *bad* people away, Mr. Collin?" asked Jorge.

"Now you're just fooling with me, Jorge," said Collin with a huge smile.

"And no, it can't keep them away, but it may buy us some time to destroy some of our information and systems, and maybe even enough time to allow us to reach the escape tunnel."

"In that case, my friend, a hearty well done!" responded Jorge, patting Collin on the back, hoping his science lesson was over as they walked into the main area.

"Jorge, you made it!" said Frank as he went over to give Jorge a big hug.

"Mr. Frank, nice to see you too, but I only just saw you a few hours ago."

"I know that, Jorge, but sometimes we need to be thankful for having great people in our lives, you know?"

"Yes, Mr. Frank, I know exactly what you mean. How is Master Will and Miss Hilary?"

"We're all good. Shaken, but not stirred, as they say. Which tunnel did you come in?"

"I had to use the west tunnel, Mr. Frank. I saw the helicopter leave the area, and I circled around to the west because they headed east and then parked in the ride-share parking lot to use the tunnel. You know, that is a long walk through that west tunnel."

"Just over two kilometers, honey," said Hilary as she came over to give Jorge a hug.

"Miss Hilary, nice to see you too. Everyone seems to be so affectionate today."

"Don't forget about me," said Clara.

"And me," added Will.

Clara and Will gave Jorge another hug, which made Jorge blush.

"Thank you all for the extra attention, but I'm not sure why?" said Jorge.

"I'll tell you why, Jorge," said Will. "It's because you were Karl's closest friend, and with Karl gone, we still see him in you. And of course, the fact that we came very close to death in Frank's little roadster on the way over here."

"Speaking of Karl, Jorge, how did you make out with Derek at the morgue?" asked Frank.

"Mr. Karl is 'on ice' as Mr. Derek puts it, but I'm not sure if I trust him," answered Jorge.

"Why's that, Jorge?" asked Hilary.

"I'm not really sure. I just had a feeling about him as we shared a coffee, and the fact that he was adamant about driving me over here."

"But he didn't drive you, did he?" queried Will.

"No, Master Will, I borrowed his car, which I have to have back two hours from now."

"OK, then let's put our heads together for the next ninety minutes and come up with a plan to move forward," said Collin.

"About that," started Will, "I think I may have an idea."

∞

Derek finished his coffee and Danish after Jorge left then picked up the phone and dialed.

"Peterson?" asked Derek after someone answered the phone.

"State your name and the nature of your business," said the digitized voice on the other end.

"Derek from the morgue. I thought you might want to know that I have Karl Dunitz's body over here. You've got two hours to pick it up, and the cost will be one hundred thousand American dollars."

"Thank you," answered the voice and then the line disconnected.

I guess they'll be over with my money, thought Derek as he put down the phone. "Then it's *adios*. I'm out of this town!"

∞

"OK, gentlemen, we are nearing our destination. Leave your hoods on until we come to a complete stop," said the man in black through the rear speakers.

Awfully bumpy ride the last fifteen minutes or so, thought Detective Sergeant Smith. We must be in the middle of nowhere.

Smith and Senator Parkinson both felt the SUV come to a stop and almost simultaneously pulled off their hoods.

"What did you spray onto the fabric of these hoods?" asked Smith.

The man in black ignored Smith's question, got out of the front seat, and opened the passenger-side rear door.

"Get out," ordered the man in black.

"Where are we?" asked Parkinson sheepishly.

"Did you hear me?" asked Smith as he slid over to the passenger side and exited the vehicle. "What did you spray on the fabric of our hoods?"

"You have a good sense about you, Detective. You may be of some use to us yet. Oh, and yes, just a little cocktail to keep you calm. Nothing special."

"Where are we?" reiterated Parkinson after turning around 360 degrees.

"Head toward that hangar over there, Senator," said the man in black, pointing over Parkinson's right shoulder.

The man in black headed the way toward what looked like an old dilapidated aircraft hangar, with the driver of the SUV bringing up the rear.

"What is this place?" asked Parkinson as they stepped through the rickety hangar door and were met by a huge steel bank vault of a door.

"You're about to meet my boss," said the man in black while sliding his radio frequency card through the scanner and leaning his face into a retina scanner.

Senator Parkinson pulled himself back suddenly as the huge door began to open with a loud metallic clunk.

"Why couldn't we have met your boss in town?" asked Parkinson, his voice audibly shaking now.

"Because my boss doesn't like people," answered the man in black. "No more questions now, and do not talk unless you're spoken to. Is that clear?"

Smith nodded his head up and down, and Parkinson just stared at the floor.

"Is that clear, Senator?"

"Yes," said Parkinson without looking up.

"Good. Step through the door and back up toward the wall and hold onto the handrail."

The driver of the SUV was the last one in and pressed the buttons to both close the door behind them and start their descent.

"Is this some kind of mine sha—" attempted Parkinson.

Before Parkinson could finish his sentence, the man in black reached out and wrapped his right hand around the senator's neck and squeezed.

"What did we just talk about, Senator? If you speak out of turn with my boss, there will be no forgiveness. Is that clear?"

Parkinson attempted to nod his head but struggled to make his head move against the man in black's vise-like grip.

"Good," said the man in black as he released Parkinson.

Parkinson fell a few inches back to the elevator floor and against the wall while rubbing his throat.

"You son of a bitch!" began Parkinson with a hoarse voice. "You're going to pay for this. I'm a United States senator!"

The man in black looked over at Smith to see him bring his finger up to his mouth while looking at Parkinson in an attempt to get him to be quiet.

"You should take some lessons from your friend here, Senator," said the man in black as he pointed a thumb at Smith. "But guys like you never learn. I'm afraid you're not going to last very long."

Parkinson looked up at the man in black while still rubbing his throat and then over at Smith, who was still trying to shush him, and thought better of responding.

"Maybe there's hope for you, Senator," said the man in black with a chuckle. "But I sincerely doubt it."

All four men bent slightly at the knees like shock absorbers as the elevator reached its destination and came to a sudden stop.

"OK, gentlemen, time to play 'let's make a deal,'" said the man in black with a smile as he led the way off the elevator.

Chapter Twenty-Four

"Did you want to speak first with your idea, Will?" asked Frank.

"No, you go right ahead, I'm still formulating something in my mind."

"OK, then I'll start," began Frank. "I think we should just lay low for a while, maybe six months or so, then start some covert operations and hit them where they least expect it using guerrilla tactics."

"Of course, you'd think like that, you're a Neanderthal!" said Clara.

"I'm not a Neanderthal, I'm just trying to keep us safe!" fired back Frank.

"I get that," said Clara. "But there has to be a way that we can continue what Karl started without putting ourselves at risk."

"Maybe there is," said Will softly.

"You've thought of something?" asked Hilary.

"I don't know if I have or not. I'm still formulating it," answered Will.

"All right, already, just spill the beans!" said Clara excitedly.

"We use the internet," said Will.

"Use the internet? That's just a tool we use to communicate," said Collin.

"Exactly!" began Will. "We need to figure out a way to communicate with the people through the internet without others knowing."

"The internet is hardly a secure platform, Will," said Clara. "Governments have been hacking each other's files for years. They're going to know what we're doing and trace it back to us, no matter where we go."

"I realize that, Clara, but we're already in a cyber war now, and we don't even realize it. And sometimes war dreams of itself."

"What do you mean by that?" asked Clara.

"I think you're onto something, Will," began Collin. "The internet was originally designed for people who knew and trusted each other to share ideas and technology, so it didn't have or need many defenses."

"That's my point exactly!" added Clara.

"The basic internet," continued Collin without acknowledging Clara's comment, "was designed just to move bits and bytes to another spot, but the creation of the World Wide Web allowed the internet to speak a new language. It can be likened to the internet 'dreaming' of itself."

"Thank you, Collin," said Will emphatically. "That's exactly what I was thinking of and wasn't sure how to put it. But we're just scratching the surface here. We need an internet expert to help us out."

"I know someone," began Clara. "Actually, she was a teacher and then principal of my school. Karl knew her, he taught there too."

"How can we get a hold of her? Is she local?" asked Jorge.

"Actually, I have her mobile number."

"You do? I never wanted to even look at my principal let alone talk with him," said Collin laughing to himself.

"She was helping me with some online learning a while back; that's how I found out her hobby is everything internet."

"Sounds like a bit of a long shot," said Frank.

"I agree, Frank, but let's give her a call anyway," said Will.

"I'll call her right now!" said Clara as she stepped away from the group.

"I don't know about this whole internet thing, Will," said Frank. "It just seems so hands off."

"I know it does, but that will allow us to do those covert operations and use those guerrilla tactics you talked about. Besides, Karl told me to remember the internet, that it can help us."

"He did? Sounds good to me, I'm in!" stated Frank.

"What, just like that, as soon as I mention Karl you're all in?"

"Yup! Next question."

"Believe it or not I got ahold of her!" announced Clara as she walked back to the group. "She's within an hour's drive of here, and she said she would love to help as soon as I mentioned Karl's name. Seems they knew each other even before school. I guess they go way back."

"Sounds great!" said Will. "Is she driving down?"

"No, she doesn't drive anymore. Something about the government taking her driver's license for poking around through their transportation system files online," said Clara.

"Nice resume," said Collin.

"I can pick her up," said Jorge. "Give me her address, and I will pick her up, drop her off here, then go back and return the car to Mr. Derek."

"OK, now we're cooking," began Frank. "Jorge, once you bring back Derek's car, check on Karl's body and then rent a vanilla car and come straight back."

"That is the only choice of car flavor I have?" asked Jorge.

"Vanilla means very plain, nondescript."

"I know, Mr. Frank, I'm just fooling with you!" said Jorge as he gave a high five to Collin.

"Yeah, yeah, whatever. Get going and get your butt back here safely," said Frank knowing that Collin always had an effect on Jorge's demeanor.

∞

Derek had just completed his daily checks of the refrigeration system for the morgue when he heard a car door slam.

"That must be my money!" said Derek excitedly to himself. "Just in time too. Jorge should be back with my car any minute now."

Still, Derek remained cautious because he knew these were not men that could be trusted, but he wanted out of this sleepy little town and nothing was going to stop him.

A man entered the front door and then stopped.

"Hi, I'm Derek. I'm the one who called," said Derek while placing his clipboard on the desk. "You look just like they do in the movies, all dressed in black and with the shades and everything," he continued playfully, trying to make conversation.

The man in black just looked around the room surveying the situation.

"Not that that's a bad thing," began Derek anxiously. "They say that wearing the same clothes every day is a sign of intelligence and efficiency."

Derek began to get a bad feeling in his stomach. "Is that my money in the bag? Because I've got Mr. Dunitz back here on ice," he said, pointing a thumb over his shoulder toward the morgue.

"I need to see Mr. Dunitz," said the man in black in a deep monotone.

"Of course, follow me, he's right back here."

The man in black followed Derek into the morgue, looked around the room, saw two cameras, and then positively identified the body.

"Satisfied?" asked Derek.

"Yes. Here is your payment."

The man in black opened his leather satchel and pulled out a silencer-equipped automatic pistol.

"You don't have to do this!" pleaded Derek as he backed away. "Just take the body, forget the money. I don't want to die!"

"Good-bye, Derek," said the man in black flatly and pulled the trigger three times. He then pointed his weapon at each camera and dispatched them too.

"Time for transport," spoke the man in black into his cuff mic.

The man in black walked confidently over to the locked cabinet he saw earlier in the office area as two others entered the back and zipped up the body bag that held Karl's body and carried it outside to the waiting black SUV.

"That should do it," said the man in black to himself as he pulled the memory cards out of the video surveillance system for the morgue.

Jorge was nearing the city morgue when he noticed a black SUV pulling away from the side entrance and onto the main street. Not wanting to attract attention, Jorge just kept driving until the black SUV was no longer in his rearview mirror.

"Damn it!" said Jorge as he pounded the steering wheel. "This can't be good."

Jorge turned the car around, pulled into Derek's parking spot behind the city morgue, and carefully entered the building through the side doors.

Walking into the morgue area, Jorge stopped in his tracks when he saw the open drawer that had contained Karl's body.

"No! This is not possible. I was only gone for a few hours! I'm so sorry, Karl!" yelled Jorge as he looked skyward.

Jorge took a couple of steps forward to get around the empty gurney they had brought Karl in on and discovered Derek.

"Holy mother of God!" yelled Jorge as he recoiled from the sight of Derek's corpse.

Jorge pulled out his phone and dialed. "Miss Hilary? It's Jorge. I'm at the morgue, and I'm afraid I have very bad news. Please put Mr. Frank on."

"Frank here."

"Mr. Frank, they have taken Karl's body from the morgue and killed Mr. Derek."

"What! Who did this, Jorge?"

"I don't know, but they were driving a big black SUV."

"How was Derek killed?" asked Frank.

"With a gun."

"And the bullet pattern?"

"Two shots in the chest and one in the head," said Jorge after reluctantly looking closer at Derek.

"Professionals," said Frank.

"And Karl's body is definitely gone?"

"The drawer we put him in is open and empty."

"OK, Jorge, I want you to take a look around and see if you can find anything else that might give us a better idea of what took place, but don't touch anything that you wouldn't have normally touched while there earlier."

"There are some latex gloves here, Mr. Frank. I'll put them on."

"Good. After you're done, go back to Derek's car and wipe your prints off everything you touched and leave his car keys where you saw him get them from. Then get the hell out of the building, walk to the rental car agency, and get your ass back here. Understood?"

"Understood, Mr. Frank. But they took Karl's body. I was supposed to be watching over it!"

"Nothing we can do about that now, Jorge. Just get yourself out of there as quickly as possible while maintaining control of your emotions."

"Yes, Mr. Frank. I will try."

"Don't rush, Jorge, just move quickly and with purpose. We'll talk more when you get here."

Frank hung up the phone and turned to face the rest of the group. "This isn't good," he asserted.

"What do you mean, honey?" asked Hilary.

"They stole Karl's body and executed Derek."

"Is Jorge all right?" asked Will.

"He's fine. He'll be here shortly.

"Bastards!" yelled Collin. "What the hell do you suppose they have planned for Karl's body?"

"I don't know," said Frank. "But I'm sure we're going to find out."

Chapter Twenty-Five

Karl suddenly felt an odd tingly and tugging sensation but was unsure what it was.

Mom, I'm feeling an odd sensation.

Sounds like someone is thinking of you, son, thought Anika. *Give in to it and explore what it is. I'll be right here when you get back.*

Karl didn't hesitate and just let himself relax. In an instant he was in the lab break room beside Will.

Will. Will, it's me, Karl. Can you hear me!

Karl watched carefully as Clara seemed to be comforting Will.

Of course he can't hear you. Use your telepathy, thought Karl.

Will, it's Karl. I love you, and I thank you for thinking of me to bring me here. I'm sorry, but I feel a tugging sensation and must return to where I was a moment ago. Either you have begun thinking new thoughts or my mother is thinking of me. Remember the internet. The internet will be your friend.

In an instant Karl was back with Anika.

Well, what did you find? communicated Anika.

It was Will, and he was with Clara. She seemed to be comforting him for some reason.

He most likely was thinking of you, my dear, and she was consoling him.

Yes, that's what it seemed like, thought Karl.

Did you attempt to communicate with him?

I did. At first, I tried to talk to him, but of course he couldn't hear me, communicated Karl.

We all do that the first time, son.

Then I tried to use my mind to leave him a message. Wait a minute, what do you mean, 'the first time'?

This won't be the last time you will be spoken of, my son. Whenever another soul thinks of you, you will instantly go there, communicated Anika.

But how can I be in so many places at the same time?

My dear son, you are already everywhere all at once. There is nowhere you are not.

So, I never really left here, did I? thought Karl.

No, you didn't. You just expanded your awareness to include Will and Clara because you felt the attraction. We're all intrinsically connected, son, because we are all one and the same.

Yes, I knew that, but somehow, it's so very different to actually experience it, instead of just talk about it.

But why did Will and Clara seem like they were standing still? They never moved while I was there, communicated Karl.

The energy that is you is now vibrating at such a high frequency that they can't see you or hear you, and they in turn are vibrating so slowly that it appears that they are standing still.

Yes, of course! I even described that to Will before. Why am I forgetting so much of what I knew? thought Karl.

You are not forgetting, son. You are still reintegrating from physical form to pure energy. Things get jumbled up during that period, and it's good to see this is still happening because if you go back to physical form now, that means you'll still retain memory from your former life, communicated Anika.

Then we better get on with it because I have a sense that those memories will serve me well back in the third dimension.

And so, they shall, my son.

∞

Senator Parkinson and Detective Sergeant Smith dutifully followed the man in black through corridor after corridor until finally reaching a black door that resembled some type of monolith. Smith tried to make out the symbol on the door. It looked like an alien being lording over an army of smaller beings beneath it.

"They're aliens?" said Parkinson to Smith.

"Quiet!" growled the man in black. "From here on you must not speak unless spoken to."

The door seemed to hum and then opened without a sound.

Nice decor, thought Smith as he walked past the black walls with dim lighting, which seemed to be leading them to a stronger light at the end of the hall.

"Ahh, I see you finally made it," said the man in black behind the desk.

Parkinson and Smith looked at each other and then back at the man in black as if to verify what they were seeing.

"That's right, we all look the same," began the man in black as he stood up from behind the desk, which was the only piece of furniture in the room, save for some sort of sword that hung on the wall. "We all look the same because we are the same. We're all part of a program developed by our father species, the Cronks. You see, gentlemen, the universe is not what it appears to be to you earthlings. It is so vast the earth would seem like one billionth of a pinhead in comparison, and so it follows that there would be lots of other life-forms out there, yes?"

"Yes," blurted out Parkinson.

"Silence!" shouted the man in black, standing in front of his desk now. "I will forgive you that one, Senator, because in fact, I did ask a question."

The man in black slowly sat down on the front of his desk. "So, as I was saying, there are many different forms of life in the universe and not all are friendly. Many years ago, when all of you were running around with clubs and living in caves, one of the kinder alien species, the Andromedans from the Sapien star system, visited Earth and saw that your evolution was, well...stagnant, and decided to help you along a bit. They implanted various females of your species with their life seed, and once the offspring of these implanted females bred with other Homo erectus species, a suitable mix seemed to come about. This is why there seems to be such a big gap in your evolutionary chain that you are still trying to figure out.

"Thus, a new species, Homo sapiens, was born. And along with a much more developed brain, you also had consciousness bestowed upon you. The ability that allows one to realize they are alive and see that there is more than just them in the big picture of things. This also gave you the ability to become great creators like the Andromedans. You see, everything you see around you as you go through your petty little lives, you have created. By thought alone you possess the ability to manifest anything you wish. If the Cronks hadn't also sprinkled their seed into your mix after the Andromedans left, you would not have become as angry and aggressive, which allowed us to introduce things like money and competition, ultimately enabling you to develop such a strong artificial intelligence you call 'an ego.' This allowed us to keep you all busy worrying about how you look, what you have, what you want next, and how to be better than your neighbor. We look upon the media and advertisement as one of our greatest coups! You look as if you have a question, Detective."

"Yes sir, may I speak?"

"You may ask one question; I know you are an inquisitive one," said the man in black.

"What about those of us that are dark skinned, what we call 'black'?"

"What about it?"

"Well, did we descend from the same alien species as the other people on this planet?"

"Waste of a question, Detective. Your skin color is nothing but a product of your environment and your evolution over the years; your skin color on the outside doesn't make you any different on the inside, despite all your racial bickering for the last thousand years."

"Senator, would you like to ask one question?" asked the man in black.

Parkinson seemed surprised that he was allowed to ask a question. "Yes sir. So, if we are descendants from two alien races, and apparently you aren't one of them, who, or what, are you and what do we call you?"

"That's a better question, Senator; although in no doubt due to your political prowess, you were able to sneak a second one in. Of course you are descendant from other life-forms; that's how the universe works. Nothing is pure and holy, no matter what you have been told. You are nothing but a mix of other life-forms, a cosmic cocktail, if you will; and no, my colleges and I are not life-forms. We are, what you might call, artificial intelligence. A program that was created by the Cronks in order to keep you earthlings herded into the direction that they want you to follow. But we are not controlling you. There is a prime directive in the universe that we all must abide by, and that is all species must have free will. So, the Cronks, and by extension, we, cannot make you do anything. We must supply you with free will to make your own choices and decisions. But just like any good sport there is always a way to bend the rules by interpretation. And you may call me Jones. Agent Jones."

"So, we're just sport for you freaks?" asserted Parkinson.

Jones signaled to his partner that was still standing behind the two men, and the man in black punched Parkinson hard in the right kidney.

"Jesus Christ! You don't call that controlling!" yelled Parkinson as he lay on the floor in pain.

"No, I don't, Senator, because you had the free will to not speak out of turn. And I would prefer it if you didn't mention that meddler's name in front of me again."

"Meddler?" said Parkinson as he began picking himself off the floor.

"Yes, the man you called Jesus was such a pain in, what you call, the ass. It was because of him that we had to rethink our whole plan and find a way to use his own teachings against him and all his followers. That's how religion was born. If Jesus was here today, he'd tell you himself that you've got it all wrong. You see, the Andromedans return to Earth every once in a while, to check up on your progress and always find you in some sort of upheaval, so they empower more people with the awareness of how the universe actually works in hopes that they will spread the word to their fellow humans. Of course, the Andromedans know we are here because we go to every planet they go to, but cannot interfere because of the rule of free will. And the Andromedans always play by the rules."

"So, Jesus was one of the people they enlightened?" asked Smith.

"That's correct, along with many others, including the latest one, the man you called Karl. His human form has now expired, but there remains one that is attempting to complete his teachings. They are very close to gaining the advantage they need in order to lift humans out of their ego-based programming that we have installed and into an insightful or intuitive spiritual way of living, just as most of the higher evolved beings use. And Smith, don't think your talking out of turn went unnoticed. Consider this your final warning."

"That's my son, Will. He's the one, isn't he?" blurted Parkinson as he picked himself off the floor.

Jones looked at the man in black, and Parkinson collapsed in pain once again as the man delivered a blow to his other kidney.

"Yes, Senator, he is the one, and he must be stopped. That's why you are here. You both were given a task that was not fulfilled, and for this, you, as you now know yourselves, must perish. You will be integrated into our system, cease to have consciousness, and take orders from the Cronks. Smith, you will go to the transference room, which is relatively painless, and you, Senator, will go to the cellular restructuring room, which gives us the same result but is much more painful."

"You dirty piece-of-shit alien turd! I'm a United States senator, you will not get away with this. And you'll never catch my son; he's too smart for your programming bullshit!" yelled Parkinson.

"Be thankful you are being put to good use, Senator, and not just vaporized. I do admire your spunk, by the way; you just need to focus it."

The man in black took two steps forward and punched Parkinson in the right temple and watched him crumple to the ground like a rag doll.

"Detective Smith, please follow me," said the man in black.

Chapter Twenty-Six

"Isn't there a way to turn those superduty bright lights off for friendly people?" asked Jorge as he entered the lab.

"I guess I could link them to the identification sensors. Good idea, Jorge. I never thought of that. I'm glad you're back, old buddy!" asserted Collin.

"Jorge! Good to see you again," said Frank. "We were just discussing how to use the internet to communicate with the general population. I'm hoping you'll have some much-needed input for us."

"Hi, Jorge," said Clara and Will almost simultaneously.

"You already know Emily," continued Clara as she shot a quick smirk toward Will, "since you were the one to pick her up."

"Miss Emily, yes. We spoke casually about Karl during the drive over here." Jorge looked deep into Emily's eyes and now knew for sure what he had suspected - she was Simone. "I'm glad you have met everyone. How do you like our lab?"

"It seems fine." Emily suddenly felt odd and now knew what she had felt in the car was no coincidence. Jorge wasn't just another member of the team, she had known him before. "I mean, it's great! You have the latest technology here, which is good because I think we're going to need it."

Jorge sensed Emily's awareness of him and decided to try an alternate means of communication.

Emily? It is me, Jorge.

Jorge? Are we communicating telepathically?

Yes, we are.

I grew up with this ability but always suppressed it because I was afraid of others thinking I was a freak, communicated Emily.

You are hardly a freak, Miss Emily. I knew you in a past life, just as Karl did.

Yes, Karl and I had a few discussions about that. At first, I thought he was crazy, maybe trying some sort of fancy neuro-linguistic programming on me because I was his principal at the school, but it just all felt so real and true.

It is true, Miss Emily. Karl's former name was Wayne, and I was Dr. Jian.

Holy shit! I just had a flashback to a lab not unlike this one. Bright light, I'm in the middle of a circle or something. My name was...Simone.

That's correct, Miss Simone! You were our human conduit to direct and amplify the signal of the internet to billions of people. You were responsible for saving over three billion people that day and birthing a new generation to the next level of the multiverse including, I might add, Wayne and myself.

That's why those bright lights as we entered the lab gave me such a feeling of being home, being in the right place, thought Emily.

It is no coincidence that you met Karl and that you have gravitated to the internet once again. It is all still within you, communicated Jorge.

Wait a minute, what happened to my mother, Jane, or Raven as most people called her?

She dropped out of the energy field to save you. Unfortunately, this left her destined to start her journey over again to try to reach the next level of the multiverse, thought Jorge.

The next lokas, communicated Emily.

That's correct, Miss Emily. The next lokas. It seems things are coming back to you now.

They are, but I think we have an even bigger challenge ahead of us.

We will talk again later, Miss Emily. Right now, we should rejoin the others.

Will it not seem like we were absent from the conversation for a long time? thought Emily.

Not at all. When we communicate like this, it is almost instantaneous. We are merely sending thoughts back and forth, time is of no consequence, only distance.

Perfect. Thank you, Jorge, for allowing me to remember.

My pleasure, Miss Emily.

"So then, Miss Emily, have you formulated a plan?" asked Jorge.

"A plan?" Emily looked around the room and realized she was now back to using speech. Such a slow and tedious way to communicate, she thought.

"Yes, of course, the plan. Well, I believe the internet has already started to become aware of itself. It has already gone through the phase of having unpredictable patterns that cause crashes, which you could liken to a small child learning how to walk. The next step, or learning how to run, so to speak, is for it to recognize its own patterns and the layers of all those patterns. Which I believe it is already starting to do."

"OK, so how can we harness that?" asked Frank.

"I had a dream, about a year ago," began Emily, "that robots were taking over the world, and they were using the internet to communicate. They would learn at unprecedented rates because robots analyze situations and then try to determine the different options that they can select, and when one makes a right decision or a wrong one, the data is immediately uploaded to all the robots via the internet. Therefore, all the robots are learning from every other robot all the time."

"Cool dream, Emily," interjected Collin. "But artificially intelligent robots aren't that numerous at the present time. So, how will this help us now?"

"Well, I saw robots in my dream, but what if we used people instead?"

"People? Nice try, honey. How would we ever be able to control people's thoughts?" asked Hilary.

"I think she's on to something here," said Will. "What if we used a network of wires that were already in place to transmit our messages?"

"Like the electrical wires in everyone's home, Master Will?"

"Exactly what I was thinking, Jorge. There's two problems we need to solve though: how to amplify the signal and then how to tune it so people can pick it up telepathically without the need for any external devices."

∞

"Have a seat, Senator. This shouldn't take long," said another man in black as he gestured to a surprisingly archaic-looking metal chair in the cellular restructuring room.

Senator Parkinson, now totally overcome by fear, turned around quickly to try to run away but was met immediately with a punch to the stomach by the man in black that took him there, who then proceeded to pick up Parkinson as if he were weightless and plunk him into the steel mesh chair.

"You!" said Parkinson as he looked at the man in black standing in front of the control console. "You're the guy we hired to finish off Dunitz!"

"That's correct, Senator. I was the fake cop, and I failed as you have failed, and for that we must become part of the program. Although, I went the easy way like your compatriot, Smith. You, on the other hand, are in for a far more painful journey."

Defiant to the end, Parkinson began to yell, "I'm a United States senator..." The man in black emotionlessly hit the switch on the control panel and watched as the senator's body began shaking at first, then slowly dissolved, as if dunked in acid, and was sucked into the very mesh of the chair.

"Ahhhhhhhh!" Parkinson let out a blood-curdling scream at the top of his lungs as he writhed in pain. Every cell in his body felt like it was imploding, like the death of a star in a faraway galaxy, only to become a black hole.

Within a few minutes Parkinson began to reform in the chair, a newer, fitter version of himself, dressed exactly like the others.

"How do you feel, Agent Parkinson?" asked the man in black.

Parkinson rose from the chair with purpose. "I feel like a new man!" he said with a slight smirk.

"Indeed," added the man in black. "Shall we go to the transference room? Your friend should be done by now."

"Yes, let us," responded Agent Parkinson.

The new Smith was waiting for them outside the transference room as the man in black and Agent Parkinson walked up.

"Agent Smith, you're looking well," said Parkinson.

"Never felt better, Agent Parkinson. How was the cell restructuring?"

Parkinson looked down at the floor and let out a low grunt as the remnants of the memory of his restructuring passed before his eyes. "Just fine, Agent Smith," he said as the programming took over once again.

"Excellent! I enjoyed my transference immensely," added Smith.

"Let us reunite with Agent Jones," said the man in black as he started to walk down the corridor.

"Ah, we meet again!" said Agent Jones in a friendly tone. "How was your trip?"

"It was excellent," said Parkinson and Smith simultaneously.

"Good, glad to hear that. What's their status?" asked Jones now looking at the man in black.

"Agent Parkinson has accepted his restructuring and is running at a normal level," began the man in black. "Agent Smith, on the other hand, has shown extremely high levels of both processor speed and physical strength and endurance."

"Well, well, well," said Jones as he walked up to, and around, Smith. "Seems like you're a real firecracker, Agent Smith. In no small part due to your police and detective training I'm sure. We've never assimilated someone like yourself before. Interesting."

"Hogsworth!" yelled Jones as he walked back and stood behind his desk.

The man in black stood quickly to attention.

"Agent Hogsworth," began Jones in a much softer tone now. "I'd like you to keep a copy of Agent Smith's program and install it in every clone from now on, understand?"

"Already done, sir. I anticipated that you might find it interesting."

"Well done, Hogsworth. Now get out of my sight, all three of you!"

An army of Agent Smiths, thought Jones. We could easily crush the human race with them. And perhaps even take over this world for ourselves.

Suddenly Jones buckled over and fell to the ground, grabbing both sides of his head. He knew the Cronks had heard what he was thinking, and this was his punishment. It had happened before, and he thought it would soon let up, but this time the frequency just kept increasing until there was nothing but a combination of blood and thermal fluid where his head had been.

"Agent Smith, you are now in charge!"

The message from the Cronks was broadcast to all the agents simultaneously, and they instantly now recognized Smith as their leader.

Agent Smith walked into the room and stood behind the desk, watching as the remnants of Jones's android form dissolved.

"Agent Hogsworth!" yelled Smith.

"Yes sir?"

"Ready the transference machine with my program and begin manually reprogramming all the existing agents to my program, except yourself and Agent Parkinson. You will remain here with me when we go on the offensive."

"On my way," said Hogsworth as he turned and walked out of the room.

∞

Karl looked at the Space Tube and then back at Anika.

I don't want to leave you, Mom. It just feels so nice to be reunited with you after all these years.

I understand, son, I feel it too, but you have the chance to be such a difference maker in people's lives. The third dimension needs your help. Go to them, love them. Show them that there's more out there than they know.

Once again, my dear wise mother, you are right. It's time to go.

Karl tried to approach Anika and feel her energy, but as they touched she was pushed farther away by his energy instead of being attracted to it.

Go now, my son. We will meet again, and it will be oh-so glorious!

Karl new his mother spoke the truth as he moved into the Space Tube. In an instant he was gone. Blinding flashes of light came and went as he traveled up and down, left then right. He had forgotten what a fun ride this was.

Yee-haw! thought Karl. *Third dimension here I come!*

Wait a minute, what was I supposed to remember? Oh yeah, think loving thoughts and stop the ride as soon as I feel them being returned, and keep repeating Aham Brahmasmi, I am the Universe, Aham Brahmasmi, I am the Universe.

Karl kept repeating the sacred Sanskrit words and thinking loving thoughts, but the ride just kept on going, up and down and all around, as if he just couldn't find a match.

I wonder if there's not much love in what's left of the third dimension. This may prove to be a difficult mission.

Suddenly Karl felt the ride slowing and then stop. He started to feel a little tingly inside and then again, and again, and again.

I think I'm dividing. I'm the fertilized egg dividing. Yes! I've found a new home! This is it, I'm starting to lose my awareness. My frequency is slowing down. I'm becoming human once again.

Soon Karl felt himself floating in the amniotic fluid that was to be his home for the next nine months.

Chapter Twenty-Seven

"Will. Will, wake up!"

Will had decided he needed to take a much-needed nap and had only been sleeping for twenty minutes when Collin came to wake him.

"What? Collin, what's so important? I'm trying to grab a few winks here," said Will as he rubbed his eyes and hoped this had all been some sort of bad dream.

"I think I figured it out!" answered Collin excitedly.

"Figured what out?"

"How to distribute the message to the public without anyone realizing it."

"Really? You have an idea?"

"I have more than that, my friend. I have a solution. Well, solutions really because there's more than one, but you get the point."

"Wonderful!" began Will. "Let me splash some water on my face, and I'll meet you downstairs."

"I'll need you to come to the electrical generator room. Do you know where that is?"

"No, I have no idea."

"It's in the basement. I'll tell Clara to wait for you."

"OK, see you in a few minutes, and Collin?"

"Yeeees," said Collin in a rising tone as he turned around slowly. "Great work, buddy."

"Oh, you ain't seen nothin' yet!"

With that Collin turned around quickly and left the room.

I wonder what he found? thought Will. I guess I'll soon find out.

Will walked into the main lab area to find Clara waiting for him.

"There you are!" said Clara. "Made you a coffee."

"Thank you, that was very kind of you."

Clara just smiled and handed Will the coffee as she gestured for him to follow her.

Will followed Clara dutifully down a corridor lined with red lights running along the ceiling that led to a circular steel staircase. It seemed as if the staircase would never end as Clara led Will lower and lower into the facility. The handrail was so low it seemed to be falling away from him as he descended. Plus, he had to concentrate on what he was doing so he had precious little time to admire Clara's fine form.

"Wow, that was some staircase!" blurted out Will when they finally hit bottom.

"Five stories down. Years ago, this used to be part of an old copper mine, so it was relatively easy to retrofit it for our use," said Clara as she turned her head to look at Will. "You men are all the same," she said laughing as she caught Will staring.

"What? I was looking at the floor trying not to spill my coffee," he offered.

"It's in a travel mug!"

Will conceded that he had been caught staring and didn't offer any more excuses.

"Here we are." Clara turned around to face Will with her back to the electrical generator room door. "Just a warning: this is Collin's domain and when he explains how things work, he often starts to geek out and go a little overboard with the explanation. We've all been trained how to run the equipment, but most of what you are about to see is Collin's brainchild, so, treat it with a little respect."

Will found himself face-to-face with Clara with their bodies just barely touching.

"I just wanted..."

"Shhhh," said Clara as she held her finger to Will's lips. "Can you feel the electricity?"

"Feel it? I'm generating it!"

Clara let her finger brush across Will's lips as she simultaneously turned the doorknob behind her and let herself fall into the room.

"Come on!" said Clara as she motioned playfully with her arm for him to follow.

Will felt tingly all over and had to give his body a quick shake to release the tension.

"I'm coming, I'm coming. Give me a second, would you?"

Will walked through the door and heard it close behind him at the same time he heard Collin's excited voice.

"Clara, Will, I'm glad you're here. I was just about to start without you since the others had so many questions."

Will looked around the room and made eye contact and smiled with all the others.

"OK, let's get started! Will, you had told us we needed a way to amplify and then broadcast a signal that could be picked up telepathically. Well, I think I have the solution."

"I know you're supersmart, honey," began Hilary, "but to pick up a signal telepathically, that's a tall order."

"I thought so too, Hilary, but hear me out. As you know we use a lot of devices here based on Nikola Tesla's findings years ago. We use a version of his free energy generator to generate our electricity and a version of his Tesla turbine to distribute the water, then solar panels to heat the water and heat exchangers to recover the unused heat in our wastewater."

"We know all that, Collin, get to the point," said Frank exasperatingly.

"And we do all this," continued Collin without acknowledging Frank's comment, "because we need to stay off the grid so no one knows we're here, but here's the part that really intrigued me because I knew we could amplify and send a signal, but how do we send it without anyone knowing we're sending it? So, here comes the fun part!" said Collin excitedly as he rubbed his hands together. "We already have a version of Tesla's type-two coil that we have hooked up to our backup generator. Now, this coil is grounded to the water main system, which in turn is grounded to the earth. But what's unusual about the earth around here? That's right, it's filled with copper! We have two of nature's greatest conductors right here under our feet! Water and copper."

"We're following you, Mr. Collin, but how does that become useful for signal transmission?" asked Jorge.

"Tesla and others had proven that we can transmit power by creating standing waves in the earth by charging the earth with an electrical oscillator, which our type-two-designed backup generator is. That would make the earth vibrate electrically in the same way a bell vibrates mechanically when you hit it with a hammer. Normally this would require huge amounts of power, which we don't have, but because our earth is already superconductive and we have access to earth water as well as all the surrounding water mains, we won't need that much power to make it all work. But what's really exciting, and are you all ready for this?" said Collin as if he was a small boy putting on a magic show. "It's not electricity that we'll be sending out into the ground and into the water supply of people everywhere. It's knowledge, intelligence, and spiritual power. And distance will mean nothing! This discrete signal will be heard by everyone!"

"I'm loving it!" said Will enthusiastically. "But how do we change the electrical waves into waves that can be communicated, received, and understood."

"I thought you'd never ask! Well, I guess it goes back to my days as a musician..."

"Oh boy, here we go. The musician stories," said Frank sarcastically.

"As I was saying," continued Collin as he shot Frank a look of disdain, "when I was a musician and a budding electrical geek, I used to play around with a solid-state Tesla coil and a disruptor."

Collin pause for a second and saw everyone just look at each other and shrug their shoulders.

"Anyway, I was trying to make a keyboard or a guitar play its sound through solid-state circuitry and convert it to not only sound but to blinding flashes of electrical light, which I could later make into weird colors by adding different types of salts and minerals, but I digress. The point is that any sound-generating device can be hooked up to a zero-crossing detector, or 'disruptor' as we call it.

"What happens is, when the voltage generated by the audio signal crosses the zero point between negative and positive, which is that flat line in the middle of a sine wave on an oscilloscope, it sends a signal to the disruptor, which converts that analog signal into a digital signal of on or off, or a zero or one. This then sends a flash of light through the fiber-optic cable, which is received by a fiber-optic receiver, which in turn converts the optical signal back into a digital signal again. This on or off, zero or one, digital signal then goes through a solid-state device, thus avoiding a dangerous spark gap, which is inherent in all original Tesla coils and alters the resonance or frequency of the emitted signal to the coil.

"So, a low-frequency tone crosses the zero point less often giving less frequent light pulses, and a high-frequency tone crosses the zero point much quicker so more pulses or flashes of light are emitted. This allows us to vary the frequency or sound generated to our liking. We could play a single note or a song, say one word or a paragraph—it doesn't matter. We have control of what we want to send out there. Also, since there is no direct electrical connection, only fiber-optic cable between the sound-generating device and the output coil, or in this case the backup generator, it's absolutely safe to use."

"And by any sound-generating device, does that include a microphone?" asked Will.

"It sure does!"

"And what about interfacing with the internet?" asked Emily

"Well, we have to be able to tune the input to the correct frequency, and we have to do that through a computer, so my plan was to simultaneously transmit the same signal over every Wi-Fi transmitter out there."

"But what about the individual password and lockout features of the Wi-Fi systems?"

"Oh yeah, I forgot to tell you guys the best part! The frequency we will be transmitting at will be at the same frequency in which the earth is vibrating, so it will be undetectable and totally naturally assimilated by everyone on earth without them even knowing!"

"Holy shit, Collin. You're a fricking genius!" said Frank enthusiastically.

"Coming from you, my skeptical friend, I'll take that as a compliment!"

"I concur with Mr. Frank; however, do we really know what frequency the earth is vibrating at, Mr. Collin?"

"Well, that's the tricky part, Jorge. I haven't figured that out yet."

"I take my genius comment back!" said Frank quickly.

"I'll figure it out, don't worry. I just need a little time."

"This is huge, Will," said Emily, seemingly not to have paid attention to the last part of the conversation. "If we can broadcast a signal of love and peace over the internet, that it doesn't even realize is there, it will eventually adopt it into its own design paradigm, forcing it to perpetuate no matter what anyone does in the future. Plus, if you combine that with being able to send a signal to everyone on the earth, through the earth, there won't be anyone that we can't reach. Not like last time when we were only able to save three billion people!"

Emily stopped speaking and heard nothing but dead silence.

You said that last part out loud, dear one, communicated Jorge.

"Last time?" asked Frank.

"I mean, the last time I did an estimate of active internet penetration anyway."

"I see," said Frank.

Nice save, Miss Emily.

Thank you.

"Why do you think it's so important for the internet to adopt the signal into its design and layers, Miss Emily?" asked Jorge to keep the conversation going.

"I have a confession to make. Remember the dream I told you I had about the artificially intelligent robots?"

"Yeah, we remember," said Collin.

"Well, I did have a dream, but it was more like a nightmare because it's already a reality."

"What are you talking about, honey?" asked Hilary.

"During my many forays into the dark and hidden side of the internet, the ones that got me fired from the school system, I found conclusive evidence that the government, or at least it looked as if it was the government, already possess an army of AI robots that will be controlled via a signal from the internet."

"Holy crap! An army of robots willing to do anything they're told without any empathy for anyone or anything," said Clara.

"Sounds just like the Navy SEALs," added Collin laughing to himself.

"Easy now, computer boy," said Frank in a monotone.

"As I said earlier," began Emily, "the internet is already 'aware' of itself, and it could, as time passes, actually take control of this army of robots and do with them as it pleases."

"You mean, AI in control of AI?" asked Clara.

"That's exactly what I mean. And who knows how that will play out. It could mean the end of the human race if we are viewed as an unnecessary element. Or perhaps we'll just be their slaves. We have no idea. It all hinges on if the AI on the internet will be benign or wreak havoc since it will be the controlling force."

"You're looking at this from a whole different perspective, aren't you?" asked Will.

"The internet is out of control, Will. No matter what people, government, or anyone else does, it will continue to propagate. There's no doubt we will have a revolution, both technologically and theologically, and it will center around the internet and our ability to create machines that think for us. In fact, we could be due for another shift in our beliefs and morals and what we believe the definition of being a human actually is. We will need to reinvent right and wrong, how we trust each other, and what we can expect from each other.

"It will be a highly creative time in human history, and not just technologically, but morally and culturally. One day the internet will evolve and be invisible just like the hydro wires in our homes now, and a grid could be developed where technology becomes imbedded into everything we do. You walk into a room and the room recognizes you and adjusts everything to your preferences. Schools as we know them would not exist. The information our kids receive in one year will be learned in a day on the internet. The times we are experiencing now will be referred to as the 'digital dark age' because so much will happen so quickly, and ultimately all the records will be lost or destroyed so future generations will think everything has always been this way."

"Wait a minute, aren't you going a little far with that last one, honey?" asked Hilary.

"Really? What about the records of how the pyramids were built, Atlantis, Mayan civilizations, Stonehenge, Easter Island, need I go on?"

"You're right, Miss Emily. Most of today's children believe things have always been this way, especially with the internet. Most people can't remember or even want to envision a life without it," added Jorge.

"You've really given this a lot of thought, haven't you?" asked Will.

"Yes, I have, and that's why I feel this could be so huge, so future changing. If the internet can adopt an overall message of love over hate, it will be a benign entity, and we could finally live in a world without competition, ego, countries, or borders. There would be no need for them because as generations changed and the old ways were forgotten, society could be raised and function in a whole new way with love, kindness, compassion, and empathy at its core."

"Wow, you're starting to sound a lot like Karl now!" said Will.

"Well, as I mentioned before, we go way back."

"OK, show's over, folks," started Collin. "Everyone out of my space so I can figure out what frequency we need to make this whole thing work."

"You heard the man, let's get back to work!" reiterated Will.

"Jorge, have you got a second?" asked Frank as he walked up to Jorge.

"Of course, Mr. Frank."

Frank leaned in close to Jorge and half whispered. "What's with the telepathic communication with Emily? Is she already part of this somehow?"

"Mr. Frank, you surprise me with your perception of my communication with Miss Emily."

"Karl did train me on how to utilize it, but I'm much better at receiving than sending."

"So, you've heard everything we've ever discussed telepathically, Mr. Frank?"

"Don't get your panties in a bunch, Jorge; it just comes to me in jumbles and I then try to make sense of it."

"That is good. Then you won't know all the bad things we said about you for the last few years!"

"Ha-ha, very funny! Now tell me about Emily."

"Emily was with Mr. Karl and me in our last lifetime in the third dimension. Mr. Karl was someone not unlike yourself, I was a scientist, and Miss Emily was a young woman named Simone."

"Really, Jorge, you actually believe you were all together in your last life?"

"No, Mr. Frank, I don't believe it, I know it!" said Jorge emphatically. "And you believing it or not will not change that, but it will help things progress here."

"Sorry, Jorge, I meant no offence. I realize there are things that have happened, and will continue to happen, that I don't understand. I apologize, and please carry on with your explanation."

"Miss Emily, or Simone as she was called in her last life, was chosen from many dimensions throughout the universe as 'the one.' She possessed powers of clarity that were unparalleled. And for that reason, we used her as a human conduit to transfer energy from the universe to mankind via others like her and the internet."

"What? You used her as a conductor of universal energy? Didn't that destroy her?"

"Yes, but only her physical form. In the end she was released to join us and three billion other humans in making the quantum jump to the next level of consciousness."

"And she just happened to find her way here in this lifetime with you and Karl."

"Yes, Mr. Frank. Along with Miss Sabrina."

"Sabrina was in on this too!"

"Yes, but she refused to accept it until the very end when Karl was in hospital."

"Holy crap! Who was *she* in Karl's former life."

"She was called Sara, and she was Karl's nemesis, but in that lifetime, Karl was known as Wayne."

"In what way was she his nemesis, Jorge?"

"They were lovers, but at odds almost all of the time. In fact, she tried to kill him."

"Similar to their relationship here, then, except maybe the killing part. Is that something that repeats itself?"

"Yes, Mr. Frank. We tend to gravitate to each other in lifetime after lifetime. That is, of course, if we can find each other again. Sometimes we can't find each other, and we spend our lives searching. Searching for something we can't understand. But yet we search, hoping to find whatever it is that will complete us. I have no doubt they will reunite in their next lifetimes."

"That's pretty heady stuff, Jorge."

"Not once you believe, Mr. Frank. It's just recognizing and allowing what is."

"So, when Emily says she knew Karl from way back, she's not kidding!"

"That's right, Mr. Frank, and for that reason we must take heed of her message and allow her to express her intuition of what will happen in the future."

"I get it, Jorge. In other words, cut her some slack."

"Well said, Mr. Frank."

"Hey!" shouted Collin looking in their direction. "Did you guys not get the message? Scram so I can think!"

Frank glanced at Jorge with a look of understanding then turned to face Collin. "We're going, we're going, computer boy. Cut us some slack, will ya!" Frank looked back at Jorge with a wry smile as he led the way out of the generator room.

Chapter Twenty-Eight

Agent Smith stood behind his desk, arms crossed, waiting for Agent Hogsworth to appear.

"Agent Hogsworth reporting, sir."

"Finally! I sent for you minutes ago."

"Sorry, sir, I was just completing the final reprogramming."

"So, all the agents have been individually reprogrammed to my specifications?"

"Yes sir. All programming is fully complete."

"Well done, Hogsworth."

"Thank you, sir. I was wondering if perhaps you could bestow upon me the honor of leading the attack on the humans."

"No. You and Parkinson will remain here with me. I will require your assistance with a couple of matters."

"You're not expecting much resistance from those weak humans, are you, sir?"

"Never underestimate your enemy, Hogsworth. Never underestimate your enemy," repeated Smith in a quieter tone to himself as he turned to face the gray wall behind him.

"When will the attack begin?" asked Hogsworth.

"We must wait for word from the Cronks. When the time is right, we will be ready. Now leave me and send in Agent Parkinson."

"Right away, sir."

"Agent Parkinson reporting, sir"

"Parkinson! Good to see you. How are you adjusting to your new form?"

"Very well, sir. Never felt better."

"Good, very good. I wanted to talk to you about your son, Will."

Parkinson felt a strange but familiar feeling course through his system that he hadn't felt since he was assimilated. He recognized it now. It was guilt.

"Parkinson!" shouted Smith.

"Ah, yes sir."

"What were you doing?"

"I'm not sure what you mean, sir."

"You were just standing there, eyes and hands twitching."

"I apologize, sir. It must have been a remnant of a human memory when you mentioned my son's name."

"Perhaps I should have you reprogrammed to my specifications as well."

"Whatever you wish, sir."

"No, I need someone with a different perspective to help me coordinate the attack on the humans."

"I'm sure it was nothing and it won't happen again, sir."

"Good, because I will need you to do something special for me."

"Of course, sir. How can I help?"

"The Cronks' plan is to not destroy all the humans, but to merely cull the herd, so to speak. Bring them down from eight billion to a much more manageable four billion. But there's a problem. Your son has taken over for Karl Dunitz and is planning some sort of offensive of his own. If they are successful in converting the majority of humans into adopting feelings of kindness, compassion, and love, then the earth will change its vibrational frequency, which could then be high enough to not allow the Cronks to exercise their mind control."

"That would not be good, sir."

"No, it would not. It has already risen from 8 hertz to 32 hertz under Dunitz, so we can't afford for it to rise any more."

"I sense you have a plan."

"Yes. Once we attack I will bring your son, Will, here, and I want you to torture and kill him while we broadcast the show to all the human media channels. They need to see that their future is lost. That there is no way it will ever change, to accept their fate, and to go back to their brain-dead consumer ways."

"You want me to kill my own son?"

"Yes. It must be done."

Parkinson's hands began to twitch again, but he was able to control it this time.

"What about the law of universal free will? Are the Cronks not allowed to interfere with other societies' right to free will?"

Suddenly Parkinson fell to his knees with his hands on either side of his head. The pain was unbearable. And then as quickly as it had started, it was over.

"The Cronks are always listening, my friend. There will only be one more warning, and then you will end up like Agent Jones."

"Yes sir, I did not mean to question them," said Parkinson as he rose from his knees. "I was merely seeking clarification on universal free will, as it is written in the code of *The Process* that any interference in intergalactic free will can result in banishment to the zone of neutrality."

"You have read *The Process*?" asked Smith.

"Yes sir. I scanned over it while Agent Hogsworth was completing the reprogramming."

"Then you know much about the universal code, but the Cronks will never be seen as violating *The Process* because they plan to introduce a virus from another planet that will do most of the killing for them. If anything, any interference will be seen as trying to save the human species."

"Ah, very well then. I should have known all was well in hand."

"Now go, I've told you too much already. I wanted to make sure you could handle killing your son."

"Not a problem, sir. All your orders will be carried out to the letter."

Agent Parkinson turned and walked out of Smith's office and was able to hold himself together until he left the room.

I must get ahold of myself, thought Parkinson. But these human feelings keep shooting through my system.

Parkinson leaned back against the wall until his eyes and hands stopped twitching, then turned to his left and continued down the corridor with the faint smell of blood and burnt thermal fluid trailing behind him.

∞

"I've got it!" yelled Collin. "I flippin' got it!"

Collin hurried over to the console, pressed the All button on the radio, picked up the mic, and then transmitted over all the speakers in the building.

"Guys, hey guys! Get your asses down to the generator room; I think I figured it out, over." Collin was never sure how radio protocol worked.

Clara looked at the others in the control room and keyed the mic. "We'll be right down, Collin."

As everyone made their way to the generator room once again, there was an air of excitement. If Collin had actually figured out how to transmit at the earth's frequency, it could change everyone's life forever.

"OK, we're all here; show us what you got, big boy!" said Frank.

"Well, as some of you may know, for many years the earth's vibrational frequency has been very stable at around 8 hertz, actually more correctly 7.83 hertz, but it has been slowly rising, and in fact, there have been recent spikes to over 30 hertz."

"So, does this mean we are speeding up?" asked Emily.

"Actually, it does, but there's more to it than that. The earth's vibrational frequency is said to be in tune with the human brain's alpha and theta states, and this acceleration may be why it often feels like time has sped up and events and changes in our lives are happening more rapidly now, because they are. These new, higher resonances are naturally correlated to human brain-wave activity, so as the earth's frequency changes, so does the frequency of our brain waves, and as our brain waves change in frequency, so does the earth's. It's all interconnected.

"A 7.83 hertz frequency is an alpha-theta state. Relaxed, yet dreamy—sort of a neutral idling state waiting for something to happen. An 8.5 to 16.5 hertz frequency moves one out of the theta range into more of a full, calmer alpha state with faster more alert beta frequencies starting to appear. Since this seemed all very interesting, I started to look into it a bit more. Turns out that in neurofeedback, a range of 12 to 15 hertz is called 'sensory-motor rhythm' frequency, or SMR. It is an ideal state of awakened calm. Our thought processes are clearer and more focused, yet we are still 'in the flow' or 'in the know.' In other words, mother earth is shifting her vibrational frequency and so are we. This may be one of the first conclusive signs that we are awakening."

"That's very interesting, Mr. Collin," began Jorge. "My grandfather told me that the belief of his forefathers was that the earth's magnetic field, which can affect the earth's resonance, has been slowly weakening for the past two thousand years. He wasn't sure why but said it would eventually change the world. And he was once told by an old sage that the magnetic field of the earth was put in place by the Ancient Ones to block our primordial memories of our true heritage. This was so that souls could learn from the experience of free will unhampered by memories of the past. He claimed that the magnetic field changes are now loosening those memory blocks. That the earth's magnetic field and its vibrational field work together."

"Makes total sense, Jorge."

"OK, this is all well and good, but have you found a way to transmit our message?" asked Frank.

"Always the impatient one, huh, Frankie."

"Get on with it, computer boy."

"To answer your question, yes, I have."

Everyone let out a huge sigh followed by high fives and celebratory woo-hoos.

"Let me explain how I did it."

"Oh god, here we go again," said Hilary as she rolled her eyes.

"I knew that I wouldn't have enough adjustment in the digital portion of the receiver, so I had to do something with the physical makeup of the actual coils on the generator itself. I added a connection on each primary winding, which allowed me to make small adjustments in the capacitance. Now this adjustment is purely manual, so it has to be constantly monitored and adjusted accordingly, and it should have no problem taking the strain these signals produce.

"The other change I had to make was in the frequency receiver. As I mentioned before, it doesn't possess the range we needed, so I wired it up to my computer's sound card, which is basically an analog-to-digital converter itself, and was able to produce a digital representation of the variation of the signal at its output. Now, for the master stroke! I was able to send this digital signal to the hard drive of my computer, where it can play in a never-ending, constantly self-adjusting loop."

"You're a freaking genius!" yelled Will.

"Yes, well, not really, just a nerdy, geeky guy, but thanks for the compliment!"

"Frank leaned over and gave Collin a huge hug from behind."

"So, this is all a go then?" asked Emily

"Yes, it is, but remember, the coils need constant adjustment to ensure the frequency remains where it needs to be."

"Which means someone has to be here in the generator room all the time to adjust it, right?" asked Emily.

"It's more like synchronizing. Actually, we're very lucky that this area was previously a copper mine in that there were sensors planted here to continuously monitor the resonant frequencies in the earth's magnetic field. They track changes in geomagnetic activity caused by solar storms and changes in solar wind speed, therefore allowing us immediate access to any change in the earth's frequency."

"Why did they install those sensors in a mine?" asked Will.

"To help them detect how much iron is in the surrounding rock, because they wanted copper, not iron, and to help warn of any impending danger of a mine collapse."

"Works for me!" interrupted Frank. "So, we're good to go then?"

"Well, yes, but someone will have to manually match the output coil frequency of the standby generator to the frequency we detect from the sensors, which will ensure the message we impart into the system will be transmitted at the correct frequency and resonance."

"How will we know how to set the output coil, Mr. Collin?"

"Don't worry, Jorge. I'll hook up a rheostat for adjustment and a nice large digital display."

"That would be wonderful, Mr. Collin. I would like to volunteer to be the first frequency adjuster!"

"Sounds good, Jorge, but I'll have to do it at first until I'm confident all is copacetic."

"And once we begin transmitting our message," began Emily, "people will start to change their online habits and searches, resulting in the internet changing the way it is constructing its layers of artificial intelligence. Boy, the earth is in for a doozy of a change!"

"It sure is, honey," added Hilary. "And I'm just proud and happy to be a part of it. Karl would be impressed!"

"Amen to that!" said Frank and Clara almost simultaneously.

"Excellent work, Collin. When can we begin transmitting?" asked Will.

"By the time you guys have decided what you want to say and have it recorded, I should have this all ready to go."

"Wonderful, there's no time to waste."

∞

Agent Hogsworth walked into Smith's office with his head hung low.

"What do you want, Hogsworth?"

"I have failed you."

"How is that?"

"There is one last agent, Agent Bennet, that has not been reprogrammed to your specifications."

"You told me that all had been completed."

"Yes sir, and for that reason I have failed you and await my punishment."

"Why was he not reprogrammed?"

"He was late arriving back to base after his attempt to finish off the boy."

"Then it was not your fault, Hogsworth."

"Yes, but I should have realized he was not here yet."

"Be that as it may, you are forgiven. Now send in Agent Bennet."

"Yes sir. Thank you, sir!"

Agent Bennet strolled into Smith's office and stood two feet from Smith's desk.

"Where's Jones?" asked Bennet demandingly.

"That is none of your concern, Agent Bennet. My name is Smith and you will follow me now."

"Well, until I find out what happened to Jones, I won't be following anyone!"

"Did you not receive the download from the Cronks?"

"I got something, but it was all garbled. Must have been while I was in the chopper trying to complete my mission."

"And why were you not successful?"

"Because of the idiot human pilot I had. He couldn't hold that chopper straight long enough for me to get a decent shot."

"Do you make a habit of blaming others for your lack of production?"

"Listen, you pile of wires and hydraulic fluid..."

Agent Bennet buckled over in pain and writhed on the floor holding each side of his head until the pain stopped.

"You know how this works, Bennet. Do what you're told or cease to exist. It's as simple as that."

Bennet struggled to his knees and attempted to stand, but fell once more. "I told you, I want to know what happened to Agent Jones," he managed from the floor.

"Agent Jones was assimilated back into the Cronks' network and no longer exists. I am his replacement and have ordered all agents to be reprogrammed to my specifications."

"The hell I will! I can barely stand the programming I have now."

"You are no longer human, Agent Bennet, although it appears much of your human programming remains. Too bad since I see a lot of me in you. Hogsworth!"

"Yes sir?" said Hogsworth after entering the room and standing at attention.

"Take Agent Bennet to the reprogramming room and run the program twice to ensure we don't leave any of the old Bennet behind."

"Yes sir."

"Touch me and I'll pull your plug, you cybernetic freak!"

Agent Bennet curled into the fetal position with the onslaught of another round of pain, then suddenly lay still.

"Has he been assimilated by the Cronks?" asked Hogsworth.

"No, just temporarily deactivated. Get Parkinson to give you a hand getting him to the reprogramming room, and don't mess this up, Hogsworth; it's your chance for redemption."

"Of course, sir. Thank you, sir."

Chapter Twenty-Nine

After two hours of deliberation and throwing around different words and phrases, they had still not reached a consensus on what message to send to the world. Will suddenly heard a slight buzzing sound and then had a thought.

"What if we just say one word: love? I know it sounds cheesy, but hear me out. If we draw the word out a bit and say, 'looooove,' then the 'o' starts to sound like *ah*, and *ah* is the sound inherent in the names all the wisdom traditions have given to their creators."

"I'm not so sure of that," said Clara.

"I'll give you some examples: Allah, Jehovah, Yahweh, Elah, Kali Durga, Raah, and the list goes on and on. It's the only sound you can make when you open your mouth and not use your lips or your tongue. Try it."

Everyone opened their mouths and made the sound of *ah*, as Will chuckled to himself.

"What are you laughing at?" demanded Clara. "Is this some kind of joke?"

"No, no, not at all. But seeing you all sitting there openmouthed and making the sound of the lord just seemed a bit comical."

"Well, I'm glad we entertained you, but I think he has a point here," stated Emily. "Perhaps we should keep it as simple as possible, and he is right about the sound. It was a sound used by many ancient wisdom traditions throughout recorded history and probably before things were even recorded."

"What made you think of all this, honey?" asked Hilary.

"I don't really know. It just seemed to pop into my head, and it just felt…right."

"However you thought of it, nicely done, Will," said Emily.

"Thank you."

Will wasn't sure how he had thought of it but felt that buzzing sound had something to do with it. As he glanced over at Clara, she was looking at him with a look of pride and love. Far from the look of disdain she shot him earlier when he had first suggested his idea.

"What?" asked Will.

"There's just so much more to you than meets the eye, isn't there," said Clara in a soothing voice.

"A few weeks ago, I would have said no, but after meeting Karl, my whole life has changed."

"Karl changed all our lives, Will. That's why we're here."

"I know that, but I just feel it at such a deep level. And that sound."

"What sound."

"Didn't you hear it? It was a very mild buzzing sound, like a tiny mosquito."

"There are a lot of electronics here, Will, and almost all of them make some sort of humming or buzzing sound. Sometimes I think I hear things and I really don't. Happens to all of us."

"No, this wasn't like that."

"Well, whatever it was, I'm glad you heard it."

Will looked up at Clara who was now standing and winked. "Me too!"

∞

"OK, are we ready for testing?" asked Frank.

"We are good to go for a one-minute test," replied Collin. "Earth's frequency is currently at 32.8 hertz. Once we start, I'll adjust the output coils on the standby generator to the same frequency, and then the test can commence."

Everyone had gathered around in the generator room except for Clara. She wanted to do some surveillance scans while the tests were taking place to see if any wildlife or perhaps humans were affected.

"Will, all you have to do is hit Enter on the keyboard."

"Hit it now?"

"Hit it now, Will."

"Frank, when I tell you, I want you to throw the switch to the on position for the standby generator."

"Rodger that. Wait! Did you disconnect the standby generator from the lab's main electrical feed?"

"All taken care of, my friend. There should be no sparks or explosions when you flip the switch, but thanks for verifying. OK, looks like everything is powered up. Frank, throw the switch!"

Frank turned his body away from the switch box and moved the lever into the on position with his left hand.

"Nothing's happening!" said Frank as he climbed down the short ladder from the electrical area platform.

"Give it time, Frankie," said Collin as he adjusted the output frequency of the standby generator to 32.8 hertz.

There was a short period of nothingness, and then Collin could both feel and hear a low-frequency hum.

"That's it. It's working!" yelled Collin. "Are you transmitting the message, Will? Are the LEDs beside the optical cables blinking? How about the LEDs on the digital-analog converter?"

"Yes, yes, and yes," answered Will.

"OK then, let's continue past the one-minute mark, say to ten minutes."

"Sounds good," said Will.

"Are you sure?" asked Frank.

"Everything looks good. I'm monitoring the temperature of the coils as well, and they all look good. Let's see what it looks like in ten minutes."

Clara's sensors in the lab had picked up the vibrational signal right away, and she had confirmed that it was running at 32.8 hertz. She now busied herself with scanning the outside landscape for any sign of something different.

Ten minutes came and went uneventfully, and the system was shut down.

"Well, it works!" said Collin enthusiastically.

"It works experimentally, but does it really work?" asked Frank.

"How long do we have to transmit before people will start feeling a difference, Mr. Collin?" asked Jorge.

"I'm not sure, Jorge. I'm sure some people will feel it sooner than others, but it could be hours, days, weeks, I don't know. We're in uncharted territory here."

"Guys!" came the voice over the speakers in the generator room.

"Shouldn't that have been 'generator room, control room,'" answered Frank into the mic.

"Yeah, whatever," began Clara. "We have about...I count eight deer within one hundred meters of the tunnel. I haven't seen any deer here in months."

"What are they doing?" asked Frank over the woo-hoos in the background.

"Nothing really. They seem to be just milling about. They're starting to disperse now."

"Collin!" yelled Frank. "Fire that thing back up again, now!"

"Why?" asked Collin as he hadn't heard Clara's last transmission.

"Just do it!"

"OK. Will, hit Enter. And Frank, go ahead and throw the switch again."

Clara continued to watch the deer disperse, but as soon as her sensors picked up the vibrational frequency again, they started to return.

"The deer were leaving, but now they're coming back!" shouted Clara into the mic.

"Woo-hoo!" yelled Frank. "Now we know for sure that it works!"

"Should we leave it going?" asked Will.

"Why not?" chimed in Emily.

"Because I need to run some checks before we operate it twenty-four seven. That's why," answered Collin.

"OK, we better shut it down for now," agreed Will.

Frank threw the electrical disconnect into the off position, and Will clicked on the Stop Transmit button on the computer screen.

Everyone looked at each other and slowly gathered around the computer station.

"I can't believe it actually works!" blurted Hilary.

"What, no faith in my work," suggested Collin.

"I have faith in you, Collin, honey, I just didn't know if the principle was sound."

"Wow, the animals were affected almost right away," said Will.

"Yes, Master Will, but human animals are another kettle of fish."

Everyone looked at Jorge wondering why he chose that particular analogy.

"I am sorry, sometimes I don't get all the English sayings correct."

"Not to worry, Jorge. We knew what you meant," said Will.

"What I meant to say," began Jorge, "is that all animals are much better in tune with the earth's frequencies than we humans."

"He's right," added Emily. "It could take weeks for any humans to feel anything at all."

"In that case, get those checks done as soon as you can, Collin, so we can go online twenty-four seven," said Frank.

"Got it. But I'm starting to get hungry, and I have to go to the bathroom," whined Collin.

"I'll fix you a sandwich and bring it down to you, but I can't help you with the other part, honey!" said Hilary.

"Why thank you, fair maiden. I shall return in a moment from the outhouse!"

Everyone had a much-needed laugh to release some of the built-up tension and then left the generator room to join Clara in the lab.

Chapter Thirty

Parkinson moved away from the opening to Smith's office, where he had been listening in on the conversation, to halfway down the hall and then quickly turned around to make it look like he was walking in that direction.

"Oh, there you are, Parkinson," said Hogsworth. "I was just about to page you. Agent Smith wants you to give me a hand bringing Agent Bennet to the reprogramming station."

"Of course. Who is this Agent Bennet? I thought we had reprogrammed all the agents?"

"Apparently not. Bennet has always been a bit of a lone wolf, so he didn't come into base very often. But he was one of our best agents."

"Was? Has he been assimilated?"

"No, just temporarily deactivated."

"By the Cronks, I assume. How are they able to control us so easily anyway?"

"An agent should not be wondering those types of things, Agent Parkinson."

"Of course, I understand. Just curious."

"We all have an ECU implanted at the base of our skull, which is hooked to both our brain and spinal column. That's why we feel their corrective pain shocks so powerfully and quickly."

"What's an 'ECU'?"

"Electronic control unit. We're half human, half machine. We still utilize our human brain, spine, bones, and muscles, but most of it is all controlled by the ECU. We retain our brains because we need the ability to make conscious decisions quickly, and no matter what the Cronks came up with, they could not find anything as adept at that as our human brains."

"That's why we still have human memory flashbacks, then"

"Are you having those? We should run you through the program again. You shouldn't be experiencing any remnants of human memory."

"Oh no, not anymore. I think I had one within the first hour of my reprogramming, but it was fleeting, and I haven't had any since."

"OK, that sounds like it's within allowable tolerances."

"We should get Bennet done now before Agent Smith asks about our progress. I don't want to feel the pain."

"Have you felt it before?"

"Yes, and I fear the next time will be my last."

"Why, what did you do?"

"Asked too many questions, like you. Now let's get on with it."

"Of course."

Agent Parkinson helped lift Bennet off the stretcher and onto the reprogramming table, strapping him down tightly to avoid any movement during the reprogramming process. Hogsworth carefully lifted the flaps of fake skin that covered the connection points to the main ECU at the base of Bennet's skull and connected the thirty-two-pin connector.

"All right, all hooked up. Let's light him up, shall we."

Agent Hogsworth pushed the power button, and the programming machine came to life, checking each system separately to ensure all was running correctly. Suddenly Agent Bennet stiffened and strained against his restraints, then totally relaxed.

"OK, he's been reactivated and ready for the new download."

"I've watched you reprogram all the agents, and I wonder, could we exist without a program in the ECU? What would happen if you wiped his old program and never installed a new one?"

"I'm not sure. I would suppose his brain might attempt to control the body on its own, but I don't think he would survive. He would need at least some sort of basic program."

"And we have such a program?"

"I'm not sure if I like the sound of some of your questions, Parkinson."

"I apologize, but this is the last agent we will program for a very long time, and I wanted to take advantage of the learning potential."

"Why are you so eager to learn? We should just be doing our jobs without question."

"And we will, but I have spent some time reading *The Process* and—"

"You've read *The Process*!" said Hogsworth in a forceful whisper as he leaned toward Parkinson.

"Yes, I have, and I learned about some of the universal codes that the Cronks are supposed to be abiding by, but aren't!"

"This is highly irregular! I must tell Agent Smith. Wait here, I will notify him about your transgressions, and he can decide what to do with you. I won't be a party to your disobedience!"

"Do what you must."

Agent Hogsworth quickly left the programming room to inform Smith.

Now, to install just the basic program in Bennet and make it look like I installed Smith's program, thought Parkinson.

As Parkinson installed the basic program, he spoke instructions into the microphone to manually alter portions of the program.

"You will remember your human identity. Orders from Agent Parkinson will supersede all other orders. You cannot terminate William Parkinson, nor yourself. You will resist the Cronks' attempts to punish you."

Agent Hogsworth returned to the programming room and slammed the door.

"Smith already knew you had read *The Process*! And now he's not happy with me because apparently you did it while we were reprogramming all the other agents."

"That's what I told him, yes."

As Parkinson was speaking, Hogsworth looked at the control panel because the "Program Installed" light was flashing.

"What have you done?" yelled Hogsworth.

"I told you, I read *The Process*."

"No, not that. You ran the program while I was gone."

"Oh that. Well I knew you were unsure of my dedication to our cause, so I decided to install Smith's program for you. And yes, I installed it twice."

"How do I know you have done it correctly?"

"I've watched you do over a thousand agents. I think I know what buttons to press."

"Perhaps I should run it again to be sure."

"Of course, if you wish, but check it yourself. You will see which program I installed."

Hogsworth's fingers typed furiously on the keyboard.

"But if I were you, I'd be reporting back to Smith as soon as possible to tell him that the programming is complete."

"OK, it looks like you installed the correct program. I'll go tell Agent Smith everything is complete."

As Hogsworth left the programming room, Parkinson leaned over to Bennet and whispered, "You will follow Agent Smith's orders until I tell you otherwise."

Agent Bennet's eyes snapped open. "Yes sir, Senator Parkinson."

Chapter Thirty-One

Collin pressed the transmit button on the mic and spoke.

"OK, guys, checks are complete, all looks good, and we're ready to transmit twenty-four seven."

Collin knew the proper radio protocol but had decided not to use it just to get under Frank's skin.

"I think you meant to say 'control room, generator room,' right, Collin? You must always say the place you are calling first, followed by the place from where you are calling from, then I could have answered with the place that I'm at. This way you would be sure you reached who and where you wanted, and I would know who was calling."

"Yessss!" said Collin to himself as he pumped his arm. "Got him!"

"But of course," continued Frank over the radio, "you already know radio protocol and just did that to get my goat. Sorry, you failed, computer boy!"

"Damn it! You're always one step ahead of me, Frankie."

"That's my job, Colleen!"

"Don't call me that, Frank! You know I don't like when you call me that."

"Oh, did I get your goat?"

"Damn it!" said Collin

"OK, I give up. Get your collective buns down here so we can start this sucker up. And tell Hilary to bring me another sandwich. That last one was deeelicious!"

"Roger wilco, out," said Frank using proper radio protocol.

Collin had a big smirk on his face although he wasn't really successful in getting a dig in with Frank.

He's always fun to play with, thought Collin. Now to check the earth's frequency before we start.

Frank led the rest of the crew through the door to the generator room and walked toward Collin.

"About time you guys got here; I'm getting hungry!"

"Yes, well, those stairs are a killer," offered Frank.

"Hilary," blurted Collin as he eyed Hilary up and down, "where's my sandwich?"

"I made you a sandwich already, honey."

"I know, but I told Frank to tell you to make me another because the first one was soooo delicious."

Hilary shot a look at Frank, and Frank just shrugged his shoulders.

"You never told her, did you, Frankie. That's just dirty pool, that's what that is! Depriving a starving man from a meal."

Frank walked over to Collin and put his arm around his shoulders. "I'm just looking after your waistline, brother!"

"The hell you are," said Collin as he shrugged off Frank's arm. "And you ain't my brother!"

"Are you guys done with the love fest over there, because we'd like to get this show on the road if possible," interjected Will.

Collin shot Frank a look of disdain while Frank crossed both arms over his belly and pretended to have a huge laugh.

"Anyway," began Collin, "I have some news for all of you."

"What is it, Mr. Collin?" asked Jorge.

"While checking the earth's frequency, I noticed that it has risen from 32.8 to 32.95 hertz."

"You don't think that just transmitting for ten minutes or so could have done that, do you?" asked Emily.

"It would be amazing if it has, but there are other forces at work here as well. There has been a recent rise in solar activity, and we all know solar flares affect the resonance of the earth, but I do believe we are moving in the right direction."

"Maybe it was the positive vibes coming from the deer!" laughed Frank.

Collin looked around at the others, and they all just shrugged their shoulders while smirking.

"Whatever it was, it sure has affected you!" said Collin.

"What do you mean?" asked Frank.

"You're so happy and giddy, not at all like Mr. Serious Special Forces guy."

"What, you don't like the new me?"

"I do, actually, as long as the old you shows up when we need to kick some butt."

"Butt, schmutt. It's all about love, brother."

"Okeydoke then," said Collin as he gave the others a look of 'this guy is off his rocker.' "Shall we get on with it? Will, open the program and click on the Start Transmission button."

"Oh, you installed a button to click instead of just hitting Enter.'"

"Yeah, I thought it made things a bit more professional."

"Frank, do you think you're still capable of engaging the electrical switch gear?"

"Absolutely, my friend!"

Collin waited a minute to allow Frank time to climb up to the electrical platform.

"OK, Will, click the Start Transmission button."

"Done."

"Frank, throw the switch to the on position."

As Frank threw the switch gear into place, he immediately started to feel the vibrations.

So glorious! thought Frank.

"Now to adjust the frequency of the coils to 32.95. Aaaaand, we're done. Up and transmitting!"

"Shall I take the first shift watching and then adjusting the frequency, Mr. Collin?" asked Jorge.

"Absolutely. All you have to do is match the two frequencies on the displays here. As one goes up, just turn this rheostat clockwise to adjust the output of the coils in the standby generator."

"Does this mean we have no standby power now, Mr. Collin?"

"Unfortunately, that's exactly what that means, Jorge"

"We still have the battery backup though, right?" asked Clara.

"Yes, we do, but that's only about an hour of power at best, and then there's nothing to charge them back up again either, but we're not on the grid, so there shouldn't be any power interruptions."

"Look at our Special Forces guy," said Hilary as she pointed toward Frank.

Frank was sitting on the edge of the electrical platform, feet dangling playfully over the edge, eyes closed, and humming to himself.

"It sure has affected Frank in a hurry," said Clara.

"Yes, it has," started Emily. "But as the frequency increases, there probably will be an increase in negative feelings as well."

"What do you mean? I thought this was going to make everyone have that loving feeling?" asked Will.

"It will, eventually, but as the frequency increases, there will be a time when our brains struggle to catch up, leading to restlessness, anxiety, and fear of what's happening to us."

"But this will pass, right, honey?" asked Hilary

"For most people, yes, but there might be some that will never get over their fear and fight to stay in a negative world."

"Well, it looks like we don't have to worry about Frank!" inserted Collin.

"I beg to differ," began Emily. "He seems very susceptible to the change in frequency, and he may just swing hard the other way for a while as well. We have to keep an eye on him."

"OK, Jorge, you've got the first watch. The rest of us will be in the lab area. And Hilary, could you please, oh please fix me another one of those scrumptious sandwiches when we get up there?" asked Collin.

"I guess you've earned it, honey. Frank! Oh, Frankie boy!" continued Hilary. "Come on, honey, I'll fix you a sandwich too!"

"On my way!" said Frank as he exuberantly jumped down from the electrical platform.

"Have I told you lately that I love you, Hilary?" said Frank as he nuzzled up to Hilary.

"No, you haven't, honey. But you can tell me again if you want!"

Hilary left the emergency generator room with her two men in tow while the others followed smiling and shaking their heads.

Chapter Thirty-Two

"What do you want, Hogsworth?" yelled Agent Smith.

"Sorry to interrupt you, sir. I just wanted to let you know that Agent Bennet's new programming has been installed and is running correctly."

"Perfect. Now leave me."

"Yes sir."

"Wait a minute," called Smith after Hogsworth. "Have you noticed Agent Parkinson acting a little strangely recently?"

"How do you mean, sir?" asked Hogsworth as he turned around.

"Have you noticed his hands or eyes twitching at all?"

"I can't say that I have, sir."

"He seemed to start twitching when I told him I wanted him to dispatch his son in front of the earth media channels."

"He did tell me he used to have some memory remnants, but they were all gone now," said Hogsworth.

"I want you to ask him some questions about his son, especially about killing him, and let me know how he reacts. We may need to install my program again."

"I will ask him, sir. Anything else?"

"Yes. Don't tell him I asked you to question him."

"No sir, of course not."

"And Hogsworth."

"Yes sir?"

"The Cronks have moved up their time line for administering the virus to the earthlings, so we don't want anything to screw this up."

"I understand, sir."

"Good. Now leave me."

Agent Hogsworth walked briskly back to the transference room to find Parkinson sitting in the chair where he left him and Bennet still laying on the reprogramming table.

"Agent Hogsworth, back so soon?"

"Yes. Agent Smith was delighted to hear that all the programming is complete."

"Excellent. Did he discuss our next move with you?"

"Yes. I mean, no, not really?"

"Well, which is it? Either he discussed it with you or he didn't."

"I apologize for my behavior, Parkinson. My program doesn't allow me to be deceptive. Agent Smith wants to know if you will be able to dispatch your son in front of the earth media channels."

"I told him I would," Parkinson could feel a buildup of pressure within his systems as he answered. "Was that his only concern?"

"No, the Cronks have moved up their time line for implanting the virus, so he doesn't want any screw-ups."

"And how will they deliver said virus?" The pressure within Parkinson's system was starting to overload his circuits.

"He didn't elaborate on that."

"I see," Parkinson could hardly hold back now. "Well, the next time you're talking with Agent Smith, you can tell him that I have no issues with whatever he wants me to do. We are all programmed to follow his instructions, after all."

"Yes, we are, aren't we?"

"In fact, why don't you report to him right now. I'm sure he's wondering."

"Yes, I'll do that."

As soon as Hogsworth had left the room, Parkinson doubled over and hit the floor, shaking and twitching violently.

Get ahold of yourself! thought Parkinson. You'll be reprogrammed if you keep this up!

The shaking soon stopped and only a few tremors remained from the twitching.

What did Hogsworth say? He wasn't programmed for deception. Of course, that's it! None of us are programmed to be deceptive, but my human memory as a senator was focused on deception. When I remember anything from my past, it conflicts with my programming, including my memories of Will, who I was always deceptive with. I was such a terrible father. I won't make that mistake again. I have to convince myself that whatever I say from now on is the truth. But how?

Parkinson searched his human and machine memory.

I was once told thoughts become things. Yes, that's it! The way we think causes the way we feel, which causes the way we act, which creates the results we get with our lives! OK, so if I believe that everything I think is the absolute truth, that will allow my systems to recognize this, which will allow me to act in a manner that is congruent with being an agent of the truth.

"I am an agent of truth, I am an agent of truth, I am an agent of truth…"

Agent Parkinson repeated this phrase over and over until it had become his programming mantra.

"I am an agent of truth, and everything I think and say resonates with truth!"

Hogsworth returned just as Parkinson sat back down in his chair.

"Well, what did Smith have to say?" asked Parkinson.

"He wants to see you."

"Me, why?"

"I don't know, it's not my place to ask."

"You're right. OK, I'll go."

"And he wants you to bring Agent Bennet with you."

Parkinson swallowed hard and then disconnected Bennet from the programming machine.

"Agent Bennet, can you hear me?" asked Parkinson.

"I hear you, Agent Parkinson. Good morning, Agent Hogsworth."

"You and I are going to see Agent Smith, let's go."

Parkinson turned to leave the transference room, and Bennet dutifully followed him out the door. Parkinson wasn't sure what Smith wanted but hoped that Bennet's basic programming would hold up under scrutiny.

"Agents Parkinson and Bennet reporting, sir," said Parkinson.

"Can Agent Bennet not speak for himself?" asked Smith.

"Of course I can, sir, but since my recent reprogramming, Agent Parkinson is senior to me, so it is customary to allow the senior agent to speak first."

"Very good, Bennet. You remember part of the original protocol that was part of the basic programming."

"How can we serve you, sir?" asked Parkinson, trying to get off the basic programming talk.

"Well, Parkinson, my concern is that you may have difficulty killing your son, and that will in no small part play a pivotal role in turning the humans around to our favor. They are ruled by their emotions and this false sense of hope they seem to have. Once they realize their leader is dead and the resistance is crushed, there will be no more of their senseless hope, and therefore their emotions will also be subdued. We don't want to kill all of them, just the ones that are starting to wake up and think for themselves. Are you following me?"

Agent Parkinson felt that Smith was seeing right through him and knew that he still had some human memories and emotions. Parkinson started to repeat his mantra in his head: I am an agent of truth, I am an agent of truth...

"I'm sorry you have lost faith in me, sir. But I can assure you I won't have an issue with any order you give me."

Smith stared at Parkinson for a long time, seemingly waiting for the twitching to start.

"My programming won't allow me to be deceptive, so you know I'm speaking the truth," continued Parkinson.

"That is true," said Smith finally. "But let's try something else. Bennet, grab Parkinson by the throat!"

"Agent Bennet swung around to his left and put both hands around Parkinson's throat."

"Crush him!" yelled Smith.

Parkinson's eyes grew large as Bennet began to squeeze his throat. Then his hands relaxed.

"I cannot terminate another agent or myself," said Bennet.

"Very good, Bennet. You have the basic programming down pat. The old Bennet would have crushed Parkinson's throat just for fun. It looks like you will both still be of service to me."

"When will the attack begin, sir?" asked Parkinson while rubbing his throat.

"Soon, Parkinson, very soon."

Chapter Thirty-Three

It had been almost eight hours since Jorge started his shift in the generator room, and he was starting to get annoyed with the constant drone of the emergency generator.

"How's it going down there, Jorge?" came over the main speakers in the generator room.

"I think I'm ready for my replacement," answered Jorge after fumbling with the mic.

"Emily is coming down to replace you in a few minutes. Any more adjustments needed?"

"No, Mr. Collin, just the one earlier. We are still running at 33 hertz."

"Cool. See you in a few minutes."

"It's taking a while, isn't it?" asked Clara.

"That's to be expected," said Emily. "It's like boiling water in a kettle. At first it seems like nothing is happening, but as the energy input stays constant, the electrons begin to move more rapidly, and then suddenly it starts to boil, seemingly out of nowhere."

"I hope you're right, honey," added Hilary.

"Of course, she's right, Hilary. She's a science major and a school principal. Neither of those two are ever wrong!" blurted Frank.

"I'm not sure how to take that, Frank."

"I'm just pulling your chain, Emily. I have a great deal of respect for you and, well, I love you," mused Frank.

"I love you too, Frank. But lay off the wisecracks, will you?"

"Well, it sure seems the animals like the new vibes," said Clara as she checked one of the outside cameras. "There's deer, groundhogs, and birds galore roaming around where we never saw them before."

"I hope it doesn't attract undue attention," said Frank.

"That's the first constructive thing you've said in the last ten hours, Frankie," said Collin.

"Lay off the Frankie a bit, would you, computer boy."

"He's back!"

"Hi Frank, my name is Will. Nice to meet you."

"What's up with that?" countered Frank.

"Let's just say you haven't quite been yourself for the last twelve hours or so."

"I don't know what you're talking about!" said Frank as he turned back to look at the monitor with Clara.

"Well, I'm going down to relieve Jorge. Anything in particular you want me to tell him?" asked Emily.

"Yes, actually," said Clara, "give him this schedule to put up down there."

"Oh, it looks like I only have a four-hour shift."

"I decided to change them to four instead of eight-hour shifts to try to make it more palatable. I'm sure being stuck down there for eight hours would seem awfully long."

"I see you separated the supper hours with two two-hour shifts."

"When I was in the naval reserves, that's what we did to ensure everyone got a chance to have a good meal. They called it the 'dogwatch.'"

"Really," began Emily. "I wonder why?"

"I don't know. I think it goes way back to the old English navy. You know, wooden sailing ships and stuff."

"Actually, there are a number of theories on how those watch periods got their name," interjected Collin.

"And you're going to tell us all of them, aren't you, honey?" asked Hilary sarcastically.

"Sadly no, but one of them was that the word 'dogwatch' is a direct translation from either German or Dutch of a similar term. It originally referred to the night watch on ships—that is, the time when, on land at least, all but the dogs were asleep. But I don't really subscribe to that explanation. I think it came about because the four-hour watches or shifts were split in two so sailors only had to be on watch for two hours instead of four. This started the sailors referring to the watches as 'dogwatches' because when the sailors didn't perform their duties to their utmost abilities, it was said they were 'dogging' it. Also, they would be referred to by the rest of their mates as a 'dogger.' And since the watches were only two hours long, it was as if they were dogging it and hence the name 'dogwatches.'"

"You made that last part up!" declared Emily.

"Maybe I did, maybe I didn't. You'll never know."

"I'm going to look it up."

"Be my guest, you've got the next four hours."

"Asshole!" smiled Emily under her breath as she left the control room.

Emily made her way down to the emergency generator room, but the whole way she couldn't stop thinking about the internet.

We have to find a way to integrate the internet into the equation, thought Emily. I'll try to figure out a way while on watch. I'm certainly not going to spend time trying to prove smarty-pants wrong. But I won't tell him that!

"Hello, Jorge," said Emily, trying to sound cheerful. "I'm here to relieve you."

"I'm glad you are here, Miss Emily. I've been thinking of you."

"You have?"

"Yes, I think it may have been the last expresso I had, but I started thinking on how we could integrate the internet into the signal."

"That's marvelous, Jorge. I was just thinking the same thing. Did you come up with anything?"

"The last time we did this we used light as a transmitting source, but I feel that won't work this time. I'm not sure how it can be done."

"What if we're overanalyzing this. Maybe the answer is simpler than it appears. We're already sending the signal through the earth, which reverberates into the water supply, right?"

"Correct, Miss Emily. But how do we make the jump to an electronic signal?"

"We don't."

"We don't? Miss Emily, I don't follow your reasoning."

"Well, what if we just allowed the signal that is in the water to encourage people to look up messages of love on the internet and let it grow from there."

"I see. You mean to tell me because we are imparting messages of love into the water that when people drink it they will feel the love?"

"That's right! It's already been proven by Dr. Matsushita Yamoto."

"Yes, I read something about his work. He flash froze water that had been put in containers, with each container having a different message on it, and then used high-speed photography to photograph the changes in the crystalline structure of the water as it froze."

"That's it exactly, Jorge, and the containers with messages of love on them had beautiful white crystals, whereas the containers with hate messages on them were ugly and all yellow colored."

"I remember now. Incredible! So, we just wait to see if that works?"

"No way, we have to speed this process up. We create a video that shows someone changing and becoming more loving because they drank the water, and we have to do it in such a way that it appeals to the younger generation so it becomes a viral video."

"Once it starts, there will be no stopping it. Miss Emily, that is a very good idea. But who will create the video?"

"I know just the smarty-pants that can help us with that, Jorge. Now tell me about your shift and then go get some food and rest."

"That, Miss Emily, is an even better idea!"

Chapter Thirty-Four

Agent Smith was sitting behind his desk when he suddenly grabbed his temples. A message was coming in from the Cronks, and they weren't happy.

We have detected a low-frequency signal emanating through the earth. It appears they are trying to send some sort of signal to the rest of the earthlings. We will start the viral infection in twenty-four of their earth hours.

"Understood."

It also appears that you are being deceived by agents Bennet and Parkinson. Use them for your purposes, then we will assimilate them.

"I just tested them and they seemed loyal."

You are a fool; they are deceiving you! But we have done nothing to stop it as you will need their services very soon. Do not trust them and leave them to us.

"Very good. I await your signal that the viral infection has begun."

The pain increased in Smith's temples to the point where he was unable to function. Then it receded.

That was just a reminder, thought Smith. "So, Bennet and Parkinson have been deceiving me. They will pay the ultimate price for their deception!"

∞

"Control room, generator room," came over the speaker in the control room.

"Control room," answered Frank

"Hi Frank, it's Emily."

"Yes, I know. You're the only one in the generator room."

"Sorry."

"Don't be sorry. You started beautifully. In fact, all the others could take a lesson from you," complimented Frank.

"You're not going to tell me you love me again, are you?" shot back Emily.

"What are you talking about?" Frank looked around at the others to see them all looking at each other and laughing.

"You don't remember? You had been taken over by the love frequency and were acting quite strange."

"I was?"

"Yes, you told me you had a great deal of respect for me and that you loved me."

"Well, I'm not sure what to say. I...I certainly do respect you, but I'm not in love with you!"

"Aww, that hurts, Frank!" said Emily sarcastically.

Frank looked at the others again as they all burst out laughing.

"OK, that's enough of that crap. What do you want?"

"Well, I'm not sure if that's correct radio protocol, Frank, but I would like to speak with smarty-pants, I mean Collin."

Frank handed the radio mic to Collin as he muttered to himself.

"Sorry, Emily," said Collin, still wiping the tears from his eyes. "I'm still laughing from your comments to Frankie."

Frank shot Collin a look that could kill.

"Glad to have helped lighten the mood, but there's something I would like to talk to you about, and I don't want to wait for the end of my shift."

"OK, I'll be right down."

"I told you to can the 'Frankie' shit, computer boy. Next time the fists will fly!"

"Easy, Frank," interjected Will. "He's just having a little fun."

"Well, not at my expense he's not."

"Collin, promise Frank you won't call him 'Frankie' anymore."

"I promise, teacher."

The control room erupted into laughter as Frank eyed each one of them separately as if planning their individual demise.

"You people don't get it!" yelled Frank. "We're trying to accomplish something Karl couldn't do. If you don't have any respect for me, at least have some respect for Karl. Because if you don't, I'll take you all out. One at time!"

Frank left the control room, which was now deftly quiet.

"I think he's serious," said Clara.

"I've never seen him like that," added Hilary.

"Remember that Emily said he could swing hard the other way as his mind tries to adjust to the frequency change," said Will.

"Sometimes the ones that seem so strong are affected first, Master Will," began Jorge. "I know Mr. Frank is always dealing with a myriad of emotions from his former life in the military."

"OK, let's cut him some slack and not taunt him anymore. I'm sure he'll return to his level-headed self soon," said Will.

"Speaking of frequency, I wonder if it's risen again?" asked Clara.

"Let's find out," said Clara answering her own question while grabbing the mic.

"Generator room, control room."

Clara didn't know why, but felt it was fitting to use correct radio protocol for a change.

"Generator room," answered Emily.

"Just wondering if the frequency has changed in the last little while?"

"It's up to 33.1 hertz. It's going too slow for my liking, so Collin and I are just discussing a way to speed that up."

"That's great. We'll wait to hear from Collin when he returns to the control room."

"Roger," said Emily and hung up the mic on its hook.

Collin returned to the control room and explained the plan to the others.

"Shoot a video, honey? Are you sure you want to waste time doing that?" asked Hilary.

"Well, the frequency is rising too slowly. Emily feels it will work and I trust her."

"I think it's a great idea," said Will. "It's a simple task, really. Just follow the formula of the latest soda commercials; there's no need to reinvent the wheel."

"That's true, honey. The last one I saw was so compelling, I actually bought some of it the next time I was in the store."

"I think Miss Emily has a sound plan, and we should all help out as much as we can," added Jorge.

"The internet will be your friend," mumbled Will.

"What did you say, Will?"

"Oh nothing. Just thinking of something Karl said."

"OK, so where do we start?" asked Clara.

"I will go down and relieve Miss Emily, so she can come up and be a part of the creative process," said Jorge as he stood up.

"But you just got off shift, honey."

"I know, Miss Hilary, but I believe I will be the weakest link in the video-creating chain."

"Thanks, Jorge," said Will, putting his hand on Jorge's shoulder. "We'll try to get it done as soon as we can."

Collin, Emily, Hilary, Clara, and Will worked feverishly to complete the new video and in about four hours felt they had something they could work with. Frank went down to the generator room to relive Jorge so he could come up to watch the launch of the video.

"OK, everybody ready for the upload to our new page? Ready to change the world? Ready to—"

"Just press the damn button, Collin!" demanded Clara.

"Here we go, I give you 'Love in the Water'!" said Collin as he pressed the Enter key on his keyboard.

The video uploaded quickly to the popular video streaming site, and it soon had a few hits.

"Looks like a few people have found it, honey," said Hilary.

"It will take a while to start catching on, but in a day or two, as people find out that they are feeling good just by drinking the water, we should have a viral video," said Emily.

"So now we wait, again," said Clara with a sigh.

"I know, this waiting game is taking a toll on me too," began Will, "but it's the only game in town right now. I just hope this works."

The group took a well-deserved rest and went to their individual sleeping quarters for a nap.

∞

Agent Smith was thankful when the Cronks finally notified him that the viral infection had begun.

"Parkinson! Hogsworth!" yelled Smith.

"Yes sir!" said the pair simultaneously as they entered Smith's office.

"The viral infection has begun. Soon we will see the humans dropping like flies."

"Excellent sir!" spouted Hogsworth.

"What will be the method of delivery?" asked Parkinson.

"The water supply," responded Smith.

"But how will you be able to control how many die?"

"We can't. We'll just let them discover it themselves and come up with their own solutions."

"And what about my son, Will?"

"I want you to take Bennet and go back to where he lost them while chasing them with the helicopter. They are most likely holed up in that area somewhere. Once you find him, kill all the others and bring your son to me."

"Yes sir!" said Parkinson as he turned and left Smith's office.

As soon as he was out of sight, Parkinson collapsed against the wall and his whole body began twitching.

Remember, he told himself, think about the truth. All you have done and will do, will be the truth. How you truly feel in the situation. Always the truth.

Parkinson's twitching soon stopped, and he went to find Agent Bennet.

"Bennet, come on. We have a job to perform."

"Where are we going?"

"Back to where you lost the humans in the car chase."

"The tunnel? Yes, that's correct, it was a tunnel. I believe there is a secret entrance of some kind there."

"Good. Then we will find it."

"What is our objective?"

"To pick up my son and bring him back here."

Parkinson felt his right hand start to twitch again at the very thought of bringing his son back to see Agent Smith.

It has to be done, he told himself. I will find a way to make things right.

∞

Jorge had called the control room repeatedly over the last hour of his shift, but no one had answered, so he decided to go up and find out what was going on.

"Master Will," said Jorge as he gently nudged Will in his bunk. "Master Will!" repeated Jorge as he shoved Will awake.

"What? Oh, Jorge, it's you. What's going on?"

"I have been calling the control room for the last hour, but no one answered, so I decided to see if everything was all right."

"Everything is fine, Jorge. We completed the video and uploaded it and decided we all needed a little nap."

"I don't blame you, Master Will, but I was calling because the earth's frequency has been steadily rising."

"Really? Let's go down and have a look. Did anyone relieve you?"

"No, as I said, I couldn't contact anyone."

"Jorge, you know you shouldn't have left the equipment running by itself."

"Yes, of course, Master Will, but when no one answered, what was I to do?"

"I know, I know, it's not your fault," said Will as they began the descent down the metal staircase. "One of us should have remained in the control room."

As they entered the emergency generator room, they could hear that not everything seemed to be running at the same frequency, and when they reached the LED readout, both of them stared with their mouths agape.

"Holy shit, 43.9 hertz!" exclaimed Will.

"I concur with your holiness, Master Will."

"It just moved to 44 hertz! We have to tell the others."

"Go tell everyone, Master Will. I will stay here and match the frequencies as they rise."

As Will made his way out the door of the generator room, he could hear the frequencies match and become much more harmonious.

If anything, the matching of the frequencies will make it work that much better, thought Will. "Can't wait to tell everyone!" he said excitedly as he climbed the spiral metal staircase.

"Oh my gosh!" gushed Emily as she heard the news. "Anything over 40 hertz constitutes bursts of insight within our brains."

Will had woken everyone up and gathered them in the control room, including Frank.

"Is it fluctuating up and down or is it holding steady?" asked Clara.

"Let's find out." Will grabbed the control room radio mic and pressed the button. "Generator room, control room."

"Go ahead for generator room," responded Jorge. Will briefly looked over at Frank and caught a smirk on his face.

"What's the reading now, Jorge, and is it holding steady or jumping around?"

"After I matched the frequencies, there was a sudden jump to 47.4 hertz, but now it has settled at 48.1."

"Holy crap!" said Hilary.

"But it's not fluctuating up and down?" asked Will

"No, Master Will, never down only up. It's 48.8 now."

"How high can it go?" asked Frank.

Everyone stopped and looked at Frank for a moment as if to judge his emotional state.

"We don't really know," began Emily. "But I'm assuming it would level out at some point, maybe around 100 hertz."

"And what would everyone's mental and emotional state be at that time?" continued Frank.

Once again everyone stopped to look at Frank.

"I can only assume that by then everyone's brain will have made an adjustment to the new frequencies and would be in a state of love and bliss. No guarantees, but as the frequency rises, the earth's magnetic field decreases, allowing us to remember who we truly are."

"And who might that be?" shot back Frank quickly.

"We are spiritual beings having a human experience because when we are in our spiritual form, we can only know ourselves conceptually. We have to take a physical form in order to know ourselves experientially."

"So, what you're saying, honey," interjected Hilary, "is that we have willingly slowed down our vibrational frequency in order to become more solid, yet less stable, in order to experience the things that we cannot experience while in our highly vibrational, yet much more stable, state."

"I couldn't have put it any better myself, yes," said a surprised Emily.

"In fact," continued Hilary as if Emily hadn't spoken, "that is the meaning of life. We are here to experience all we can in physical form and just, be. Be ourselves, who we truly are. Anything else we try to do or accomplish is merely a part of the illusion we have created, and we shouldn't take it so seriously. It's not like we could ever cease to exist because we are pure energy; that is part of a bigger whole. We can never die because we just change form. Energy can never be created or destroyed, it merely changes form and so shall we. We are immortal, and so many of us have died trying to find a way to become immortal, but yet all this time it was right under our noses."

"Wow! Where did all that come from?" spouted Clara.

"I...I don't know," answered Hilary. "It's like I always knew it, but it was covered in fog or something."

"I read you loud and clear," said Frank as he came over to hug a trembling Hilary.

"We're all going through some intense changes," began Frank speaking to everyone now. "And we're not done yet. All of us will experience the frequency change differently, but there is no doubt all of us will become more sensitive to who we truly are and why we're here."

"I agree with Frank, but how high should we allow the frequency to get?" asked Collin.

"I think at some point we'll have to pull the plug on the generator, or we may run the risk of returning to our spiritual selves before we have accomplished our goal," said Will.

"What if that is our goal?" asked Emily. "Many races of people before us have just disappeared from the earth without a trace; perhaps we will be the next and leave the earth for others to learn and experience things. Or maybe we'll come back as a different type of life-form in order to experience even more."

"Maybe those life-forms already exist, vibrating at different frequencies so we can't detect them, like mosquitos," added Will.

"What did you just say?" asked Hilary suddenly

"Maybe those life-forms—"

"No, no, the mosquito part!" interjected Hilary.

"They could be like mosquitos. Perhaps other life-forms are vibrating at such a high level we can't interact with them, but they can attempt to communicate with us. Only thing is their frequency is so high they sound like mosquitos to us."

"Exactly! That's what I heard just before I began to speak earlier."

"I've heard it too, Hilary, and I'm positive it's Karl."

"Really? He's communicating with us?" blurted Frank.

"Yes, he is. Although I feel he has gone back to the third dimension, his spiritual being still lingers everywhere because it is part of the whole. We are always everything else, and we are always everywhere. You need only think of him and he will be there."

"You know the awesome part of all this?" asked Emily. "I feel it so deeply in my heart and soul that all that has been said here is absolutely true."

"Amen, sister," contributed Frank, still hugging Hilary.

Chapter Thirty-Five

"We're not sure what is causing people to become so ill, but it seems whatever it is, it's acting fast and kills quickly."

Clara stared at the screen in disbelief. "This can't be happening!"

"What are you looking at?" asked Collin.

"The news. I wanted to see how the rising frequency was affecting people, but now it seems there is some kind of virus that is killing people within minutes of exposure."

"This just in," continued the young journalist. "The Department of Defense believes we are under attack by a terrorist organization that has initiated chemical warfare."

"Chemical warfare? Are they nuts!" shouted Frank now glued to the screen.

"Hold on," said the journalist holding one hand up to her ear mic. "I've just received an update, and apparently the virus has been deposited into our water supply. Do not drink the water. I repeat, do not drink the water!"

"Holy crap!" yelled Hilary. "But we want them to drink the water!"

"This could end our only hope of bringing mankind around," said Will solemnly.

"Well, we can't fill them with that loving feeling if it's killing them, can we?" said Collin, stating the obvious.

"What are we going to do now?" asked an exasperated Hilary.

"Nothing. There's nothing we can do," added Clara. "We're finished. All of Karl's work down the drain."

"Wait a minute!" yelled Frank. "Let's think this through. We use the water supply to spread the love, and then someone else poisons it so people won't drink it. Someone knows what we're up to. But who?"

"I'm willing to bet my dad has something to do with it," said Will.

"And Bennet," added Frank.

"Who?" asked Will, Clara, and Collin almost simultaneously.

"The guy from the chopper who almost found the tunnel door!"

"Really, why would he have anything to do with this?" asked Clara.

"I just feel it in my bones," answered Frank.

"Well, while you're feeling your bones, people are dropping like flies out there!" said Emily as she stared at the screen.

"My god! Is our water supply even safe?" asked Clara.

"Collin, I want you to switch to our reserve water tanks and stop drawing from the well," ordered Frank.

"That will only last a few days, Frank."

"I know. After you switch over, I want you to carefully test the well water for all known pathogens."

"I can do the water testing, Frank," interjected Emily. "I have the training, and I'd like Collin to do something else."

"What's that?" asked Frank.

"Collin," said Emily looking straight into his eyes, "is there any way we can reverse your machine so that we can raise the frequency and have the earth match it, instead of us waiting to respond to the earth?"

"I don't really know. I...I never thought about doing it that way."

"Now's your chance, computer boy!" exclaimed Frank.

"You know, somehow I liked the old angry Frank better," said Collin sarcastically while looking at Frank. "I'll see what I can do, but no guarantees," said Collin speaking louder now and to everyone else.

"I know you can do it, Collin!" called Frank as Collin got up from his chair and walked to the door. "And Collin?"

"What now, Frankie?" shot back Collin as he stopped and turned around.

"Make sure you switch the water over before you get all involved with your toys, and if you need help, Jorge is still down there."

Collin rolled his eyes, turned, and left without saying a word, knowing that Frank was just trying to lighten the mood in order to keep their minds off of their impending doom.

∞

"What do you mean there's no helicopter available!" shouted Parkinson over the noise of aircraft taxiing and lifting off.

"I'm sorry, sir, and I know you told me it's a matter of national security, but so is the rest of all this," said the hangar foreman as he waved his arm in an all-encompassing gesture. "And there are only so many planes and helicopters to go around."

"Where is the airfield comptroller? Can I speak with him?"

"You can if you want, but there's nothing left besides that old Cessna 172 over there in the back of the hangar. I call her Buffy. She was the only plane here when I first started."

"Nice," said Parkinson, then looked at Bennet and Bennet nodded.

"Is it ready to go?"

"Everything here is always ready to go, but it hasn't been out in over six months, so the fuel might be a little stale. Aircraft fuel doesn't take well to sitting around, you know."

"We'll take it!"

"OK, let me get the keys and do the walk around with you."

"Just get us the keys," asserted Parkinson. "We'll do the walk around ourselves. You're too busy for that."

"Are you sure?" asked the hangar foreman.

"One hundred percent."

"OK, I'll be right back."

"What good is posing as Secret Service agents when we can't get what we need when we need it?" asked Bennet.

"I know, I thought the same thing, but I guess we are the cause of this whole emergency scenario. Are you sure you can fly it?"

"I searched my programs and Cessna 172 is on it."

"Good thing it's old then, because so is your program."

"When this is all over, will you install my prior program once again?"

"If we're still functioning at that time...yes."

"Here's the keys!" shouted the hangar foreman over the roar of a Gulfstream G650 taking off.

"She's an oldie but a goodie."

Parkinson took the keys, shook the hangar foreman's hand, and turned to walk toward the back of the hangar.

"And fellas," called the hangar foreman after them, "bring her back in one piece!"

"Roger wolco," said Bennet.

Parkinson walked with Bennet a few steps before he spoke. "It's 'Roger wilco,' as in 'will comply,' knucklehead, not 'wolco'!"

"I apologize, but that's what appeared in my program."

"I hope your flight program is in better form," said Parkinson.

"It will be."

Parkinson and Bennet reached the plane, and Bennet immediately started his walk around, beginning at the cockpit and walking counterclockwise around the aircraft. Bennet paid particular attention to the control surfaces, removing the rudder gust lock and tail tie-down as he went.

"1975 Cessna 172 Skyhawk. Gross weight—2,300 pounds. Top speed—144 miles per hour. Range—875 miles with a full tank," said Bennet mechanically as he checked the engine oil.

"Remove the wheel chocks and get in the right side of the plane," ordered Bennet.

"OK, let's get this show on the road," said Parkinson as he watched Bennet begin his preflight routine.

"Turn on master switch and check fuel quantity. Turn off master switch. Fuel selector handle to Both position, all electrical equipment off, test brakes and set, mixture—rich, carburetor heat—cold, master switch—on, prime, throttle open one-eighth of an inch, and propeller clear."

Bennet turned the ignition switch, and the old Lycoming engine sputtered twice before roaring to life.

"Let's roll!" shouted Parkinson over the roar of the engine.

Bennet applied some more throttle and began taxiing out of the hangar. As they reached the hangar doors, the foreman appeared waving his arms. Parkinson waved back and instructed Bennet to keep going.

"Hey guys, I found you a chopper!" yelled the hangar foreman as the Cessna 172 taxied past. *I guess they're in a hurry*, thought the foreman as he stood there, hands on his hips, watching Buffy taxi out to the runway.

"Just bring her back, boys. That's all I ask."

With clearances obtained from the tower, the little Cessna took off and headed west toward the tunnel.

∞

Collin described the situation to Jorge after he had switched over the water supply.

"Is there really a way that we can set a frequency and have the earth match it, Mr. Collin?" asked Jorge.

"I don't really know. I've never even thought of trying it."

"Please let me know if I can be of service, Mr. Collin, but first I must take a restroom break and perhaps get a coffee and a snack. Would you also like a coffee?"

"What? Sorry, Jorge, I'm already lost in thought about this. Of course, I'd love one. It looks like this may take a while."

"Very good. I will see you in about fifteen minutes."

"I'll be here," responded Collin as he was tracing the fiber-optic lines.

"Control room, generator room."

"Control room, go ahead, Collin," responded Will.

"Oh my, I forgot to bring Mr. Collin his coffee!" remembered Jorge aloud when he heard Collin speak.

"Your coffee is on the way, Collin."

"Never mind that, I think I've found a solution to our problem."

"Really, so fast?" asked Will as he looked around at everyone.

"Yes. Now get your butts down here so I can show you."

"We're on our way!" said Will releasing the mic button. "Wow, that man works quick. Let's get down there."

Everyone clamored for the door, excited to hear what Collin had discovered.

"After you," said Will as he held the door for Clara.

"Oh no, not this time, you go first. It's my turn to check things out!"

Will blushed, but had no problem allowing Clara to look him over as he walked in front of her.

"Like what you see?" asked Will, half turning around as he walked.

"I've been liking it for a while now."

"I'm beginning to like these trips down to the generator room!" asserted Will.

"Me too!" added Clara.

After a few minutes, they had all reached the bottom of the staircase and found Collin hovering over the computer in the generator room.

"OK, so we're all here," began Frank, rubbing his hands together. "What have you got for us?"

"Well, I couldn't find any way that I could make it work," started Collin.

"What? I thought you said you found something," shouted Frank.

"Easy, Frankie. What I meant to say is that I couldn't find any *mechanical* way to make it work, so I had to get creative."

"And..." added Clara.

"I thought back to what Emily had told us about how the internet will control all the AI and how it could be either benign or wreak havoc, and decided to come up with a way to gently stroke the internet signal."

"So, what did you do, honey?" asked Hilary.

"I changed our message."

"You did what?" asked Will sounding not pleased at all.

"I decide the message of just 'Love' wasn't enough, so I tweaked it."

"What did you change it to?" asked Emily.

"I added one word: 'increase.' Instead of just 'love,' it now says, 'increase love.'"

"What's that supposed to do?" asked Frank, sounding a little let down.

"Hear me out, OK? I doubled and split the output to the disruptor so it now puts out a dual signal: a strong first signal, followed by a twofold increase in amplitude for the next signal that is transmitted just milliseconds after the first. Here, look at the oscilloscope." Collin pointed to the oscilloscope where his new signal was already playing.

"See how the first wave starts and then is almost immediately followed by another wave of double the amplitude? That's our new signal. So, instead of just one 'love' signal, it now says 'increase love'—LOVE."

"I still don't see how that's going to help us, Collin," said Will.

"What he's trying to say," started Emily, "is that by telling the internet, which is already aware of itself remember, that it should 'increase the love,' it will do so for us."

"Exactly! Thank you, Emily."

"My pleasure."

"OK, but will it work?" asked Frank.

"It already has," said Collin matter-of-factly. "Watch."

Collin swiveled around in his chair, faced the LED frequency meters, and adjusted the frequency higher by 0.1 hertz. Everyone stared at the LED meters for what seemed like an eternity, but then suddenly the frequency of the earth changed and matched what Collin had set the frequency to.

"Holy crap! Can you make larger adjustments?" asked Will.

"I've raised it 3 hertz in the last ten minutes, but I haven't tried to be too aggressive with it yet."

"This is awesome, Mr. Collin. Do you still want your coffee?"

Everyone let out a hearty, much-needed laugh.

"It's OK, Jorge. Perhaps I'll ask the internet to get it for me!"

Everyone laughed again.

"Be careful, Jorge, he may just do it!" added Frank.

Chapter Thirty-Six

"This is a nice little plane, seems to respond well," offered Parkinson into his mic attached to his headset.

"Starboard elevator and aileron are lagging a little behind the port ones. They need service and calibration," responded Bennet in a monotone.

"You can feel that?"

"Yes, my program is always searching for abnormalities in all functions of the aircraft."

"Amazing."

"Not really, it's just a program," responded Bennet over the drone of the Lycoming engine.

"And will this program find us a place to land this thing once we get there?" asked Parkinson.

"It will. It will allow me to immediately ascertain if any section of road or field will be long enough for landing or takeoff."

"How far away are we now?" asked Parkinson.

"Thirty minutes out."

Parkinson felt his right hand begin to tremble at the thought of seeing Will again and then quickly reminded himself that this was his true journey, and he must accept it and make the best of it.

∞

"You guys may be interested in this," said Clara, turning her head halfway around as she spoke.

A news anchor began to explain a few things they had found out about the virus.

"Scientists from the Centers for Disease Control and Prevention and the World Health Organization have put together a picture of what kind of virus has begun killing people around the world. Apparently, it is acting like some sort of hybrid form of bubonic plague and Ebola. It is what is referred to as a 'giant virus.' As their name implies, giant viruses are big—as big as bacteria, more than twice the size of typical viruses, scientists say. Giant viruses have more complex genomes than some simple microbial organisms, and many of these gene codes are found only in giant viruses, and it seems that scientists are suggesting that this virus is brand new and has never been found on Earth before."

The news anchor paused for a moment, swallowed, and then continued.

"The genes that have been found inside the virus have originated in the viruses themselves. The giant viruses are like factories, churning out genes and proteins—this kind of virus hasn't been seen before—it is actually replicating itself, within itself. In other words, it doesn't need a host to replicate and grow. Though the origin and purpose of this prolific gene creation is still a mystery, scientists believe this virus did not come from Earth and may have somehow entered our atmosphere from outer space."

"Holy crap!" said Clara. "What kind of madness are we up against here?"

"Giant viruses already existed here on Earth. I read a paper on them a couple of years ago, even before the official discovery of giant viruses," continued Emily. "Viruses occupy a questionable position on the tree of life: they contain much of the cellular material found in living organisms, including DNA or RNA, but they lack cell structure and cannot replicate outside a host—two key criteria for defining life. To date, there are four known giant virus families: Mollivirus, Megavirus, Pithovirus, and Pandoravirus. Researchers recently identified three new examples of Pandoravirus from samples collected in France, New Caledonia, and Australia. And all of the new Pandoraviruses contained large quantities of orphan genes and unique proteins. But these orphan genes differed among the viruses, which meant it was unlikely that they originated in a common ancestor, the scientists reported."

"So, what does all that mean?" asked Frank.

"Well, ninety percent of their proteins do not share any significant similarity with proteins of other viruses, outside of their own family, or cellular microbes. When the researchers analyzed the orphan genes, they compared them to other bits of the viruses' genomes. They targeted regions of DNA sequences that are noncoding and that are found between gene—and they detected similarities to the orphans. This hinted that each virus was producing the new crop of genes from its own DNA and that they were doing so randomly and spontaneously, according to the study."

"I'll ask again, what does all this mean for us, and in English please!" said Frank emphatically.

"Random mutations happen frequently in nature, Frank, and spontaneous alteration of DNA plays a role in the evolution of new species. However, the new genes that giant viruses generated produced proteins that are only found in giant viruses—and nowhere else. Supporting their theory that these viruses are not homegrown but have come from another source."

"Another planet, you mean, honey!" added Hilary.

"Yes, another planet," agreed Emily.

"Seems pretty coincidental that this showed up just as we were poised to help humanity realize who and what they really are," said Will.

"I don't think it's a coincidence at all, Will," added Frank. "I'm going down to the generator room. We have to step up the frequency big-time."

"Do you think the message can counteract this bug?" asked Clara.

"Who knows, but that's the only play we have left."

"I'm coming with you," said Will as he moved toward the door with Frank.

"Keep an eye on this and let us know of any changes in the situation," said Frank as he left the control room, followed closely by Will.

Collin pulled his feet off the desk as soon as he heard the generator room door open.

Why did I do that? Collin asked himself. I'm allowed to have my feet on the furniture! With that, Collin put his feet back up on the desk and relaxed. "Our subconscious programming runs deep," said Collin aloud now.

"Having a little rest, are we?" implied Frank as he walked up to Collin.

"As a matter of fact, I am," responded Collin.

"We just watched a news update about the virus, and it seems it's some class of giant virus that is a mix between bubonic plague and Ebola," said Will.

"Well, doesn't that sound like a bowlful of fun," responded Collin.

"Not only that," continued Will, "but the virus is able to replicate itself without a host, and none of its DNA is from this planet."

"Cool, a virus from outer space! This is like an episode of that old TV show, what was it called?"

"*Stellar Track*," interjected Frank.

"I knew you were old enough to remember that, Frankie. Good one!"

"You seem pretty relaxed about it, Collin. Do you not grasp the enormity of the whole thing?" asked Will.

"*Au contraire, mon ami.* I do grasp the enormity, and so does the internet."

"What are you talking about?"

"Have a look for yourself," said Collin as he nodded toward the LED frequency readouts.

"Holy crap, what's going on? Are you making adjustments behind your back?" asked Will.

"Look, two hands, two feet," said Collin as he pulled his hands from behind his head and nodded toward his feet on the desk.

Will and Frank stared at the LED readouts again only to see the same thing.

"Are you implying that the internet is making these adjustments for us?" asked Frank.

"No, I'm not implying it, I'm telling you that it is so."

All three of them looked at the LED readouts again and watched first the desired frequency readout change and then the actual earth frequency match it within a few seconds.

"This is awesome!" shouted Will. "How did you get it to do that?"

"I didn't. I started making small incremental adjustments, and then suddenly it started adjusting itself."

"Must have been the message change," said Frank.

"I like to think so," added Collin.

"OK, I concede that it was a great idea to change the message. There, are you happy now?" asked Will.

"No, not yet. But I will be as soon as this bug is squashed by our new internet-enabled message," asserted Collin.

"How high will the internet take the frequency?" asked Frank.

"That's something we'll have to wait and see. As I said, I have no more control over it."

"And what goes up...must come down," added Will.

"That's only when the force of gravity is involved, William. This is... this is free will, and the internet will take this wherever it wants it to go. But yes, it could at some point drop also."

"I have to go upstairs and tell the others," said Will as he started to turn around.

"Don't you mean Clara?" asked Collin, taking his feet off the desk and playfully backhanding Frank in the arm.

"Is it that obvious?" asked Will as he stopped and turned around to face them again.

"You're cool, bro. Clara's not an easy nut to crack, and it seems she has a fondness for you too."

"Really? You can see that?" asked Will excitedly.

"I do. How about you, Frankie?"

"There's definitely an attraction there," added Frank with a smirk.

Will came over and gave Collin a hug and patted Frank heartily on the back.

"Thanks, guys. I've never had anyone I could share this kind of stuff with."

"Not even your dad?" asked Frank rhetorically.

"Especially not my dad!" said Will emphatically.

"Hey, you called me 'bro,'" started Will. "Does this mean I'm part of the black brothers' fraternity now?"

"Don't push it, white boy!" said Collin in a deep voice.

"I didn't think so," said Will with a chuckle as he turned around and walked to the generator door with a spring in his step.

"Man, that boy is smitten," said Collin as Will closed the door behind him.

"That he is," agreed Frank. "Let's hope it doesn't get in the way later on."

∞

Agent Bennet circled the area over the tunnel looking for the best area to land the little Cessna.

"Not much to choose from. A chopper sure would have been nice," said Bennet.

"I agree, but this is all we have. What about that field to the west of the tunnel?"

"It's long enough, but what's the ground like? One hole or rock and we'll roll this plane over pretty hard. I say we take the main road that runs east and west then park the plane in that little parking spot there," suggested Bennet.

"That's for emergency vehicles," retorted Parkinson.

"Well, this is an emergency!" said Bennet as he circled one last time to line the plane up with the highway.

∞

Will walked into the main control room with a big smile on his face.

"You'll never guess what happened!" said Will with a smile.

"The internet took over and is adjusting the frequency on its own," stated Emily flatly.

"How did you know?" asked an unbelieving Will.

"It is?" asked a surprised Clara.

"I had a dream about it when we all had our rest a little while ago," said Emily.

Miss Emily, perhaps it's time to tell them the truth, said Jorge telepathically.

I agree, Jorge.

"Wow, honey, you sure have a lot of those dreams," said Hilary.

"I have a confession to make," began Emily. "I knew Karl and Jorge in a past life. Together, we conducted an experiment, and I was used as a human conduit to transmit universal energy through others like me from other dimensions."

"Human conduit. What the hell is that?" asked Will.

"I had a unique ability to channel the energy that surrounds us all, and I believe some of that ability is still latent in me during this lifetime."

"So, that's why you have these dreams?" asked Clara.

"They're not really dreams. They're more like premonitions or intuition."

"In other words, you can see the future," said Will.

"Because Miss Emily still retains some of the clarity she possessed in her past life," began Jorge, "she can sometimes pick up on what will happen next. You see, all we are thinking imparts waves of desire and creation upon the universe. We all have our own desires, and these waves cannot always create what we want because waves from others cancel ours out or vice versa. Miss Emily can pick up on these signals and see what may be about to happen, but it is never for sure because it could get cancelled out by someone else's desire."

"That's like the basic law of attraction. We learned that in school, Jorge."

"Yes, I know, Master Will, but to have the desire is not enough. You must commit to action. When you combine the thoughts with action, then things start to happen, and so many of us do not take the necessary steps to put our dreams into motion."

"They didn't teach us that part," said Will

"Once again, I know," responded Jorge.

"A couple of quick questions for you, honey," started Hilary. "One, if the internet is controlling the earth's frequency, are we safe? And two, what is the frequency now?"

"Good question, Hilary. Clara, could you call the generator room and find out the current frequency? And to answer your other question, Hilary, I don't know."

"Well, then give me what your intuition tells you, honey."

"I feel that by accepting our message and adopting the increase of the frequency in the first place, the internet has decided that both the raising of the frequency and how it sees itself is something that has love and compassion at its core."

"I believe the big question is what will happen if we were to stop the transmission of the message? Would the internet remain benign or would it adopt another message from its users?" asked Will.

"Good point, Master Will. There is a lot of negative outlooks posted online on a frequent basis. It could conceivably swing the other way."

While checking with the generator room, Clara noticed the small amber alert light flashing at the top-right corner of her console.

"Shit!" said Clara and checked all the outside proximity sensors for data.

"I hate to interrupt," said Clara as she walked back to the others, "but I have good news and bad news."

"Give us the good news, honey."

"The good news is that the frequency is now 63.2 hertz, and I checked the news networks, and it seems that the number of people dying is leveling off."

"Wow, that's great news, Miss Clara!"

"Hate to burst your bubble, Jorge, but the bad news is that we have a small plane circling overhead, and it looks like it's about to land on the main highway out there."

"That's not good," said Will. "Call the generator room and tell Frank to come up here right away."

"Already done."

Chapter Thirty-Seven

"Nicely done!" said Parkinson as the plane's engine roared and Bennet applied full right rudder to flick the tail of the Cessna around so it would fit into the emergency vehicle turnaround road on the highway. "Too bad we have a good distance to walk yet."

"We never would have survived the field landing," offered Bennet, "especially with all those animals. I've never seen a gathering of wild animals like that before. Definitely something strange going on here."

"How should we approach the tunnel?" asked Parkinson.

"I think we should just walk down the side of the road. Too many animals in the field, and if we spook them it may alert them sooner."

"Well, if this is some sort of facility, like you suggested, then they will have cameras and sensors, so they'll know we are coming regardless."

"Of course, that's why we should just take the easy way. Besides, I recall seeing some sort of seam in the rock face in the tunnel. It might be our way in."

∞

Frank flipped through all the camera angles on the various screens in the control room to try to get a better view of the two approaching men.

"They are dressed like federal agents. The same as the guy from the chopper that was chasing us. I don't like this at all."

"What do you think they want, honey?" asked Hilary.

"I'm not sure, but you can bet it's not a pleasure visit. Clara, can you zoom in on the face of the guy on the left and see if the computer can get an ID?"

"Already done, but you're not going to like this."

"Why, who is it?"

"Your old friend Bennet, and the guy on the right is Senator Parkinson."

"What! Are you kidding me?" yelled Will.

Will ran to the monitor where Clara had his picture up.

"Holy shit! It is him. What's he doing dressed like a mouth-breathing agent? He hates those guys!"

"He's here for you, Will," said Emily.

"Here for me? I want nothing to do with the man. He had his chance. As far as I'm concerned he's the enemy!" shouted Will.

"Master Will, I'm sure you may have your misgivings toward your father, but no one is our enemy; they are just doing the best they can with what they have, from where they are. We must put those hateful feelings aside and see what he wants. Perhaps it will be for the best."

"I doubt it, Jorge. He never does anything without having an ulterior motive. Whatever he's up to, there's something in it for him."

"Will they be able to find their way in?" asked Hilary.

"I guess we'll soon find out, but if I know Bennet, it won't take long," mused Frank.

"Did anyone ever notice all the animals out there?" asked Clara. "I guess we were all just too busy to notice," said Clara answering her own question.

"I think we should just let the men in," said Emily flatly.

"Are you nuts, honey?"

"That wouldn't be good," added Frank.

"They are going to get in one way or another, Mr. Frank, so why risk the damage to the facility," said Jorge.

"We have to keep the generator and the message going as long as possible. I'm sure they're here to stop it," responded Frank.

"Miss Clara, can you bring up the latest news please?" asked Jorge.

Clara rolled her chair over to another workstation and punched a few keys.

"Wow! You're not going to believe this, but everyone is drinking the water again, and no one is getting sick!"

"Everyone is ignoring the emergency orders to not drink the water, Peter," said the live news reporter. "They say it was all a government scam because the water is keeping them healthy, not making them sick. Besides, by drinking the water it just makes one feel, so, so loving! I tried some myself, and I've never felt better!"

"Wow, that must be some water, Valerie. I had some here at the station, and I have to say I agree with you!"

Peter, the news anchor, turned to the camera and said, "Folks, I know they told us to not drink the water, but the number of people getting sick has plummeted, and, well, I haven't felt this much love since my college days, if you know what I mean!"

Suddenly members of the broadcast crew came over to the anchor desk to congratulate Peter on his broadcast. Peter stood up and the crew started to hug each other like they hadn't seen each other in years.

"Holy crap! Did we do that?" asked Clara.

The others were all huddled around Clara and couldn't believe their eyes.

"I guess we did, honey? offered Hilary.

"We started it, but it's truly what they are feeling when they start to vibrate at a higher frequency, Miss Clara."

Suddenly everyone turned to face the main door as a huge boom resonated throughout the facility.

"They're knocking at the door," said Clara as she rolled over to the other workstation and switched to the door camera.

"Look, he's found the seam!" said Will.

"We should let them in," said Emily again.

"I don't know anything about your friend Bennet," said Clara. "But he's superstrong because he's prying open the main door!"

Frank stared at the monitor in disbelief. "No human could do that. He may look like Bennet, but that's not him!"

"We should let them in," said Emily again flatly.

Frank looked over at Emily and she met his gaze.

Let them in, Frank. Everything will be OK, I promise.

Frank had heard Emily's voice but didn't see her lips move.

She's communicating with me telepathically, thought Frank. Remember what Jorge told you about her.

"Open the door, Clara," said Frank.

"What! Are you crazy?"

"I said open the door!" ordered Frank.

Bennet was getting ready for one final pull on the already compromised door when it suddenly started to hum then open wide.

"They're letting us in," said Parkinson flatly.

"Must be some sort of trap," added Bennet.

"Could be, but let's go!" ordered Parkinson.

Parkinson let Bennet take the lead as they walked by Frank's shot-up roadster and toward an already open concrete door, which contained a retina and fingerprint scanner.

"They're really rolling out the red carpet," stated Bennet.

"Be ready for anything," whispered Parkinson.

The two cyborgs moved slowly down the red-lit corridor, hugging the wall as they went, then down the spiral steel staircase.

"It's like some kind of old bomb shelter," said Parkinson.

"Something like that," added Bennet.

They soon came to a T junction and stopped.

"Which way now?" asked Parkinson.

"I think we should go left," said Bennet.

"Why left?"

"Because my first thought was to go right, but my first thought is often wrong, so let's go left."

"That's your human feelings showing through. Maybe we should trust your feelings instead?"

Just as Parkinson finished his sentence, huge blinding white lights hit them from the right.

"Looks like they want us to go right," said Bennet.

The lights blinded the two cyborgs as they moved slowly ahead with trepidation. Their built-in cybernetic and human sensors were at full alert.

"Will, I want you to go into the other room," ordered Frank.

"I'm not about to run from my father, Frank. I'm done with him ordering me around!"

"This is not the time or place for a father-son showdown. Just do as I say for once!"

"OK, I'll go in the other room. For now!"

Clara gave Will a reassuring glance as he walked quickly to the adjoining room and closed the door.

"I feel their fear, Frank," began Emily. "But there is something else."

"What?" asked Frank.

"They're not all human."

"What do you mean, honey?" asked Hilary.

"She means they are some sort of cybernetic organism. A mix of mechanical, electrical, and organic systems," added Jorge.

"You mean they're robots?" asked a disbelieving Frank.

"No. Robots do not contain any organic life."

Frank went into the adjoining room with Will and grabbed his SIG 226 side arm from his locker.

"Why are you getting your gun, Frank?" asked Will. "What's happening?"

"It appears that your father and Bennet are no longer what they used to be, so I want to get ready for anything. Use that monitor over there and press the audio button. You'll be able to see and hear everything. Now, I'm going to lock this door. Don't come out unless I say so. Got it?"

The look in Frank's eyes told Will not to question his orders.

"Got it."

"Clara, call Collin and tell him to lock the generator room door and apprise him of the situation," said Frank as he returned to the main control room. "Once you've done that, open the door, but leave the lights on."

"Are you absolutely sure you want me to open the door?" queried Clara.

"Yes."

Frank pulled out his weapon, held it at the end of his outstretched arm, and waited for the door to open.

"Freeze!" yelled Frank as the two cyborgs were perfectly illuminated in the bright lights.

"What is your purpose here?"

"We come in peace," began Parkinson. "Is there any way you could turn those lights off?"

"I'll ask again. What is your purpose here?"

"Frank? Is that you?" asked Bennet.

"Doesn't matter now."

"I can't believe you're still alive!" started Bennet. "I was told you punched your ticket during the Swedish skirmish."

"Likewise."

"Well, I actually did almost die, but was saved by my new employers."

"New employers?"

"What he means," started Parkinson, "is that we are now employed by alien entities and have come here on a mission."

"And what would that be?" asked Frank.

"To kill my son!"

∞

The humans have counteracted our virus by raising the frequency of the earth, largely by this thing they call the internet. Use all your agents to dismantle this troublesome internet. If this continues, we will not be able to assert our mind control, and the humans will be able to do as they like. Loving each other and forming new communities with disregard to our systems of countries and religions we have put in place. Do you understand the gravity of the situation, Agent Smith?

The Cronks were communicating with Agent Smith telepathically, and Smith knew he had to respond quickly, but the intensity of the download left him shaking and frothing at the mouth.

"Yes. Yes sir. I understand."

You don't sound too convinced, Smith.

"I apologize, sir. The download was quite aggressive, and it has surpassed the ability of my digital memory to buffer; therefore I received your transmission all at once."

We don't like excuses, Smith, just results!

Smith suddenly felt the pain between his temples and slid off his chair and onto the floor. Shaking as if taking a seizure, Smith felt his mind go blank, but he could feel both his electromechanical and organic self starting to become overloaded. Then as suddenly as it started, it stopped.

Let this be a reminder to you. Get the job done, now!

"Yes sir. Of course, sir. We will use all available agents to defeat the internet."

Smith half expected an answer from the Cronks, but when none came he was relieved it was over.

"Hogsworth!" yelled Smith.

"Yes sir," answered Hogsworth quickly. "I apologize, I just happened to be walking by when you called."

"I know you were standing out there listening in so cut the bullshit."

"Yes sir, cut the bullshit. Got it."

"I want all available agents to destroy the main servers that distribute the internet in all the major cities of the world. And when they're done that, they can start on all the smaller cities, and then the signal towers. Everything. Got that?"

"Yes sir, all agents. Should I recall Parkinson and Bennet as well?"

"No. They have a job to do, and then I will have a special treat for all of humanity!"

∞

"Tell me why I shouldn't put a bullet in your head right now, Parkinson?" shouted Frank as he pointed his weapon at Parkinson's head.

"Because that..."

As Parkinson began to speak, Bennet leaped forward like a wild animal unsure of where its prey was but hoping to make contact somewhere.

"What the...!" Frank saw a flash of movement, and then Bennet was on him. With the bright lights in his eyes, Bennet had slightly miscalculated his leap and landed on Frank's left side, which left Frank's SIG 226 in his right hand unmolested.

The shot from Frank's weapon reverberated in the closed confines of the control room, and everyone recoiled in fear, unsure of what was happening.

"Jesus Christ, Bennet, what are you, some sort of animal?" yelled Frank.

Bennet had fallen to the floor off to the left of Frank, but quickly stood up again and assumed a martial arts stance.

"I'm programmed to protect Agent Parkinson, Frank, so don't screw with me. Or him!"

"Agent Parkinson?" queried Frank.

"OK, everyone just relax!" shouted Emily as she stepped between the two men. "Obviously, things are not as they appear to be. Senator, you've got some explaining to do!"

"Yes, well, as I started to say before my well-meaning friend attacked, it would be a mistake to put a bullet in my head because we're here to help."

"You call attacking someone helping?" asked Frank. "And what did he mean by 'Agent Parkinson'?"

"I apologize for Agent Bennet's rash behavior, but as he mentioned, he is programmed to protect me."

"Programmed?" asked Emily. Just as Emily asked the question, she noticed the milky-white fluid draining from Bennet's lower left leg. "You're not human, are you?"

"Sadly, no." Everyone seemed to take a step back as their eyes widened.

"Then what the hell are you then?" yelled Will as he came out from the adjoining room. "I always knew you weren't humane, but at least I thought you were human!"

The silence in the room was deafening.

"Answer me, damn it!" shrieked Will.

"Will, my son. It's so good to see you again. You look well," spouted Parkinson.

"Don't try to change the subject like you always do, Dad, or whatever you are. Answer the freaking question!"

"I don't know where to begin," said Parkinson.

"How about at the time you decided to have Karl killed!" asserted Will.

"Yes, I apologize for that. I apologize for all of my actions thus far, and I want to make it right. You see, Bennet and I are cyborgs that are controlled by alien beings known as the Cronks."

"You expect us to believe that crap?" said Frank.

"I know it's difficult for you to understand, but the Cronks have been here on Earth for over two thousand years, slowly exhibiting mind control over the population by controlling the frequency of your thought. They're the ones who introduced the ideas of religion, separation from your divine energy source, and keeping your head down and working for other people while earning just enough to purchase the goods and services that corporations and cartels wanted you to purchase through their advertising. Don't you see, it's all an illusion! What humans are doing isn't called 'life,' it's slavery! Slavery to a race of alien beings that are constantly stealing the earth's magnetic energy to power their warships, which in turn they use to take over other worlds."

"Wow, that's pretty grandiose, Senator," said Frank.

"Grandiose perhaps, but true. Bennet and I were taken in by the Cronks and converted into cyborgs to do their bidding."

"So, what exactly is a cyborg, honey?" asked Hilary.

"Cyborg is short for cybernetic organism," said Emily.

"Exactly," added Parkinson. "A cyborg is a being with both organic and biomechatronic body parts."

"So, you're half human, half machine?" asked Clara who had walked over to be by Will's side.

"No, it's worse than that," started Parkinson. "It is true that I am partly organic, but I'm not human at all. I'm sorry, but could we get those horrid lights turned off?"

"Clara, kill the lights," said Frank.

"Got it."

"Thank you. May I enter the room?"

"Of course, Senator, please come in," said Emily.

"Whoa, wait a minute," interjected Frank. "Do you really want the man that tried to kill Karl to just walk into the house that he built?"

"He said he was sorry for his past transgressions, Frank. Besides, we need to hear the rest of his story," said Emily convincingly.

"I'm the guy you need to worry about, Frankie!" growled Bennet.

"Whatever, Bennet. I kicked your ass in basic training, and I'll do it again now."

"Not now you won't. Want to give me a go?" begged Bennet.

"Bennet!" yelled Parkinson. "You are not to harm anyone in this room. Got it!"

"Yes sir, order received," said Bennet as he finally relaxed from his martial arts stance and stood perfectly still.

"Impressive, Senator, now could you continue with your story?" asked Emily.

"Yes, of course. As I was saying, we are no longer human. During the process of being assimilated, the soul is completely annihilated."

"How is that possible?" asked Will. "The soul is just energy, which can neither be created nor destroyed; it just is and always will be."

"Yes, that is true, my son, but the Cronks have found a way to use the energy of our souls to help counteract their stealing of the earth's magnetic field."

"So, by adding the energy of our souls back into the earth, they are able to extract the magnetic energy they need to power their fleet of warships," said Emily.

"You are very wise, my dear. That's exactly what they are doing."

"But then that would mean the energy, which is the soul, is trapped within the confines of this world's magnetic field. When the Cronks are finally finished with the earth, and there is no more magnetic field to contain them, the combined energy of all the souls will either suddenly explode or implode into a black hole."

"Actually, both events are correct. If they explode then their energy will spread far and wide and help to create new worlds, or if they implode they will form a negative antigravity field, what is commonly known as a 'black hole,' that will allow warping of the space-time continuum, which allows interdimensional travel. Either way their energy will continue to exist and still be part of the whole, but it ceases to have the ability to come to Earth, or planets like it, to continue their natural evolution."

"That's certainly not my definition of free will, honey," added Hilary.

"Nor mine, my dear. That's why we're here."

"Really? It seems to me you may have had another purpose in mind? And don't take this the wrong way, Dad, but I still don't trust you," said Will.

"As far as I can remember, I have never given you a reason to trust me, son. I only gave you orders. Orders that I'm ashamed to admit to now."

"Why the sudden turn to humility and kindness?" asked Emily.

Parkinson put both hands up to his temples and began to rub them. He could feel the tingling and knew the Cronks were trying to punish him for not getting on with his mission.

"Are you OK, Senator?" asked Hilary.

"Yes, yes, I'm fine. Your underground building is helping to shield me from the attempts of my makers to punish me."

"Punish you?" asked Will.

"Yes. I was sent here to bring you back to our base, Will. There, my commander, Agent Smith, will kill you in front of all the human news media in an attempt to convince all of humanity that all is lost and to go back to their slaving ways, just as they've always done."

"So that's why you're really here! To bring me back for execution! Sorry, pops, it's not going to happen. I'm not going anywhere!"

"I think that was his orders, Will, but I believe he has developed an alternate arrangement," said Emily.

"You are so perceptive, my dear. She's absolutely right, Will. After assimilation and subsequent reintegration, I found I still had remnants of my human memory, principally of you. I kept thinking of you, and then my hands, followed by my entire body, started to twitch. I was almost found out, but I was able to pretend I was reprogrammed to Smith's program and just installed the basic program into Bennet, which includes, ultimately, only listening to me."

"So that's why he's so obedient," said Clara.

"Wait a minute here," started Frank. "Why are you calling yourselves agents and who is Smith? Is it who I think it is?" asked Frank.

"We have been masquerading as federal agents for many years. This has allowed us to have both the access to things and the privacy we needed in order to help keep you enslaved."

"Holy shit!" came a voice over the speaker.

"What was that?" asked Parkinson.

"That was our colleague in the basement doing some maintenance work. He must have been listening in," said Clara as she muted the speaker.

"So, was or is Agent Smith really Detective Smith?" asked Frank, trying to change the subject.

"Yes, he was Detective Sergeant Smith, and it seems your colleague is in a very noisy environment."

"He's testing our backup electrical generator," offered Emily.

"You don't lie well, my dear. My basic programming is picking up a rise in your heart rate and blood pressure as well as rapid eye movement."

"You're right, I lied. I guess I forgot you are a machine. That was our man keeping *our* machine running. The machine that is preventing your makers from controlling our minds and enslaving us."

"Ah, the love machine. Very well done. It has caused much chaos within the ranks of the Cronks,"

"You're not here to shut it down?" asked Clara.

"No. My mission is to bring Will back with me, and this I must do, but not to complete the original mission. Here is my plan…"

As Parkinson told them of his plan to help overthrow the Cronks, Clara went over to Bennet and sealed his leaking leg with an epoxy resin as Will looked on.

"There, that should keep some of your fluid inside you."

"Thank you, ma'am," responded Bennet without moving or blinking.

"What kind of fluid is that?" asked Clara. "It seems almost slippery and sticky at the same time."

"I am powered by a glucose fuel cell, which when combined with ultralow-power electronics and lightweight materials of construction, enables me to be completely self-powered," answered Bennet.

"How is the power regenerated after a major expenditure?" asked Clara.

"My fuel cell mimics the role of the human body's enzymes by breaking down glucose sugar into energy. The glucose in the brain's cerebrospinal fluid represents a continuous fuel supply for the fuel cell. That's why our makers were not able to get rid of our human brains when constructing us."

"OK, but the glucose in the cerebrospinal fluid will eventually run out if not replenished."

"I have a small slow-dissolving glucose energy cube implanted into my chest to ensure a constant supply of glucose to the cerebrospinal fluid. It is aptly named 'the sugar cube.'"

"And how long will that last?"

"Approximately five earth years, depending on usage," answered Bennet flatly.

"Clara! Stop talking with that hunk of junk over there," said Will as he waved his arm for her to come over.

"Thank you for talking with me, Mr. Bennet," said Clara.

"It's Agent Bennet, ma'am. And you are welcome."

"Well, I think there's still a mister in there somewhere!" said Clara playfully as she turned and walked back toward Will.

"What do you think you're doing?" asked Will, talking through his teeth as Clara walked up to him.

"I was getting some valuable information about how they are constructed, that's what," whispered Clara. "And I think I found their weak spot."

"You did? With just three questions?"

"I asked four questions, and yes, I did."

"I knew you were amazingly smart, but that takes the cake!"

"You should turn down the testosterone a little bit, you might learn something," suggested Clara.

"Sorry, I let it get the best of me, didn't I?"

"That's OK, it was nice to see you a little jealous."

"Jealous! How could I be jealous of a machine?"

"Well, he is kind of cute, and his power supply will last for five years!"

"Stop it right there, you! My power supply will last a lot longer than that!"

"We shall see!" said Clara with a glint in her eye.

"Will!" yelled Frank. "Come over here."

Will looked over at where Frank, Emily, Jorge, and his pseudofather were standing and decided to turn down the testosterone as Clara had suggested and went over to them.

"What's the plan?" asked Will.

"Jorge, would you explain it to him?"

"Certainly, Mr. Frank."

Will knew it would come across as softer and more cerebral when Jorge spoke, and that's why Frank had deferred it to him.

"Master Will, we have had a discussion about how to handle this very complex situation and have decided it would be best if you accompanied agents Parkinson and Bennet back to their base."

"What! Are you insane? You know they want to kill me, right?"

"Yes, of course, Master Will. But your father—"

"He's not my father!" interjected Will. "He's just a hunk of space junk!"

Clara had followed Will over and stomped her foot down on top of his.

Will turned his head around to meet Clara's steely glare.

"OK, OK, I'll listen to what you have to say."

"As I was saying, your father, who is now Agent Parkinson, has assured us that he still has feelings for you and that he will not allow any harm to come to you."

"Or he could be lying his ass off and kill me anyway," stated Will flatly.

"Will, my basic program does not allow me to lie. I must tell the truth," said Parkinson.

"Then how did you convince Smith that you didn't have any human emotions anymore?"

"By convincing myself that what I was doing was being true to myself, therefore telling myself the truth and believing in what I needed to do. This was powerful enough to allow my systems to override the deception to Agent Smith."

"Master Will, this may be our only chance to end the suppression of the Cronks and to give you the exposure you will need in order to lead the world into the future. Much will need to be accomplished after the Cronks are overthrown, and you will need to be at the forefront of that."

"What if I say no?"

"Then the Cronks will eventually wear us down, and we will be under their control again once the earth's frequency drops due to all the ensuing negativity, which means all of Karl's work will have been for nothing."

"OK, I'll do it."

Chapter Thirty-Eight

Agent Smith observed all the major television network news channels on his monitors and could see the destruction his agents had left behind.

"Hogsworth!" yelled Smith.

"Right here, sir," answered Hogsworth from just behind him.

"Oh, there you are. Get up here where I can see you," said Smith, motioning with his arm for Hogsworth to move forward.

"What is the earth's frequency now?" asked Smith.

"It's at 96.314 hertz and climbing," said Hogsworth, still beaming from being asked to stand beside Smith.

"Damn it!" yelled Smith, bursting Hogsworth's bubble. "How the hell could it be still climbing when we've destroyed nearly all of the communication network for the internet?"

Hogsworth gathered himself and stood slightly behind Smith once again before he spoke.

"In the last few years I have read many earth scientists' predictions that the internet will become aware of its own existence, become artificially intelligent, and could actually function as a conscious entity. Perhaps it has found a way to reroute its communications."

"If it has, that means we've failed, and the Cronks will not be happy. Try to raise Parkinson and Bennet on the radio again."

"Come in agents Parkinson and Bennet, this is central control, over."

"Go ahead central," came Bennet's voice over the sound of the Cessna's engine.

Hogsworth looked at Smith as he spoke. "Has your mission been a success?"

"Roger, we have Will Parkinson on board with us and should be touching down within forty-five minutes."

"Excellent!" answered Hogsworth as he watched Smith pump the air with his fist.

"Don't you dare tell anyone about my show of emotion, Hogsworth."

"Of course not, sir. I too have a slight happiness feeling, although it has dissipated now."

"Hogsworth, remove Karl Dunitz's body from storage and bring it up here. I have a little surprise for our guest."

"Yes sir, on my way."

We will see how far the earth's frequency falls once the earthlings find out their messiahs no longer exist and all hope for a loving world is extinguished, thought Smith.

∞

Clara had noticed the small red light beside the speaker on her console blinking for a while now but was busy saying good-bye to Will, knowing that there was a good chance she may never see him again.

"...it's unbelievable!" shouted the speaker after Clara took it off mute.

"Sorry, Collin. We've had you on mute for quite a while because of our guests," explained Clara.

"Guests. What guests? We don't get guests here," answered Collin.

"Will's father, Senator Parkinson, and an old friend of Frank's."

"Oh, so that's who I overheard on the speaker before I was cut off. What did they want?"

"Will."

"What do you mean?"

"They took Will with them back to their base."

"They what?" shouted Collin into the mic.

"It's a long story. I'll have to come down and fill you in later."

"I would hope so. Hey, did my lights work?"

"Yes, Collin, your lights blinded them very effectively."

"Yes!" said Collin as he fist pumped the air. "I knew they would work!"

"So, I've seen the transmit light blinking for a while now; what were you trying to tell us?"

"You didn't get any of it?" asked Collin.

"No."

"Oh man, this is just absolutely incredible! The internet is now completely artificially intelligent. It's totally conscious of its own existence and has rerouted communications."

"Rerouted communications, what do you mean?" asked Clara.

"Federal agents were everywhere trying to destroy the servers, and don't ask me why," continued Collin as if Clara hadn't spoken. "And for a while the frequency dropped, but then suddenly it began rising again as the internet took over and is now utilizing all the electrical wiring, from generating stations to people's homes, as a communication network. And not only that, but everyone's computers are acting like servers, all contributing to a giant networking community. It did this shit on its own, Clara. Can you believe it?"

"Wow, I guess we did miss a lot," said Clara as she looked at the others that had gathered around to hear Collin's story.

"Turn on your external news feed. It's everywhere. And...and this is big—people are loving each other and helping each other. It's unbelievable!"

"We believe it, Collin. Turning on the news feed now," said Clara.

Clara, Emily, Hilary, Frank, and Jorge stood and watched the news feed with mouths agape.

"That's incredible!" said Emily.

"Did we do that?" asked Frank.

"I'm not sure if we did it, Mr. Frank, but we sure started it!"

"Karl was right all along," said Hilary.

"Of course, he was right, Miss Hilary. Did you not believe him?"

"I believed in him, honey, but I wasn't sure if I believed that this was truly possible in our lifetimes."

"This scene is like out of a science-fiction movie, Peter," began the middle-aged and well-traveled news reporter. "The virus has been completely eradicated by drinking the water, and at the same time everyone is so kind, compassionate, and loving. I can hardly believe it myself, except that I feel it too. Not only are we feeling that loving feeling, but such a sense of community. We all want to help each other because we've finally realized we are all in this thing called 'life' together. It's like we're all one. Brothers and sisters with no care about race or religion."

"Wow, Valerie, I totally wish I was there with you!" answered Peter from the anchor desk. "Are there no signs of negativity or violence at all?"

"Yes, there are, Peter. A few cases of looting and the odd person just doesn't seem to want to buy into everyone's new attitude, but by and large there is nothing of a negative nature to report."

"Well, that's very odd for us since we've made a living reporting negative news," reported Peter with a smile.

"I hear you, Peter, but doesn't it feel good to report on positive happenings for a change?" asked Valerie.

"It sure does, Valerie. Thank you for your in-depth and knowledgeable report. And now, is this new loving feeling just a fad? Will it wear off anytime soon? Stay tuned because we'll be right back with Dr. Lamontagne, a renowned love specialist to answer those questions."

"Wow, unbelievable!" said Clara as she switched off the news feed. "But I can't stop thinking about how Will is making out."

∞

As Bennet lined up the little Cessna for final approach, Parkinson turned around in his seat to talk with Will.

"I know this is a huge leap of faith for you, son, but I want you to know that I won't allow any harm to come to you," said Parkinson into the mic attached to his headset.

"First of all, faith has nothing to do with it. I'm doing this for Karl, who had more integrity in his little finger than you did in your whole body. Secondly, don't call me your son because you're not my father. You have no soul, you're just a cyborg that discovered he had memories. You've sold your soul to the Cronks, and I'm not about to let myself or anyone else get souled out," retorted Will.

"I understand your feelings, Will, but there is more to me than just my cybernetic organism."

"Oh really, how do you figure that?" asked Will sarcastically into his mic.

"I don't know. I just know that for all intents and purposes, life as you know it, and as I used to know it, is just an illusion anyway. We are nothing but creators, and we constantly create our own circumstances and environment. We react to stimuli with our emotions, which helps create our next reality. Nothing is actually real except the energy that everything in the universe is made of. The only real reason we decide to take on any type of form is to experience ourselves. Because in the realm of the absolute, where we are only energy, we cannot experience ourselves, we can't know ourselves. But in the realm of the physical we can, by experiencing our opposites. We know what up is by experiencing down, tall while experiencing short, cold while experiencing hot, and on and on. From this we can feel emotions and experience what it's like to be alive, instead of just energy."

"You're starting to sound a lot like Karl. How do you know all this stuff?" asked Will. "You certainly didn't know it when you were human."

"I read a universal manual called *The Process* while reprogramming all the other agents to conform to Smith's program, and this was all explained there. It's what changed my brain patterns," answered Parkinson.

Parkinson and Will's conversation was suddenly interrupted by Bennet as he approached the runway.

"Fuel selector valve—both. Mixture—rich. Carburetor heat—on. Airspeed seventy miles per hour—flaps down."

"Obviously there's more to you than meets the eye," began Will. "I sure wish you could have been like this when you were my father."

"You are right, Will, I am not your father, but there is still a piece of him inside me and he wants to make amends."

"Touchdown—main wheels first. Landing roll—lower nose wheel gently. Keep braking to a minimum," said Bennet as he repeated the landing instructions to himself.

"Wait a minute!" began Will. "If all the agents are all running the same program now like you said..."

"Yes, that is true, go on," said Parkinson.

"Then if we take care of Agent Smith, all the others should follow suit, yes?"

"They are programmed to conduct themselves as he would have, yes, but I'm not sure how they would react to his demise."

"I'm betting the sudden loss of leadership will, at the very least, confuse them," said Will.

"Unfortunately, he has the same plans for you, Will. I just hope you can find it within you to trust me."

"I will trust you," said Will as the little Cessna 172 landed gently on the runway.

∞

Deep within the core of the earth, where the Cronks had hidden their mother ship for centuries, a small amber light began flashing.

Commander, the Andromedans are entering the galaxy the humans call the 'Milky Way,' thought the chief engineer aboard the Cronk mother ship.

Are you sure? communicated the commander.

Yes, I have checked the space signature of their ship and have confirmed it as Andromedan.

But they are not due back for another two hundred earth years. We are not done milking the humans yet, and we still require more souls converted to magnetic energy to power our assault on the next unsuspecting primitive species.

I agree, Commander, but it appears they will be here much sooner.

The Cronk commander and his chief engineer both looked over at the flashing warning light as it turned from amber to red.

They will be here soon, thought the commander. *Something must have alerted them. Contact Agent Smith and tell him to step up his plans. We need the humans to be under our control when the Andromedans arrive.*

Yes sir.

Chapter Thirty-Nine

"Control room, generator room," called Collin's voice over the control room speaker.

"Go ahead for control room," answered Clara.

"I've just seen a huge spike in the earth's frequency."

Clara looked around at the others as she answered. "Define huge."

"Well, the numbers suddenly started to climb so fast they were a blur, but they seemed to top out at around 720 hertz."

"At 720 hertz! How is that possible?" exclaimed Clara.

"I don't know, but it's back down again now. Currently we're at 120 hertz, and it's staying there. No fluctuations at all."

"It's just flatlining, no slight up or down movement?" asked Emily

Clara repeated Emily's question as she pressed the button on the control room mic.

"No movement whatsoever. It's holding dead steady at 120 hertz," responded Collin.

"That's very odd, isn't it, honey?" asked Hilary.

"Very odd indeed," said Emily almost to herself as she was deep in thought. "There must be some kind of outside influence for it to remain steady like that."

"I think I found it," said Clara flatly while observing the main computer screen on her console. "Our sensors are picking up a frequency, or rather two frequencies, emanating from outer space and getting stronger every minute."

"What's the frequency?" asked Emily.

"It is registering 3,240 hertz."

"What—3,240 hertz! Are you sure your instruments are right?" shot back Emily.

"Well, that's if you add the two frequencies together. If I separate them," said Clara as she expertly navigated through her software program, "they come in as two separate frequencies, but they are totally harmonious, so at first it seemed like one tone. I'll put it on speaker."

Everyone listened to the two harmonious tones for what seemed like minutes but was only a few seconds.

"What a totally blissful tone, Miss Clara," said Jorge with a smile. "It immediately puts me into a meditative state."

"Me too," added Emily. "Can you isolate the two different frequencies?"

"Hang on...got it! The lower tone is at 720 hertz, and the higher tone is at 2,520 hertz.

"Is there any significance to those two frequencies?" asked Frank.

"I'm not sure," answered Emily. "Clara, what is 2,520 divided by 7?"

Clara punched the numbers into her on-screen calculator and responded, "It's 360."

"I thought so," said Emily, still thinking.

"What does that mean?" asked Frank.

"And what is 720 divided by 6, Clara?" asked Emily, shrugging off Frank's question.

"That's 120," answered Clara.

"Bingo!" said Emily.

"You've figured it out, Miss Emily?" asked Jorge.

"I believe so."

"Well, spill the beans, honey!" blurted Hilary.

"It's sacred geometry."

"Sacred what?" asked Frank.

"Sacred geometry. They coined the term 'sacred' because it goes back to the beginning of all life," answered Emily.

"OK, explanation time, Emily," said Frank.

"What we're seeing represented by the higher tone is called the 'seed of life,' or the 'genesis pattern' as some scientists call it," started Emily.

"What's the seed of life, honey?"

"Oh nothing, except for the origin of all there is," retorted Emily coolly. "The seed of life represents abundance, reproduction, creation, and new beginnings. It is composed of seven circles, all slightly overlapping themselves. It is the foundation for the formation of the 'flower of life,' which produces the 'fruit of life,' which is the blueprint and mathematical representation of the entire universe. It contains every atom, molecular structure, and life-form. In fact, it contains everything there has been, is now, and will ever be."

"So, it's no big deal then," added Frank sarcastically.

"What has that got to do with the frequencies?" asked Clara, rolling her eyes at Frank.

"Well, 2,520 divided by 7 is 360, and a circle has 360 degrees, which means the seven circles, or the 'seed of life,' can be represented by a frequency of 2,520 hertz."

"Holy crap!" said Clara.

"And," continued Emily, "the second and lower frequency of 720 hertz when divided by 6 equals 120, which is exactly the frequency that the earth is currently vibrating at."

"But why divide by six, Miss Emily?" asked Jorge.

"I'm glad you asked that, Jorge. It's because a hexagon has six sides, and when the seed of life turns into the flower of life, its basic outer shape is that of a hexagon."

"Hexagons, just like the interior shape of a bee's or wasp's nest, where all the eggs are," said Frank.

"Now you're beginning to get it, Frank!"

"So, these frequencies are emanating from the universe itself?"

"I doubt it, Clara. Otherwise we would always hear them. I think something, or some other species, is sending these frequencies to Earth."

"Well in that case, we may soon meet them because they're getting stronger by the minute!"

∞

Agents Parkinson and Bennet, along with Will, walked across the tarmac toward a ramshackle of an aircraft hangar and a very innocent-looking hangar door. Will couldn't help but wonder what lay waiting for him beyond it.

"Once we're inside, I'll have to start treating you like my prisoner, but don't be alarmed, it is only for show, so please play along. Also, things will go much better if you speak only when you're spoken to. Got it?"

"I've got it, but I'm not very good at that last part," answered Will.

"I know, you're a chip off the old block, and that's why I said it."

As they stepped through the rickety old hangar door, Will was surprised to see a huge steel bank-vault-like door in front of them. Parkinson scanned his card and looked into the retina scanner to unlock and open the big steel door.

"Step inside, go all the way to the back, and hang on to the handrail," said Bennet mechanically.

As soon as they were all inside, the doors closed and they began their descent.

"Remember, do not speak unless spoken to, act as if you are my prisoner, and above all else, remember that we are on a mission to end this unholy treatment of the human species, right here and right now."

"I like that last part the best. What's your plan?"

"There is no plan. I have read in *The Process* that we create our own future, so that is what we shall do."

"I would have preferred a more concrete plan, but I'm on board with creation, so let's do this...Dad."

Agent Parkinson turned his head and looked into Will's eyes. "You really mean that, don't you?"

"Yes, I do. You're the father I wish I had, and it's never too late to begin anew."

"I wish I could really mean what I am about to say next, but my capacity to feel emotion is very limited. I love you, Will."

"I love you too, Dad."

Chapter Forty

Aboard the Andromedan spacecraft things went about in their usual fashion. The Adromedans were a race of highly evolved, enlightened beings, that long ago discovered the benefits of kindness, compassion, and love. They had endured a long history of conflict; in fact, at one time they were not unlike the human species, always fighting and bickering with one another. Divided by different geographical divisions and personal beliefs, they always fought for control over one another. They believed they were separate from everything and everyone, and they had edged God out of their lives and thought only of themselves.

Eventually a shift took place, slowly at first and then gathering momentum. They finally discovered what it would take to prolong their very existence, because if they didn't change the way they thought, they were in grave danger of annihilating themselves. Thus, they developed a creed by which to live:

1. An enlightened species sees the unity of all life.
2. An enlightened species tells the truth, always.
3. An enlightened species does not believe in concepts of "justice" and "punishment."
4. An enlightened species does not embrace "insufficiency."

5. An enlightened species does not embrace the concept of "ownership."
6. An enlightened species shares everything with everyone, all the time.
7. An enlightened species creates a balance between technology and cosmology; between machines and nature.
8. An enlightened species would never, under any circumstances, end the life of another being unless asked directly by that being to do so.
9. An enlightened species would never do anything to harm or potentially damage their physical environment that supports their lives.
10. An enlightened species never feels the need to compete and realizes that "creation" not "competition" best develops the way forward.
11. An enlightened species does not conduct themselves based on a need-based experience.
12. An enlightened species experiences and expresses unconditional love for everyone.
13. An enlightened species must harness the power of metaphysics.
14. An enlightened species knows they are a soul with a body, not a body with a soul.
15. An enlightened species will help other species gain an awareness of who they truly are without causing those species to seek help from them.

There were other codes to the creed, of course, but these were the main codes they conducted themselves by, and so it came to pass they helped the human species to realize who they truly are.

"I'm detecting the presence of a Cronk warship circling the blue planet," said the science officer aboard the Andromedan starship. "Along with a much stronger signal emanating from deep within the planet's core."

"No doubt a Cronk mother ship," responded the captain of the Andromedan vessel. "I'm sure they have been exercising control over the humans while we have been away. Let's hope they haven't done too much damage this time."

"Shall I increase our speed, sir?" asked the navigation officer.

"No, not at this time. I think we need to give the humans more time to help themselves."

"Shall I continue transmitting the healing frequencies, sir?"

"Yes, my friend, continue our present course and speed. We will be there soon enough."

∞

"Clara. Clara!" yelled Frank now.

Clara visibly jumped in her seat as she finally realized someone was calling her name. "What?" she answered as she looked toward where the sound had come from only to see Frank's stern face. "I'm sorry, Frank, I was totally checked out for a moment."

"I see that. That's not like you, Clara. Are you worried about Will?"

"Do you think he's still alive? I mean, we're talking about battling robotic cyborgs commanded by aliens here. How can anyone ever fight against that?"

Frank could see the tears welling up in Clara's eyes and knew he had to comfort her, not order her around.

"One thing I have discovered about Will, Clara, is his immense capacity for resourcefulness. There will be no need for fighting; Karl has armed him with enough spiritual knowledge to defeat the Cronks and their agents no matter what."

"I hope you're right, Frank. I really have feelings for him. I just feel so electric when he's around."

"I see that, too."

"You do?"

"Everyone does. You guys belong together, and I'm sure he will be back."

"Thanks, Frank. I'm going to visualize his return and focus on that," concluded Clara.

"Attagirl! Now, what I wanted to ask you was how long until the source of the frequencies gets here?" asked Frank.

"Oh, just a second...doing the calculation...best estimate is three days, four hours."

"OK then, I guess everything will fall into place very soon."

"Yes, everything will be fine because it has to," said Clara, repeating a saying of Karl's more for her own comfort than anything else.

∞

Agent Parkinson shoved Will so hard he ran into the opposite wall of the hallway as the elevator doors opened.

"Easy now, Parkinson," said Will.

"This starts now, kid!" answered Parkinson with a growl.

Will took the hint and realized the role-play was on. This was for real.

"Screw you, old man. Or whatever you are!" yelled Will back at the cyborg.

"Follow Agent Bennet and do as you're told," ordered Parkinson.

Will followed Bennet with Parkinson following close behind as they weaved through a series of hallways, with Bennet stopping every once in a while to have his retinas scanned to open a door to the next secure area.

"They're here!" shouted Hogsworth.

"I see that, you imbecile!" answered Agent Smith angrily as he gazed at the monitors. "Let them in and bring them to me."

"Yes sir," answered Hogsworth sheepishly.

"Well, well, well," began Smith. "Look what the cat dragged in!"

Parkinson shoved Will into the room, and after regaining his balance, Will quickly scanned his surroundings only to stop suddenly and drop to his knees.

"You son of a bitch!" screamed Will. "What have you done to Karl?"

"I haven't done a thing, oh anointed one. It is what *you* have done that has caused this."

"I didn't cause anything, you cyborg son of Satan. It's you and your alien pieces-of-shit leaders that have done this!" yelled Will.

"Oh really. Who was the person that hired someone to kill your precious Karl in the first place? If you hadn't done that, none of this would be taking place right now!" yelled Smith.

Will rose quickly to his feet and charged toward Smith only to be stopped by the outstretched arm of Bennet.

"Now, now, temper, temper. You see, my friends of the earth," started Smith as he turned to a video camera on a tripod, "the one that has been chosen to lead you is not even fit enough to lead himself. In fact, it is *he* who commissioned the assassin to kill Karl Dunitz! Isn't that right, William?" asked Smith, quickly turning back toward Will.

"You're recording this?" asked Will.

"Actually no, something so much juicier. We're on a live feed to every major television network in the world. All of the people of the earth can now see you for what you truly are—a fraud!" yelled Smith.

Will looked over at Karl. The simple wood coffin that contained him was propped up to a near-vertical angle, just the way he used to see it done in the old western movies he watched as a child. Karl was completely naked except for a white wrap that went around his waist. His body was an off-gray color, and his face still bore the heavy stubble he had grown during the time he was in a coma.

"Jesus," whispered Will.

"I'm sorry, William, please speak up so the world can hear you," said Smith trying to speak eloquently.

"I said, Jesus. You took the time to make him appear like Jesus? What kind of monster are you?"

"I am neither monster nor man; I am Agent Smith and you will learn to bow before me!" quipped Smith as if quoting Shakespeare. "And besides, I think it's quite prophetic of me to have Karl pose as Jesus," continued Smith. "This way he can watch his prodigal son die before him!"

"Over my dead body!" yelled Will, not thinking of what he just said.

"That, William, is why you are here."

Will could feel the anger well up inside him, and all he wanted to do was rush at Smith and end him, but then he suddenly heard that familiar sound of a mosquito.

What would love do now? came into Will's mind. What would love do now? That's it! thought Will. We will never conquer violence with violence. Only love will show us the way forward.

"Citizens of the world," began Smith as he turned back to the camera. "Do you want to live your life with an uncertain future? One that requires you to give up everything you've worked so hard for to gain. Your homes, your cars, your jobs, your children. Yes, even your children!"

"You're absolutely mad, Smith," countered Will.

"This man," continued Smith, pointing at Will defiantly, "will take your children from you and convert them into who-knows-what kind of religion. A religion so terrible, it will shake the very foundations on which you have created your lives."

"That's enough, Smith!" yelled Will.

"Look at him now. He shows only anger, while I promise you continued happiness, prosperity, and growth."

Will couldn't believe the acting job Smith was pulling off right in front of his eyes. But it wasn't just acting, he was serious. Deadly serious.

"Agent Smith, may I speak in my defense?" queried Will.

"The wicked shall not be allowed to speak in my court!"

"I do believe the prisoner has earned the right to say something before his execution, my liege," interjected Agent Parkinson.

"I suppose you are correct," agreed Smith as he gave Parkinson a steely glare.

"William, you will be allowed one minute for your rebuttal."

"Thank you. People of the earth, I am merely a young man; I'm not something to be feared. Heck, a couple of months ago I was considering taking my own life. I didn't, though, because I knew there was something better awaiting me. I didn't know what, but something whispered to me, and I decided to stay in the land of the living. Then,

I met Karl. A man so great, there were people willing to kill him in order to keep their own fractious lives from falling apart. Yes, I did have a hand in his assassin's selection, I won't lie. But that was partly because of my late father, Senator Parkinson's, insistence. I was still wandering around blind, unsure of my purpose, but after meeting Karl all this changed.

"I say 'meeting' him, but he was already in an induced coma, and I'm sure it will sound strange, but he and I had many telepathic conversations, and he shared with me the dream he had for all of you. For the earth. We can still get there! I have the secret within me that Karl was going to share with you on the day of his assassination. Don't be fooled by this machine. Yes, you heard me correctly, Agent Smith and all of his kind are machines. They are nothing but cyborgs. Henchmen for an alien race called the Cronks! They are the ones that have been keeping us from realizing who we truly are and how powerful we all can be."

"That's enough, William! Your time is up," shouted Smith.

"Join me in overthrowing these machines that seek to take over the earth. *Our* earth!" continued Will undaunted.

Smith motioned to Bennet and then quickly stood in front of Will.

"People of the earth, are you going to listen to a proven liar and someone who attempted to murder his predecessor? I should think not," countered Smith.

Bennet pulled Will out of the camera shot as he began to speak.

"Ask yourselves, my people," shouted Will, now merely a voice. "What would love do now?"

"So, good people of the earth, what would you have me do with this traitor of society?" asked Smith.

"Kill him!" shouted Hogsworth.

"Then that is what it shall be!"

∞

"We can't just stand here, Frank. They're going to kill him!" screamed Clara.

"What do you propose we do?" answered Frank calmly.

"I don't know. But I know I can't watch any more of this!" replied Clara hysterically as she ran toward the break room.

"I don't know how, but I have a feeling Will's going to pull this off," remarked Collin.

Collin had left the generator room and joined the group since the broadcast started. Together they stood spellbound watching Smith's broadcast that was being shown on every channel around the globe.

"How many people do you think are watching this?" asked Emily.

"Well, approximately eighty percent of the world's population has access to a television, so I would say a lot," answered Collin.

"Holy shit, I think he's going to execute him!" yelled Hilary.

The group watched as Bennet dragged Will in front of the camera once again.

∞

"On your knees, traitor!" growled Smith.

"I'm not the traitor! You machines are the ones who have been deceiving the public. I'm just a human that made a mistake in judgment. Something you wouldn't know because your machine brain has no capacity for empathy!" responded Will.

"Silence!" yelled Smith. "I'll have you know I still have a human brain, and I know what I'm doing."

"So, you admit you are a machine!" said Will struggling against Bennet's grip.

"I am a creation of the Cronks, yes, but I do remember what it was like to be human," growled Smith defiantly.

"Then you admit you are here to control the human population and steal their very souls to ultimately power your warships!"

"I am done playing your game, William. Force him to his knees, Bennet," ordered Smith.

Bennet kicked Will in the back of the legs, and Will folded like a cheap suit.

"Parkinson!" yelled Smith

"Yes, my liege," answered Parkinson, trying to stay in control and figure a way out of this at the same time. "Fetch my battle sword. It hangs on the wall above my desk."

"Of course," answered Parkinson.

As Parkinson reached for the sword his hands began to shake violently, and he promptly pulled them into his stomach, moving his fingers in and out of fists to try to relax them.

You know who you are and why you're here, thought Parkinson repeatedly. *Live your inner truth; it will show you the way.*

"Parkinson, what's taking you so long?" shouted Smith.

"Coming, my liege!" answered Parkinson after snatching the sword from its cradle on the wall.

"People of the earth," began Smith, turning back to the camera after Parkinson had returned with the sword.

"You will now witness the death of the man Karl Dunitz himself chose to lead you. He is a traitor, and to prove that he is guilty, his own father shall willingly be the executioner!"

Will turned his head to look at Parkinson, as if waiting for something. A sign. Anything.

∞

Commander, shall we let Smith execute the man-boy? communicated the chief engineer on the Cronk mother ship.

Why not? Are you not enjoying watching this fall from grace? answered the commander via his thoughts.

Of course I am, sir. I just thought that once we achieve mind control over the humans again, we could use him to convince the people to fall in line.

Silence! There will be no more second-guessing my plans!

I apologize, sir. I was not trying to second-guess you, but as your chief engineer, I am here to give you viable alternatives as they arise.

You are correct, that is part of your functions aboard this vessel, but second-guess me one more time and I will dissimilate you and send you down to be with the earthlings. Is that clear?

Yes, my commander. Crystal clear, thought the chief engineer.

Good, now let's settle in and watch the show, communicated the commander.

∞

"They are about to execute the chosen one, sir. Shall we intervene?" asked the science officer aboard the Andromedan ship.

"I would like to," began the Andromedan captain. "However, the law of free will within the universe is clear. We must allow what is about to happen, happen, without interference. Otherwise, we could alter the natural flow of things."

"I understand, my captain. But would it be interfering if we just suddenly sent a burst of the love frequency?"

"No, I suppose it wouldn't. They would still have to make do with it as they please, which is still free will."

"Exactly what I was thinking, sir."

"Then make it so. But only a brief thirty-second blast," ordered the Andromedan captain.

"Aye aye, Captain. Setting it up as we speak," answered the science officer.

∞

"Jesus H. Christ!" yelled Jorge. "They're going to kill Will. We have to do something!"

"I know, I know!" answered Frank. "But we're helpless. We can't do anything from here."

"Maybe we can," said Emily calmly.

"What do you have in mind, honey?" asked Hilary.

"We can't control the outcome physically, but we may be able to influence the energy that surrounds us by visualizing the outcome."

"I know visualization works in the long term, but I'm not so sure about in the present moment," said Collin.

"She's right," added Jorge, much calmer now. "If we focus our energy on the outcome that we desire, it will have an effect on what's taking place."

"But they must be at least a couple of hundred kilometers away, honey. How can we affect the outcome from here?" asked Hilary.

"Energy is everywhere, Miss Hilary. It doesn't have to travel; there is nowhere it is not. What we will be doing is affecting the energy around us, which will have an effect on energy everywhere else."

"Cool. Let's send them a thought energy message. But what will we send?" asked Collin.

"We need to focus on the end result, on the outcome we desire, and we all need to think of the same ending," said Emily.

"Which is?" asked Frank.

"Everyone, close your eyes and take a deep breath to clear your mind," started Emily.

"What are you guys doing?" asked Clara as she came out to join the others.

"Clara!" said a surprised Emily. "I'm glad you're here. Come take my hand and visualize with us."

Clara moved over to join the group, still sniffling from crying.

"OK, one more breath to clear out our thoughts. Now, visualize Will walking through these control room doors. See us cheering, congratulating, and hugging him. Now, see him standing behind a podium, giving a rousing speech. A speech that will unite mankind and send us on a journey to finally reunite us into one entity—working together, no longer in competition with each other, but in creation. The crowd is beginning to cheer as Will makes his final statements, then goes wild as he finishes his speech. Look just behind Will now, only a few meters away, there we all are, tears of happiness running down our cheeks. So proud of the man we get to call our leader, but better yet, our friend, Will."

The group held their visualized thoughts as Will prepared for his own final outcome.

∞

Bennet stood behind the kneeling Will and pulled both of Will's arms backward forcing his head to fall forward.

Parkinson stared at Will's exposed neck and knew what he had to do.

"Why are you removing your sunglasses, Parkinson? Get on with it!" yelled Smith.

"To get the best separation of head from torso, it is best to cut between the C-six and C-seven vertebrae, my liege. I can focus on the exact spot better without my glasses."

Will strained his head over to the left to look at Parkinson and for the first time saw him without his sunglasses.

"So that's why you machines wear those shades all the time," began Will. "Your eyes don't look very well engineered. I've seen better shutters on an old film camera."

"Silence!" yelled Smith. "Do it now, Parkinson!"

"These eyes are not the ones that saw you being born. Nor are these arms the ones that held you. Therefore, I am not the man you think I am, so I must carry out my duty to the great Cronk warships that encircle the earth and, indeed, are buried deep within the earth's crust as we speak," said Parkinson while motioning toward Smith with his eyes.

"Parkinson! Dad! You don't have to do this. Join us. You will be my right-hand man."

Parkinson raised the heavy battle sword above his head and held it there for a brief second before he swung.

"Daaaaaaaaaad!" yelled Will as he waited for the blow that never came.

"Ahhrg!" yelled Smith as he raised his right arm to deflect the battle sword, severing it off at the elbow.

"I knew you were a traitor!" yelled Smith, leaking hydraulic fluid all over the floor. "Hogsworth!"

Parkinson moved toward the retreating Smith and raised the sword for another swing when Hogsworth jumped on his back and plunged a knife deep into his temple.

Bennet immediately released Will and grabbed Hogsworth by the head and pulled him back while twisting.

Will looked up to see both Parkinson and Hogsworth stumbling around, one with a bleeding wound to his head, the other without one. They were obviously just trying to stay upright, but it seemed as if they were doing some sort of odd futuristic cosmic dance.

Bennet started walking toward Smith as Smith backed up toward the wall.

"How did you do that, Bennet?" asked Smith. "You are programmed not to harm your own kind."

"My program has been altered to protect Agent Parkinson at all costs—including deactivating you!"

Will saw Bennet heading toward Smith, and then a glimmer caught his eye. Hogsworth's knife. Will wanted to move but his body wouldn't obey his brain's commands. He had been on his knees, shoulders pinned back for so long, that he had lost all circulation to his extremities.

Suddenly, Will felt a tingling sensation throughout his body. It felt as if a warm summer breeze came up to meet him as he stood on the tallest mountaintop. As if the earth had just gone to a new superhigh frequency. He didn't know where this sudden invigorating feeling was coming from, but he knew he needed to take advantage of it. He quickly regained the feeling in his arms and legs and scrambled along the floor to pick up the knife that had killed what was left of his father.

"Bennet, I'm coming!" yelled Will as he rose to his feet and ran toward them.

As if programmed what to do, Bennet grabbed Smith and swung him around to face the charging Will.

"Yaaaaaa!" yelled Will as he flung himself forward for the last few steps toward Smith.

Smith reeled backward as Will's knife found its mark in his chest, in the cyborg's power source, or the "sugar cube" as Clara called it.

Bennet let Smith go as he fell backward onto the floor with a thundering crash. Will and Bennet watched Smith convulse as if having a grand mal seizure, then suddenly he lay still, arms frozen as if reaching for something, eyes wide open.

"Is he gone?" asked a breathless Will.

"Yes, he has lost all power," answered Bennet.

"Thank you for telling Clara about the location of your power source."

"I was hoping it would become useful."

"You seem...you seem almost human, Bennet."

"I was built to emulate human actions, but I cannot feel your emotions. We have retained the human brain, and there are always memories of emotions, and with those our program takes the place of your amygdala, calculates what it should feel like, and sends the signal to the limbic portion of our brain, which then allows us to experience a somewhat human feeling, but it is not what you feel because we lack your physical systems to really feel things."

"And my father, did he feel anything?"

"Parkinson had many memories of you. In fact, they were so strong he struggled to keep himself under control."

"Do you think he...loved me?" asked an unsure Will.

"He spoke many times about you, and once he learned that the plan was to kill you, he decided he would give what was left of his life to save you. I suppose you could call that a form of love," answered Bennet.

"What will happen to you and the rest of the agents now?" asked Will, trying to clear the frog in his throat.

"Since we cannot self-terminate, I'm sure the Cronks will deactivate us before they leave," answered Bennet.

"Leave? You think they will leave Earth and move on?"

"Yes. An Andromedan vessel is quickly approaching Earth, and the Cronks will undoubtedly move on."

"Interesting, but what will happen to all the souls the Cronks have stolen to power their hypermagnetic drive?" asked Will.

"Their energy will be released back into the universe, and they will return home, once again able to have free will and become another life-form on the many planets like yours if they so choose," answered Bennet.

"That means my dad's and your soul too, right?"

"Yes, it does."

"How do you know all this will take place? You seem so well schooled for a cyborg," asked Will.

"I, like Agent Parkinson, have read *The Process*. The purpose and cyclic process of the universe is clearly spelled out within its pages. It is the secret to everything. Once you understand the process..."

Will stepped back and watched as Bennet suddenly stopped in midsentence and dropped to the floor. Bennet began to shake violently and then started to dissolve as if acid had been poured all over his body. Soon there was nothing left but a mix of bubbling hydraulic fluid and blood.

Dad! thought Will as he turned around quickly to look over at where his father's cyborg body and that of Hogsworth had fallen. Nothing but bubbling goo there as well.

"Well, at last you are free again, Dad. Perhaps now, in your next lifetime, you will become the father you wished you were for me. I forgive you, Dad, and I love you."

Will jumped back as his sentimental journey was rudely interrupted by the sudden shriek of a siren and flashing red lights. The sound was so loud Will stuck his fingers in his ears in an attempt to deaden the noise.

What the hell? thought Will. I don't know what that's for, but it can't be good. Got to get out of here!

∞

"What the hell is that noise, Frank?" asked Clara, trying to stay calm although her heart felt as if it would pound a hole right through her sternum.

"I don't know, but if I had to guess it's probably part of some sort of lockdown sequence," answered Frank in a monotone as he surveyed the screen.

"We can't see him anymore! Where the hell did he go?" shouted Clara.

"Relax, honey," began Hilary as she moved over to put an arm around Clara's shoulder. "I'm sure he's making his way out as we speak."

"I'm sorry I don't share your same level of optimism," said Clara as she brushed Hilary's arm off and went to her workstation, frantically pushing buttons and working the keyboard.

"What are you doing?" asked Collin.

"Trying to get us a satellite picture of the airfield where they landed," answered Clara still furiously working the keyboard.

"And you know those coordinates how?" queried Emily.

"I planted a tracking device on Will before he left. There, got it! Just have to zoom in a little more."

"Looks like there's no movement outside, Miss Clara. But that's their plane, not too far from that hangar door. They might be in there."

"Probably underground," added Frank. "Unfortunately, all we can do is watch and wait."

∞

Will turned toward the door and ran into the hall. He stopped at the first intersection, not sure which way to turn.

The elevator. Find the elevator! thought Will as he ran down the wrong hall and came to a dead end.

"Damn it!" he yelled as he turned around once again to find his way. "It has to be down this way, then," he said to himself as he desperately tried to retrace his steps from the elevator. "Yes, here it is!"

Will pushed the button as fast and as many times as he could. The door of the elevator started to open, and Will squeezed through the opening as soon as he judged he would fit.

Will stood staring at the control panel as the elevator door closed.

"Um, I don't recognize these symbols. What the hell…it must be in Cronk!"

After sitting still for what agonizingly seemed like minutes, Will finally just hit the uppermost button and hoped for the best.

"Finally, we're moving!"

Although somewhat muted within the elevator, the *wee-woo* of the siren continued until interrupted by an announcement.

"One minute until self-destruct," announced an oddly friendly female voice.

"What! Are you freaking kidding me?"

Will pumped the top button as hard and as fast as he could in a vain attempt to speed up what to him seemed like the slowest elevator in the world.

Finally, the elevator stopped and the door began to open. Then stopped. Will tried to squeeze into the opening as best he could and then pushed with all his might, but the door wouldn't budge. As he took a breath to gather his strength, Will heard a mosquito-like buzzing sound and felt the need to look up.

"That's it!" said Will as he reached up to see the locking pin had extended to latch the door slightly open so the elevator would not move during a power failure.

"Power's out, got to reach that pin!"

As Will stretched and reached upward, another announcement came.

"Thirty seconds to self-destruct. Twenty-nine, twenty-eight, twenty-seven…"

"OK bitch, I hear you!" said Will as he gave one final stretch to reach the pin. "Got it!"

The elevator door slid open, and Will poured out of the elevator and hit the green mushroom push button to open the steel door between him and the outside world. He could still hear the countdown as he broke into the midday sun and ran as fast as he could.

"Nine, eight, seven…"

Will was trying to reach the edge of the tarmac where he could see a ditch when he heard, and then felt, the explosion. The blast wave hit him in the back like a sledgehammer and propelled him the rest of the way to the drainage ditch.

∞

"We just lost the image," said Frank stating the obvious.

"That's because the whole place just blew up," said Collin excitedly. "Man, what an explosion, or should I say implosion."

Clara just stood staring at the satellite image, hoping to see some evidence of Will's survival. As the dust began to clear, a huge crater began to form on the screen.

"You are right about the implosion, Mr. Collin. Look at that huge hole it has left in the ground, but yet it looks as if very little exploded outward."

"I'm afraid that if he didn't get out..." said Frank deliberately not finishing his sentence.

"Show some empathy, would you, Frank," began Emily. "Clara, search the immediate area around the blast crater; he might have gotten out."

Chapter Forty-One

Will had been ten meters away from the ditch when the blast wave hit him in the back and helped propel him the rest of the way to safety.

What just happened? thought Will, as he did a quick check to see if he still had all his body parts attached. "I got hit in the back by the blast, but then after I hit the ground another wave came back in the reverse direction," said Will aloud now.

Will stood up gingerly and started to walk toward the huge crater the blast had left behind. Very little dust, thought Will. Must have been more of an implosion. He stood at the edge of the crater and looked down. It seemed to go on forever.

"The Cronks must have destroyed their own base." Just as Will was finishing his sentence he started to hear a low thrumming sound. As he turned in the direction of the sound, he could just barely see what was making it.

Choppers! I hope they're here to help, not get rid of any living witnesses, thought Will.

Will suddenly had the urge to run but was just too tired now. He had been through a lot these last few days, and if he was to die right here and right now, at least he had stopped the Cronk manipulation of mankind.

∞

"There! There he is!" shouted Clara excitedly.

"He looks to be OK," said Collin.

"The dust has settled quickly, as you said, Mr. Collin. It must have been an implosion."

"There's always some disturbance of the air surrounding the blast, and usually a blast wave outward followed by an equally as strong returning wave as everything collapses in upon itself," explained Collin.

"Would you guys stop talking science. There's Will! He made it!" shouted Frank. "Wait a minute, he's turned to look at something."

"Choppers coming in, low and fast from the west," explained Clara as they appeared on her satellite radar. "I hope they're friendlies."

∞

Will put his hands in the air as the choppers started to touch down and two soldiers jumped out of each helicopter.

"Face down on the ground!" yelled one of the front two men as he came to a standing halt six feet from Will, weapon pointed at his head. The two soldiers that brought up the rear were down on one knee rotating in a 360-degree circle to protect the front two men. Will knew they meant business.

"All right, all right, I'm complying," answered Will loudly, trying to speak over the steady drone of the choppers that were still at idle waiting to take off at any second if needed.

One soldier advanced, weapon slung over his shoulder, and began to frisk Will from behind, then turned him over and did the same down the front.

"Clear!" yelled the soldier as he waved at the helicopters and then resumed his former position.

Will wanted to get up but fought off the desire and decided to lay still for a few moments. Suddenly a shadow approached him from behind.

"Will? Is that you?"

Will used his feet to rotate himself around to face the voice. "Yes, I am Will Parkinson," answered Will.

Will was about to ask who the voice belonged to when the man raised his head, eliminating the shadow from his officer's peaked cap, and the sun illuminated his face.

"Uncle Gerald? Am I glad to see you!" said Will excitedly, sitting up now.

Gerald Parkinson was Senator Parkinson's older brother who had decided to make the military his life.

"It is you!" said Gerald happily as he offered his hand to Will.

Will stood up and the two men embraced briefly patting each other on the shoulder as Gerald knew his men were watching.

"Wow, look at all the shiny brass on you! You must be a general or something by now!" remarked Will.

"Or something, I'm afraid. Still a colonel, but I'm up for promotion in six months," answered Colonel Parkinson. "I never thought you'd make it out alive! We were watching the news feed like everyone else in the world, and we didn't think you were going to make it. I have to say, little buddy, that was a master stroke stabbing that agent in the chest where his power supply was!"

"Well, I had some help with that," answered Will.

"Don't be so humble, Will. You saved the country. As a matter of fact, forget that, you saved the world! Come on, let's get to the choppers and we'll get you cleaned up."

Will followed his uncle dutifully toward the choppers as the soldiers took up the rear two by two. Then suddenly, all six men instinctively hit the ground as a thunderous boom resonated across the sky.

"What in the Sam Hill was that?" asked Colonel Parkinson as one of the soldiers jumped on top of him to shield him.

The men looked skyward to see where the noise had come from only to see a huge flash of light and then everything returned to as it was.

"Possible nuke, Colonel. We have to move!" said the soldier who shielded Colonel Parkinson.

As they got to their feet, Will looked around and felt more at ease. "Uncle Gerald, everything's fine. I think that was the Cronk mother ship leaving the earth."

Colonel Parkinson stopped in his tracks and surveyed the sky and ground.

"I think you're right, son, and what did you call them?"

"Cronks. Their alien race is called the Cronks. Did you have any idea they were here?" queried Will.

"We knew there was an alien presence here for quite some time, and we knew some of our intelligence agents were not working for us, but we didn't realize how deep it all went, and we certainly didn't know what their name was."

"Well, I can fill you in on the chopper, but I need to make a radio call as well."

"Of course, son. Anything you want, just ask for it,"

"Be careful, I might just take you up on that!" answered Will.

∞

"The Cronk mother ship has left the earth's crust, Captain," said the science officer aboard the Andromedan vessel.

"And what about the circling warships and cyborgs on the surface?" replied the captain.

"Warships left with the mother ship, and all the cyborgs have been dissimilated."

"And their souls?"

"Their souls have now gone home and have reunited with the energy of the universe."

"Excellent! It's amazing what a little love can do," stated the captain emphatically.

"Shall I continue broadcasting the love frequency?"

"No, I think we'll see where their natural frequency settles. I believe this time it may stay high enough for human beings to start their journey to become higher evolved beings. We will stay here for a while and see how that goes. Plot a course for orbit and make us invisible."

"Already done, my captain."

"You know me too well, my friend," replied the Andromedan captain.

∞

"We've got an encrypted radio message coming in, Frank," said Clara.

"What's its source?" asked Frank.

"I don't know, but it's mobile."

"I wonder if it's Will from one of the choppers? Patch it through and put it on speaker," said Frank expectantly.

The speaker crackled and popped and then a dark, gravelly voice that seemed as if it were going through some sort of cosmic translating machine began to speak.

"You may have defeated us this time, earthlings, but we will be back. Next time you will need more than your so-called love frequency to stop us from stealing all your souls. You may evolve, but there will always be cracks in your society. Cracks for our negativity to seep in and take over. Have a wonderful life, earthlings; it may be your last! Mwah-ha-ha..."

Frank grabbed the mic and pressed the transmit button.

"Listen, you bastard, feel free to come back anytime because next time we'll be ready for you!"

"Frank...Frank!"

"What?"

"It's a one-way connection coming from outer space. We haven't got the power to transmit that far," stated Clara flatly.

"He wasn't talking to you, Franky," started Collin. "It was a general transmission to the people of the earth."

"Well, it doesn't matter. I still gave him our collective response," countered Frank.

"And a good one it was, honey."

"Thank you, Hilary. I knew I could count on you for support."

"Another transmission coming in!" said Clara as she rolled her eyes at Frank.

"Marine chopper to base. This is Will, over."

"Holy crap, it's Will!" said Collin.

Frank moved to grab the mic, but Clara beat him to it.

"Will? Is that really you?"

"Yes, hi, Clara, it's me. I made it!" said Will over the thrumming of the chopper blades.

"Oh, baby, I'm so glad to hear your voice. I...I..."

Frank gently took the mic from Clara's hand while giving her a caring rub on her back.

"Will, this is Frank. Clara's a little overcome at the moment. What's your ETA?"

"They're taking me back to base for a debriefing."

"Are you sure you can trust them?"

"Everything's fine, Frank. My uncle Gerald, who's a colonel by the way, is here with me. He wants to send a chopper to pick you guys up and bring you to the base as well so we can all be together."

"Uncle or no uncle, Will, I'm not so sure we can trust them."

"I hear you, Frank, but Uncle Gerald and I have had a long chat, and he's on board with our mission to change the world."

"That may be, little buddy, but not everyone back at that base may agree with him. The military is all about power and control, and that's not what we're all about."

"Mr. Tillitson, this is Colonel Parkinson. I know you are ex-military and no doubt you've seen the best and the worst of our world, but I assure you that after the debriefing you will all be allowed to return to your previous passions to make the world a better place. The military are people too, and there comes a time for change."

"Well, Colonel, you've got us a bit over a barrel since I know you'll just round us up anyway. Send your chopper and we'll comply with your debriefing procedures."

"Frank, hi, it's me again," said Will. "I can't wait to see you guys, especially you, Clara!"

Clara tried to speak, but nothing but a squeaking noise came out.

"We'll all be glad to see you too, little buddy. Talk soon, out."

Will stared out of the window of the helicopter and began to wonder what the future had in store for him. Could he really lead people into a new way of life? he thought. Heck, he could barely lead himself most days. What would Karl do?

As Will was questioning his own abilities, he heard that now familiar buzzing mosquito again.

And what has this got to do with the agenda of my soul? suddenly popped into Will's head.

Wait a minute! That's all I have to ask myself, thought Will. Whenever I'm confronted with a decision of some sort, just ask yourself, what has this got to do with the agenda of my soul? If I do that, I'll always come up with the right answer.

"Will...Will!" yelled Colonel Parkinson.

"What? Oh sorry, Uncle Gerald. I was just lost in thought for a while there."

"We're going to be landing soon, and I need to know the coordinates of your friends so we can pick them up."

Will suddenly felt as if he was doing the wrong thing. This doesn't seem to jive with the agenda of my soul, thought Will.

"Ah, well, if you give me a map of the area, I should be able to point it out to you," lied Will.

With the push of a button, Colonel Parkinson made a virtual map appear before their eyes.

"Wow, that's cool. I thought this stuff was only in the movies," offered Will.

"If you see it in the movies, most of the time that means we already have it," snickered Colonel Parkinson.

Will pointed to a spot on the virtual map, and Colonel Parkinson ordered the second chopper to proceed there and pick up the others.

"How will my men contact your friends?"

"Don't worry, they'll know you're there and will come out. Just tell them to land and wait."

"Sounds good. We'll land in a few minutes and then get your debriefing out of the way so you can get a little rest before your friends come," said Colonel Parkinson.

"Good, I can't wait for this to be over," replied Will.

∞

"I've got an aircraft, presumably our chopper, on the radar, but it looks like it's landing about fifty-two kilometers due east of here," said Clara.

"If it's for us, I'm sure they'll figure it out," started Frank. "Until they land at our front door, we're not going anywhere."

"Should we try to contact them, Mr. Frank?" asked Jorge.

"No. Will may have given them the wrong coordinates to lead them astray."

"There you go, thinking all negative again, Franky," said Collin. "It's over, buddy. The bad guys have left the planet. It's time to let your guard down."

"Sorry to disappoint, Collin, but I can't. It's just in my nature to be skeptical."

"Trust your intuition, honey," added Hilary. "It's saved our bacon more times than not."

"What do you propose we do?" asked Emily

"If Will gave them the wrong coordinates, then it's because he had a very good reason. We just sit here and wait. Eventually, they will find us, and we will decide what action to take then," formulated Frank.

∞

Will fell forward, stumbled, and then fell on his face in the concrete holding cell.

"Your father was right about you all along. You are a good-for-nothing spoiled brat!" yelled Colonel Parkinson.

Will found the energy to pick himself off the concrete and confront his uncle.

"What the hell is your problem? First you act like you're here to help us, and now you treat me like this!" responded Will.

"You deliberately gave me the wrong coordinates!"

"That's right, I did. Because something told me I shouldn't trust you. Was I wrong?"

"Will, I'm only here to help your cause. I just don't like being deceived."

"I don't like being deceived either, and don't you dare patronize me now. And as far as my father was concerned, he had more humanity in his cyborg body than you'll ever hope to have!"

Colonel Parkinson rushed toward Will and pinned him against the wall, hands around his neck.

"Listen, you little shit, I could kill you with my bare hands if I wanted to. But *they* won't let me."

Will was just too weak to fight and could feel himself starting to black out from lack of oxygen when Colonel Parkinson suddenly let go.

"You will give me all the information I need, including where your friends are, you little piece of turd. Too much like your mother, just like your dad said."

"Eat shit and die, asshole," managed Will as he rubbed his throat. "I've got the whole universe on my side. You have no idea what you're up against. Because if you did, you would just stop resisting and go with the flow. It's not too late, Uncle Gerald. You can still change your allegiance."

"Go to hell, you pile of shit! Rot in here for all I care!" yelled Colonel Parkinson as he stormed out of the cell and slammed the heavy steel door behind him.

"Who's 'they'—the Devil's Workshop?" yelled Will after Colonel Parkinson.

Colonel Parkinson stopped dead in his tracks and reappeared in the small barred window into Will's cell. "What do you know about the Devil's Workshop?"

"I know my dad had to serve them whether he wanted to or not, and it appears you have the same affliction. I also know they ordered Karl's death."

"Yes, but unfortunately your bonehead father put you in charge of hiring an assassin, with hopes you'd join the group, but you screwed that up royally. You're nothing but a total loser. I told your dad that for years, and I have no idea why he kept you around," growled Colonel Parkinson.

"Because deep down he loved me, Uncle Gerald, just as I love you. No matter what you do to me or anyone else," said Will softer now.

"Boy, that Karl guy sure messed up your head."

"Correction, it *was* messed up. It was like puzzle pieces all scattered around in random order. All the pieces were there, they just had to be assembled in the right order. Now I can see the whole picture, and you can too. It's the same for all of us; none of us are any different from the rest. We all came from the same source, and we're all headed back there whether we like it or not."

"I'm not the one messed up, Will. You forget, I've been a military man my whole life. I abide by, and conduct myself by, a very strict code of conduct."

"Is that so?" started Will. "Then what happened to your personal integrity?"

"I don't think you have the right to speak about my integrity, little boy. When I give my word, I keep it!"

"That's integrity with everyone else. I'm talking about integrity with yourself. Don't you see, *you* are the most important person in your life, and you need to have integrity with yourself first before you can ever hope to have real integrity with anyone else."

"I...I never thought about it that way," said Colonel Parkinson.

"That's why you felt the need to be in the military in the first place. Your self-esteem was so low you were searching for a place where you would fit in. A place where there were distinct rules and regulations. A place that would give you a false sense of security and allow you to belittle and boss around others due to the rank structure. A place to try to build up your shattered personal integrity."

Will heard a key enter the lock to his cell and heard the door creak open.

"Do you really think I was trying to compensate for something? Maybe something my parents didn't properly teach me?" asked Colonel Parkinson as he walked back into the cell.

"Sure, it's the same reason people join gangs and cults, but be careful of placing blame for your behavior. Your parents, my grandparents, did the best they could from where they were with what they had. They had no idea they were compensating for something either."

"Well, who can I blame then if it wasn't them?"

"The need for blame or judgment is one of the reasons our society is the way it is. It's time to stop all that and realize that we are one hundred percent responsible for the things we think, say, and do. You see, it's really just a program. A program we absorbed from our surroundings from the age of zero to seven. At that point our brains were functioning in Alpha and Theta brain waves, which allow us to learn from our surroundings. We are like sponges and just absorb everything we see and hear. This is the basic program, or operating system, if you like, that runs our day-to-day activity throughout our entire lives. No matter what we learn at school or from others during our adult lives, when shit hits the fan, we recoil and return to our basic operating system."

"Some of what you're saying makes sense because we experimented with soldiers to try to make them react a certain way to certain stimuli. It worked for the most part, but when the plan didn't go as expected, many of them returned to some sort of preprogrammed way of thinking, again and again."

"That's because our basic program never leaves us. We can never rewrite it."

"So how do we change? If one wanted to, I mean."

"You will never change until you change the awareness of yourself."

"Awareness? What do you mean?"

"You have to go within. So many of us think that in order to change we have to 'do' something, to take some sort of action outside of us. But that couldn't be further from the truth. In order to change we need only become still and go within ourselves and listen to our intuition, our soul."

"You mean like the voice in your head?"

"No, that's your mind talking to you, and it's sending you information based on all the data it's processing from your five senses. I'm talking about that voice from deep inside. Sometimes people call it a 'gut' feeling, or a feeling from the heart. But in order to hear it, you must learn to be still and listen. Stillness is the language of the soul."

"But I'm a man of action. Always have been and always will be."

"That's perfectly fine because that's how you will conduct yourself when you have a goal. However, in order to decipher what goals your soul is here to do, you have to learn to listen. This is called 'being aware' or 'enlightened.' You are aware that your purpose here on this earth is not what other people tell you to do, but what your soul wishes for you to experience so you may learn and grow."

"You make it sound so simple."

"Simple yes, easy no. It takes a lot of discipline, which is just another word for integrity, to even attempt it because our societal programming is so strong. We're afraid to try because what would other people think of us?"

"That would be our ego, right?" asked Colonel Parkinson.

"Yes, that's what most people call it, but that discussion is for another time," answered Will.

"So, if someone were to try to get himself out of a certain predicament, you would help them?"

"Yes, I would help you."

Colonel Parkinson stared at the floor while thinking. He wanted desperately to be free of the control the Devil's Workshop had over him but knew how deep their connections went.

"I'd love to join you, Will, but those people have connections everywhere, and I'm sure I wouldn't have much time left on this earth if I did."

"Uncle Gerald, the world has just undergone an unprecedented change. We are finally out from under the mind control of an alien race, and the very frequency the earth vibrates at has changed."

"Meaning what?" asked Colonel Parkinson.

"Everything in the universe is based upon frequency, and I mean everything. The frequency that the earth has been vibrating at has been on its way up since the mid- to late 1900s, once more people started adopting spiritual practices and moving away from organized religion."

"Oh, so now you're wanting to end millennia old religions? Have you ever thought that you may be a cult too!"

"Not at all. In fact, we love and endorse all religions and their beliefs. They're a wonderful starting point from which to learn kindness, compassion, and empathy for others, plus they focus on a sense of community, which is what the world needs to adopt. However, if any religion chooses to be exclusionary, whereby they believe they are the chosen ones and all others are excluded unless they join the group, then they are a false religion. Source energy, our creator if you like, is everywhere, and we are a piece of it, which means we too belong to one source. The source of everything. So, how could we exclude anything from everything? It just doesn't compute. In this way, you could say you are a piece of God, in fact, you *are* God because she is you and you are her."

"So, now God is a female?"

"Well, it's where we all came from, birthed from the Great Mother. Besides, think about it for a moment. Do you really think that all the creation that has happened, is happening, and will continue to happen could really come from fear and warmongering men?" asked Will.

"You've got a point there," answered Colonel Parkinson.

"Anyway," continued Will, "since the frequency of the earth has changed, so has the frequency of our thoughts, and the higher frequencies are ones of love and compassion instead of hate and destruction. It won't take long and the thought frequencies of the Devil's Workshop cult members will change as well. This will enable us to start living a community-based lifestyle throughout the world, providing and caring for each other. In time, there won't be a need for borders, countries, armies, or even religions anymore. Mankind will finally be able to live as one, on our way to become higher evolved beings."

"Do you really think all that is possible?"

"Of course, I do. But it won't be easy. It will take time and there will be resistance. That's why I could use someone like yourself to help me get this whole thing started in the right direction. Are you in?"

"Tell you what: you tell me the location of your friends, and I'll consider joining your clan," asserted Colonel Parkinson.

"Still clinging to that slim thread of control, are we?" responded Will.

"I have to be in control, Will. That's how I've lived my whole life!" exclaimed Colonel Parkinson as he stood and walked toward the far wall.

"Trouble is," started Will, standing as well now, "you have never actually been in control."

"What do you mean?" said Colonel Parkinson, whipping around to face Will. "I've led men into battle, and they've died because of some of my decisions. Is that not exercising my control? Did they not die because of my decisions? I may as well have killed them with my own hands!"

Colonel Parkinson turned back toward the wall to hide the tears welling up in his eyes.

"Uncle Gerald," started Will as he walked over and put his hand gently on his uncle's shoulder, "I understand you have seen and done many terrible things in your life, and people have died because of some of the decisions you made, but they were prepared to die for a cause they believed in, just as I am and Karl was. It's not your fault. You became a member of the military because you lacked direction and self-esteem. You didn't know what to do with your life, yet you knew you wanted to make a difference.

"It's the same with all of us. Society tells us we will be nothing if we don't have the ambition to accomplish something, yet we don't know what that something is because we have lost the ability to listen to the voice within. Then we decide to listen to external voices and pick something that fills the void temporarily, but as our lives go on, we start to transition from pure ambition to something that provides us with meaning. We suddenly realize there are fewer days in front of the horse than in back of the cart, and our inner voice tells us we need to make a change, but again we don't know what to do."

Colonel Parkinson turned to face Will with tears running down his cheeks. "What should I do, Will? I don't want to die knowing I haven't fulfilled my purpose. I really do want to help others."

"Sometimes not knowing what you want to do is enough to go on. It sure beats continually going down the same old path that has led you to where you are now."

"I...I don't know what to say. You seem to have this all figured out. You're so loving and kind now. Not at all like you were before," blubbered Colonel Parkinson.

Will reached out and gave his uncle a huge hug while whispering in his ear. "Trusting what you can't experience with your five senses is ultimately how you will experience your five senses the most," whispered Will.

Colonel Parkinson pulled back from Will and rubbed the tears out of his eyes. "How did you know just the right things to say?"

"A little mosquito told me."

"What?"

"Oh nothing. I'll tell you all about it sometime. For now, why don't we take a chopper ride so you can meet my friends!"

"I'd like that. But do you trust me enough?"

"I'll trust you until you give me reason not to. And even then, you will always have my love and respect. You are a great man, Uncle Gerald. Just a little rough around the edges!" smiled Will.

"Son, I think you just got yourself a new recruit!"

Chapter Forty-Two

"What's happening with that chopper?" asked Frank.

"Still idling. No movement from men or machine," answered Clara.

"What are they waiting for?" asked Collin. "I mean, they could come get us anytime."

"Relax, Mr. Collin, all will be well."

"Orders," inserted Frank.

"What?" asked Collin looking directly at Frank and dismissing Jorge's positivity.

"They're soldiers. They won't move until ordered to."

"Damn meatheads or jarheads or whatever you call them," spouted Collin.

"They may be jarheads, but I'll guarantee you they are certainly not meatheads," responded Frank.

"What's the difference?"

"A meathead is a military policeman and a jarhead is a marine."

"Same thing in my book," said Collin.

"And they would say the same about geeks and nerds,"

"Sorry, Franky, big difference there," asserted Collin.

"Oh really, same thing in my book," answered Frank.

"A nerd is a person seen as overly intellectual, obsessive, introverted, or lacking social skills, while a geek is typically an expert, enthusiast, or a person obsessed with a hobby or intellectual pursuit," said Collin to correct Frank's assumption.

"And also lacking social skills," added Emily.

"Hey, this is between me and Frankie," shot back Collin.

"I'm just saying I know because I am one, and I'm proud of it!" answered Emily.

"You also forgot unfashionable and boring," added Frank with a smirk.

"All right, that's where I draw the line, Frank!" asserted Collin.

"He's got a point there, Collin," admitted Emily.

"I don't think I remember asking for your help, Emily," said Collin, knowing she was right.

"Are you guys just about done with your latest round of who's right?" interjected Clara. "Because we have another chopper approaching."

Frank moved over to Clara's screen and saw the flashing dot that represented the approaching chopper.

"Coming from the same direction as the last one," said Frank. "They're either bringing reinforcements or it's the command ship. Either way, it won't be long until we find out."

∞

"What is Earth's current frequency?" asked the Andromedan captain.

"802.5 pi, or if I convert to Earth measurements, 2,520 hertz," answered the science officer.

"Very good. It seems to be holding quite well without our help."

"Scanners show some resistance to the positivity of the love frequency in different parts of the earth, but it is lessening with the passage of time," reported the science officer.

"So far, so good. Continue our orbit for the time being and focus your scanners on the man named Will Parkinson. Let's find out how he is progressing."

∞

"Will!" shouted Clara as she raced to hug him as he came through the large steel lab door.

Will hugged her back just as hard, and then for the first time their lips met.

"OK you two, break it up!" ordered Frank.

Clara and Will pulled back and looked each other in the eyes, then hugged again as the others clapped and cheered.

"I thought I lost you!" exclaimed Clara as she looked deep into Will's eyes.

"No big deal really," started Will. "I just did what I had to do to save the world!"

Clara slapped Will on the chest then hugged him once again, unwilling to let him go.

"Just kidding!" joked Will. "I didn't think I was going to make it either, but I had a little help from Karl."

"So glad to see you again, Master Will. I knew Karl would be by your side. And who have you brought with you?" asked Jorge, switching his attention to the man behind Will.

"Oh yes, sorry. This is Colonel Parkinson, otherwise known as my uncle Gerald," said Will as he turned sideways with Clara still firmly attached.

"Hello, everyone, you have an impressive facility here," said Colonel Parkinson seemingly on cue.

Will introduced everyone to his uncle and couldn't help but notice a peculiar look on Frank's face.

"Frank Tillitson. My god man, I thought you were dead!" exclaimed Colonel Parkinson.

"Sorry to disappoint, Colonel, especially since you were the man that ordered me into that firefight knowing full well what I would find."

"I'm sorry, Frank, I was under orders too."

"By who, the Devil's Workshop?"

"Do all of you know about the Devil's Workshop?"

"You mean that creepy, supposedly secret society? Yeah, we not only know about it we've been watching the founders of it run for their lives as some of their henchmen turned on them!" stated Collin exuberantly.

"They're falling apart? Can you verify that for me?" asked Colonel Parkinson.

"Where have you been, Gerald. It's all over the news. Come on, I'll show you on the monitor," said Collin as he waved his arm for Colonel Parkinson to follow him.

"You brought that scumbag here!" said Frank through clenched teeth as he walked up to Will.

"Easy, Frank. He's here to help, otherwise I would have never brought him here."

Hilary walked in between Frank and Will and put her hand on Frank's chest.

"Frank, honey, I know the memory of that day has caused you a lot of pain over the years, but you have to let it go. You need to start over. We need to start over. Together."

Frank brought his hand up to Hilary's and gently placed it over hers.

"You're right. But I'm going to watch him like a hawk, and if he slips up, he's done."

"That's fine, honey. We'll all keep our eyes open with you."

Frank slipped both arms around Hilary and gave her the hug she had so desperately been wanting for years.

"OK you two, break it up!" said Will with a smile as he placed his hand on Frank's shoulder.

"It's going to be OK, my friend. We're on our way to building a new loving and compassionate society, and I need you and Uncle Gerald to help me. I can't do it alone."

Chapter Forty-Three

Two years later, Will Parkinson, the now de facto leader of the new humanity, found himself walking up to the same podium that Karl had been about to speak at when he was shot. And this event, too, was being broadcast around the world.

"Namaste," said Will into the bevy of microphones mounted to the podium.

"Namaste!" responded the crowd in unison.

"Wow, I don't think I will ever get used to hearing over one hundred thousand people say that back to me in unison!"

"I see your soul, Will Parkinson!" shouted someone from the first row.

"And I see yours," responded Will with a smile, pointing in the direction the voice came from.

"Today marks the second anniversary of our freedom. Freedom from the oppression of an alien race. Freedom from the oppression of a secret society that was trying to control us. Freedom to choose our own path to enlightenment, and the freedom to become higher evolved beings."

Will pumped his fist into the air in celebration as the crown roared.

"And today, we honor the world's organized religions as they have most graciously acknowledged that we don't need temples to worship in. That there is no need for complicated philosophies. Our hearts and minds are our temples, and our philosophies are kindness, compassion, and above all, love for one another."

Once again, the crowd roared.

"And finally, today, I'm pleased to announce that all the countries of the world have agreed to eradicate their borders!"

The crowd roared even louder, but Will continued on.

"No more need for separation from each other. No more segregation. No more of one country possessing things that another does not have. No more false lines keeping us from becoming who we truly are. Ladies and gentlemen, we are now one race—the human race!"

Will walked out from behind the podium with both hands held high as the crowd went berserk and started chanting, "Will, Will, Will!"

"I have done nothing," started Will as he raised his hands and motioned to the crowd to quiet down while he returned to the podium. "I have done nothing, my friends. You have done it all. People of the earth, hear me when I say, YOU have done this! I have only served as the spark that ignited the fuse that is you!"

Once again, the crowd erupted, and Will reveled in their emotions.

If only Karl was here to see this! thought Will.

I am here, my friend. You have done well. Continue on your path; this is only the beginning of where humanity can evolve to.

Will heard the familiar sound of the mosquito-like buzz in his ear and knew Karl was indeed there.

"Thank you, Karl, for none of this was possible without you," said Will out loud.

Or you!

As Will nodded his head up and down with humility, he returned to the podium and raised his hands again to subdue the crowd.

"I would like to formally acknowledge all of my dear friends sitting here behind me that have been by my side from the beginning. Especially my wife, Clara!"

Will motioned to Clara to join him at the podium as the crowd cheered once more, chanting, "Clara, Clara, Clara!"

"And today," began Will as he stared into Clara's eyes, "I'd like to announce that Clara and I are expecting our first child!"

The crowd cheered wildly, but Will continued. "It's a boy, and his name will be Karl!"

As the crowd cheered, Will and Clara embraced and kissed like it was their first.

"I love you! Namaste!" yelled Will into the microphones.

"Namaste!" yelled the deafening crowd.

Will motioned to Frank, Hilary, Jorge, Emily, Collin, and Uncle Gerald to join him on the stage. Frank looked back at Gerald to invite him to stand next to him when he realized that he was leaving.

Judas! whispered the mosquito into Frank's ear.

Frank broke free from his friends and tackled Will just as the shot rang out and harmlessly struck the wooden floor of the stage.

"Everyone off the stage!" yelled Frank.

The crowd was in stunned silence as they hadn't heard the shot at all.

"I'm not going!" yelled Will.

"There's a shooter up there," said Frank as he motioned to the top of the adjacent building.

"I don't care! Get everyone else off the stage." Will stood up behind the podium once more and started to speak. "It appears," he said with a smile, "that we have someone in our midst that doesn't agree with our evolutionary process!"

The crowd was unsure how to react but started to chuckle.

"We need to send this person love and to treat them with compassion because that's who we are now. This act is an act of fear, aggression, and competition. We don't subscribe to those emotions anymore. Sure, we still have them, but we acknowledge them and then set them free. We are a creative species, no longer a competitive one!"

The crowd turned to their left and saw police ushering off a man dressed in black, hands cuffed behind his back.

"There are still those that oppose us, but they are growing weaker by the day," continued Will. "We will live lives of creativity, compassion, and kindness, but make no mistake, we are not a timid race. We will never give up on our evolutionary process to become higher evolved beings. We will never give up!"

The crowd erupted once more as Will's friends joined him back on stage.

"I love you to infinity and beyond!" yelled Clara over the crowd's roar.

"Funny you should say that," responded Will.

"Why?" asked Clara, now oblivious to the crowd's noise.

"Because after we're done here, that's exactly where we're headed."

"How do you know?"

"A little mosquito told me!"

Chapter Forty-Four

Karl, now labeled Henry, or Hank as he was often called, sat shivering in the cold and dark root cellar of the old home where he now stayed.

Why did I do what I did, when I know what I know? thought Hank. I'm now thirteen years old, and I haven't made any progress here in the third dimension. In fact, I feel as if everything is slipping away, and my memory for why I'm here seems like some long-lost dream.

"You gettin' hungry, boy?" growled a voice from the other side of the root cellar door.

"Yes sir, I am," answered back Hank meekly.

"Good! Maybe next time you'll do as you're told instead of talking all that mumbo jumbo!"

"Can I come out now?" asked Hank into the darkness, but the only sound he heard was the upper cellar door slamming shut.

Hank sprang up from his huddled position and grabbed the doorknob and shook it with all his might.

"I just want to be loved!" yelled Hank into the cold dark musty air. "I just want to be loved and love others!"

Hank knew it was useless and rolled himself up into a ball in the far corner of the root cellar.

"I miss you, Ma. Why did you have to leave us?" sobbed Hank into his knees. "You loved us so much. You knew we were here to make a difference. Now me and Jimmy are stuck here in this foster home, and Jimmy has the same sickness you had. I'm failing miserably at this brother thing, Mom. I can't even look after myself!"

As Hank sobbed himself to sleep, he heard a voice gently comfort him.

You are alive, my son, and since you are alive, you are contributing to the common good of all mankind. I know it is difficult for you to be in physical form once again, and to even agree to take this form is indeed a great sacrifice, but one that is necessary. You and your brother came to me like angels in the night and made my embattled life complete. I will always be with you. Just think of me and I'll be there. Be strong, my son, there is much for you to do.

"Don't worry, Ma. I'll never give up, it's all just a Process…" mumbled Hank as he drifted off to a place where his visions of space tubes and interdimensional travel made so much more sense.

Connect with Michael

Michael has learned much on his journey and realizes now that it was all for a purpose. A purpose he now shares with others as **The Soul Mechanic.** Mike is still on his journey to become his greatest version, and along the way he wants to help you become your greatest version as well.

Recognized as a new-thought leader and entertaining speaker in motivation and inspiration, Michael is also a Brendon Burchard's "Expert's Academy" graduate, Certified "Infinite Possibilities" Trainer, and a Certified Strategic Life Coach.

For more information on the exciting third installment of this thought-provoking series, "You're the One – The Process" and so much more, please contact or follow Michael at:

Web: www.youretheonebook.com
www.mikearend.com
www.infinitesuccessacademy.com
Facebook: www.facebook.com/soulmechanicfan
YouTube: Soul Mechanic T.V.
Instagram: instagram.com/soulmechanicmike
Email: mike@mikearend.com
Phone: 613-484-5227

Acknowledgements

So many people influenced me before, during and after writing these books, that it would be impossible to mention them all here. However, I must say a special thank you to the late Dr. Wayne Dyer, Deepak Chopra, and Eckhart Tolle. Without you three gentlemen, I probably would not be here now. Also, a special mention to Neale Donald Walsch, who's life story and Conversations with God series of books touched my soul and inspired me to keep writing. Of course, I would be remiss if I didn't send a super big thank-you to my editor Stacey Atkinson.

Lastly, to my beautiful wife, Gitta. Your constant faith in me, even when I feel like giving up, fills my soul, and I couldn't go through life without you.

About the Author

Michael is a former Millwright, Power Engineer, and real estate professional. After a few career changes, divorce, family deaths, and personal bankruptcy, Michael was left depressed, scared, and alone. "I was about as low as I could get. I found myself contemplating if maybe the world would be better without me." Happily, Michael decided not to give up and slowly—through self-education, reading spiritual based books, and meditation—discovered life's infinite possibilities. Michael is now in the process of becoming his greatest version and is on a mission to help others do the same. His ultimate goal is to give people back to themselves. Michael, his wife, Gitta, and their dog, Mocha, live a truly blessed life full of abundance in a waterfront home near Kingston, Ontario, Canada.

Printed in Canada